Also by Ted Cross:

The Immortality Game

The Chronicles of Xax
The Shard
Lord Fish

THE SHATTERED SPIRE

Ted Cross

THE SHATTERED SPIRE

Copyright © Ted Cross, 2022

This book is a work of fiction. Names, characters, businesses, places, events, and incidents are the product of the author's imagination or are used fictitiously. Any resemblance to actual persons, living or dead, events, or locales is entirely coincidental.

All rights reserved. Except as permitted under the U.S. Copyright Act of 1976, no part of this publication may be reproduced, distributed or transmitted in any form or by any means, or stored in a database or retrieval system, without the prior written permission of the publisher.

Published by Breakwater Harbor Books, Inc.
Scott J. Toney and Cara Goldthorpe, Co-Founders
www.breakwaterharborbooks.com

Visit tedacross.blogspot.com for the latest news, book details, and other information

ISBN: 978-0-9909877-6-5 (paperback)
ISBN: 978-0-9909877-5-8 (ebook)

Cover art by Jay Epperson

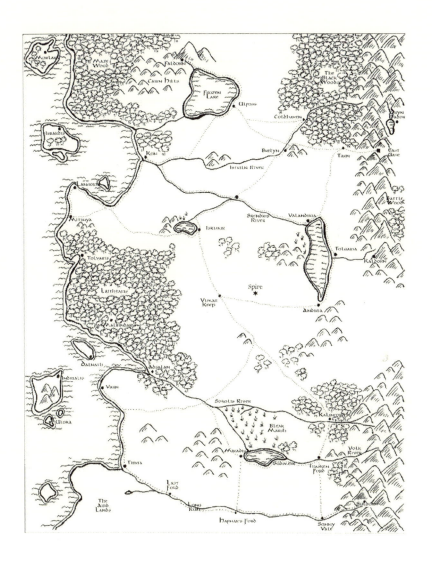

Prologue

The stonecutter had planned it perfectly, arriving on a tired horse on a cloudy, moonless night so his son would not yet be able to lay eyes upon the greatest wonder of the realm. Oh, it had been there, a void looming in the darkness—they could feel its presence. The boy had wanted to go to the spire then, but the stonecutter had hurried him toward the stables. The lamp-lit inn sat by the side of the flagstoned trade road that ran between the great cities of the inland sea to the east and Vimar Keep to the west.

The night in one of the inn's tiny rooms had been more restful than any he had known for years, even those nights spent exhausted from hard labor in the mines. The magic of the spire cradled them and gave them restful and pleasing dreams.

It was a hard life cutting blocks of marble from the quarry. The stonecutter had endured by holding tightly to his dream of bringing his son to see the Peace Spire. A week before his son's twelfth name-day—a week before the boy must himself begin laboring in the quarry—the king's man had agreed to give the stonecutter that week for himself. He had wasted no time, renting a pair of brown nags and setting off the same day so they could reach the spire and still have time to return by week's end.

This morning the boy had wanted to rush straight out to see the spire, but the stonecutter had forced him to sit at one of the trestle tables in the large common room and eat a hearty breakfast. He wanted to give the sun time to crest the wall of mountains to the east. The first view of the spire should come in sunlight, he thought.

Now the stonecutter paused just outside the door of the inn, savoring the moment. A path led around the side of the inn toward the ancient monument. He looked at his son, seeing the excitement plain on the boy's face. The boy smiled, and the stonecutter, normally taciturn, could not help but grin in return.

He nodded his head and said, "Come."

They rounded the corner and the stonecutter saw that many other pilgrims were already swarming about the base of the spire. He heard his son gasp.

The stonecutter had not seen the monument for nearly twenty years. As he drew his eyes up the length of the spire, he snapped his hand to his mouth to stifle his own gasp. He had expected beauty, but even his own memories left him unprepared for what he now saw. The height of the spire, its red granite rising up and up seemingly to touch the sky, did not surprise him. Neither did the enormous teardrop crystal at its tip. It was the dazzling shimmer of colors that stole his breath. The sky hung cloudless overhead and the sun striking the crystal caused a burst of rainbow colors to dance in the air above the grassy fields.

"Father," whispered the boy.

"Yes," he answered. He knew he was grinning like a fool but he didn't care.

"I want to go closer."

With his heart thudding in his chest, the stonecutter felt the power of the spire surge through his blood like a raging torrent, filling him with energy and strength, and the confidence that he could accomplish anything he desired. He had felt it all his life, but it was never so overwhelming as now, so close to the source.

The boy had set off down the path and was even now crossing the small arching bridge over the stream that flowed behind the inn. The stonecutter hurried to catch up. He took a deep breath and smelled the sweetness of grass and rich earth. His knees often pained him these past few years, but the energy from the spire filled him to overflowing so much that he leapt over the bridge in two quick hops.

"Do you feel it?" he called to his son.

The boy laughed aloud. "I could push a marble block all on my own."

They passed other pilgrims, some of them laughing and others gazing openmouthed into the sky.

As they drew close to the monument, the stonecutter grew even more excited. "Look, Son. This is what I wanted to show you."

The base of the spire was a wide slab of carved red granite and marble perhaps fifty paces across. Its sides were covered with intricately carved bas-relief scenes from the lives of a myriad of tiny figures. The stonecutter stepped close and ran a hand over a picture showing stocky bearded figures wielding picks and awls within a mine.

"Dwarves."

"And these are elves here, Father! They look so real. How could they carve in such detail?"

The stonecutter wished he knew. He had cut stone all his life, yet he could never mimic the delicate strength of these carvings. Tracing a finger down the trunk of a tree in a forest scene, he marveled at the fantastic skill of some ancient master who had managed to turn rock into thousands of perfect leaves. He took a deep breath, filling his lungs with the smell of cold stone.

"Look up there," said the stonecutter, pointing.

The spire's presence was intimidating when viewed so close. It towered into the sky, and the stonecutter felt his neck creak from staring up the dizzying length of red stone. Large runes were etched into the mica-flecked granite, each rune lined with silver that somehow never tarnished.

"What do they say?"

"You know the story, my son. It was always your favorite."

"Tell it again. It's different hearing it here."

The shimmering colors in the sky were hurting the stonecutter's eyes, so he dropped his gaze back to the carvings.

"What do you see in these?" he said.

The boy pursed his lips and examined the rounded base of the monument. "They are beautiful beyond anything I have seen."

"They show scenes of peace," said the stonecutter. "You won't find war in any of these pictures."

The boy nodded and said, "Here, let's sit while you tell me the story."

The stonecutter joined his son on a length of smooth gray stone set back about ten paces from the base of the spire. More such benches surrounded the monument, most of them occupied by other pilgrims. The stonecutter tugged at his beard, trying to figure out the best place to begin.

After some minutes he asked, "Do you remember when man arrived in these lands?"

His son nodded. "Arrival Day is now twelve hundred and thirty-seven years past. The great King Aronis led our people through the great pass where East Gate now stands."

"Yes," said the stonecutter, "though it was the wizards who showed us this realm, where we could not easily be attacked and where the Peace Spire had already stood for more than five thousand years."

"'Twas the elves and dwarves who built it," the boy exclaimed.

The stonecutter chuckled. "I thought you wanted me to tell it?"

The boy nodded and waved a hand impatiently for his father to continue.

The stonecutter combed his fingers through his graying brown beard. "Long and long ago there was a terrible war between the two races that dwelt in these lands. They were deceived, drawn into war by the wizard Bilach, whose lust for power had caused him to turn to evil, though his fellow wizards knew it not at that time. The dwarves marched on the forest of Laithtaris with fire and axe, and the arrows of the elves turned the sky dark at midday. With both sides terribly bloodied, Bilach struck with his own army, secretly gathered from among the orc tribes that infested the mountains. The elves and dwarves had no choice but to put aside their grievances and unite against Bilach. Victory seemed assured for the hosts of evil. Their numbers seemed endless. Yet the allies defended stubbornly and at last Bilach's forces broke and fled back to their reeking caverns. The allies were too exhausted and heartbroken to rejoice. Then it was that the remaining wizards brought the elf queen and the dwarf king to council and told them that they should together construct a monument to peace so that they might put aside their grudges."

The stonecutter pointed at the flat land around the spire. "This place they chose because it lies midway between the capitals of the two races. The wizards asked..."

"Father! What's wrong?"

"In the sky there," said the stonecutter, pointing to the northeast. "I thought it was an eagle, but it seems too large now."

He stood up from the stone bench and his son stood with him. Whatever it was, it was blacker than night. It looked like spilt lamp oil slowly spreading, until it drew close enough that the stonecutter could see vast bat-like wings, though no bat could ever grow so large.

Murmurs of confusion rose among the gathered pilgrims. A man shouted, "Dragon!"

"It can't be," whispered the stonecutter.

"There's no such thing as dragons," said the boy, his voice breaking. "You always said so."

Screams broke out all around and people began to run toward the inn.

"They are only legends," said the stonecutter. He shook his head at the impossible sight. The inky stain became the unmistakable form of an enormous jet-black dragon. It seemed to hover motionless on its outstretched wings even as it loomed larger.

"No such thing," said the boy, panic clear in his voice.

"Run, my son," whispered the stonecutter. He reached out his hands and shoved at the boy, though he could not take his eyes from the dragon. The monster wriggled sinuously and then folded its wings and plunged like a dart toward the crystal atop the spire.

"Father!" screamed the boy. He had begun to run but then turned back when he saw his father had not joined him.

As the dragon neared the tip of the spire, it again spread its wings and pulled out of its dive. It seemed to the stonecutter that the beast dropped something, though at this distance he could not tell for sure.

Then the world seemed to explode.

One moment the stonecutter was on his feet, and the next he was face down in the earth. The force was unimaginable. He spat dirt from his mouth and pushed himself up from the rumbling ground, shaking his head to try to clear it. A high whine was the only sound in his deafened ears. My son, he thought, and he frantically searched the ground around him. He saw the boy lying unconscious about ten paces away. He scrambled to his feet. Dizziness nearly overwhelmed him as he weaved toward his son. Something hard struck his shoulder and knocked him back to the earth. He clawed over the hard ground, trying desperately to reach the boy. A large chunk of rock shattered his leg.

In terrible pain, the stonecutter reached out, grabbed his son's foot, and used it to pull himself closer. A head-sized piece of granite smashed into the ground two paces away, and tiny fragments stung the stonecutter's forehead. He turned himself onto his back to stare at the sky. A dark cloud hung in the air where the top of the spire had once been. More debris rained down all around.

Out of the corner of his eye, the stonecutter saw the dragon banking around in a lazy arc. He ignored the beast and watched as the spire, which even strong winds had never been able to move, swayed slowly back and forth. Cracks ran through the red granite near the base. Though he still could not hear, the stonecutter felt the ground thrum as the entire structure snapped and began to topple.

Tears mingling with the blood flowing down his cheeks, the stonecutter pushed himself over and lay his body atop his son's, as if he could protect the boy from the collapsing tower with his love. He couldn't hear his own voice as he whispered his last words into the boy's ear: "I'm so sorry, Son."

1
IMRIC

Imric's stomach rumbled at the smell of roasting lamb and onions. He knelt on the greasy tiles of the noisy kitchen and hissed at the dark-haired girl peeling carrots on a cutting board across the aisle. "Soot."

The girl looked at Imric and wrinkled her nose at him before turning back to her carrots.

"Come on, Soot. I don't want my dam to catch me here again," he said.

Soot waited for pot-bellied Davit to pass by with a tray of fresh-baked bread before dropping the knife and kneeling down near Imric. "She's right. No little prince should be skulking 'round the kitchen getting grease on his fine clothes. Now go away. Meri says I'd best have all the carrots and potatoes done by third bell."

Imric peered into Soot's hazel eyes. Though more than a year younger than Imric's thirteen years, Soot was taller by an inch. This bothered Imric greatly, though he would never admit it. Despite Soot's lanky, black hair and sharp face, Imric thought she was the prettiest girl in the castle. He said, "When can you get away? Livia says a wizard has come and will see my father today. I want to listen."

Soot smirked. "You and your stories. If a wizard's come to Tolgaria, don't you think we'd have heard by now? We hear everything in the kitchen. Anyway, I thought all the wizards were dead."

"Livia says there are two of them still. She says this one was her tutor, back when..." Imric hesitated, remembering the always-whispered stories he had heard about his birth, then continued, "...back before I was born."

"You've caught me in too many of your fairy stories for me to believe you now," Soot said. "It don't matter noways. Meri will have me scrubbing pots 'til—"

"Sooty!" The shout came from across the room, and from the sound Imric knew it was Soot's mother Meri. "Stop lazing about and get back to work!"

Soot gave Imric a small shove as she stood up. "Go on and see your wizard. You can tell me about him tomorrow."

Meri waddled around the nearest table and stopped when she saw Imric. "Sooty, go fetch me six onions. Young lord, you had best run along now. Remember what happened the last time your dam caught you here?"

Imric scowled and nodded. He gave Soot a last glance before heading out the doorway. *I'll just have to see the wizard myself then*, he thought. This was the most exciting event in years as far as he could remember. He ran up two flights of stairs and stopped near a wooden door. When he was sure no one was watching, he opened it and slipped inside.

An arrow slit high on one wall let in a feeble ray of light, enough for Imric to see the cloakroom was deserted. Huge oaken wardrobes lined the walls. Imric approached the largest and swung open one of the doors. This room had not been used for years, so the wardrobe was empty. He climbed inside and shut the door behind him. Though it was dark inside, he confidently knelt and felt about on the back panel until he heard a tiny *click*. The panel slid aside, revealing a pitch black crawlspace. He had discovered the first secret panel by accident three years ago while playing with Soot. Imric still felt a thrill each time he came here, though the first time he had opened the secret door it had taken all of his courage to crawl into the dank stone passageway behind the wardrobe. There was no fear now; he had been exploring the tunnels almost every day since he had found them.

He clambered into the passage and slid the panel shut. A cool draft wafted against his face as Imric crawled forward across the cold stone. A faint light appeared ahead of him. As he drew close to the light, Imric's hand touched a blanket laid out upon the floor. He found another blanket crumpled near the wall and quickly draped it about his shoulders before sitting down. The light came from an intricately carved marble screen, through which Imric could peer down into the large green-tiled throne room of the castle. He was disappointed to see that the chamber was mostly empty. His father usually held court here each day between lunch and fourth bell, and Imric had expected the room would be packed in anticipation of the wizard's arrival.

The marble screen was set in the wall behind and just to the left-hand side of the throne, so Imric always had a great view of the happenings in his father's court. Except for holiday feasts, this was the only way for him to see his father.

Imric lay down upon the soft wool and wrapped the second blanket tightly about himself. I'll just have a short nap, he thought. Surely the wizard will come soon.

He woke to the sound of someone rapping on the panel of the wardrobe. He shook his head and rubbed his eyes. The sound of many voices came from the throne room. Imric sat up and groaned when he saw the packed crowd below. I hope I didn't miss the wizard.

The rapping sounded again through the stone crawlspace. Imric ignored it as he scanned the faces in the throne room, searching for anyone who stood out from the usual group of lords, knights, merchants, and ladies. He sighed when he saw the throne stood empty, certain now that he had not missed anything.

The rapping became a pounding, and faintly Imric heard his sister Livia's voice. "Imric, are you there?"

He had known it was her from the moment he had awoken. Soot knew how to open the panel, and the only other person he had ever shown the hidden passage to was Livia. He quickly scooted across the cold stone and slid the panel aside. "What do you want?"

His twenty-year-old sister stood in the open door of the wardrobe, limned by the wan light from the arrow slit. She had long hair of the same startling silver color as Imric's. He could barely make out her long face with its prominent nose and pinched lips. Imric thought Livia always looked angry, but he knew she just liked to hide her mouth. She had told him once she didn't like her crooked teeth, but Imric loved her dimpled smile.

"Is there room in there for me?" she asked. "Father won't let me in the throne room and I simply *must* see what happens."

"Thought you were scared of the dark?" Imric grinned but then waved her in. He enjoyed teasing his big sister, but he also adored her. She was the only member of his family who cared for him. "Close the door behind you."

Livia looked pale but determined as she climbed into the hole beside Imric and pulled the panel shut. "How can you see anything?" she whispered.

"I don't need to see," he replied. "It's just a short crawl."

A few moments later they huddled together on the blanket before the marble screen, the second blanket pulled tight around their shoulders.

"What a splendid view," murmured Livia.

"You don't need to whisper," Imric said. "They won't hear us out there if you just keep your voice down."

"I wonder who built this passage."

Imric was about to give some of his theories, but at that moment a hush fell over the crowd in the room below and the page announced the arrival of King Varun Kaldarion and Prince Balmar, the oldest of their brothers.

Varun walked quickly up the center aisle, not pausing as he usually did to share a few words with a favorite or two in the crowd. His erect carriage and shaggy mane of gray hair made him appear taller than his medium height. He wore a silk crimson tunic over black breeches and tall leather boots. Imric thought his father looked grim today and he wondered why. King Varun was a man who liked to smile.

Eighteen-year-old Balmar stared at the floor and grinned sheepishly as he trailed after his father. He had a lantern jaw, a protruding brow, and a perpetually confused look in his eyes. Ostensibly the heir to the throne, Balmar was feeble-minded from birth, and it was forever whispered that King Varun would pass him over for his second son, seventeen-year-old Darus.

As Varun stepped up to the throne and Balmar slunk to his seat, Livia said, "Why does Father always make poor Balmar attend court? It's humiliating."

"I suppose he thinks Balmar might learn something eventually," Imric replied.

"It's Darus who needs to learn how to rule," Livia snapped. "Instead he spends all his time off playing soldier at East Gate."

The immense fortress of East Gate guarded the only pass through the vast wall of the Hellisgaard Mountains that formed the eastern border of the Known Lands. The only serious danger to the realm came from the barbarian tribes who lived beyond those mountains.

Darus seemed to prefer the harsh military life at East Gate to the politics of the capital. Imric had not seen Darus in more than four years now.

"I hope he never comes home," he muttered.

Livia put her arm around Imric's shoulders and pulled him closer. They huddled this way for several long minutes as the crowd below grew restless. The rising murmur was cut off at last when the page cried out, "Milord, the wizard Xaxanakis!"

Two guards came through the entrance practically dragging a middle-aged man with shoulder-length black hair and a short beard. The man was dressed plainly in black tunic and trousers, leather traveling boots, and a green travel-worn cloak. Imric frowned. He had expected someone grand and...wizardly. This man seemed just like any other commoner.

"Xax!" cried Livia in a hushed voice. "Have they arrested him?"

"He doesn't look like a wizard to me," Imric muttered.

"How do you know what a wizard should look like?"

Imric shrugged. "Shouldn't he be older, at least? He looks younger than Father."

"Hush!" Livia waved a hand at him as the guards deposited the wizard a few paces before the king. "Aww, poor Balmar!"

Balmar had risen from his seat and gazed in confusion at the wizard. For a moment it looked as if he might go to Xax, but he caught his father's disapproving look and fell back into his chair.

Livia whispered, "He was only five when Xax had to leave. Surely he barely remembers him."

When the guards released his arms, Xax straightened himself up and brushed out the sleeves of his tunic before looking up at the king. "Nice way to greet an old friend, Varun."

King Varun leapt from his throne and stalked up to the wizard. "You knew what would happen if you ever returned here. I swore you would be flayed alive if you dared show your face again."

Xax wiped spittle from his face with one sleeve. "Still deceiving yourself over that tragedy, I see. Trust me, I have better things to do with my time than watch you wallow in self-pity. If I came here, it's because I feel an obligation to try to save the good people of this realm. You must let me speak with you in private, Varun."

"If you value your hide you might, for once, try some courtesy."

"I am not your subject," the wizard said with a tight smile.

Varun's face turned beet red, his fists clenched at his side. He swayed as if he might fall before steadying himself. "Say what you have to say and be quick about it."

The two men glared at each other for half a minute before Xax broke the silence. "Your people are in grave danger. You must prepare for what will come."

"Danger?" the king scoffed. "Twelve hundred years since we arrived in these lands. The greatest danger we face is boring ourselves to death. What danger?"

Imric had to read Xax's lips to understand what he whispered. "The tower has fallen."

"The tower has fallen," repeated Varun. "Which tower? Is my castle being undermined by dwarves?"

The audience tittered, but Xax pointed a finger in the king's face. "You know which tower, Varun. The tower that has protected the Known Lands all these centuries."

The king whirled about and strode back to sit on his throne. He gazed at his son Balmar, who was slumped in his chair trying to look invisible, before turning his attention back to the wizard. "I believe our army at East Gate protects our lands well enough. Regardless, what is wrong with the spire? Has the earth given way beneath it?"

"You understand nothing," Xax said. "The barbarians will be the least of your worries. It's your own troops that are the danger. Led by your own son."

"Darus?" Varun cried, leaping up again. "He is my only true progeny. He idolizes me. Why in the name of Aronis would I need to fear him?"

Imric felt his sister stiffen beside him at their father's words. The king had always favored Darus over the rest of his children. Imric was used to being ignored, having been disavowed at birth, but Father's blunt words had to sting for Livia. He put an arm around her shoulders and squeezed.

"Such self-deception you practice," Xax said. "Are you truly so blind? Do you believe Darus left for East Gate out of boredom? The martial spirit? Adventure?"

"Get to the point," the king growled.

"Jealousy has eaten like a worm at his gut. He believes he should be your heir. And that you have never announced it has driven him half-mad. How does the magic of the tower treat those with rage in their hearts? You know. We all know. I helped imbue the spire with its magic in the first place. The magic amplifies his fear. It makes him feel sick and weak. He went to East Gate like so many others, because it lies beyond the influence of the magic. Now that the spire has fallen, there is nothing to prevent his return."

"Good!" the king cried. "I should like to see him home again."

Xax's shoulders slumped and he shook his head. "You believe this can end well? I have seen it, Varun. Do you understand?"

King Varun stiffened and remained silent for a few moments, glaring at the wizard. "Your visions are not always accurate. Betimes they are riddles whose true answers elude you."

"Would that it were so this time," Xax said. "No, this vision was all too clear. The fall of the spire will destroy your realm."

"The spire! The spire!" the king shouted. "How has it fallen? Would we not feel it if we lost the magic?"

"Do you not? Even now your blood pounds in your chest. Is it not at such times when the magic fills you? Yet you feel nothing. All your life you have lived with it. Can you truly not feel that it is gone?"

Imric was both fascinated and terrified by what he was hearing. Like everyone else in the realm, he had lived with the magic of the Spire of Peace his entire life. When he ran up the tower stairs or chased other children in the yard, the magic flowed through him and gave him strength and courage. It was as much a part of him as breathing. Would he really never feel it again? Could its loss cause the destruction of everything he had known? He had run up the steps on his way to this hideout, and thinking back he realized that he had not felt the normal burst of energy and confidence that he always felt when exerting himself. He wondered how he could have missed it at the time. He felt Livia shiver beside him and knew she was having similar thoughts.

King Varun slumped in his throne, looking suddenly much older than his forty years. "When did it happen? Who destroyed it? And how did you come to be here so quickly?"

Xax began to pace before the throne, gesticulating with his right hand as he spoke. "My vision came more than a month ago. I hurried here as fast as my feet could take me, but I was too late. I saw your city gates in the distance early this morning when I felt it happen. Felt the spire fall. You *must* prepare if you are to have any chance!"

"Tell me how to prepare. And for what? Will Darus march to attack his own father?"

"Darus will march, that much the vision made clear. But there is a far graver danger first. The tower was destroyed by a dragon. I know not—"

The wizard was interrupted by laughter from the assembled courtiers, and Imric felt a smile steal over his own face. Everyone knew dragons were only legends. Faerie tales to scare young children before bed. He tugged at Livia's shoulder and whispered, "Your old tutor has lost his mind." Through the shadows Livia's face looked troubled.

The king stood and held his arms up to still the laughter. "Explain yourself, wizard. There has never been a dragon in the Known Lands."

"The memories of man are short," Xax said, with iron in his voice. "Certainly there have been dragons here. Only not since the coming of your ancestors. Let me assure you, there is a dragon here now, and a most terrible one it is. Larger than any I have seen. And some vile magic is aiding it. A dragon's strength alone would not have been able to fell the spire."

The king turned his back on Xax, and Imric saw his mouth twitch back and forth between a grin and a scowl. He spun back around and thrust a finger at the wizard. "You play a dangerous game with me. Let's pretend for a moment that you speak true. What would you have me do about this dragon?"

"What else?" Xax said. "Flee! Save your people! Your best chance lies north to Valandiria and then northwest, perhaps to Brelyn, or west to the coast. It may be too late, but it's your only chance."

"You really have lost your mind, Xax," the king said. "Run away? From one dragon? All the people of the realm? And what about Darus? You just told us he would be coming with his army. If we go north we'd be marching directly toward him."

Xax shook his head vehemently. "He comes later. You have time. And the vision didn't make it clear why he was marching. It may be that he will join with you."

"If this…dragon is so dangerous that an entire people must flee before it, why not go into the mountains? Kaldorn is close. The dwarves have no special love for us, but they would not turn us away. Their tunnels run deep and could surely shelter us until the danger is passed."

"Kaldorn will fall," Xax said. "This too I have seen. No, north and west is the only way."

"Enough!" the king cried. "This is too much even for you." He snapped a finger at his nearest guards. "Show him to his old chambers and be sure he remains there. We'll speak more on this later, wizard."

"You are being foolish," Xax said over his shoulder as the guards led him away. "There will be no later!"

The king waved a hand dismissively and slumped in his throne. "Out! Everybody out!"

As a cacophony of voices filled the chamber and people began to file out, Imric turned to his sister. "Can any of this be true? Please tell me Xax has lost his mind."

"I..." Livia shook her head and started over. "Xax is the wisest person I have ever known. I must go and speak with him." She let the blanket slide from her shoulders and turned to crawl down the dark passage.

"Wait! The guards won't let you into his rooms."

"Perhaps they will. How does this blasted panel open?"

Imric crawled alongside Livia. "Press here, see?" They had to shield their eyes as light flooded in. "Livia, I can help you."

"What do you mean?"

Imric smiled. "Follow me. I'll show you."

2
VILLEM

Sir Villem Tathis tugged on the reins to pull his pony to a stop. Around the bend in the steep defile rose the towering gray walls of East Gate. Two weeks of travel and he was here at last! A tingle of worry shivered down his spine. Would they accept him into their ranks? It could not be often that those of noble blood joined their army, especially one so young at just fifteen summers. Except for Darus Kaldarion, naturally—the prince had not just been accepted but had become their leader. Villem assumed he would be brought before Lord Darus, and what reason could Darus have to reject another member of the nobility? Surely Villem would be useful to the army of East Gate?

When he looked around at the stark emptiness of the place, it made his stomach churn. Does nothing green grow here? To leave his childhood home in lovely Iskimir for this dead and dreary fortress was depressing.

Two days ago, Villem had drawn near the small town of Tarn, and the magical torture from the Spire of Peace had released its grip on him after more than a month of agony. Villem rolled his shoulders back and drew in a deep breath, happy to be free from the gut-twisting fear and weakness the tower's power had forced upon him.

Here he could at least breathe freely and hold his head high again, however drab and lifeless the place might be.

He nudged the pony's flanks to get it moving and glanced back at his warhorse, led by a long tether. A gorgeous roan mare, it plodded along stoically, two large packs slung over its back. Villem hated treating the warhorse this way, but he hadn't dared take more than the two steeds from his father's stables.

Villem turned his attention back to the looming walls. He heard the clanking of chains before he saw the rusted iron portcullis begin to rise. Had they seen him coming? Soon enough, nearly a dozen soldiers on horseback trotted through the gate and headed straight toward Villem, who tugged the reins to halt again. Or at least he had assumed they were soldiers. Now that they drew closer they looked more like bandits. They wore a ragtag assortment of clothing, mostly worn leathers, though a few had bits and pieces of chainmail armor beneath their tunics. One man seemed to be missing an arm. Another was grossly fat, and…yes, another was even a woman! Villem's hand found its way to the hilt of his longsword. Surely these could not be members of the famous East Gate army? Were these lot what Lord Darus would send to greet him?

As the band drew closer, they looked as if they meant to pass by Villem altogether. *So they weren't sent for me after all*, Villem thought, uncertain whether to feel relieved or even more offended that Darus's men were ignoring his arrival.

The members of the small band all stared at Villem as they began to pass, until a short, dirty blond man near the rear held up his hand and whistled the group to a stop. He pointed at Villem. "Haven't seen you before. What's your business at East Gate?"

Having a grimy peasant address him in such a commanding tone chafed at Villem, but he understood the need to prove himself to Darus's men before he could claim his rightful place. "I am here to see your lord, Darus Kaldarion. I will offer my services as a knight."

A few of the horsemen began to chuckle until the blond man cut them off with a wave of his hand. "A knight, you say." He paused a moment to examine Villem's warhorse and packs. "We could use another of those. Especially now." He flung his hand out to encompass the other riders. "We are heading out on the very first expedition of the new war. I think you should join us."

War? Villem had heard nothing of a war brewing. And why would they be heading the wrong way? The barbarian tribes lived beyond East Gate. And join with this rabble? Villem's stomach went queasy at the thought. "What war is that now? The news hasn't reached us back home yet."

The blond man jerked a thumb over his shoulder. "Fall in with us then, and we'll tell you on the way."

Villem's eyes flicked toward the gate to be sure it was still open. He felt a powerful urge to kick his pony into a trot to get away from these vagrants. "I appreciate the offer, but I would like very much to meet with Lord Darus. I'm certain he'll be able to fill me in and provide me with a proper command."

The blond man scowled. "You misunderstand, good man. I am Orderic, one of Darus's lieutenants. I have full authority for recruitment. So you are falling in with us now, or you are with the enemy and will be treated as such."

Villem's mouth fell open and he couldn't speak for several moments. He felt his face flush with anger and embarrassment. "I…I am of noble blood. We—"

"That is of no matter to us here. Even Darus had to prove himself before he was treated as more than a common recruit. You need to learn your place quick, or you won't be liking the consequences." Orderic again jerked his thumb over his shoulder. "Now fall in, on my orders. I plan to make town by nightfall."

To give himself time to think, Villem examined the other members of the ragged band. Each was more astonishing than the last. There were eleven of them. The smallest one looked to be no more than ten years old, if Villem judged his age right. The woman had a collar about her neck, and a thin leather tether drooped from the collar and led to the saddle of the huge horse holding the grossly fat man. Although now that Villem looked closer, he wasn't sure the fat man was a man at all. The grimy face looked manly enough, but the tunic was distended by what looked like a mammoth bosom. Villem thought he couldn't be surprised further until his eyes settled on the one-armed man. Under the grime and huge scowl, the figure was so slender and had such luminous eyes that Villem thought it may just be the first time he'd ever laid eyes on an elf. Elves were all but legends in the Known Lands. Faerie stories. Hidden away in their forests, having nothing to do with the realms of man. But Villem would swear no man had such eyes. The elf sneered at Villem and spat in his direction.

Orderic laughed. "Making friends with Miranvel already! We're all going to get along famously. Come, let's go. We'll have us some fun." Orderic whistled and nudged his horse forward, hooves clacking loudly on the hard road of the rocky defile. The elf Miranvel continued to glare at Villem for several more moments before kicking his horse to get it moving.

Villem looked longingly to where the portcullis was now grating its way downward. Nothing about these people felt like the proper army he had thought to find here. He dreamed of making a run for the gate but knew it was futile. Would this ragtag band truly murder him if he defied them? He imagined they would do so happily. He blew out his breath and clucked at his pony to turn it around to follow the others.

3
IMRIC

Imric and Livia huffed up the last of the steps to the top floor of the castle. They paused on the landing to catch their breath.

"The spire truly is gone," Livia said.

Imric nodded. Climbing stairs had never been like this before. All his life, when Imric began to exert himself, the magic of the spire had filled him with energy and strength. It had always been a pleasure to run through the hallways or clamber up staircases. Now it was a chore.

"I think I want to take a nap," Imric said, breathing heavily.

Livia gave him a small shove with one hand. "Don't be silly. Xax's room is not so far now."

She took off walking and Imric had to scurry to catch up. They rounded a corner, and Imric saw two guards standing outside a door near the end of the hallway. Livia abruptly halted, and Imric bumped into her.

"That's his room," Livia said, pointing to where the guards were standing. "What should we do now? I'm certain they won't let us in."

Imric studied the hallway. It had a burgundy carpet and four sets of wooden doors along the sixty paces of its length. There was a small archway at the end, just past the guards, and Imric could just make out a spiral stairway through the arch.

"Where does the arch lead?"

"It's a guard tower," Livia said. "Xax's room is a corner room bounded by two of the castle walls."

"That's not good," Imric said. "What's that door just before the wizard's?"

"Across from it, or the one on the right just prior to it?"

"On the right."

"It's the library," Livia said. "That's why Xax's room is here, to be near the library."

"What's a library?"

Livia blew out her breath in exasperation. "I've spent so much of my time there, and you don't even know about it. Come on, I'll show you, if you like."

They trudged down the hallway. The guards eyed them warily, and as they drew closer, Imric recognized one of them. It was Wilor, a nearly deaf old man with one milky eye and a bad drinking habit. Wilor was surly with most people, but for some reason he had always seemed to like Imric. He gave a sour grin as the pair drew closer.

Livia halted outside the door to the library and fished a key out of her pocket. She unlocked the door and it creaked open to show a small room, perhaps five paces to a side. The burgundy carpet looked newer than in the hallway. The walls to the left and right each had stone shelves lined with musty tomes. Two smaller shelves were set in the far wall, with a reading lectern in the middle. A small table with two wooden stools stood in the middle of the room, and a single book lay on the table, along with an oil lamp and a pair of candlesticks.

Livia approached the table and ran a finger across the book. "It's what I've been reading lately."

Imric sniffed the cold air and promptly sneezed. It was dusty in here. He was dumbstruck by the number of books. He hadn't realized so many existed in the whole world. There had to be two or three hundred of them. "How many of these have you read?"

"All of them, of course," Livia replied. "Even the boring ones. Many of them I've read multiple times."

Imric shook his head. "You're as daft as Balmar."

Livia scowled. "This is how one gains an education. Something you clearly don't appreciate. It's very sad to not know the pleasures of reading."

With only the bit of light from the torches in the hallway, the room was rather dark. Livia fished out her matches and soon had the lamp shining cozily on the table.

Imric pulled the door shut and began searching over the shelf on the left, since its wall adjoined the wizard's room. He had first discovered a secret passage, purely by accident, at the age of ten. That exciting discovery had led to him searching far and wide throughout the castle, and he had found many more such passages since. He'd never gotten as far as this wing, though. He had no idea if the king who had ordered the castle to be built had purposely designed the castle to have these passages, or if the architect had put them in on his own, but he had learned a lot of the tricks used and he knew what to look for. This shelf was built solidly into the wall, though, so it didn't look promising. Imric tugged on each shelf to see if any were loose, and he peered carefully along all edges to see if he could spy any cracks. There were none.

He gave up on this shelf and looked around to find Livia seated at the table reading her book. He shook his head again. Livia was the smartest person he knew, and he was sure that she must get some of that from these books, but reading was so boring. He couldn't understand how anyone would choose to do it on purpose. He glanced at the two smaller shelves along the back wall. They didn't look any more promising than the shelf he had just examined, but the lectern drew his attention. Like the shelves, it was set against the wall, but it was made of wood. Its top was flat and slightly tilted, with a front edge to hold a book for easy perusal. He knelt near the lectern and began feeling around the base near the wall.

"Ha!" he cried.

Livia jumped up from the table. "You found something?"

Imric got on his knees and looked more closely at the back corner of the lectern, where he had felt movement. He found a small slider, similar to others he had found in other places where he had found passages. Pressing it hard with his finger, he pulled the slider toward him. There was resistance at first, but then it clicked into place. Before trying anything further, he moved to the other side of the lectern and found a similar slider, and he snapped that one into place as well. He tried pulling the lectern away from the wall, but that wouldn't work. Next he tried to slide it to one side or the other, but again he had no luck.

"I'm sure pushing it wouldn't work," Livia said, and placed her hand on the wooden panel that was the lectern's front. The panel shifted slightly under her touch.

"That's it!" Imric brushed Livia aside and put both hands on the front panel. He found that it could swing upward from the bottom, revealing a hollow interior… and a dark hole in the wall behind it.

Livia clapped her hands together. "You did it! Where does it go?"

"Hold the panel so it doesn't hit me," Imric said. When Livia had grasped the panel, Imric crept through the hollow and peered into the gloom. "Too dark. I need light."

"I'll get the lamp," Livia said, and propped the wooden panel against Imric's back.

After a minute, Imric grumbled, "What's taking so long?"

"I'm lighting candles. Don't want the room to be pitch black once the lamp is gone."

Imric listened impatiently until finally Livia pulled up the panel again and handed him the flickering lamp. He shifted his body to be able to pull the lamp though and into the dark hollow beyond the wall. He stuck his head out and peered around in the wan light. There was a narrow stone passage running left and right, with the back wall less than a pace beyond the wall of the library. This looked very promising. Imric inched himself forward until he could pull his whole body into the passage.

"Be careful!" Livia hissed. "There could be rats, or…or worse!"

"I'm fine," Imric grumbled. He looked longingly to the right, wishing he had time to explore the whole passage. He'd come back to it another time. For now he turned away and began stalking down the passage to the left, toward the wizard's room. He paused when he realized Livia hadn't followed. "Aren't you coming?"

Livia's face looked pale and she shook her head vehemently. "I can't go in there."

"I don't want to talk to this wizard by myself. It's fine in here, just a little cold. Look, no rats or spiders." It wasn't exactly true; he did see plenty of spider webs, but he hadn't spotted any actual spiders yet.

"I'll wait here for now. You find the way into Xax's room, and then I'll come."

Imric sighed. Finding a new secret passageway was the most exciting thing in the whole world. How could his sister be so afraid? He shuffled along the narrow passage, brushing away cobwebs and holding the lamp high so he could see. He trailed his left hand along the wall, feeling for any changes. The stone was icy cold and slightly damp. Suddenly he saw tiny eyes ahead of him, gleaming in the lamplight. So, there were rats in here after all. It scampered off into a crack, and Imric decided it was best not to tell Livia about it. Ahead of him the passage came to a dead end, and he understood he must have come to the outer wall of the castle. The stone beneath his trailing fingers changed to wood, and he abruptly halted and began feeling around the edges of the stone and wood. It took only a minute to find the outline of the wooden portal set in the stone wall. It was similar in size to the panel of the lectern.

Imric tried pressing against the wood, but it wouldn't budge. Next he began feeling across the wood panel, and this time his fingers discovered a catch, similar to many others he had found over the years. He smiled and was about to move the catch when he realized he might startle the wizard. The man might even scream and attract the attention of the guards. He had to proceed cautiously. He slid the catch aside and found that the panel could be pushed out slightly and then slid to one side. It was dark inside with a musty smell that he recognized as clothing. He knew instantly what he had discovered, because the designer of these secret passages had loved using large wardrobes. Imric guessed that nearly a third of the passages he had discovered involved such wardrobes. He decided he'd better get Livia before going farther.

It took some effort to coax her into entering the dark passage. "He'll want to see a friendly face," Imric said. "He doesn't know me." He offered his hand to help her through the narrow passage through the book stand.

"I'm bigger than you are. I can't fit through there."

"You're quite slender, Sis. I know you can do it."

Livia scowled but grasped Imric's hand and allowed him to ease her through into the passage. "I thought you said there were no spiders."

"I haven't seen any, and I broke up all the webs. Come on, it's just a short walk and we'll be there."

Livia refused to let go of his hand. Imric held the lamp higher and shuffled along the passageway until he reached the entrance to the wardrobe.

"You go first," Imric said. "It's just clothing in there. He should see your face first, and try to be quiet so he doesn't yell and bring the guards."

"Hold the lamp close," Livia said. "I want to see what's in there."

Imric did as directed, and Livia spent a minute inspecting the inside of the wardrobe.

"I already looked," Imric hissed. "No rats, no spiders."

Livia gave him a sour look, then proceeded to crawl into the wardrobe.

"Ease the door open, gently," Imric whispered.

Livia pressed against the doors, but they refused to budge. She pushed harder, and this time they popped open. The first thing Livia saw was Xax sitting on the edge of a bed, staring at her as if she had been expected. She gave a tiny yelp.

"It's wonderful to see you again, young lady," Xax said. "Do please come out."

Livia clambered out of the wardrobe and stood before her old tutor. "It has been so long."

"That it has," Xax replied. "And I'm very sorry for abandoning you when you most needed me."

Imric scrabbled through the wardrobe and came up beside her.

"You...you had no choice. I was only seven, but still I knew you were forced to leave." She turned to Imric. "This is my brother, Imric. The very reason you had to go."

"Good t-to meet you, my lord," Imric stuttered.

Xax smiled. "I'm no lord. Please just call me Xax. My full name is Xaxanakis, but shorter names are easier for people. I saw you briefly as a newborn babe. I'm happy to see you have thrived."

"Xax," Livia cut in, "were you expecting us?"

"I was expecting someone to come through that wardrobe. I don't know if you remember, but I sometimes have visions. One I had recently showed me sitting on this bed and someone opening that wardrobe door. I only saw the hand, and it looked feminine. I reasoned it could only be you, the one person in this place who was likely to have missed me."

"I did miss you." Livia went to Xax and embraced him awkwardly. "I don't know how to act around you now. I've lived with only memories of you for so long."

"Please, sit," Xax said. "I'm sure we have much to talk about." He indicated a chair near a writing desk.

Livia glanced at Imric, who motioned for her to take the chair and promptly plopped himself down on the carpet before the bed. Livia pulled the chair around to face Xax and sat down.

"Now," Xax said, "what is your plan?"

Livia shook her head. "I hoped you'd tell us. How can we help you?"

Xax pursed his lips and thought for a moment. "You could find my walking stick. That would be very nice. The guards took it from me and I haven't seen it since."

"That's all?" Livia asked. "Don't you want us to help you escape?"

Xax laughed. "Oh, my dear, I sure have missed you. It's too early to escape. I must be here to help you when the time comes."

"What do you mean?" Livia asked.

Xax suddenly looked grim. "Have you heard nothing of the news I brought?"

"The dragon," Imric said.

"Ah, good, so I don't need to repeat everything. It's tragic, but this city is going to be destroyed. I imagine within the next few days. I had hoped the dragon would find the city mostly deserted when it arrives, but your father, sadly, doesn't wish to pay me any heed. Many innocent people are going to pay the price for his pride."

"Is there nothing we can do now to help people get away?" Livia asked.

"We could—" Imric began, but his heart leapt into his throat when he heard the sound of someone fumbling at the door. "Hide!" he hissed at his sister, then dove for the wardrobe.

When inside, he paused to see if Livia was following, but she had crawled under the bed, so Imric shut himself inside the wardrobe just as the bedroom door swung open.

"Time for your supper," chirped a merry voice.

A very familiar voice. Imric pushed the wardrobe door open a crack to see if any of the guards had followed her in, but none had, so he pushed the door open wider. "Soot, am I glad to see you."

Soot's eyes widened and she jerked to a halt, nearly dropping the tray of food. She rolled her eyes. "Why am I not surprised to find you here, you little rat!" She skirted wide around the wizard and placed the tray on the small stand beside the bed. "Always sneaking around where you don't belong!"

"Come on, Soot," Imric said. "You like sneaking around in my tunnels just as much as I do. Anyway, I told you there was a wizard."

Soot sniffed, but her eyes had a glint in them that told Imric she was just peeved at having been startled by his sudden appearance. "I haven't seen any sign of a wizard. Not even one little spark of magic." She glanced hopefully at Xax.

"I thank you for bringing my supper, my dear," Xax said. "I'm afraid there is another rat crawling about beneath my bed."

Livia made an appearance on the far side of the bed and smiled sheepishly at Soot.

"The both of you, eh?" Soot said. "I should have known."

"Please don't tell the guards," Livia said. "Xax was my tutor years ago. I just want to speak with him."

Soot glanced at the door and bit her lip. "I won't tell them as long as you promise to tell me everything later."

"I will," Imric said, and gave her a nudge toward the door. "Now go on before they get suspicious."

Soot went to the door, then stuck her tongue out at Imric before closing it behind her.

Xax had scooted over to the food tray and was nibbling on a piece of bread that he had dipped in the soup. "Does anyone want some? No? Good, because I'm starving."

Livia returned to her chair, and Imric sat down again.

"We really want to help," Livia said. "Can we do anything?"

Xax carefully chewed his food and swallowed before answering. "It's unlikely you can do anything to convince tens of thousands of people to pick up and leave their city. Not without the king's say so. No, the best thing you can do is prepare yourselves for a sudden departure. Find my walking stick if you can. Get a small bag and put the things you value most in it, but no more than you can easily carry. Some food and water." He pointed at Imric. "You like secret tunnels. Do you know any that lead out of the city?"

"I…I'm not certain," Imric said. "I found one that goes on and on for a long ways, but it has a cave in and I was afraid to crawl over the rubble in case more came down and I got trapped."

"That sounds promising," Xax said. "We need options. Now, go on and leave me to my supper. When the dragon arrives, come to me, and bring your bags and my stick." Xax nodded at Imric. "I hope to have a chance to get to know you better, young man. And Livia, I long for the opportunity to make up for lost time."

4
VILLEM

Questions roiled through Villem Tathis's mind, but it didn't look like he would be getting answers anytime soon. The column of riders retraced the road that Villem had taken over the past couple of days, but at a more relentless pace. They didn't stop for lunch, but simply took hard cheese and even harder bread from their saddle bags and kept riding. Villem trailed at the rear of the line, just behind Miranvel, the elf whose left arm had somehow been removed at the shoulder. The elf clearly despised him, which made it that much easier for Villem to keep his mouth shut.

With little to do besides eating the dust of all the riders before him, Villem studied them more closely. Ahead of the elf rode the two women. Someone had called the big one Wide Willa. Villem had never known a woman could get so huge. It wasn't all fat either—in the years spent training to become a knight, Villem had become a good judge of bodily strength, and Wide Willa was sheathed in muscle like the strong men he had seen during festival days. He hadn't heard the name of the woman who never left Willa's side. A narrow leather tether trailed from Willa's horse and attached to a boiled leather collar around the dark-haired woman's neck. This woman was astonishing to Villem. She was one of the loveliest women he had ever seen, with an elegant face, high cheekbones, and sensuous lips. He had thought her some sort of slave, but she seemed far from miserable. She smiled and laughed more than anyone else in the band. And whenever she needed to heed the call of nature, Willa simply loosened the tether and let the woman go off on her own. The rest of the party was too distant to make out new details. The young boy rode near the front of the column and never spoke a word as far as Villem could tell. He couldn't tell anything about the characters of the other men, since they rode in silence and gave nothing away.

It had taken just over a day for Villem to reach East Gate from the village of Tarn, but this band reached the hamlet just as the sun was setting. Villem's muscles ached from the relentless hard riding. He wanted to fall off his pony and sleep for a week.

Tarn was a drab place of small huts, not one building with more than one story. Windows were kept shuttered, so darkness would become complete once the sun finished setting. When he had passed through on the way to East Gate, Villem had stopped in the small tavern to have a pint of mead and ask a few questions about East Gate and Lord Darus, but the townsfolk had been so reticent that he'd quickly finished his drink and departed to camp in a nearby grove of cedars.

The party came to a halt outside the tavern and dismounted with a spate of groans. Villem was happy he wasn't the only one with sore calves. Being new to the group, he felt he had to stand back and wait for instruction. A few of the men began stabling horses, but it was clear the stable was too small to hold all of their beasts.

The leader of the group, Orderic, approached with a grin. "You're still with us? We rode hard. Glad to see you can take it. Look, I have a small task for you." He pointed a thumb over his shoulder at the horses. "We need to stable the rest of these—yours as well. See that barn over there?"

Villem followed Orderic's pointing finger and saw the dark silhouette of what he assumed must be a barn past the outskirts of the town. "I see it."

"Lead the rest of the horses there. Take care of them; you know what to do, saddles, blankets, rub them down, feed them. We'll bring you some hot grub and ale. When farmer Mac shows up, tell him he'll get his standard rate. Tell him it comes from Orderic. He won't give any trouble. There's only three rooms in the tavern, so you'll be sleeping in the hayloft of the barn, just like most of them." He waved a hand at the other members of the band.

Villem wanted to protest. He was tempted to say that he was a noble and this wasn't how it worked. But he saw the wicked glint in Orderic's eyes and kept his mouth shut. Sore and exhausted as he was, he had a lot of work to do to prepare all these horses for the night. He nodded at Orderic and tugged the reins of his pony and warhorse to get them moving. He collected the remaining line of horses and headed for the barn. The next couple of hours went by in a blur of blisters and utter exhaustion as he rubbed down the weary flanks of horse after horse. He loved horses, so he didn't blame them for his misery. He would treat them well if it killed him.

It was a long while before others showed up with his dinner. Clearly they had already supped, and the bowl of stew one of the men handed him was cold. At least the ale wasn't too sour. He was so hungry at this point that the congealed glop actually tasted good. Villem had assumed the two women and the boy would get rooms at the tavern, but they were all here. He wasn't familiar enough with all the men to know who had gotten rooms, but Orderic was one, naturally. Miranvel wasn't here, which was a relief. Wide Willa led her woman by the tether up into the hayloft by the rickety ladder, and a couple other men followed. Villem eyed the loft with envy, but he had more work to do on the horses before he was finished. Only the boy seemed willing to help, though only on his own horse. Villem had already rubbed that one down, but the boy gave him a glare and picked up a brush to do it again. Villem found feed bags and grain, so he set about feeding the mounts. The boy didn't help with that.

As Villem was finishing up, the farmer finally appeared. "Just call me Mac," he said, after Villem had passed along Orderic's words. "Always happy to meet a new member of the watch."

"Not sure I'm a member yet," Villem said. "Twas my first day."

"A little hazing, eh? They all go through it."

Mac seemed friendlier than any of the other townsfolk he had seen, so Villem ventured to ask a few questions. "Do you know these people?" He indicated the hayloft where all the others had gone.

"Not well," Mac said. "I've seen a few of them now and then. The watch doesn't come this direction very often. Spend most of their time out east with the barbarians."

"Why are they coming this way now? They talked about a war."

Mac shrugged. "No idea. Haven't heard nothing about no war."

Villem thanked him and headed up the ladder to the loft. It was too dark to see much. Bodies were strewn about in the hay, and Villem couldn't find a decent spot to lay himself down. In the end he perched himself on a pile of straw near the edge of the loft, hoping he wouldn't tumble off in the night.

The band started off early in the morning, grabbing only a few apples and boiled eggs from the tavern to break their fast as they rode. The group continued to ignore Villem, with one exception. A willowy blond man named Eiric had introduced himself and shook Villem's hand, thanking him for taking care of his horse the night before. Villem supposed that was a good sign.

He groaned as his arse and thigh muscles renewed their protests against the abuse of too much time in the saddle. Miranvel, again riding just in front of Villem, kept looking off to the north, but all Villem could see was a distant dark line of trees. He thought back to the geography lessons of his childhood and realized with a jolt that these trees must be the legendary Black Woods, the setting of so many bedtime tales. The woods were supposedly haunted by all manner of ghosts and foul undead creatures. He didn't suppose the stories were true, but he wondered why the elf was so interested. Still, he didn't dare ask. Miranvel drew forth a wicked looking dagger and began to sharpen it with a whet stone as he rode. It was difficult to do with one arm—he had to wedge the whet stone into a specially made leather holder attached to the saddle so he could run his blade along it. After half an hour of this, he pointed the dagger at the distant wood line and held it that way for half a minute before sheathing it.

Three members of the band, including the leader Orderic, began discussing something as they rode, but they were up at the front of the line and Villem couldn't hear what they said. A farmer working his field raised a shovel and waved it at them, so Orderic turned the group aside to pull up near the man.

"News, old man?" Orderic asked.

"Have you heard?" said the farmer. "The magic is gone! The Colquitt boy rode by this morning shouting the news."

Orderic nodded and waved to the farmer as he kicked his steed forward. Villem was stunned. The magic of the spire gone? That couldn't be true. The band was riding on with no discussion and no sign that they even cared about what the farmer had said. They must know he's spouting nonsense, he thought. When several minutes passed in silence, Villem couldn't take the suspense anymore. He nudged his pony forward, passing by the elf and several others until he drew abreast of Eiric, the only one who seemed willing to show any sort of friendliness.

"Eiric, why does no one react to what the farmer said? He's crazy, right?"

Eiric tilted his head at Villem and squinted. "I thought you knew already, seeing as how you rode from this direction. Tevin rode in yesterday morning with the news. Why do you think we're riding this way?"

Villem gaped, his mind roiling. "You're…you're saying it's true? The magic is truly gone?"

"Aye. Or at least that's what Tevin told us, and he's a serious fellow. When he speaks, no one discounts him."

"Who's Tevin?"

Eiric pointed to the head of the column. "One of the scouts. Up there speaking with Orderic now."

Villem seemed to be having trouble catching his breath. He had no idea how to react to this news. It still seemed impossible. The Spire of Peace had been around for thousands of years, even before men had come to this region. Did it still stand but somehow the magic had stopped working? If it had been destroyed, what could have done such a thing? An earthquake?

He thought of home, the beautiful town of Iskimir by the lake, and the castle where he had lived all of his fifteen years. He missed it, though he harbored anger against his lord father. And his mother. Could he return home now, despite what his parents had done to him? One thing was certain, he was thrilled that there would be no more gut-churning fear and weakness caused by that damnable magic. A sudden thought came to him. "Eiric? What did you mean about why we are riding this way? Are we all heading home now that there's nothing to prevent us?"

Eiric squinted at him again. "Are you daft, boy? You heard Orderic mention the war. Does that sound like we're headed home?"

"But what war? I haven't heard any news of war."

Eiric threw his arm out to encompass all of the view to the south. "There! All of the land that abandoned us. Outlawed us. Exiled us.

Perhaps you've come too recently to understand, but do you imagine we feel kindness toward these people? They don't give a damn about us, that's for sure."

"You can't mean that you intend to war against our own folk?"

"Oh, aye," Eiric said with a nasty grin. "We'll set things straight. Darus will be the new king before long, as he should be, and we'll finally get what we're owed."

"What's that?"

Eiric spat onto the ground. "All these fancy lords and ladies will bend the knee to Darus or get what they deserve. And we, the faithful, will be the new lords…as we deserve."

Villem drew his mounts to a halt, and Eiric cackled with laughter. The rest of the column passed by as Villem stared at the ground, horrified by what he had heard. Yes, he resented what had happened to him that had forced him to leave behind all that he had known in his life, but he felt no hatred for the people of the Known Lands. To bring war to these beautiful lands was unthinkable.

He fell in place behind Miranvel again, but he swept his gaze from side to side, wondering if there was a good way to escape these lunatics. He looked behind at his warhorse and knew he had no way of getting away short of abandoning his pony and most of his equipment. Even then he wasn't certain they wouldn't catch him. At least one of the men, Tevin, was a scout by profession. Villem feared to make the attempt for now, but he promised himself he'd find a way.

When the sun hit its zenith, Orderic called a halt and everyone pulled out whatever they had for a hasty lunch. Villem wished he had more. He had been reduced to bread and cheese prior to his arrival at East Gate, and he'd been given no opportunity to replenish his supplies.

"Do you realize where we are?" Orderic shouted. He spun in a slow circle, his arms spread wide. "That oak there sat on the borderline. And we feel nothing. The magic *is* gone." He laughed and others in the band joined in with him, laughing and twirling about as if half mad. Villem shook his head and continued chewing the moldy cheese. He studied the lay of the land. It was mostly flat with some gentle rises here and there. A few stands of oak, cedar, and ash. No sign of people except a lonely cabin tucked away in the middle of the nearest stand of trees.

Orderic drew near and followed Villem's gaze to the cabin. He grinned broadly. "Oh, yes! Time for your initiation, young Villem. You will kick off the war for us."

Villem had been in the act of swallowing a mouthful of bread, and he choked so hard on it that Orderic had to pound his back several times before he could clear his airway.

"Nothing easier," Orderic said. "Doesn't look like a farmer, but perhaps a woodsman or small craftsman of some sort. Burn it down, Villem. Burn it down."

"They are innocent folk," Villem protested. "They've done nothing."

"They are the enemy," Orderic said. "Lessens must be taught."

Villem's spinning mind grasped at anything that might deter this insanity. "Darus wouldn't want this. He'll want his subjects to love him when he assumes the throne."

Orderic laughed. "Darus doesn't give two shits about love. They'll love him plenty once they fear him enough." The laughter stopped abruptly and Orderic looked grim as he pointed at the cabin. "You'll do this, or you are one of them. And you'll pay just like they will for all these centuries of pain they've inflicted upon us." He snapped a finger at Miranvel. "Light a torch, elf. And go with this lad to see he does his proper duty."

Miranvel's eyes gleamed as he stared at Villem, and he smirked at what he must have seen in Villem's eyes. With his one arm, Miranvel needed help from a man he called Meldon to get a torch lit and pass it to Villem, who took it reluctantly.

"On foot," Orderic said. "We'll mind your steeds."

Villem slid to the ground, careful to keep the fire away from his pony. He walked slowly toward the cabin, Miranvel falling in behind him. He hoped no one was home. The place was constructed from cedar beams and looked well built, though it had clearly been here a very long time. It was small, looking to be just a single room. There were no windows, and just one door that Villem could see, covered only by a tanned hide. A large pile of split wood was piled beside the door.

Villem thought about calling out to whomever occupied the cabin but decided against it. He turned to Miranvel. "It's for me to do. Wait here and let me finish it."

The elf hissed at him, his hand on the hilt of the dagger at his side.

Villem walked on, his knees rubbery with fright. He listened to see if he could hear the elf following, but he heard nothing. He stopped short of the doorway and tried to see through the edges of the hide, but there was nothing but darkness. Villem sighed. Whoever lived here must be gone. He hated to burn the place, but at least no one would be hurt. He pulled aside the hide and took a step inside. There was a decent number of furnishings, all gorgeously crafted of wood. The occupant must be a carpenter, he thought. He heard a groan from one corner, and his heart caught in his throat. A large man with an enormous red beard sat up from a cot, a large bearskin pooling at his waist.

"What's this?" the man said, his voice slurred.

Villem saw a wooden cup on the small stand near the cot, along with a large wineskin, and he realized the man was drunk. "Sir, you…you must get away from here." He scanned the room but saw no other exit than the main door. "You must run…or they will kill you."

The man rubbed his eyes with a fist. "Get out of my home. Leave me be."

Villem looked back at the doorway and a chill ran down his spine. Miranvel stood silently on the other side of the hide. Villem began to pant. He dropped to his knees near the drunk man. He whispered, "Is there any other way out of here? You see that man out there? He'll—"

The drunk man punched Villem in the face. It was a clumsy blow that glanced off one cheekbone, but it sent Villem sprawling backwards, the torch flung off to one side. The drunk roared and clambered to his feet, eyes blazing. "You dare!" he shouted.

Villem scrambled backward. He heard laughter from Miranvel, but the elf did not enter the cabin.

"You dare!" the man shouted again, snatching up an axe.

Villem had never felt such terror. He scrambled to his feet and reached for a sword hilt that wasn't there. The sword was still strapped to his pony. He glanced at the dropped torch, which was busy setting a small cabinet ablaze, but it was out of reach. The drunk hefted the axe over his head and advanced on Villem. All Villem had was the small dagger he used for eating, but he snatched it from his belt and lunged forward quickly under the man's reach, lowered his shoulder, and slammed into the man's belly, driving him backward to fall in a heap together with Villem on top. Villem didn't want to stab the man, so he brought the pommel of his dagger down hard on the man's temple.

The man cried out and all the fight seemed to drain out of him. Villem sat on the man's abdomen and felt sick as the man began to weep with great shuddering sobs, his hands held to his forehead.

Smoke began to fill the room from the growing fire. Villem lurched to his feet and stared down at the man. "I'm sorry. You must get out of here." He turned and stumbled out of the doorway, brushing by Miranvel. He weaved his way to the woodpile and fell to his knees to vomit.

The cabin began to burn in earnest now, and smoke roiled from the doorway, but still the man did not make an appearance. Miranvel took a few steps back, and Villem had to crawl away from the woodpile to escape the heat. He heard rasping coughs from inside the cabin, and suddenly there came soul searing screams. In horror, Villem leapt to his feet, pressed his palms to his ears, and scrambled back toward his pony and horse, tears streaming down his face. He didn't want to hear or see what happened to the poor man. It was all his fault. He should have prevented this somehow. He crashed into the flank of his pony and gripped the saddle with both hands to hold himself up.

"You did well, kid," Orderic said, and clapped a hand to his back.

With an animal growl, Villem turned and punched Orderic as hard as he could, sending the man sprawling in the dirt. He lunged forward, intending to pound him to a pulp, but a tangle of strong arms caught him and slammed him to the ground. At least two men sat on him while multiple hands pressed him down. Through his tears of rage and fear, he heard them laughing. Never in his life had Villem felt he actually hated anyone, but at this moment he would have gladly murdered every member of Orderic's band.

5
IMRIC

Imric stood at the crenellations gazing out at the city of Tolgaria. He was in a foul mood, so the beautiful sight soothed his nerves. The tower upon which he stood was one of the broad, squat ones, and a dozen more graceful towers clustered all around him, seeming to touch the puffy white clouds that filled the sky. Even from his short tower the view was splendid. The sea filled the horizon beyond the city walls, and dozens of fishing vessels skimmed the placid blue waters. The city itself was enormous. He'd heard that nearly two hundred thousand people lived here, and he could believe it. They were like tiny ants swarming through the narrow streets far below. Most of the city proper was made from marble brought up from the vast quarries to the south—the walls that surrounded the old city, most of the buildings, and even the street pavings themselves. Down among the colorful pavilions and kiosks and tiled roofs, the city gleamed white from the marble, though if he looked closely, he could see striations of red or pink where different kinds of marble had been used. Beyond the walls, ramshackle wooden houses marched on as far as Imric could see, except where limited by the seashore on one side and the line of the river on the other. He loved this city, and each time he came up to look at it he wondered why he didn't do so more often.

He noticed there were more guards than usual on the walls, most armed with crossbows. Some of the towers now had ballistae set up, with deadly-tipped bolts set into the grooves of their wooden frames. His father may not believe in the dragon, but he was taking preparation seriously. Imric simply could not take the idea of a dragon seriously either, even with Xax's warnings. The man could be getting addled in his old age. Imric frowned. But what about the vanishing of the magic from the Spire of Peace? That was real. He shook his head and looked again at the vastness of the city. Even if a dragon did exist, it couldn't possibly get away with attacking a place like this. It would be filled with bolts and quarrels in an instant.

"Livia told me I could find you here."

Imric turned and saw Soot climbing the last steps of the spiral staircase that led up onto the tower. In her arms was an enormous gray cat. Soot was breathing hard, just as Imric had when climbing up here himself, a reminder of the disappearance of the magic that had sustained them their whole lives.

"What do you want?" he grumbled.

"Why so moody?" She joined him in gazing out at the city, one hand stroking the lazy cat.

Imric scowled and shook his head. "I can't get to it."

"To what?"

"Xax's walking stick. It's in the room below us. A guard told me so. I've been searching all morning and can't find any way of getting in."

Soot smiled. "Maybe not every room in the castle has a secret passage."

"You're such a big help. Don't you have chores?"

"Mama gave me free time until next bell."

"And you're wasting it here with me?"

Soot sighed. "I'd suggest we go do something fun, but I'm beat from climbing all those steps. I really don't like losing the magic. Maybe you can tell that wizard to build the spire again."

Imric glared at Soot. "It took decades to build and needed the cooperation of legions of elves and dwarves, not to mention several wizards. Don't you know anything about history?"

Soot shrugged and scratched behind the cat's ears. "Not much, I guess."

Imric thought back to the similar conversation he'd had with his sister, and suddenly he felt ashamed that he had also brushed off the importance of learning history. Livia knew so much about everything, and was that so bad? Why couldn't he ever have the energy to study such things? Whatever he did know he got only from what Livia told him.

He heard a commotion coming from the stairwell, so he motioned to Soot to follow as he walked over to peer down the curve of stone steps. Someone was pounding on a door, and he assumed it could only be the door to the room he so desperately wanted to sneak into. He looked at Soot and placed a finger to his lips, then began sneaking down the steps. He went down only far enough to be able to peer through the bend of the stairwell and see the part of the landing below where a balding man in expensive clothing stood near the wooden door, hand raised to knock again. The door swung open and Imric was astonished to see his father.

"Tarl, what is it?" the king asked.

"The dragon, sire." The man was sweating profusely from his journey up the stairs.

Varun Kaldarion's eyes widened. "It's here?"

Tarl waved a hand as if to brush away an evil thought. "No, sire. It attacked Andiria."

Imric's breath caught in his throat. Andiria was one of the three huge sister cities of the realm. At the far northern end of the inland sea sat Valandiria, ruled by his Uncle Erol, the duke of the north realm. The capital city, Tolgaria, sat on the east side of the Sea of Alia, just below the mid-point. Andiria lay at the southern tip of the sea, a day's ride away. It was ruled by a cousin that Imric had never met.

The king remained silent for a few moments. "Did they drive it off?"

Tarl fumbled for words. "I...I only have the words of a few panicked riders, sire. They say..." he drew a shuddering breath, "...they say the city is fallen. They say a river of refugees follows on the road. The—"

The king cut Tarl off with a hand gesture. He looked pale. "I must go out into the city. Reassure my people. This is the time they need me most."

"Sire! We must flee, like the wizard said. Head north to safety."

The king shook his shaggy gray mane. "You go ahead and flee, Tarl. Take your family and go. This is the moment to show my people what kingship truly means. Go on." He waved a dismissing hand at Tarl.

"But, sire!"

"I said go."

"Aye, sire." Tarl scurried off down the stairs.

Varun turned back into the room, though he left the door open. Imric inched down the stairs, wishing he could see inside the room, but it was too dark inside. He didn't want his father to spot him. This wasn't the moment to raise his ire. It only took a few moments for the king to reappear, and in his hand was Xax's walking stick. Imric didn't know what to think. It seemed impossible to be able to get the stick from the locked room, but would it be any easier to snatch it from the king himself? Perhaps Varun meant to bring it to Xax, now that the dragon had turned out to be real? Maybe he's going to Xax now? These thoughts sent Imric's blood racing. *Now we'll see something!* The king and the wizard united together could surely do something to stop the dragon.

As Varun plunged down the stairs two at a time, Imric waved to Soot to follow. "Hurry," he hissed. "We have to keep up with him."

"I'm not chasing after the king," Soot said, dropping the cat on the landing as they hurried by. "You go right ahead."

"Come on, Sooty! We have to see what happens. I bet he's going to the wizard."

The king had outpaced them, and when they came to the next landing he was nowhere to be seen or heard. This was the level where Xax's room was, but Imric should have been able to see the king down the long hallway if he had gone that way.

"What is it?" Soot whispered.

"He's…he said he's going out into the city. We'll go ourselves." This was a sobering thought, tinged with excitement. He had never left the palace in his entire life. He'd watched the city from the battlements enough times to feel he knew some of the directions, but actually going out into the streets on his own was something he'd rarely even contemplated doing.

"You're mad," Soot responded. "I'm going back to the kitchens." She headed for the stairs again and Imric hurried to follow.

"Soot! This is the adventure of a lifetime. We must go!"

"My mama would kill me," Soot said as she continued to clip down the stairs.

"When she hears the king is out there rallying the people, she'll probably go out herself. Everyone will."

Soot sniffed loudly. "She'd never do that."

Imric felt desperate. He didn't want to go into the city by himself. "Help me find, Livia, at least."

Soot groaned. "All right, but then you're on your own."

It wasn't difficult to find Livia. She was in her room on the bed, reading a book by lamplight. She sat silently gaping at Imric as the words tumbled out of him.

"Men on horses have come. The dragon destroyed Andiria. Father took Xax's walking stick, and he's going out into the city to…to…to help the people. I want to go see."

Livia set the book aside, took a deep breath, and stood up. "You can't go dressed like that. Let me get my cloak. Perhaps I have something here you can use."

Imric wrinkled his nose. "Not some of your clothes."

"Look, I have this old riding cape. It would look fine on you."

It was a green silk-looking thing but didn't look too terrible to Imric, so he let Livia fasten it about his neck. He noticed Soot was still there, standing silently by the door. "I thought you were going to the kitchens?"

Soot looked sideways at the door. "I want to come with you."

"Great! Let's go before we miss everything."

Livia kept telling him to slow down as they headed toward the castle grounds, but Imric couldn't contain his energy and hustled onward. The girls giggled and scampered to keep up. It felt like a holiday, despite the supposed danger of the dragon.

They reached the courtyard and Imric halted. He had never gone beyond the gates. Livia put an arm around his shoulders.

"I haven't gone out much myself, except riding a few times, and always under escort. If Father hears I went out without guards, he'll skin me alive."

Imric looked at his sister, then at Soot, and grinned. "Come on!"

The guards at the gates stood in clumps gossiping about Andiria and the dragon, so the trio passed through without incident. They passed over the dry moat on the drawbridge, and for the first time Imric's feet touched the marble street. A hush seemed to have fallen over the city. Whenever he looked down from the ramparts, he saw the streets swarming with people, but now he saw only a few dozen, all of them shifty-eyed and in a hurry to reach their destinations. Imric sensed their fear, and it wiped the grin from his face.

Livia pointed to a nearby block of marble where protesters were allowed to stand to shout their grievance at the castle. It was empty now. "We can wait here for Father to come. He shouldn't notice us, and we can follow him."

Imric stood nervously between Livia and Soot, shifting from foot to foot. He took Livia's hand, as he had done often as a little boy. For some reason it didn't make him feel childish now. Some city folk began to gather in the small square before the castle gates. They murmured and muttered together, but no one got rowdy. It took more than an hour before the king and his retinue appeared, and by that time quite a crowd had gathered. When the men-at-arms and knights stalked through the gates, the crowd silently moved aside to form a path for them, and when the king appeared they roared out a desperate-sounding cheer. King Varun Kaldarion's face lit up with a massive grin, and he pulled forth his famous sword, gifted by the dwarves to the first king of the Known Lands, Aronis Kaldarion, more than twelve hundred years ago. He thrust the sword above his head, where it caught the sunlight, and shouted, "Fear not, my people! The great beast will meet its doom upon this blade!"

The cheer grew to a roar, which Imric ignored when his eyes fell on the figure that scuttled through the gate behind the king. It was Xax, wearing his travel-stained cloak, his walking stick held loosely in one hand, a grim look upon his face.

A troop of guards lined the path for the king as he made his way through the crowd of cheering city folk. Several courtiers walked with him, though Imric noted many of them looked as if they wished they were anywhere but here. His brother Balmar stamped along at the rear of the group, not far from Xax.

"Come!" Livia cried. "I want to speak with Xax."

The crowd began to fall in behind the royal group, so the trio had to struggle to push their way forward to reach the wizard.

"Xax!" Livia shouted. She cried his name three times before he heard and turned his head, a look of surprise on his face.

"You shouldn't be here, little ones," he said. He eyed the crowd behind them. "Too late now, I suppose."

"Is there some way we can help you?" Livia asked.

"I don't know," Xax said, shaking his head. "We need to get far away from here. You should have brought the bags I asked you to make up."

Livia looked at the sky, then back at the wizard. "When will the dragon come?"

"I don't know when, but I know it will. And we don't want to be here when it does."

"All of these poor people," Livia said, staring around at the crowd.

"There's nothing we can do if the king won't listen," Xax said.

They trudged forward following the king's retinue. The streets beyond the castle gates were mostly empty, though people threw open their second-floor shutters to watch and cheer the king's passing. Imric could tell by the expression on his father's face that he was unhappy not to be drawing crowds. He saw the king speaking and gesturing at two men, who then ran off in different directions. Suddenly a huge hand grabbed a bunch of Imric's hair and pulled him painfully upward.

"Hey, little rat."

"Balmar, leave him alone!" Livia shouted, punching their brother in the shoulder.

Imric rubbed his scalp after Balmar let him go. He didn't interact with his brother often, but he didn't hate him. He knew that Balmar was only mimicking the way he'd seen Darus treat him. Darus was the true bully. Balmar was just simpleminded.

"Why you here?" Balmar asked.

"We're worried about the dragon," Livia said. "We want to see what Father is going to say to everyone."

"We will kill the dragon," Balmar boasted, though Imric thought he saw worry in his eyes.

"Your father is mistaken, young man," Xax said, walking along with the aid of his stick. "No one is going to kill this dragon anytime soon."

Balmar looked angry. "Fa-father says his sword can slay the dragon."

Xax stared sadly at Balmar for a few moments as he trudged along. "It's true that only a blade like his could pierce the hide of the beast. But it would mean getting in very close and striking true in order to have any chance."

"Father is brave!" Balmar exclaimed.

"Mmmm," Xax mumbled. "That he is. Brave but foolish."

The streets of Tolgaria were a tangled maze of alleyways, except for the road from the castle gates that led to the main gates of the city. It was the widest lane in the city, about twenty paces across. Imric was happy to see everything up close for a change. The buildings formed a continuous wall to either side, broken only by the narrow alleyways. Almost all the buildings were two stories tall, made of marble or stone, with red-tiled roofs. When he peered down alleyways, he saw they were strung with clotheslines from window to window all along their lengths. The roadway, though made of marble, wasn't nearly as slick as he had imagined it would be. The marble was carved in rough patterns that helped his feet keep their grip. Imric wrinkled his nose; the city smelled like a privy.

"How can anyone stand to live here?" he asked Livia, waving a hand in front of his nose.

"You're spoiled from living in the castle," she replied. "They get used to it and don't even notice the smell after a while."

"Where are we going?"

Livia shrugged. "Near the city gates is one of the larger squares. I assume that's where we're heading, but I'm not really sure."

In the distance to both sides, trumpets began to sound.

"Father's trying to call people out," Livia said.

"Look at them!" Imric said, pointing to the most exotic-looking group of people he'd ever seen.

There were seven of them, standing by the side of the road ahead, watching the royal procession. Their skin was the color of creamed coffee, and all of them were thin and wore strange clothes made of rough spun wool. Imric had seen plenty of interesting people in his father's throne room, but none like these.

"Are they barbarians?" he asked Livia.

"I...don't think so," she responded.

Xax stepped in closer. "They are nomadic tribesmen from the Arid Lands far to the south. You won't see many of them in the Known Lands. They might be an embassy, or traders."

They were just passing the nomads now, and Imric eyed them with great interest, trying to soak up every detail.

"Stop staring, Imric," Livia said. "It's rude."

"Do you think they're dangerous?" Soot asked. It had been Soot who had told him most of the stories he had heard about the mysterious nomads. They were supposedly the greatest horsemen alive, and some of them even rode strange beasts that no civilized men had seen. Soot had told him that they got their wives from raiding other tribes, and they liked to roast babies alive on spits over their fire pits.

"You think they'd be here wandering freely if they were?" Livia said and gave Soot a light shove.

Xax tapped Soot with his walking stick. "Don't believe everything you hear. People like to make up stories about that which they don't understand. They have a fascinating culture, quite different from what you know, but that doesn't make them bad."

Imric and Soot both kept glancing back over their shoulders at the tribesmen, who were now following along behind with the crowd.

"Father should invite them into the throne room to talk," Imric said.

"I should like to see that," Soot added.

"Up ahead there," Livia said, pointing, "we're coming to the big square near the gates."

The king and some of his courtiers and knights ascended the stone stairs and stood upon the ramparts, looking back over the gathered crowd. He stood tall and gazed out over the rooftops for long moments before turning his attention to his people. He beckoned for silence and the people complied.

"Good people of Tolgaria and the realm!" The king spread his arms wide above his head as he shouted. "Rumors have brought fear to our city these past days, and it is time you had answers. You should not give in to fear, for there is nothing we face today that we cannot overcome. It is true, the Spire of Peace has fallen." Imric felt the crowd shuffling and murmuring, and he gripped Livia's hand harder. "We have all felt it. The magic has gone. And there have been riders from Andiria, our sister-city, bearing stories of a great beast. Again I say, do not fear! Andiria was unprepared, and we are forewarned. Look ye!" The king gestured along the battlements first to one side and then the other, where dozens of armored guardsmen watched their liege, crossbows in hand. Then he pointed at the nearby towers, topped by enormous ballistae. The king again raised his arms to the crowd. "Should it come, this beast shall meet its end!"

Xax twirled and bent down to face Livia and Imric. His face was pale and slicked with sweat. "Run! We must run now!" He began to push at them to get them turned about.

Soot grabbed Imric's arm. "What is it?"

The king's voice boomed on, but Imric heard none of it. He tried shoving through the crowd, listening as the pale wizard raved about being too late. Imric looked back over his shoulder, then stumbled to a halt. Where the king stood on the rampart, gesticulating at the crowd, a black dot had appeared in the sky above his head. It was growing steadily larger with each passing moment. The crowd began to take notice; men and women alike began pointing and shouting. The king seemed to take no notice but waved his arms to silence them.

A tug on his arm got Imric moving again. He was surprised at the strength in the old man's arms. "Is that—?"

"Not another word!" Xax cried. "Just run!"

Imric felt numb, as he wound through the crowd, which was growing rowdier by the moment.

"Is that it?" a woman nearby cried.

Imric desperately wanted to turn and look, to see the beast for himself. To see the guardsmen leap to the ballistae and defend the city and their king. But Xax's pulling hand was insistent, and Soot shoved him forward as she followed behind him. Livia was somehow up in front leading the way. They reached the edge of the crowd just as it began to panic. A fat woman turned to run and her bulk knocked Imric to the ground. Soot stumbled down on top of him. Screams began in earnest all about them, and the panic turned into a rush.

Xax returned and fended off two men with his walking stick before reaching down to pluck Imric back onto his feet. Imric helped Soot scramble up.

"Over here!" shouted Livia, waving them over to a sheltering wall out of the general scrum of the fleeing crowd.

When he reached the wall, Imric turned and pressed his back to it, breathing heavily. It felt like minutes had passed since he had seen the oily black dot in the sky, but he realized it could only have been a few seconds. The king was only now turning away from trying to pacify the crowd, trying to see where they were pointing. Imric watched his father's body stiffen. The dragon was no longer a small dot. It remained black as coal but had grown huge as it flew directly toward them, as if it meant to pass over the king's head.

"Head for the gates!" Xax shouted. "Run!"

Imric couldn't move. He wondered why the guards and knights stood and watched as the beast closed in. Why didn't they run to the ballistae? Why did so few of them heft their crossbows? The dragon, that had looked so large that Imric had thought it was upon them, instead grew even larger as it sped toward them. Everything seemed to be going in slow motion. The crowd became a blur around him. Hands tugged at him, but he resisted their pull. Imric watched in fascination as a valiant guardsman reached a ballista on the nearest tower and yanked the firing cord, sending a wickedly barbed bolt screaming at the dragon's scaled chest, where it caromed off ineffectively. Dozens of crossbow quarrels whipped into and around the beast, none leaving a mark, not even when they struck the membrane of the dragon's wings.

The dragon seemed so large now that it filled Imric's vision. The king stood as unmoving as a statue, one hand on the hilt of his blade, staring at the onrushing beast. The dragon opened its mouth, revealing vicious, snaggled teeth. Imric thought it meant to roar or perhaps blast out its famed breath, but instead it sped on without pause and merely dipped its head down to snap its jaws shut about his father's head. As he was jerked into the sky, the king's legs kicked and his arms flapped about. The dragon flew directly overhead at terrific speed and vanished over the rooftops, taking the king with it.

Something smacked into Imric's cheek, and when he brushed at it with his fingers, they came away sticky with blood. "Father," he whispered.

Xax stopped pulling at his arm, and Livia appeared and folded him in her arms, tears streaking her cheeks. Soot had slid down the wall into a crouch, her mouth open and eyes wide. The streets seemed suddenly empty but for a few stragglers. Guards on the walls stared after the dragon, while the courtiers and knights who had accompanied the king gazed in horror at the empty spot where he had stood mere moments before.

"This isn't natural," Xax said. "Someone guides the beast's actions."

Livia lifted her tear-stained face from Imric's shoulder. "What do you mean?"

"One tiny dot out of so many tens of thousands and it picked him out. That cannot be an accident."

Imric watched the men on the walls. A few of the knights and courtiers were filing down the stone staircase, while others stood in a huddle, some pointing out into the city. Imric followed where they pointed, off to his right, and he saw the dragon reappear at a great distance. It was circling lazily now, barely moving its wings as it glided. There was no sign of his father. The dragon opened its mouth and screeched, and even at this distance it pierced his ears so that he clapped his hands to cover them, as did everyone around him. Now the dragon arched its neck downward and sprayed a terrible, jet-black stream into the city below. Whatever it blew forth from its mouth, it billowed out into a roiling cloud that spread quickly to encompass several blocks of buildings.

Xax's eyes were wide. "We must move now!"

Imric dropped his hands from his ears and pointed one at the black clouds. "What is that, Xax? I thought dragons blew flame?"

"Only some," the wizard replied. "No time for this, run!" He snatched Livia's arm and took off at as fast a gait as he could manage.

"Let's go!" shouted Soot, pulling at his hand.

Imric took one more look at the dragon, still circling in the distance, then let Soot drag him away. They turned down the road toward the castle. Everyone they could see was pelting at full speed. A few pounded at doors, begging to be let in.

"Stay together!" Xax shouted.

They continued running until Imric saw a group of figures ahead standing in a group, gesticulating and pointing back the way they had come. He recognized them as the nomads from the Arid Lands. Imric and Soot had to stumble to a near halt to avoid running headlong into the tribesmen. He turned his head to see what the men were staring at and saw that the dragon had come full circle. It was just about to fly over the city gates again, but this time it billowed its wings out, extended its clawed feet, and landed on the top of one of the guard towers of the gate. A brave man-at-arms stood his ground mere paces from the beast and fired his ballista. The bolt shivered off the dragon's belly and clattered off into the street.

"Nothing can pierce its hide," Soot said at his side.

The dragon spread its wings wide like a great bat and screeched, forcing Imric to cover his ears again.

Someone grabbed hold of Imric's shoulder. "What are you doing?" cried the wizard. "We must keep going."

One of the tribesmen held his arms out imploringly at them. "Help us," he said in a thick accent. "We have nowhere to hide."

"No time!" Xax shouted. "Follow us if you must."

The group ran onward, but Imric couldn't help but look back over his shoulder. He saw the dragon arch its neck and then lunge his head forward to blast its breath directly down the street toward them. The jet-black stream spread into a roiling cloud and engulfed the houses behind them. Screams arose everywhere, and Imric heard a crackling and hissing sound that was unlike anything he had ever heard in his life.

"We must get off the streets!" cried the wizard. He plunged to a halt and pounded on a stout wooden door, crying out for help. Livia and the strange tribesmen did the same, choosing other doors and pounding them with all their strength. Imric and Soot stood next to Xax and looked back at the encroaching black cloud. It looked like it would reach them in a few more moments. No one opened their doors to them.

"This way! Hurry!" Xax screamed out, lurching toward one of the narrow alleyways. The nomads streamed in after him. Livia waved frantically at the stragglers. Imric took a last look at the looming cloud before dashing after Soot into the alley. As his feet pounded on the marble paving stones, he heard a loud hiss behind him and knew that the cloud had rushed by the mouth of the alley. He couldn't help but glance back, and he saw a branch of the cloud billowing down the narrow lane directly toward him.

"Faster!" he cried, and picked up his own pace, his lungs burning and a stitch eating at his side.

Someone stumbled and sprawled to the pavement ahead of him. Imric saw that it was one of the nomads. He wanted to stop and help the man up, but he was certain the black cloud was going to envelop him at any moment and fear snatched at his heart. He leapt over the fallen man, shame burning in his throat. Behind him the man's shout changed to a horrifying scream, and Imric knew he would be dead if he had stopped. The thought entered his mind that he was doomed anyway, that he could never outrun the dragon's breath. Ahead of him he saw his sister break out of the alley into a larger thoroughfare, Soot chasing on her heels. In the center of the intersection was a large marble fountain that looked as if it had not functioned for years. The wizard shouted something and then dove headfirst into the waters of the fountain. The nomads scrambled in after him, followed by Livia and Soot. Certain that the black cloud would touch him at any moment, Imric sped up even more, gasped in a deep breath, and took a running leap over the edge of the fountain.

The water was brackish and cold, and someone's flailing foot struck his head. Imric was loath to come up for air, knowing that the black cloud would have covered everything above the water. He thought, why did the wizard lead them here? A few moments of safety under the water, and then agonizing death when coming up for air?

The toe of someone's boot connected with his ear, and Imric could no longer hold his breath. Wincing with the anticipation of pain, he burst from the water.

No pain. Just the sound of panting from everyone in the fountain. He knuckled water from his eyes and looked about. Xax stood at the center of the fountain, his walking stick with its knob of green crystal held forth in one hand. The world looked strangely dim and blurry. There appeared to be a dome of some sort formed about the fountain, the dark clouds of the dragon's breath roiling around it, unable to enter.

"What's this?" said a voice at his side, and Imric saw it was Soot.

Behind Imric came Livia's gasping voice. "It's Xax. He threw up a barrier of water from the fountain."

"He saved us," said one of the nomads.

"Perhaps," Livia replied. "Though I doubt it."

Just when hope was kindling in Imric's breast, Livia's response threw a bucket of ice water on it. "What do you mean?"

"Look at him," Livia said, nodding toward the wizard. "Even minor spells are taxing, and this is no cantrip. He won't be able to hold it for long."

Imric studied Xax and saw that Livia was right. The wizard was paler than ever. He gasped wheezing breaths and the arm holding out the walking stick was shaking. He's going to collapse, Imric thought in horror.

"Is there anything we can do to help him?" Soot asked.

Livia shook her head. "No, but look, the cloud is settling."

Outside the bubble of water created by Xax's magic, the dark cloud was slowly dissipating. Imric looked at Xax again. Could he hold long enough?

The wizard looked ready to drop. His knees seemed to buckle, and his arms drooped. Xax gathered some final reserve of strength and lunged upward, his arms flew high, and his voice rang out in a shout. The dome of water blew apart into droplets that exploded outward, carrying away the last tendrils of dark cloud. Xax panted once, then staggered to his knees and collapsed.

Livia and one of the nomads lunged toward Xax and together pulled his head above the water, each wrapping one arm about his shoulders. Soot dropped to her knees to scoop up the wizard's walking stick.

The soaked group stood panting and gasping in the remaining water of the fountain, looking in mixed awe and horror at the city around them. Every surface, whether building or roadway, hissed and sizzled as the coating of dragon's breath ate away at it. A few bodies lay in the street. Imric didn't dare examine them closely, knowing he'd be sickened by what he saw.

"What is that?" he whispered.

Xax's eyes remained closed and he looked more than half dead, but he managed to croak a response. "Acid."

"Over there! Look!" cried one of the nomads.

Imric followed the man's raised arm and saw the palace in the distance. The inky form of the dragon hulked atop one of the highest towers. This isn't over yet, Imric thought. And Xax can't save us again in the state he's in.

"Mama," murmured Soot, tears streaking her cheeks.

Imric put a hand to her shoulder and grasped it. "She's deep inside the castle. I bet she's safe." He wanted to believe it. The thought of being trapped in his beloved secret passages as black clouds of acid rolled through them was too terrifying to contemplate.

"I think we should move," Livia said. "Imric, lead the way, and don't lose Xax's stick."

"Where…where to?" Imric stammered.

The six remaining nomads were helping Livia to lift Xax over the edge of the fountain. Livia nodded to the left. "That way. Toward the gates."

Imric grasped the wizard's walking stick and peered over the rim of the fountain at the pavement. The frothing and bubbling of the acid had mostly stopped now. One of the nomads stood on the marble paving without apparent harm, so Imric grasped Soot's hand and together they clambered out of the fountain. Imric studied the way Livia had indicated, a narrow lane dotted with bodies. No one living was in sight. He drew a breath, grasped Soot's hand more firmly, and started off.

"I hope the dragon leaves us alone," Soot said.

Imric shuddered. "Please let it be so."

"I need to go back for my mother."

Imric shook his head. "I'm sorry. It'll have to wait until it's safer. When the dragon leaves."

Checking once to see that the nomads were managing to carry the slumped form of the wizard, Imric led the group forward. It took two turns to get onto the road to the city gates, but before too long they were back in the square where his father had perished. They hadn't seen a living soul along the way. The huge gates hung open, the powerful oaken doors burned and pitted. Everything smelled strange, like long-spoiled eggs and something else Imric couldn't identify.

Imric's eyes widened as he stalked through the gates. Inside the city, the marble and stone buildings were mostly intact, if scarred and pock-marked by the acid, but outside the walls, the wooden buildings were reduced to sludge. As far as the eye could see stretched a blackened shambles of burnt shacks.

Livia trudged up to Imric and Soot. "Keep going. We should get as far away from the city as we can."

Imric nodded numbly and stumbled onward again. The next hour was a nightmare landscape of scorched houses and blackened bodies. The stench of death was beginning to form a sickly-sweet miasma in the air. Ahead of them, the enormous Hellisgaard Mountains looked pristine, and the sky was blue with a scattering of white clouds. The world doesn't care what happened, Imric thought.

The nomads had been quietly chattering in their own tongue, but now one of them introduced himself as Azer and asked Livia for a rest. Livia clearly wanted to continue but dragging the unconscious wizard around was taxing the strength of the men who carried him. The buildings this far out were less damaged from the dragon's breath. Though they still had not encountered any survivors, they had begun to hear the rustlings and moans of terrified people skulking in their homes.

Imric was thirsty, and they had no supplies. Livia knocked at the door of a hovel. When there was no reply, she tried the door and found that it swung open. Whoever lived here had abandoned the place in a hurry. A bench had been knocked over and various sundries were scattered on the wooden planks of the floor. Soot found a keg of water and some wooden bowls, while Imric found a bag of small green apples. The nomads settled Xax onto a cot, then righted the bench and arranged themselves around the dining table.

"Eat. Drink," Livia said. "We can't stay long. There's no knowing how long the dragon will stay quiet."

"Where are we going," Imric asked.

"Valandiria, to Uncle Erol."

"Won't the dragon go there next?" Soot asked.

Livia shrugged, a desperate glint in her eyes. "Aye, most likely. But where else can we go?"

Imric thought about the mountains and the nearby dwarven city of Kaldorn. He recalled that Xax had foreseen it would fall as well. Was nowhere safe?

"I have to go back for my mother," Soot said.

"Soot, it's not safe," Livia said. "Your mother knows how to take care of herself, and everyone who survives will head north to Valandiria. I worry about Balmar, myself, but I have to hope that he somehow survived and we can find him again."

After munching some apples and gulping down some tepid water, the group moved onward. A half hour more and they reached the edge of Tolgaria at last. Imric peered south along the edge of the city and saw the distant river that flowed down from the mountains. He turned to the north and saw the marble-paved highway snaking off into the distance.

"There are people!" He pointed at the road. In pairs or in small groups, some even in wagons drawn by mules or oxen, survivors were streaming away from Tolgaria.

"They have the right idea," Livia said. "Come, let's put some distance between us and the dragon before night falls."

6

VILLEM

The next two days were ones of pain and horror for Villem. Orderic's band kept him lashed to his pony as they made their way across the land, burning farmsteads and fields, and slaughtering livestock. The greatest horror had been at the very first of the farms. The band rounded up the entire family—the farmer and his wife, two grandmothers, and thirteen children ranging from adults to a squalling infant. Villem had squeezed his eyes tightly shut against what came next, but he couldn't close his ears. He imagined he'd never again be able to sleep at night without hearing the screams. If he took any solace at all in the situation, it was seeing that the beautiful Dinara—she who was tethered about her neck to Wide Willa—was as sickened by it as he.

The only respite from the horror was when a mongrel with black fur going to gray challenged the murderers, baring its teeth and growling ferociously. One of the men—Villem thought the man was called Simon—cranked up a crossbow and took a shot at the dog, but he only grazed the poor beast and it scuttled away behind a shed. Villem was happy at least one innocent creature escaped the massacre.

Fortunately, word must have gotten out, because the remaining farmsteads were all deserted but for some livestock the inhabitants hadn't been able to drive off in time to escape.

Being roped across a pony all day was a form of torture he had never imagined before. His wrists were rubbed raw; his stomach bruised and burned; the muscles in his legs hurt nearly as bad as his spine; and his throat was raw from vomiting and retching. They gave him no food the first day and since they never untied him, he had to relieve himself in his own pants. When they stopped to make camp for the evening, they tied him to a tree and ordered the boy Weevil to guard him throughout the night.

When he could work enough saliva into his throat to be able to do more than croak, Villem asked, "Why do they call you Weevil?"

The boy spat at Villem's boots and proceeded to pointedly ignore him.

The next day they treated him a little better, or perhaps they became tired of how badly he was beginning to stink. When the band ate their lunch in a farmhouse prior to burning it, they let Eiric help him to strip out of his befouled clothes and wash with icy water drawn from the well. Eiric dug out his pack and found fresh clothes, and he even snuck Villem a hunk of bread.

At camp that evening, Orderic had them tie Villem up near the firepit. They gave him a battered tin plate with a bit of roasted chicken and beets. He ate as if it was the greatest meal of his life, only wishing he had more.

Orderic stood near the fire and looked around at his companions. "So, what should we do with the boy?"

"Let me have him," the elf Miranvel said, a nasty grin lighting up his face.

"Come now," Eiric said, "the boy's not cut out for our kind of work, but there's no call to be murdering him."

"Don't see why not," said the scout Tevin. "We're killing everyone else we find. What's special about this one?"

Orderic held up a hand. "Riches, perhaps?" He gazed around at each companion before continuing. "He's the son of some lordling, isn't he? Even though he ran off, might be they'd pay a pretty penny to get him back alive."

Villem saw the greed light up in the band's eyes, all except for Miranvel, who scowled and twirled the knife he'd been using to eat his meal.

Wide Willa pointed over at the line of steeds. "Bet they'd want that fine warhorse back, eh?"

"So, kid," Orderic said, rounding on Villem. "Where you from?"

Villem was at a loss for words. Would his father pay a ransom to have him back? He wanted to think he would, but he had to admit to himself that he wasn't certain. What if it came to a fight? Could the small troop of soldiers belonging to his father defeat Orderic's hardened veterans? Even if they could, Miranvel would almost certainly slit his throat before they could rescue him.

"Answer me, boy!"

Villem met Orderic's gaze. "Iskimir. It's a town on a lake off to the west."

"Never heard of it," Orderic said.

One of the band members that Villem hadn't really gotten to know said, "I know the area. Grew up not far from there."

"Oh, aye?" Orderic said. "Rich enough area to pay a ransom?"

The man—Villem thought his name was Davit—shrugged. "Could be. Lots of fisher folk around there, but Iskimir was the biggest town around those parts. Heard the lord there was a tough bastard."

"Maybe that's why he run off his pup," Willa said. "Not tough enough."

Orderic scratched his chin. "How far away is this town?"

Davit said, "At least a week if we didn't stop for nothing."

Orderic shook his head. "Nah, we've got to burn. It's why we're out here. So maybe two weeks, say. I had meant to circle around south toward the big lake, but it might be worth going west if it pays. Darus needs time to get the army organized, so a couple weeks out of the way won't hurt. Where we do our burning matters less than the fact we're putting fear in their hearts."

After grumbled assent all around, Orderic had Villem tied to another tree with the surly Weevil on guard again.

Guess I'm going home again, Villem thought. Though not in any way I ever imagined.

7
KATHKALAN

Kathkalan knew that the attention he drew from men was his own fault. He could easily have chosen to dress in a manner that would hide his appearance and allow him to move among men anonymously. But he had long ago—long before men even came into the world—chosen his conspicuous style. He loved black. He didn't even know why; it had always been that way from his youngest days. The only thing not black about him was his pale skin. His long hair was as black as his chain mail, cloak, leggings, boots, and belt. He rode a black mare unmarred by any streak of white. Even his famous sword was pitch black from hilt to blade.

He disliked going out among men, but there was no getting around it at the moment. Half of the elven forest of Laithtaris had fallen within the reach of the magic of the Spire of Peace, so elvenkind knew something terrible had transpired when that magic had so suddenly vanished. Naturally it was Kathkalan, famous among elves for his adventurous spirit, who chose to investigate this mystery.

He halted his mare where the green grass gave way to ground that looked burned and blackened, though it looked different than the type of burning caused by fire. The spire should have been visible for hours, so Kathkalan knew that the massive obelisk no longer stood.

Sadness pricked his mind. He hadn't visited the place since the arrival of man in these lands, and now he wished he had. He himself had carved some of the figures into the pillar, so many thousands of years ago, to celebrate the end of war. Ten thousand years of peace, and now war was certain to return.

He had an idea of what had burned the grass, but he wanted to confirm his suspicions. Even at this distance, he could see the figures of men moving about near the burned remnants of the inn the pilgrims had used when visiting the spire. Kathkalan tapped his heels into the mare's flanks to get her moving again.

The men all dropped what they were doing as Kathkalan drew near. He knew these men had likely never seen an elf, and certainly none dressed so singularly. He saw wide eyes and open mouths as he drew his steed to a halt and examined the handful of men, looking for any sign that one might be a leader of some type. No, these were all poor common folk, laborers or farmers.

From here he could now see the broken remnants of the spire. It must have been a truly awesome sight to witness its collapse. The ground would have thundered and rolled when it struck.

"May…may we help you, lord?" said a bearded man with a small sack slung over his shoulder.

Kathkalan swept an arm out toward the broken spire. "What caused this?" It felt strange to use the language of men again after so many centuries. Of course, he could have learned what happened much earlier. He could have stopped in Vimar Keep, the first stronghold of men between Laithtaris and the spire, but he had wished to see what had happened with his own eyes.

The bearded man's eyes turned to look where Kathkalan had pointed. He turned back to Kathkalan and spoke as if amazed that anyone could yet be ignorant of what had occurred here. "The dragon. Do you not know of the dragon, milord?"

Kathkalan nodded to himself, having confirmed what he had suspected. It had been many thousands of years since a dragon last came to the lands west of the great mountain range. "Did any of you see it happen?"

The men all looked at each other, everyone shaking their heads. The bearded man said, "I don't know that anyone survived that day, milord, but many have seen the dragon. It has attacked Andiria and destroyed every farmstead and town in its path."

"What does it look like?"

The bearded man held a hand up to Kathkalan. "Meaning no offense, lord, but it's colored like you. Black as coal it is. And vast. Larger than anything I ever imagined."

An elderly woman dressed in homespun stepped forward. "You have its look, milord. Are you its master?"

Kathkalan scowled. "No one is a master of dragons."

Without waiting for a response, he turned his mare and rode toward the wreckage of the spire. Several dozen fresh graves lined a small brook behind the charred ruins of the inn. A familiar sensation tingled across his skin as he rode closer to the granite and marble base where the spire had stood. A touch of the magic the crystal atop the spire had projected across the lands. He rode on, relying less on his eyes and more on the feel of the magic faintly pulsing in his mind. When it grew fainter, he turned the mare and searched until the feeling grew stronger again.

After an hour of riding back and forth among the rubble and larger chunks of the spire, Kathkalan dismounted near the spot he figured must be the source of the small trace of magic remaining from the once powerful crystal. A chunk of red granite as large as his horse was sunk into the ground before him. He scanned the burned grass all about, sometimes using his foot to dig into a promising spot. A half hour of searching turned up nothing, and he glared at the huge chunk of granite. He placed both hands against the stone's cold flank and gave a tentative push, though he knew it was pointless. The stone wouldn't move even if he had ten of his brothers to help. Kathkalan turned and leaned his back against the stone.

A small group of men were watching him about a hundred paces away. He noticed one seemed to have a shovel. Kathkalan told his mare to stay put and walked toward the group of onlookers. When he reached them, he pointed at the burly man with the shovel. "Come," he said, before turning on his heels and heading back toward his horse.

When he reached the block of granite and turned back, the man with the shovel was trailing after, a puzzled look on his face. Others from the man's group were hesitantly drawing closer as well.

Kathkalan pointed at the huge block of stone. "Somewhere under here is a piece of crystal. I want you to dig it out without damaging it."

The man's eyes widened. "How…how do you know, milord?"

"I can feel it. Can't you?"

The man's eyes seemed to unfocus for a few moments before he nodded and said, "Aye, I do feel it. Like it was before, only weaker."

Kathkalan dug inside a small purse beneath his tunic and fetched out a large gold coin. He didn't use the currency of men much, so this coin was ancient. But gold was gold. He held it up so the man could see it. "I'll give you this if you find it for me."

The man's wide eyes grew even larger and he nodded. "Aye, step away and I'll get to work."

Kathkalan went to his mare and loosened her saddle. He fed and watered her and brushed her down before digging out some food for himself. Most of the other men wandered off, but a few still watched as the burly man shoveled away chunks of rich, dark earth from a growing hole at the edge of the granite block.

Kathkalan expected the digging might go on for a long time, perhaps even through the night, so he was surprised to hear the man call out in excitement. "Milord!"

Kathkalan hastened over to where the man was stooped down in the hole he had dug. The man had dug about a half a pace deeper than the bottom of the stone and then begun to clear the dirt from its underside. He had done a good job, and Kathkalan decided he would give the man a second piece of the gold.

"Here, milord. Look!" The man beckoned him to join him in the hole.

It would be a tight squeeze and under normal circumstances Kathkalan would demur. Instead he ignored his distaste and slid into the hole next to the man. Ducking his head to look where the man pointed, he saw the sharp edge of broken crystal jutting from the dark earth packed around the bottom of the granite block. He nodded, and the man used his fingers to claw away the dirt surrounding the crystal. The hole grew stuffy and stank of the man's sweat, but Kathkalan suppressed the urge to climb out and waited impatiently.

With a small grunt, the man finally worked the crystal free and rubbed the dirt from it. He grinned and handed it to Kathkalan. It was a slender shard of crystal about as long as the palm of his hand. Not much compared to what it had once been, yet it held a small amount of magic within it still. For what he had in mind, it might make the difference between success and failure.

When both had clambered out of the hole, Kathkalan handed the man the two pieces of gold and thanked him. The man knuckled his forehead and sketched a short bow of his head. As Kathkalan turned toward his mare, the man said, "Begging your forgiveness, lord, but are you...are you an elf?"

Kathkalan stifled a scowl. "Is it so hard to tell?"

The man looked abashed and dragged his fingers through his

beard. "I've only heard tales, and it's just that the stories always said elves had pointed ears."

Kathkalan traced a finger along the rounded top of his left ear. "Those are just tales. But, yes, I am what your people call an elf. I thank you again for your aid."

Though twilight was near, he re-saddled his mare and rode east, toward the great wall of mountains and the city of men called Andiria. He didn't ride long, just wanting to get away from the stares of men before he made camp. He did so on a patch of grass that had managed to escape the acid burn of the dragon's breath. Before settling down for the night, he sat cross-legged on the packed earth, the crystal shard in his lap, and listened in the near silence, broken only by a mild breeze. When he heard the flutter of wings, he snatched out at the sound with his tentative grasp of the magical energy that flowed through everything and called the bird to him. He was lucky that the red moon was up tonight, as otherwise his call might have gone unheeded. No one knew why, but the red moon seemed to be the source of the magical energy. Any attempted manipulation of the energy, such as melding it with their smithing of weapons and armor, worked better when the red moon was high in the skies.

A sparrow landed lightly on Kathkalan's shoulder. He turned his head so that his cheek brushed against the bird. Long ago one of the wizards of mankind had taught him this form of communication with birds. Kathkalan concentrated on forming images, the first of his mate, Alvanaria, and his young son, Linvaris, along with the home they made in Laihtaris far to the west. Somehow this tenuous magical link could direct the bird to find the object of his message. Next he pictured an image of the Spire of Peace the way it had once looked, followed by an image of its remains lying scattered upon the earth. He painted an image of a great black dragon, followed by one of his black sword. He sent a note of gratitude to the sparrow, and the bird flew off. Communicating in this fashion was difficult at best. He had to hope it would be enough. As Kathkalan settled into his blanket, he imagined Alvanaria's reaction once the sparrow delivered his images. She would be angry. He had a young son. What could he be thinking, challenging a dragon? A tinge of sadness and shame touched the excitement that coursed through him at the thought of the hunt to come.

8
IMRIC

A short time into their march north toward Valandiria, Imric realized Soot was missing.

"We have to go back," he said to Livia. "She'll get herself killed!"

"That's just what we'll all do if we turn back now," Livia replied. She grabbed Imric by his tunic and glared into his eyes. "Don't you even think of going after her. Once we're safe at our uncle's, we can consider rescuing people."

Imric nodded sullenly and looked back over his shoulder, something he found himself doing more and more frequently, and he noticed other refugees doing it as well. Looking for the dragon. Everyone was afraid that inky black shadow would materialize in the sky and grow larger and larger as it came after them.

Imric recognized one of his favorite palace guards, Wilor, plodding along the shoulder of the road still faithfully gripping his spear. The poor man looked despondent and didn't even appear aware of Imric and his sister trudging along nearby.

Evening was fast approaching, and they would need to find a place to camp for the night. One of the nomads drew their attention to something happening on the road ahead. A small crowd had gathered and appeared to be halfheartedly cheering.

When they drew closer, they saw the crowd surrounding a large figure. They passed a young man, who said, "The king! It's the new king!"

Livia pushed through the crowd. "Balmar!" she cried. "Little brother!"

Imric recognized the face of his brother Balmar as it turned toward the sound of Livia's voice. He felt ashamed that he hadn't thought of his brother since fleeing the square where their father had died. He was happy that Balmar had somehow managed to escape the city.

Livia broke through the crowd and hugged Balmar. "I'm so happy to see you."

The onlookers moved back a little to give them room. Imric heard people throughout the crowd whispering, 'The princess.'

Balmar had the usual confused look on his face, but he also looked happy. "I'm king!" he said.

Livia kissed Balmar's cheek. "Father just died, Brother. It's too soon to talk about who will be king."

Tears sprang up in Balmar's eyes. "Father…dead?"

"Didn't you see? The dragon?"

Balmar cringed and held his hands up to shield his face. Livia hugged him harder.

"You'll be safe now, Brother," Livia said. "Come with us. We'll set up camp and have some apples."

She began to walk him through the crowd and the nomads followed, carrying Xax on a makeshift stretcher. Imric sighed and trailed after, along with the rest of the crowd. When Livia chose a campsite a short time later, the crowd chose to camp alongside them. Few had any real supplies. There were no tents and few blankets. Fortunately, the summer weather was warm and clear.

Everyone was hungry but there was little to eat. Imric's group had only a few apples until a kindly old woman gave them a small loaf of bread. The woman mumbled shyly that she wished Livia could lead the people as their queen; after all, she was the eldest child. Livia smiled and gave the woman a hug, though everyone knew that tradition only allowed kings to rule the Known Lands.

Imric wondered why that was, because it seemed obvious to him that Livia was by far the smartest and best person to rule the realm now. Then again, he thought, who would *want* to rule under such impossible circumstances. How could anyone stop the dragon?

A groan to his right snapped Imric out of his thoughts. The wizard's eyes were open. He looked shriveled somehow, wrapped in a blanket on the cot that the nomads had used to make the stretcher.

"Xax, are you feeling all right?" he asked, kneeling next to him on the soft dirt.

Xax looked at him and gave a weak smile. "I feel terrible. Do you have any water?"

Imric leapt up to fetch a flask. Livia joined him and helped prop Xax up as Imric helped him sip from the flask. Xax coughed and nodded to Livia to lay him back down again.

"I never knew magic hurt so much," Imric said.

"I've told you before," Livia said. "You just never wanted to believe me."

"I believed you. I just didn't know it was so bad."

"I'll be fine after some sleep," Xax murmured.

Livia tried to coax the wizard into eating a little bread, but he refused and was soon snoring softly, wrapped tightly in his blanket.

"Time we all got some rest," Livia said.

Imric nodded, but said, "What's going to happen after we reach our uncle? Can anyone stop the dragon?"

Livia blew out her breath. "I don't know. I've read of dragons being slain, but only by dwarves, and always at a terrible cost in lives." She shook her head. "It may be that our people will have to move to new cities and towns far from the dragon's reach."

Imric was aghast at the thought of men having to desert the very heartland of their realm. He tried to remember the names of some of the far away cities. He knew Vimar Keep, of course, since it lay on the main trade route to the elven land of Laithtaris. Others such as Miradis, Tibria, and Varn he had heard about only when their lords or representatives had visited his father's throne room. There were legends of sea lords far to the west, and thinking of them excited Imric a bit, though he wasn't certain he would love the sea or not. He would like to see it though.

His eyes began to grow heavy as he imagined traveling to far reaches of the kingdom. His last thoughts before slipping off were that perhaps he could become a great knight. Surely knights could slay a dragon?

9
VILLEM

Villem felt a little better after they began allowing him to ride upright in the saddle, though the ropes rubbed his wrists, ankles, and neck raw. Two more days passed of seeing no people in the countryside, only empty farms for the band to burn. Once they came across a small two-story stone tower belonging to some minor local lord. It was deserted as well, so the marauders spent some time figuring out how to put it to the torch.

There began to be some grumbling from members of the group. There was almost nothing worth looting, and burning empty farmsteads grew stale after a while. The elf Miranvel especially seemed to be growing more and more irritable. He kept trying to start arguments with his band mates.

Villem watched everything in sullen silence. The relationship that mystified him the most was that between Wide Willa and the lovely Dinara. About half the time Willa kept hold of the tether that led to a leather collar around Dinara's neck. Other times Willa handed the rope to Dinara and the gorgeous raven-haired woman went her own way. Villem had seen enough hints to understand that there was some sort of romantic interplay between the two women, which was something new to him. It had never occurred to him in his fifteen years that two women could love one another, though he had heard plenty of jests, insults, and bawdy tales made about men doing such. He couldn't wrap his mind around why one of the most beautiful women he had ever seen would love one of the ugliest.

The boy Weevil had long ago grown tired of being stuck guarding the captive knight and had taken to maliciously pinching him or pricking him with his dagger whenever he felt the others weren't paying attention. Villem was glad the boy never spoke, because he would surely spew out a running stream of invective if he did.

Even the leader Orderic appeared to be losing interest in following their orders. They had come across another deserted farm, yet Orderic's head hung down staring at the back of his horse's head and he rode on along the dirt track rather than turning in at the farm's gate.

"Look at that!" cried the man called Davit, a dirty blond-haired man with two missing front teeth.

Villem wiped sweat from his brow and raised his head to follow where the man pointed. Ahead the road came to a stone bridge across a creek. A scattering of willow trees provided shade on the other side of the stream, where a small group of horsemen sat watching the band approach. Villem sat up straighter when he noticed the men wore armor and held an assortment of crossbows, spears, and swords.

Orderic held up a hand to call a halt. The scout Tevin pulled up next to him and they conferred in raspy whispers. Villem studied the armed men more closely. The leader appeared to be a minor noble, dressed in an old but still fine surcoat and cloak of green trimmed with gold over chain mail. Five men-at-arms were spread out along the bank of the stream, each hefting a crossbow, while four others blocked the bridge with their spears held at the ready. The last two men were clearly knights, and Villem realized he had seen them before. They had been part of a small entourage that had visited with his father for a few days, though it had been with a different lord than the one in green and gold. He remembered the knights well because one had been such a drunk that his father had kicked the man out of his household. The other knight had seemed to Villem to be a real hard case; his armor and sword were well worn and the man's stare could send chills down the spines of the bravest of men.

A frisson of hope bloomed in Villem's chest. Twelve of them, he thought, some with crossbows, and only eleven of these bandits, one of them a child. He would have discounted the two women as well, except he had seen Willa in action enough to know she could more than hold her own. Would the marauders turn tail and find another route?

Orderic finished his conversation with Tevin and turned his horse to face the rest, a bold grin lighting his face. "They may look like something, but these men up there are untried. Most of you have been at this a long time. You're veterans. Most of those men will break and run once we show them we have no fear. Don't worry about the crossbows. When the moment gets real, these men won't even aim. If they hit something it will be luck alone that does it."

Miranvel began to cackle and bounce in his saddle. His one arm reached over to pluck his deadly blade from its sheath.

"Pull on your armor, boys, and be quick about it," Orderic cried.

It was far too hot for anyone to ride in mail. Villem thought the band of warriors on the other side of the creek should attack while the brigands were dressing, but they sat still and silent for the half hour it took Orderic's band to prepare. *I hope those knights will recognize me*, Villem thought. It would be just his luck to be feathered by a crossbow bolt or have a spear jammed into his belly.

Orderic rode up to Villem and stared at him a few moments. He pointed at Weevil. "Boy, you hold his horses tight, and keep back, you hear? Don't let him run off or I'll skin you alive."

Weevil scowled and sullenly nodded, then turned to scoop up the reins of Villem's pony and warhorse.

Wide Willa drew near on her massive stallion and handed Dinara's tether over to Weevil as well. She grabbed Dinara's hand and kissed her wrist before giving a huge grin. "This shouldn't take long!" She hefted a nasty looking maul and rode up to join the rest of the band.

Villem couldn't hear the instructions Orderic gave out, though he saw all the hand pointing and understood that the band wasn't simply going to charge across the choke point of the bridge. He figured the crossbowmen might do more damage than Orderic thought if they did that. A few more pointed fingers and encouraging shouts, and Orderic and his men began trotting their horses off to the right, heading west. Wide Willa remained behind, seated heavily in her saddle, slowly smacking her maul into her hand over and over again.

"What do you think they're doing?" came a soft whisper.

Villem looked over and saw that Dinara had eased her pony alongside his. She looked frightened.

"Why did they leave Willa here?" she added.

Villem wanted to point to the stream, but his hands were bound up tight, so he nodded his head to try to indicate the path the riders were taking. "They intend to cross the stream over there. Don't want to just charge across the bridge where the spearmen and crossbowmen will be effective. The water's pretty shallow here, so it shouldn't be hard."

"And Willa?"

"I can only guess. Perhaps Orderic thought she'd have trouble making it across the stream. Probably he wants someone to guard us in case those men come after us."

Dinara looked as if she hadn't thought of that possibility. "Do you think they will?"

Villem shook his head. "I doubt it. They think Orderic's men are the real threat. Figure they can come for us at their leisure once they beat them."

"You're hoping they win."

"I don't like being trussed up, if that's what you mean," Villem said. "But I think Orderic's right. Those men haven't known real fighting in their lives. I bet they break and run." He thought about the hard case knight. "At least most of them."

Orderic's riders had reached the bank of the stream about two hundred paces down from the bridge. The lord in green and gold was calling out orders to his men, and the four spearmen and five crossbowmen rearranged themselves among the trees to meet the attack from the west. The hard case knight sat unmoving and appeared to be staring at Wide Willa.

The raiders took their time, crossing the stream slowly so the horses wouldn't slip on the mossy rocks. After climbing up the opposite bank, they fanned out and sat still for a few minutes, just staring at their rivals in the tree line. Orderic raised an arm, cried out something, and flung his arm forward. The nine riders kicked their mounts into a trot and readied their weapons.

Villem looked at the lord's men. The spearmen found places to seat their spears to meet a charge. The crossbowmen arranged themselves next to the trunks of willow trees and began planting spare bolts in the ground nearby. Willa raised her maul above her head and cried out, "Yes! Go you bastards!"

The raiders broke into a full gallop now. One of the crossbowmen discharged his weapon far too early and the bolt sailed high. The lord screamed at the men to hold their fire. The man who had fired tried at first to reload his weapon, but when he noticed the charge was growing too near, he dropped his bow and began climbing into the nearby tree. The hard case knight finally broke his gaze from Willa, nonchalantly drew his sword, and nudged his horse over behind one of the spearmen. Villem couldn't see the other knight through the drooping leaves of the willows.

Moments before the raiders hit the line of men-at-arms, the crossbowmen fired. Orderic had been mostly right, as the bolts flew harmlessly by in most cases, but one bolt struck a horse in the breast and the steed screamed and veered directly into a tree trunk. Villem didn't know who had been on the horse, but the collision was horrifying to witness, and he didn't think it likely the rider would have survived.

The other charging horses veered around the planted spears, their riders' sword arms rising and falling. Villem recognized the closest of the raiders as Davit. He easily cut down the spearman in front of him, but as he tried to free the blade of his sword, the hard case knight drew close and rammed his blade into Davit's belly. If the man was wearing a hauberk, it didn't seem to help. Davit cried out and landed on top of the spearman he had slain.

A blood-curdling yell came from nearby, and Villem saw it was Willa, who kicked her stallion into a charge and headed for the bridge. Villem realized Orderic had wanted her to hit the flank of the defenders once they were engaged. It hardly seemed necessary, as the spearmen and crossbowmen were routed, either dying or trying desperately to escape. The lord in green and gold was himself galloping away south as hard as he could.

Two riders closed in on either side of the hard case knight. Villem recognized them as Samvel and Meldon. It's all over now, he thought. Hard Case flung his shield out to block Samvel's swing, while his blade skirled off of Meldon's. With his backswing he hamstrung Meldon's horse. Hard Case pulled hard at the reins to twist his steed around. He caught Samvel turning the wrong way and slammed his blade crossways across the back of Samvel's helm. Samvel slid from the horse and Villem winced as he saw the man hit the ground headfirst.

Willa had made it across the bridge and now came up behind Hard Case, who was turning to face two other riders coming at him out of the trees. Willa's swing would have ended the fight if Hard Case hadn't been ducking his head aside to avoid the blade of one of the men in front of him. As it was, Willa's maul clipped Hard Case's helm along the side, causing the man to grunt loudly. Villem heard a horse scream, and Hard Case slid from his saddle, using his horse to shield himself from his three attackers, who seemed to have entangled themselves momentarily with each other's mounts. Hard Case leapt forward and grabbed the rear of Willa's saddle with his left hand. With his right he plunged his sword into Willa's side.

Dinara let out a scream that froze Villem's blood. "Willa!"

As Dinara kicked her horse forward, the tethers of all three horses were jerked from Weevil's hand. Villem didn't hesitate, knowing this might be his only chance. He cried out the name of his warhorse and used his heels to nudge his pony into action. His warhorse was better trained to respond to leg and heel pressure alone, but Villem had taken the time to teach his pony some tricks as well. Weevil cried out as Villem got this pony turned about and kicked it to a gallop, his warhorse bounding alongside. Villem pushed aside his curiosity about the result of the battle and concentrated on keeping his balance. As tied up as he was, it would be all too easy to slide off the side of his pony.

He tried to remember the road they had recently passed. There was the one farm that the band hadn't bothered to burn. He'd be too easy to find there, so he rode past it still at a full gallop. He wished he could look back to see if anyone was following, but the ropes that bound him prevented it. He saw a dirt track heading west and ignored it, figuring he needed to ensure he was out of sight before turning off the main road.

He rode hard until his pony began to labor under the strain. The air ahead was dark with smoke from the farms the raiders had burned that morning. Villem used his voice to ease the mounts down to a trot. He turned them down the next side road, which turned out to be little more than a goat path heading west between two fenced pastures. Now he was able to look behind and see that there was no sign of pursuit. He breathed a sigh of relief and thought for the first time that he might actually make it out of this alive.

He noticed that the darkness of the sky wasn't all smoke—dark clouds were closing in. That's just what I need, he thought. The pony slowed to a walk. Villem worked his shoulders, legs, and wrists continuously, trying any way he could to loosen the ropes that bound him. The chafing was agonizing.

The pastures came to an end and the path wended its way through a small peat bog before entering a pine wood. Fat drops of rain began to fall, so Villem was grateful for the cover of the trees. The pony gave a lurch and brayed loudly, then stumbled to a halt. Villem tried to look down past the pony's flank to see what had happened, but he was tied too tightly to be able to see. "I'm sorry," he muttered, wishing he had given the pony a name. The poor beast was trembling with fatigue and perhaps with pain as well. If Villem didn't work his way free, the pony would eventually collapse, and Villem would likely break a leg or worse.

His warhorse had halted nearby and cropped at the grass just off the path. The poor pony couldn't even do that, stuck as she was on the path. Villem put all his declining strength into wriggling his wrists. Blood began to trickle and spatter his saddle horn.

A low growl made him pause and look at the brush to his right. He was astonished to see the mongrel from the first farm the band had attacked. It was crouched low and baring its teeth at Villem. He noticed blood streaking the right rear haunch of the poor dog where the crossbow bolt had nicked it.

In as mild a voice as he could muster, Villem called out, "Hush, boy. Hush! I mean you no harm." He had no idea if the dog was male or female, but he didn't know what else to call it for now.

The dog skittered forward a bit more and looked plaintively up at Villem. It seemed half-starved and its graying black coat was covered in nettles and burrs.

Was it Villem's imagination, or did the rope seem to give a little about his wrists? The blood seemed to be helping. Villem redoubled his efforts and felt certain that the rope was indeed beginning to loosen.

The pony's trembling became worse, and it whinnied miserably. The rain began to fall harder, and lightning flashed in the distance. A rumble of thunder made the dog whine and the warhorse give a neigh. Villem tilted his head up and let some of the rain fall into his mouth. He breathed in deeply and then cried out in pain and rage as he yanked at the ropes once more. There was a sudden give in his bindings, and with a cry of joy Villem worked one of his hands free. Pins and needles raced through his arm, so he had to wait for the pain to subside before freeing his other hand.

Lightning flashed close this time and thunder roared almost immediately, sending the yelping dog scampering into the bushes. The horse and pony both rolled their eyes in fear. Villem tried to ignore it all as he set to work on the ropes binding his legs to the stirrups. The pain in his hands was terrible, but nothing mattered to him now except to gain his freedom.

It seemed to take forever, and the rainstorm was moving well past them by the time Villem finally freed himself completely. He groaned and rolled his shoulders and kicked his legs out to restore circulation, the pain nearly making him fall off the side of his pony. The poor beast staggered and brayed loudly. Whether his legs were ready for it or not, Villem decided he needed to relieve the pony of his weight, so he took a deep breath and slid one leg over the pony's rump. The foot trying to hold him in the stirrup gave out, and Villem tumbled backward and slammed hard into the ground.

He woke to the raspy tongue of the mongrel licking his face. He tried to shift himself, but pain lanced out from his back and he groaned loudly. The dog whined and licked him again.

"Good, boy," he murmured. "Good, dog." Lying the way he was, he saw that the mongrel was actually a female. "Good, girl," he amended.

As wet and miserable as it was, he wished he could just lie here and sleep for a while, but a whinny from his pony made him realize he had other responsibilities still. He raised a hand and scratched behind the dog's ear. "Help me up, girl."

Groaning continuously, he pushed himself up to a sitting position, his back shrieking with pain. The back of his head throbbed as well, and he ran a hand through his hair. No blood, but a large lump was forming. He patted the dog again and took a few breaths to prepare himself, then rolled over onto his hands and knees. The dog barked encouragement. Villem wished a tree was nearby to help him stand. He glanced at the pony, and now he could see that the leather tether had wound itself about the pony's front right leg. He was lucky the poor beast hadn't fallen or broken its leg.

The closest stirrup seemed far away, though Villem knew it was probably no more than two paces. The dog sidled up next to Villem, seeming to offer its support, and Villem flung an arm across its back. "Good, girl," he whispered. He braced himself against the dog and crawled toward the pony. The dog seemed to understand what he wanted. It moved with him as he crawled and licked his face whenever he seemed to need encouragement. At last he could reach up and grasp the stirrup. He thought about trying to stand, then realized what he really needed to do was get the saddle off the poor pony's back. He used the stirrup to pull himself farther under the pony, where he could work at the straps. He seemed to regain some of his strength, and before too long he worked the straps free, stood himself up with a moan, and pulled the saddle off to land heavily in the muddy path.

One arm on the pony's shoulder, Villem leaned down to untangle the tether from the pony's leg. He rubbed the pony's shoulder and leaned his forehead into its mane. "I'm going to call you Zora." He didn't know why the name had suddenly come to him. Zora had been a fisherman's daughter he had thought was pretty, back when he was a young boy. They had lived in two different worlds, so he had never met her, only seen her from a distance. He wondered what had become of her. Probably married off by now, with a couple of children. The pony deserved a good name, so Zora it was. "Come on, Zora," he said, and led her under a tall pine, where he tied off the tether to a branch. The pony began to pull up great chunks of grass and eat greedily.

As Villem staggered over to the warhorse to bring it over to the pony, he wondered when he would ever get to rest. The pains and aches racking his body insisted that he collapse, but he still had so much to do. After tying off the warhorse, he dragged the pony's saddle over to another tree and began rummaging through the packs. Two of his water skins were empty, and the third was only half full.

He had watched days ago as the raiders had picked through his bags, so he knew most of his more useful belongings would be gone. Sword, bow, arrows, dagger—all gone. He found his eating knife, and he was relieved when he dug out his flint and steel. The dog rubbed up against him and nosed into the pack, as eager as him to find any food, but there was none. Villem felt bad for the half-starved animal. They would both be going hungry tonight.

He looked at the dog. "Water. Have you found any water, girl?"

He didn't expect the dog would understand him, so he was surprised when it yelped and limped off into the woods. Villem grabbed all three water skins and followed slowly. The pain seemed to lessen, but he suspected he was just getting used to it. Several minutes later he heard the dog's barks and he stumbled out into a rocky area with a tiny rill splashing down from a ridge line. The dog lapped greedily at the water, and Villem dropped to his knees nearby and began to fill the skins. "You're a real blessing, girl," he said. He needed to find a good name for her as well, but he was too exhausted to try to think of one just yet. He finished filling the water skins, cupped his hands to drink his fill, then headed back to his makeshift camp. At least the rain had stopped.

10
KATHKALAN

The next morning Kathkalan was on the road no more than an hour when he came upon a small hamlet. A collection of twelve small houses, their bases made of marble from the nearby quarries, but the upper parts framed from planks of cedar. A few farms were scattered nearby. Kathkalan was surprised to see this area looked untouched by the ravages of the dragon.

He would have ridden through without stopping if he hadn't noticed a small blacksmith forge behind one of the houses, smoke already rising above its slate roof, and the clang of a hammer ringing loudly in the early morning air. He wondered if the neighbors resented such noise so early.

He halted his horse and fished the shard of crystal from the pouch bag where he had placed it for safekeeping. The smithy had given him an idea. He spent a few moments overcoming his distaste for interacting with men, then finally nudged his horse forward and tied it off outside the hut where the smithy was located. When he came around to the opening, there was no door, so he loomed politely just outside until the blacksmith noticed his presence and stopped pounding the horseshoe he was working on.

The smith wiped sweat from his brow with a cloth and squinted at Kathkalan. "Yes, stranger? May I help you?"

Kathkalan took that as an invitation to step inside the doorway. He saw the smith's eyes widen when he finally saw his visitor clearly. "I'd like to borrow your forge for a short time, if I could. I'd pay you well for the privilege."

The man's jaw hung open for a few moments before he gathered himself to reply. "Are...are you the dragon's master?"

Kathkalan quirked his mouth. He was apparently going to get this from most men he met now. "Dragons have no masters. And no, I have nothing to do with its coming. I'm merely following it."

The smith stared at him and mopped more sweat from his forehead. "You have a death wish then. No one would follow that monster otherwise."

Kathkalan's smirk turned into a grin. "How is it your small town was spared?"

"Dumb luck, I think. We heard the noise, though we knew not what it was. The destruction of the tower. Everyone still in town came out to gape. Then we saw it. Blacker than night, moving across the northern sky fast as an arrow. Just our luck which direction it took. I think it was headed for Andiria."

"I was told that city was destroyed."

The smith nodded. "Plenty of refugees passed this way. Vimar Keep will have a city of tents and hovels outside its walls by now. Most will probably move on south, hoping they will be safe from the beast there."

Kathkalan fished two of the large gold coins from his purse and held them up. "One to borrow your forge and another for a small silver chain, if you have any."

The smith scratched the back of his head as he looked back and forth between the gold and the elf's face. "May I watch? I've heard tell that elves are the best smiths in the world, even better than dwarves for delicate work."

Kathkalan smiled again. "We're better than the dwarves at all work. Though the dwarves would never admit that, naturally. You do have silver chains?"

"I keep a few tucked away. Sometimes a wagon breaks down or a horse needs a new shoe, and while the husband deals with that, their lady often gets bored, so I show them the few niceties that I can make easily enough. Here, let me show you, though be warned, they are crude compared to the work you are used to seeing."

The smith rummaged in a wooden case and pulled forth three necklaces made of tiny silver links. He handed them over to Kathkalan, who examined them carefully. The work was slightly better than he had expected from a man, though clumsy compared to the work of his brethren or even that of the dwarves. Still, the second one he examined would suffice for what he needed. He held it up and passed the other two back to the smith. "I'll need a small sheet of silver as well, to make a clasp."

He and the smith worked through the remaining details of which tools suited the job. Then the smith sat back to watch Kathkalan get to work, starting with a tiny sanding tool to prepare one end of the crystal to hold the sheath. Kathkalan was rueful about the quality and types of tools available, but he had to make do. It didn't take him long to fashion a necklace that could hold the crystal shard, though the length of the shard was too long to look anything but ungainly. Still, it would serve. He lowered the chain over his head and saw that the crystal dangled down to his belly. The smith chuckled and Kathkalan had to laugh himself.

"It looks absurd, I know," Kathkalan said. "But it lets me keep it close." He tucked the crystal under his hauberk but above his tunic, where it could rest more comfortably. "I thank you for your aid." He handed over the two pieces of gold.

"It was a privilege," the smith said, knuckling his forehead. He pointed to the necklace. "It's from the tower, isn't it?"

Kathkalan nodded. "You can feel it."

"Aye, though only just."

Kathkalan passed him the tools he had used, then headed for his horse. The smith followed him out and gave a goodbye wave as Kathkalan set off, giving the man a polite nod in return. Reaching the road, he saw a long line of refugees streaming through the hamlet, their numbers extending as far as he could see into the distance. Those nearest stopped to gawk at his undoubtedly startling appearance.

"From Andiria?" he inquired of the nearest, a woman with a cloth bundle balanced across her shoulders.

She shook her head, her eyes wide as she stared at him. "Nay, milord. We're from Tolgaria. Twas a dragon. Great big, nasty thing. Hope never to see its like again."

Kathkalan mentally pictured the geography of the region and where the cities of men were located. Was the dragon purposefully targeting the cities of men, or was it mere happenstance? He returned his gaze to the woman. "Did anyone see where the beast flew next?"

The woman looked around at her fellow refugees and most of them shook their heads. A bald man with two young children piped up. "It set itself down on top of the castle for a good long time, milord. Those who survived were fleeing. We didn't see it move by the time we escaped."

Kathkalan nodded thanks and turned his horse about to ride behind one of the houses. He wanted time to think without all those men staring at him. He reined up and sat in the saddle for several minutes, considering his next course of action. It was possible that the dragon had simply preferred to follow the line of the lakeshore after burning Andiria and had thus come upon Tolgaria. In the tens of thousands of years that he had lived, Kathkalan had never understood dragons to be highly intelligent creatures, so he didn't like the idea of this dragon purposefully seeking out each major city of man. The dragon could go anywhere from Tolgaria. There was a river flowing down from the enormous Hellisgaard Mountain range to the east, with the largest of the dwarven cities, Kaldorn, not far away. But how would a dragon know it was there? It seemed more likely to Kathkalan that the dragon would continue its pattern and follow the huge lake north to the last of the great cities of man, Valandiria.

Having settled on that as the most probable scenario, Kathkalan now tried to determine the shortest route to Valandiria. The road he was on would pass through the ruins of Andiria, turn north to follow the lake shore until it reached the newly destroyed Tolgaria, and then continue on until it skirted the northern tip of the lake and at last came to his goal. That was a long route and would be full of refugees. If he broke from the road here and headed due north, it would be rougher country and he would have to detour around the hills and marshes that lined the western shores of the huge lake that his people called Andairon, though men called it the Sea of Alia. But he could avoid most of the refugees and the journey would likely be faster. It was an easy decision to make when it came down to it, despite a small curiosity to see for himself the destruction the dragon had wrought upon those two great cities. He clucked to his mare and turned north. Crossing the road caused an eddy of interest from the refugees, which only strengthened his determination to avoid them.

It was mostly farmland here, but not far ahead he could see the darker green of forest and he knew hill country wouldn't be far beyond that. He put a hand to the crystal dangling beneath his mail shirt, the faintest traces of strength and well-being emanating from its remaining bit of power, and he knew he was going to enjoy this part of the journey. He was always happiest off on his own.

11

VILLEM

Villem could barely move when he woke the next morning. He groaned loudly, waking the dog who had snuggled up next to him for the night. Nearly every part of Villem's body ached, though his wrists, lower back, and the back of his head hurt the most. He wondered if he would be able to stand up. The dog encouraged him with a few licks to his face.

He probed the back of his skull with his fingers and felt an enormous lump, but it was his back that worried him the most. He levered himself up slowly with one elbow and tried to roll on his side. His back sent pain lancing through his entire body, but then settled down to a low throb. That seemed encouraging, so with the dog's help (or hindrance it sometimes seemed) he groped his way first to his knees and finally to his feet.

It can't be that bad if I can stand, he thought. He tried to stretch his arms over his head and paid the price with a lightning strike of pain through his spine. His stomach chose that moment to growl loudly and the dog gave two short barks.

"Yes, I know, girl," he said, "but we have no food." He scratched behind her ear with one hand as he studied the mounts. He knew they preferred grain, but at least they could forage for edibles without too much trouble. The pony looked better, though he wasn't sure she was up to bearing his weight yet.

He took his time getting ready, walking slowly to get his legs working again. He led the steeds to the brook to drink and then scrubbed their coats with the brush from his pack. The work seemed to ease some of the ache in his muscles and back. When he couldn't put the moment off any longer, he stood over the saddle and bags on the ground and tried to summon up the strength to bend over to lift them up onto the pony's back. The pony stood patiently nearby. Villem took a deep breath and crouched low, ignoring the protests from his back. He grasped the edges of the saddle and attempted to stand. The pain was so intense that he dropped the saddle and collapsed against the side of the pony, one arm flung over its back to keep from falling. A small sob escaped his throat as he let the worst of the pain pass. The dog stared up at him and whined in sympathy.

Villem stared down at the saddle. He hated to leave it behind, if only because he had nowhere to keep the few items from the saddle bags. With a sigh, he unrolled the blanket and slipped in the essential items like the flint and steel and the water skins before clumsily rolling it back up. The blanket was heavy and bulky now. He used his eating knife to cut two lengths from the warhorse's leather halter and tied them around each end of the blanket, then managed to sling it up onto the pony's back. He had to mop sweat from his brow from the pain that caused him, but he was relieved he had managed to save some of his equipment. And he was happy that his exhaustion last night had saved his other saddle, since he had merely unbuckled it but not removed it from the warhorse. With one hand on the blanket roll to keep it in place, he clucked his tongue at his two steeds and began a slow walk down the dirt path through the pines.

Holding his back straight as he walked kept the pain to a bearable level. The dog took off ahead, smelling everything of interest, and

Villem tried to think of a name for the mutt, but the pain and weariness made the task seem impossible for now. Every name he tried seemed wrong.

He stumbled on, wracked with pain, and he thought, how did I get into this mess? It wasn't so long ago his life had seemed simple and relatively happy. He trained in the warrior arts alongside his younger brother Vonn and hunted in the woods around the great lake near Iskimir. It was true that his mother had always seemed to favor Vonn, but Villem had simply assumed it was because Vonn was the baby of the family. Nothing had prepared him for the shock of learning that he would not inherit the lordship of Iskimir from his father. No one had told him a thing until his fifteenth name-day, when he became a man—the day he assumed he would be named the heir to his father Lord Tathis. Villem could hardly believe it was less than a month ago, when it felt like years already. His father had pulled him aside and explained that Vonn had to be the heir to Iskimir. That he was ashamed of the transgressions of his youth, and sorry that he had not been able to tell Villem the truth earlier. It turned out that the woman he had lived his whole life believing was his mother was not in fact his mother. His father had impregnated one of the cleaning women in the castle just prior to his marriage, so Villem was not legitimate. He had heard the term bastard before but had never imagined it could apply to him.

That moment of revelation had set his stomach to churning, his heart going cold, and over the coming days the unfairness of it all had eaten away at him. His 'mother' had begun to treat him worse, knowing that he knew the truth now. That was when the magic of the Spire of Peace had begun to work on him, filling him with fear and making him feel overwhelmed with weakness and sick to the stomach. He had tried to stand it the best he could, but it was too much, so he had set off for East Gate without so much as a word to his family. Did I truly deserve the punishment that has followed? Everything that I was, everything that I have known is lost.

The sun was headed toward midday when he spotted a small cabin set back in the woods near a pond. A goat was tied up outside the doorway, and the dog barked and would have made a run at it if Villem hadn't called it back. Two boys of perhaps ten and eight years of age came out of the cabin and stared at the newcomers. They were joined a few moments later by a large man and a stout woman.

Villem plodded ahead until he came to the place where the path broke off toward the cabin, then coaxed the pony into turning and approached the small family. He noticed the goat was straining at its rope, trying to go to the dog, who had stopped a couple paces away, wagging its tail.

Villem put two fingers to his forehead and tipped a greeting to the husband and wife. "Good day," he said.

The woman had hold of the shoulders of both boys to keep them close. The man had a wary look on his face but didn't seem hostile. "G'day," the man said.

After an awkward silence, Villem decided the man had no intention of saying more without prompting. "Could I…could I beg some aid?" he asked. "I'm injured and have no food."

The man looked him up and down. "Where you hurt?"

Villem held up his badly chafed wrists and said, "All over, though my head and back are the worst."

"What happened?" asked the older boy before the mother clamped a hand over his mouth.

"Raiders," Villem said. "Don't know if you heard of them, but they had me captive. I just managed to escape yesterday."

"Raiders," the man repeated. "Some folks passed by and said they were burning homes and killing people. Why is this happening?"

Villem looked the man in the eyes. "Because the magic from the

Spire stopped. I don't know why, but it did. These raiders come from East Gate."

The man seemed to ponder this for a bit before responding. "Why do they need to murder folks? We ain't done nothing."

"I heard them talking when they held me captive. They blame us for them having to leave civilized lands. They want revenge."

The man shrugged. "Twern't our fault they were bad men."

Villem thought about why he had become a 'bad man', being driven away by the nausea and weakness caused by the spire's magic. He didn't feel he was bad. He had a right to be angry at his mother and father. How many of the others at East Gate were not truly bad, only driven there by circumstances beyond their control? "Whatever the reason, they are sending a whole army from East Gate soon. You may be safe out here, but maybe not. If you can think of a safer place to go, you might consider it."

"Got no place to go," the stout woman said, fear straining her voice. "Got no food to spare either, so you be on your way, mister."

The man waved an arm at his wife. "Shush, Merta." He met Villem's gaze. "She's right that we have little to spare, but we'll do what we can."

Villem nodded thanks. "If it helps, I left an expensive saddle back down the path where I slept. It's yours in gratitude for whatever help you can spare. It will fetch good coin."

"Tell me true, were those raiders following you?"

Villem's head throbbed with pain and he slumped to his knees. "They...they were in the midst of a fight when I escaped. I never saw them following."

The man glanced around at his boys. "Stiv, you and your brother fetch the cart and go get that saddle. Keep your eyes and ears open and hide if you meet anything. You know those woods, so be smart."

Merta's mouth had hung open as her husband spoke. "Rob, it's too dangerous!"

"They'll be fine. You get a pot boiling and prepare a bath for this young fellow. I'll tend his wounds the best I can. Throw the breakfast leavings to that mutt."

Merta's face reddened and she looked like she would object further, but then she turned and stomped into the house.

The boys took off running toward a small shed, talking excitedly to one another. Rob took the leads from the mounts and tied them up to a post, then squatted next to Villem and helped him stand. Merta reappeared and threw some bones and bread heels in the grass near the dog, who yipped happily and began gnawing on one of the bones.

"Let's get you in," Rob said, and let Villem lean on him as he walked him inside and helped him lie down on a bear skin-covered cot.

Vertigo swept over Villem as his head hit the soft fur, and what happened next became a blur. He heard voices and made out movement, but everything was muddled. It felt like a dream at the time, being lowered by powerful arms into a bath of lukewarm water; being scrubbed down; excruciating pain as someone plied a wet cloth to the knot on his head. He woke the next morning in a cold sweat, his body shaking. Rob must have been asleep on the floor next to him, because he sat up and put his calloused hand on Villem's forehead.

"You're in a heap of trouble, I reckon," he said. "I did the best I could, but it weren't enough."

Things faded to black again, and the next Villem knew, he was rumbling along in the back of a small cart, still wrapped in the bear skin. He heard the clopping of many hooves, and the panting of the dog running alongside. The cold sweats were gone, but in their place was a fever. He cracked his eyes and saw Rob seated on the riding board of the cart, snapping the reins at a mule.

"Where...?" he croaked.

Rob glanced back at him. "Won't be long now. I'm taking you to Lord Wotton's keep. You'll have a better chance of surviving under his care."

The next time Villem opened his eyes, it was to see a slim man with flinty eyes and a gray goatee staring down upon him from astride a destrier. He heard Rob speaking to the man but couldn't make sense of the words. But when the gray bearded man spoke, it seemed loud to his ears and very clear.

"This boy is dead. You wasted your time bringing him to me. Anyhow, I've no time for this. My liege lord has called and I must answer."

Villem's senses grew a little less foggy at those words, so he understood Rob's reply.

"He yet breathes, milord."

Lord Wotton shook his head. "Off with you now. My men will take care of this."

Villem saw Rob's ruddy face turn pale and grim. Then strong arms were hauling him out of the back of the cart. Rob didn't even protest that they were keeping his bear skin. With a sad shake of his head, Rob said, "Sorry, lad."

The two men-at-arms holding Villem laid him gently on the ground. Villem saw another soldier holding the tracers of his two mounts, and his dog darted in to lick his face.

"That's a very fine horse," Lord Wotton said. "We'll bring it along with us. The pony looks blown. Put it in the stable. We'll see if it lasts." He stared down into Villem's eyes and chewed his lip for a moment. "This one will be dead within the hour. You two fetch shovels and bury him in that tree line. Quickly now, then catch up to us. We're not wasting more time."

The two men-at-arms knuckled their foreheads to their liege, then scurried toward the small tower nearby. Lord Wotton waved an arm and cried out to the rest of his troop. Villem's mind was still too hazy to count numbers, but there must have been a score or more of soldiers and twice that number of servants and other hangers-on, all on horses or ponies, with a string of pack mules. At the lord's command they began filing down the road, kicking up a cloud of dust that wracked Villem's chest with coughs and brought on more agony.

The two men-at-arms returned with shovels, which they propped against trees before dragging Villem over to the tree line. The dog barked at them the whole way. The soldiers set to work digging just inside the woods where the ground was still damp.

Villem tried to raise a hand, but it only flopped a little. He mumbled, trying to plead with them. The men paused, leaning on their shovels and wiping their foreheads.

"This aint right, Otho," said one. "He's not even proper dead yet."

"Makes no matter," said the other, who had a large boil on his nose. "His lordship gave the orders, so we obey."

The first man scowled and shook his head but got back to digging. Soon enough the two soldiers picked up Villem—one by his hands and one by his feet—and slung him as gently as they could into the shallow grave they had dug.

The one with the boil said, "Let's hurry now. Don't want them getting too far ahead of us." He scooped up some dirt and flung it onto Villem's midsection.

The other soldier began to shovel in dirt as well, though he seemed to aim at Villem's feet, as if reluctant to throw dirt onto a still-breathing face. His dog began to growl until the man with the boil hit her with his shovel, whereupon she yelped and scurried off into the woods. A short time later the men had buried Villem's body pretty well, with only his face still clear of dirt. "Please," he tried to say, but it came out as the barest of whispers.

"Can't we just leave him like this, Otho? What would it hurt?"

Otho looked disgusted. "Stop trying to think, Jed. It'll get you into trouble. You aint doing him no favors to let him lie here and expire slowly. Ease him on his way quickly, I say. It's the kindest thing we can do." He took up another scoop of soil and plopped it directly in Villem's face.

Villem coughed and turned his head. He tried to roll himself on his side, but the mound of earth was too heavy.

"I'll…I'll go get the ponies then, while you finish this," Jed said.

"Coward," Otho muttered as he slung more dirt into the hole.

Villem shook his head from side to side, trying to create a little breathing space, hoping he could somehow still manage to breathe even after Otho finished his work. It seemed in vain, though, as dirt began to plug his nose, and his chest labored harder to try to move under the weight of the mound of earth. Darkness enveloped him as dirt covered his eyes.

Villem heard nothing now but the pounding of his heart. He sucked dirt into his mouth as he desperately tried to take in a last breath. He began to suffocate, and his entire body tried to thrash against the pressure holding it down. Everything went dark and still.

12
IMRIC

Imric snapped awake in pre-dawn darkness, surrounded by the sound of snores and the crackle of the dying fire. What had woken him? He wasn't an early riser by nature, and he had been exhausted the night before, so something must have caused him to wake. He propped himself up and looked to where his sister slept to his right. Beyond her their brother Balmar snored loudly beneath his blanket. To his left, the spot where the wizard Xax had slept was empty.

That must be it, Imric thought. I heard Xax rise. It was good that he had regained some strength. Had he just needed to relieve himself, or did he rise for some other purpose? The night was bright with all three of the moons visible. The two white moons were nearly full, and the small red moon was more than a crescent but not quite half full. Imric realized he wouldn't get back to sleep, so he pushed himself to his feet and set off to find Xax.

He wound carefully through dozens of sleeping refugees and found the wizard seated on a boulder on the side of the road, staring up at the night sky. Imric hesitated a moment, worrying about bothering the wizard, then decided to seat himself on the other end of the boulder. Xax looked at him and gave a friendly smile.

"You're up early," Xax said.

"Something woke me. I'm glad to see you're feeling better."

"The wonders of sleep. I haven't had that much sapped out of me in ages."

"You saved all our lives. It was amazing."

"I didn't think I could manage it long enough, honestly. I thought it was all over for us." Xax shook his head. "And so many did die. What a terrible tragedy."

"What will happen now?" Imric asked. "Can nothing stop the dragon?"

Xax pursed his lips and stared silently up at the moons for a minute. "As terrible as the dragon is, I believe we have greater problems."

That shook Imric, who couldn't imagine what could be worse than a dragon. "What do you mean?"

"Dragons don't tend to rampage for long. They satisfy their lusts and find a place to settle down for a long hibernation. No, what I worry most about is the realm itself. The king is dead and the succession in question. What will Darus do from East Gate? I don't foresee him accepting Balmar as king, and he has an army to back up his ambitions. The Spire of Peace…" Xax shook his head. "…it seemed necessary at the time to heal the rift after the war between the dwarves and the elves, but there was a price to pay for forcing peace upon the region. Yes, it gave thousands of years of relative calm and easy living, but it also left the people unprepared to face true aggression. It has bred the warrior out of your folk, leaving you vulnerable to someone like Darus."

Imric's memories of his brother Darus were a bit hazy, since he had been ten the last time he had seen him. "Surely Darus wouldn't attack us. He's my brother. I know how much he loves Livia as well. And…and why not let Darus be king? Wouldn't that be the best for everyone? He's a strong warrior."

Xax grinned at that. "Being a strong warrior does not necessarily make one a good king. Frankly, we'd all be better off if Livia could be allowed to rule. She is by far the wisest and most learned of the royal family"

Imric remembered thinking that last night. "She is the eldest of us. I wish she could be queen."

"Long ago I tried to convince King Aronis to accept the idea that women often make great rulers," Xax said. "I have seen it myself many times and know of more examples from history. However, it was an alien concept to your tribe and I lost that fight. I'm afraid that no matter how wise it would be to choose Livia now, it would only inflame Darus all the more. He intends to be king. I wish he would come to treat with us in good faith, but I expect it will be at the head of an army instead. And I don't see how your people can stand against him."

Imric pondered everything Xax had said while he gazed up at the myriad stars in a sky just beginning to grow lighter. He had never seen so many stars before. And the moons seemed larger and crisper than he recalled, with little marks etched onto their surfaces. "I've never seen them so clearly," he whispered.

Xax sniffed. "You've never been out of your castle before. You should see the stars in the middle of the night when there are no moons out."

"Where do they come from?"

"Heh! That is a long conversation I'm not sure you're ready for."

Imric looked at Xax. "You mean you know the answer?"

The wizard tilted his head and looked at the moons again. "Not the full answer, no, but I do know a great deal. None of your people are ready to understand all that yet."

"How do you know? Tell me one thing, please!"

"Every answer I gave you would give rise to a thousand new

questions. But all right, I'll give you one thing to ponder, if you promise to hold all your questions for a more appropriate time. It's getting light now, and we need to get moving."

"I promise," Imric said, wondering what great secret he was about to learn.

Xax pointed up into the sky toward the left. "Do you see that bright star there?"

"Yes."

"That is where I came from. Me and all the other wizards you've heard about." He held a hand up. "Remember your promise. No more questions for now."

Imric's eyes were wide. "That's not fair! A person can't come from a star!"

"You see," Xax said, "I told you your people aren't ready to comprehend all this. Now come, let's great started on breakfast."

"I don't think we have much food," Imric grumbled, but he stood up and started toward their fire.

Others were beginning to stir. Imric woke Livia and Balmar, and together everyone cobbled together a meagre breakfast. The six tribesmen of the Arid Lands made an exotic mash of some sort that intrigued Imric, though it looked unpalatable to him. As they were eating, a group of about a dozen people hesitantly approached their fire. A large bald man looked as if he would speak, then changed his mind and nudged an elderly woman forward. She looked exasperated at the man but gave a curtsy in the general direction of Livia and Xax.

"Begging your pardon, milords," she said, "but your people are desperate to know what will happen next." She flung a scrawny arm in an arc to encompass the large camp all about. "Everyone is whispering and chattering, each thinking they know what is best. Some think we should have Prince Darus as king. Others think that is heresy, since Balmar is the eldest. We hope you will settle our worries."

Livia looked to Xax, and the wizard opened his mouth to respond, but he was cut off by Balmar's angry cry.

"I am king! Not Darus. Not Darus! Me!" Balmar clambered to his feet and shook a fist at the old woman, who stumbled backward into the arms of the bald man, her eyes wide with fright.

Xax scrambled up and put a hand on Balmar's arm. "Calm down, young man. All will be well."

Balmar whipped his glare around at Xax and breathed heavily for a few moments. Then his shoulders slumped and he nodded his head.

Xax turned to the group of refugees. "I know everyone is frightened. Nothing like this has happened before to our realm. There is one answer I can give you for now—that when we reach Valandiria, the king's brother, Duke Erol, will help settle everything. A decision will be made at that time. Keep faith that all will be well."

The old woman bowed her head, and the group behind her murmured and grumbled and some nodded their heads, and they slowly drifted off to collect their belongings for the trek ahead.

Xax clapped Balmar on the shoulder and smiled at Livia and Imric and the six tribesmen, who had watched the proceedings with keen interest. "Now if only the dragon will spare us for the next three days," Xax said, "we will see if Duke Erol can indeed help us save the realm."

13
DINARA

Dinara squeezed Willa's hand and looked worriedly at her lover's pale face. Willa lay where she had fallen, though Orderic, Tevin, and Eiric had managed to lift her long enough for Dinara to slide a blanket underneath her. Dinara had done what she could to clean and bandage the deep gash in Willa's side, thankful that the thick sheath of fat had likely prevented the blade from reaching any organs. Willa drew short, ragged breaths, and she had yet to regain consciousness since her fall, though her lips moved in unintelligible murmurs now and then.

The battle had been a disaster. Davit and Samvel were dead. Simon was gasping out his final breaths even now, having been thrown hard into a tree by his dying horse. Meldon sat against the trunk of another tree, moaning and holding his shattered shield arm. Weevil was busy stripping anything of value from the corpses scattered about under canopy of the woods. There remained but three men in fighting form, plus the boy Weevil. And the elf, if he still lived. Their effectiveness as raiders was finished, and that was just fine with Dinara.

She had not known just how much difference one good man could make in a fight, and the band hadn't even managed to slay the knight who had done all this. After stabbing Willa, the man had flung his arms around a horse's neck and let it drag him out of danger before he clambered on and galloped off. Miranvel had grabbed a pony from Weevil and pursued the knight. That had been more than an hour ago, and Miranvel had yet to return.

Dinara had been agonizing for several days about finding a way to slip away from the party. Only confusion over her love for Willa and the fear of being caught had prevented her from doing so.

With one finger she traced the line of the leather collar around her neck, thinking back to when Willa had first laid claim to her. It had both horrified and thrilled her at the same time. Fear had dogged her for so long that to feel even a twisted sort of security had given her a sense of relief.

Life had never been easy up in the cold north of the realm, far outside the magical influence of the Spire of Peace. Dinara had grown up in Ulfoss, a small town of wooden huts on the shore of a vast frozen lake. Ice fishing and fur trapping were the primary livelihoods for the hardy folk who dwelled there. These people were there by choice, not forced there by the magic. The townsfolk didn't turn away every refugee from the magic of the spire. Some were decent people in bad circumstances, so the townspeople allowed everyone a chance, and only when they proved unworthy of the chance were they exiled. Most of those thieves and murderers and rapists went farther north, while some turned back and sought refuge at East Gate.

As a child Dinara had been relatively happy. The folk always commented how pretty she was, and her mother helped her to keep her fine complexion by allowing her to work indoors rather than help with the ice fishing like most of the village children.

But as she changed from a child into a young woman, fear crept into her life. The men who had once smiled and told her how cute she was now stared at her with open desire, and the women who had once sewn special dresses for her and commented on what a pretty child she had been now became jealous of her astonishing beauty and sniped at her with vicious comments and open snubs. Dinara hated being lovely.

One day, not long after her fourteenth name-day, a neighbor woman accused her of seducing her husband, and though her parents fended the woman off, Dinara could see that they were not entirely convinced of her innocence. She had made up her mind then and there to escape south. She dreamed of warmer climes and friendlier people. Surely they couldn't treat her badly down south—the magic of the spire ensured everyone behaved properly.

So, she had snuck out of the small house in the deep of night, stolen a pony, and ridden off as quickly as she could. In her fear of being caught, she took the wrong track. Rather than riding southeast toward Brelyn, she had accidentally headed east for Coldhaven, nestled alongside the Black Woods. She had never been away from Ulfoss before, so she had failed to understand her mistake until she learned from a gate guard that she had ended up near the eerie haunted woods of legend rather than the great trading city of Brelyn. The guard told her to follow the Istriln River south and she would find her destination.

Cold and half starved, she had followed the man's advice. Close to nightfall after a hard day's travel, she had been waylaid by three filthy men and barely made her escape by galloping across a rickety wooden bridge over the river. Exhausted but too frightened to try to find a place to camp, she had plodded on through a small valley between the forest and some large hills. Howling wolves in the hills and strange flickering lights in the woods gave her nowhere to turn except to search for the end of the valley. At dawn she had come up over a ridgeline to find a large dirt road. Looking both ways, she had no idea which direction to take, so she had chosen at random. She met no travelers on the road, and a day later she found herself in the tiny village of Tarn, and thus learned that she had again chosen the wrong route.

A small tavern seemed to be her only hope of succor, though she was out of funds, having used the last to purchase a bit of food before she left Coldhaven. A half dozen soldiers from East Gate had been in the tavern, on leave she later learned. They glared hungrily at her as she entered, and she had been sorely tempted to flee. But what other options did she have? Out of food and money, her only choice was to throw herself on the possible kindness of strangers. Perhaps she could trade the poor pony for a cart ride to Brelyn? As she had looked around the tavern, hoping to spot a kind-looking face, two of the soldiers had loomed over her. A loud creak from the door to one of the rooms made her look around, and she saw the vast bulk of a woman filling the entire doorframe. She mistook her for a man at first, until she heard the woman's voice boom out.

"You two go back to your drinks! The girl's with me."

Dinara was surprised to see the men back down. They cracked a couple of jokes and went back to their table, as the huge woman took Dinara by the arm and steered her to a dimly-lit corner.

"A pretty thing like you shouldn't wander about alone," the woman said.

Dinara struggled to order her muddled thoughts and could find nothing to say.

"You can call me Willa. Wide Willa those bastards like to call me, for obvious reasons, though none dare say it to my face."

Dinara took a shuddering breath. "You…you're a soldier, like them?"

"Not sure I'd use that word," Willa said. "I'm part of a team at East Gate. We do scouting and raiding among the barbarian tribes."

None of this made sense to Dinara. "But…women don't fight."

"I suppose most don't. I do."

Dinara found Willa to be irrepressible. The woman ran roughshod over Dinara's attempts to explain that she wanted to go to Brelyn or even farther south. Before she knew it, Dinara found herself on her pony, riding alongside Willa and several of the soldiers on their way to the grim walls of East Gate. Willa had a small room to herself within the fortress and installed Dinara there. Life would have been bad enough in East Gate from the icy winds and the general cold dreariness, but it was made worse by the lustful stares of nearly every man in the garrison. She found she had to either hide away in the room or remain close to Willa. Astonishing as it was, Willa several times came to blows with men over Dinara, and somehow, she always came out on top. She wasn't necessarily a better fighter than the men, but she would never back down and never quit. No matter how bloody the fight, Willa persevered.

One day Willa brought her to the courtyard where soldiers were training. She called everyone to a halt and made them watch as she buckled a leather collar around Dinara's neck and tied it off with a long leash.

"Listen here, you troll-breathed eunuchs," Willa yelled. "This woman is mine! Next man who touches her will be fed to the goats."

Dinara had not liked the collar, but there were no more incidents with the men after that. The men still stared hungrily at her and japed and jested, but they went no further than that.

It had never entered Dinara's mind that women could love one another. She had heard of such happening between men—the children she had grown up with had used that as one of their worst insults toward any boy they wished to offend. Yet, Dinara's initial revulsion at Willa's advances had evolved with time. She had gone along with Willa and the small band of scouts, led by the moody Orderic, and Dinara found herself enjoying the freedom and excitement and fear that came with their ventures into barbarian lands.

Willa was rough with the men and could do terrible things at times, mostly to barbarians, but she had a heart large and open enough to match her huge form, and Dinara had found herself growing fond of the woman, and then more than just fond.

Yet now, as she looked at Willa's pale face as she lay on the blanket in the dirt among the dry leaves, Dinara was torn. She reached out a hand to brush aside a damp hair from Willa's brow. It was the attack on the first farmstead that had shaken Dinara's certainty of her love and her desire to remain with the band of raiders. Slaughtering barbarians was one thing, but the attack on the farm became a horror beyond anything Dinara had ever imagined possible. Those children. The baby. Even the poor farmer and his wife and the two elderly women. None of them had deserved to die, let alone in the horrific manner that they had. And Willa had participated willingly, even eagerly.

Dinara hadn't been able to watch, her stomach churning. Her eyes had met those of the captive boy, Villem, and she had seen the same horror in them. She was glad he had escaped. She wished she had the same courage to make a run for it.

Love? Could she still love Willa after what she had seen? She couldn't deny the deep affection she felt, the years spent together, but however conflicted her thoughts, she knew she could no longer remain with these people. Yet, how to get away?

Orderic drew near, kicking at a loose stone. "Here comes Miranvel."

Dinara looked up and saw the elf trotting in on his pony. Half his face was badly bruised, and his expression was grimmer than she had ever before seen it. Miranvel caught Orderic's gaze and simply shook his head.

Orderic sighed. "He escaped then. Bastard!"

Dinara turned back to Willa and saw that her eyes were slitted open. She squeezed the hand she still held and traced a finger along Willa's cheek. "You're awake. I was worried."

Willa coughed and grimaced. "It takes more than that pig fucker to kill me."

Willa laid her arm out, and Dinara snuggled up close, careful not to disturb the wound when she lay her arm across Willa's belly. When Willa began to snore, Dinara eased herself up so as not to disturb her sleeping companion. She touched the hasp of the buckle that held the collar around her neck, then began to work at it. It took several minutes to get it to loosen, but at last Dinara removed the collar for the first time since Willa had placed it around her neck. She wound the tether around the collar until it was bound. With a flick of her wrist, she tossed the collar into the rushing stream and watched it sink.

14
VILLEM

Villem hacked and gagged on the earth choking him. Something warm and wet rasped across his face. He spat dirt from his mouth and breathed in air sweeter than any dessert. Gasping and panting, he tried to open his eyes, but it was too painful from the grit that filled them. He was confused by whatever it was cleansing his face, until he heard a whine.

The dog! She has saved my life once again. Despite his utter misery, Villem's heart filled with a warm glow for the poor, starving mongrel that refused to let him die. He recalled the ridged line across the dog's haunch from where the crossbow bolt had left its mark. *I could name her Scar, but that doesn't feel right. How about Duchess? I'm not much of a knight at the moment, but a knight is supposed to have someone to serve.*

He spat and spat until his mouth was free of dirt. Duchess began licking him about the eyes, and soon Villem was able to try opening them again. The grit was painful and filled his eyes with tears, but he could see Duchess standing over him, continuing to lick away the dirt from around his face.

Villem was grateful that the lord's men hadn't bothered to do more than toss a thin layer of earth over his face, else he'd surely be dead now. They had done better with his lower extremities, though—he couldn't move them much. He began wiggling his arms and legs the best he could, trying to gain more room.

Duchess's head jerked up and looked away, and she barked twice. In the distance, Villem heard a voice, perhaps that of a child. It was coming closer!

"H-help!" he cried. "Help me!" He heard a startled cry, then silence for a few moments.

"Back dog!" someone yelled, sounding like a young boy.

"It must belong to the witch," came a voice from a different boy.

"No!" Villem cried. "It's me. Help me!"

"Run!" yelped one of the boys, and Villem heard them scampering away.

Villem wept and laughed at the same time, while Duchess began to lick his face again. "Good girl. Good, Duchess." He wished he had an arm free so he could pet her. He began to wiggle his arms and legs again.

Just when he began to feel he was making some headway, he heard voices again, and Duchess again looked up and barked.

"There it is, see? Don't get too close," came the voice of one of the boys.

A man's voice responded, "It's just a mutt. Are you daft?"

"It talked, I swear!"

"It's the witch's, I tell you." So the other boy was there as well.

Villem gathered his breath and called out, "It's not the dog. It's me! Help me!"

Silence reigned for some time before Villem heard scuffling sounds. Duchess barked again.

"Easy, dog," came the raspy voice of the man. "I'll poke you if I have to."

"Don't hurt her!" Villem called out. "She's a good dog. The best!"

"Show yourself, whoever you are."

"I'm here, in the ground."

A man's face appeared, eyes widening as he saw Villem. The man was old, but he wore a conical steel helm on his head, so Villem assumed he must be a guard from the keep.

"What's this then?" the man said. "What are you doing in the ground?"

"Just help me, please!"

The man looked behind him. "You boys, come here. Nothing t'be affrighted of. Just some demon digging his way out from the bowels of the earth." The man chuckled.

"Don't want no part of no demon," said one of the boys.

"Get over here now and dig this boy out of the ground! Tis no demon, though why someone decided to bury him here is the question."

Villem saw the face of a boy of about ten years appear, joined soon after by another boy. Both boys began to cackle with laughter.

The guard whacked them with the butt of his spear. "Leave off, you idjits! Get to digging."

The boys fell to their knees and used their hands to scoop earth away from the makeshift grave. Duchess joined in with the digging, and soon enough Villem was able to ease himself to a sitting position. He groaned with pain. After brushing his hands of dirt, he rubbed at his eyes to get the last of the grit out.

"Let's get you out of there," the guard said. He gripped Villem under one arm and helped lift him to his feet. "You're a right mess. Ho there! Can't even stand. I can see why they buried you. Better get you inside and let milady decide what to do with you."

With the kids tagging along behind, chattering excitedly, the guard helped Villem stagger through the gate of the small keep and up the steps through the stout oak entry door.

"Boys, get that dog outside, and fetch a maid to clean up this mess," the guard said. "Let's lie you down on this bench so I can fetch milady. Ah, here she is already."

"What's this, Akun? I've never seen so much mud on a person. Is it a goblin?"

"No, milady. Tis a young man someone buried outside the gate."

Through slitted eyes, Villem saw a pretty girl not much older than himself, dressed in stark white linens trimmed in red.

"I don't understand. Why would someone bury a young man?"

"From the look of him, he's half dead already."

The women stooped to examine Villem more closely. "I can see nothing through all this muck." She turned to a pair of maids who had just entered, followed by the two boys. "Lidia, go draw a hot bath. We need to clean this boy up. Borun and Jessup, you boys go fetch the witch. Tell her we have an injured man."

The boys tugged their forelocks and scampered out the entrance door, while one of the maids vanished, presumably to start heating water for a bath.

"Marta, fetch a couple of blankets," the lady said to the other maid.

"Was I wrong to bring him in, missus?" the guard asked.

"No, Akun. You did well. We'll need your strength to lift him into the bath."

Villem drifted off. He came to with Akun trying to untie the muddy drawstrings of his shirt. A large copper basin stood nearby with steam pouring from its top. The young noblewoman stood off to the side, with both maids behind her.

"Milady," said the maid called Marta. "It isn't proper for us to see the man undressed."

The woman sniffed loudly. "He has nothing I haven't seen before. You two can go, but first take these muddy rags and dispose of them."

Having removed Villem's shirt, Akun now started untying his breeches.

"M-milady," Villem whispered.

"Hush now," she replied. "Let's get you clean so the witch can examine you."

Villem drifted again until he was jerked awake by the scalding water as Akun lowered him into the tub. "Aaaagh! Hot!"

"You'll survive, hopefully," the woman said. "Now scrub him well, Akun."

The guard looked miserable but did as he was told, using a scrub brush and some rags. Villem screamed when Akun touched the wound on the back of his head.

"What are you doing to the poor boy? Leave the healing to me." This came from a woman who hobbled into the room, led by the maid Lidia. If this was the witch, it surprised Villem. From the tales of his youth, he expected a crone, but this woman could have seen no more than thirty summers at most. She was homely of face and had a milky white eye, and she hobbled from a club foot. "You, go on and guard something. I can manage this myself."

Akun seemed relieved and made haste to depart. The noblewoman brought a stool so the witch could sit near the tub. The witch took up a small pitcher, filled it with the now muddy water and promptly poured it over Villem's head. He screamed in agony, fire seeming to pour through him from the knot on the back of his head. The witch ignored him and poured more water on him. She used one hand to rub his hair as she poured again and again.

"He's half dead, this one," the witch said, "and small wonder." She spread the hair from around the wound. "A wound so sour is bad enough, but on his head tis far worse. It can poison his brain and kill him quickly."

"Is there nothing we can do?" the noblewoman asked.

"Have your girls bring clean rags and something to boil them in. I need a fire as well, perhaps a brazier. Hurry now!"

The noblewoman clearly wasn't used to being ordered about, but she ran off to do as she was bid.

The witch began examining the rest of Villem's body, scrubbing it clean as she went. She scowled at the lacerations on his wrist and muttered about them being sour as well. The rope burns on his legs must have been acceptable, as she merely scrubbed them down with a rag.

The maid Marta entered, carrying a pot of water and some torn strips of white linen.

"You there," the witch said. "Get some men to empty this tub and fill it with clean water. This muck won't do. We need the boy clean."

Marta put down her supplies and hurried out.

The noblewoman returned with a steward and two other servants, carrying a brazier that they placed near the witch's stool. The witch directed them to remove Villem from the tub and lay him on the blankets. Villem was aghast at being naked in front of the women, but there was nothing he could do about it, so he endured the embarrassment in silence. The witch tucked another blanket over the top of him, then ordered the men to clean out the tub and fill it with clean water.

"You…you don't look like a witch," Villem murmured.

"Fool men will call any woman a witch who doesn't settle down to marriage and bearing children. There's no such thing as witches."

"You don't know spells?"

The woman grimaced. "Only wizards cast spells, and aint no woman been a wizard since Zoya died."

Villem had never heard of a wizard named Zoya. "When was there a woman wizard?"

"A tale you never heard, eh? Twas long ago." She paused to yell at the two maids. "More clean rags! I need many more than this!" She turned back to Villem. "She was one of that group of wizards, the only woman among them. She loved to heal. That was her specialty." As the witch spoke, she was laying out various instruments from her bag, and placing some long metal ones into the smoking brazier. "You know the war between the dwarves and the elves. The one that caused the wizards to make the magical spire afterward. The stories say that Zoya tended to the wounded of both sides, saving many of them. But tragedy struck. She was tending a dwarf warrior after a battle, and in his delirium, the dwarf pulled a dagger and struck her in the neck. And so the world lost the only woman wizard. Not a happy tale, so tis no wonder you never heard it."

"If you're no witch, what should I call you?"

"Marianna, if you like. You can call me witch as well. They all have for so long that I pay it no mind."

The servants had returned lugging the heavy tub of fresh water.

"Go on, lift him in there," Marianna directed. "And you, get more blankets. These are filthy."

After washing Villem carefully in the cold water and wrapping him in clean blankets, Marianna pulled a vial of clear liquid from her bag and beckoned the noblewoman to come closer. "I'll need your help with this. If you're too squeamish, call a servant with a strong stomach."

The noblewoman shook her head. "No, I'll help." She sat near Villem's side, across from Marianna.

"You are kind to help, my lady," Villem said. "What may I call you?"

The noblewoman smiled brightly. "Lady Sonia. And you are?"

"Villem. Villem Tathis of Iskimir.

Sonia looked startled. "I know of Iskimir, and of Lord Tathis. Are you saying you are his son?"

Villem started to nod, but it hurt the back of his head. "Aye. His son, and a knight as well."

"What is a knight doing injured and buried in the ground so far from home?"

"It's a long story, milady. Not sure I have the strength to tell it at the moment."

"Tell it later then," Marianna snapped, her voice taut with impatience. "I need you to hold him on his side so I can tend the back of his head."

The two women rolled Villem to his side on the blankets, and Lady Sonia gripped him by one arm and at his waist to hold him in place.

"This is going to hurt," Marianna said.

Villem couldn't see what she was doing, but he saw Lady Sonia's face turn pale. He heard a hiss, as of something hot being plunged into cold water. Then something poked into the wound on the back of his head, and it felt like a branding iron. He tried, and failed, to stifle a groan.

"Must you do that?" Lady Sonia asked, looking ill.

"It needs to drain. So much poison in the wound."

The brand struck again, and Villem felt himself slip into darkness.

He woke in a bed, warm inside several layers of clean sheets and blankets. His head felt heavy and swollen. When he lifted an arm to feel it, he saw bandages about his wrists, and when he felt his head, there were more cloths tied all about it.

He saw no one in the room, which was a small square of stone with a single arrow-slit window. The bed was nearly as comfortable as his own had been back home. A small table nearby held a jug that he presumed was water, as well as a small pile of white linen cloths. He dozed again until he felt someone's presence nearby. A warm hand pressed against his forehead.

"You're awake," said the witch Marianna.

"Will he live, do you think?" came the voice of Lady Sonia from somewhere behind.

"Yes. He is young and heals quickly. Bring him some chicken broth."

"I'll have it done." Villem heard Sonia leave the room.

Marianna lifted the blankets to inspect Villem's legs, gave a nod, and tucked the blanket back again.

Villem tried to say something and found his mouth was parched. He swallowed several times and worked his tongue around his mouth. "My…my dog. Is she well?"

Marianna tsked. "I'm sure your dog is fine. You'd be wiser to worry about yourself."

Silence reigned for several minutes until Lady Sonia returned, along with a servant bearing a steaming bowl that he set on the small table before departing.

"Are you able to eat?" Marianna asked. "It's better to have it while it's still hot."

Villem nodded. He wasn't sure he could keep anything down, but he desperately wanted company for the moment.

"I'll feed him," Lady Sonia said, seating herself on a stool nearby. "Thank you so much for your aid. I'll not forget it."

Marianna nodded her head. "I'll return on the morrow to check on him. Don't let him out of bed." With that she promptly strode from the room.

Lady Sonia blew on a spoonful of broth and held it to Villem's lips. He gingerly sipped at it and found it delicious. Suddenly he was ravenous. He lapped up every spoonful and was disappointed when the bowl was empty.

Sonia smiled. "I'm glad to see you eating well. It's a good sign, I think."

"Thank you for everything, my lady," Villem murmured, his eyelids growing heavy.

"Do you need the bedpan?" she asked.

It was all Villem could do to shake his head before sleep claimed him.

When next Villem awoke with a clear head, he had no idea how much time had passed. He had vague jumbles of memories, of feverish visions, images of faces—Marianna's and Sonia's mostly, though sometimes of servants as well—tending to him, feeding him, cleaning him. No one was in the room this time, and when he looked at the narrow window it was dark, just a single star glowing dimly near the top of the arch.

He heard a whine near his feet, and saw Duchess lying on the bed, head up with wide brown eyes staring into his. Villem smiled. "Good girl, Duchess." He reached a hand down to scratch behind one of her ears, and Duchess licked his forearm. "Looks like you've been eating well."

"That she has. The poor thing was nearly starved."

Villem was startled and looked around to find Lady Sonia standing in the doorway.

"You look wide awake for the first time in days," she said, drawing close to the bed. "You're regaining some of your color."

Villem took inventory of his various hurts and realized he could feel almost no pain. He felt good for the first time in ages. "I would have died without your aid, my lady."

She sat on the edge of the bed and laid a warm palm across his forehead. "You were delirious for so long. Without Marianna's knowledge of wounds…" She shook her head as her words trailed off.

"I wish I had a way to repay my debt to both of you," Villem said.

"Well, you could start by telling me what happened to you. How did you fall into such a state and how did you come to be buried outside my gate?"

Villem tried to imagine where to begin. He didn't want to admit to having been found wanting by the magic of the spire; of being driven from the realm by its magic. "I...I was captured by a band of marauders out of East Gate. My lady, they plan to war against us! Can you imagine? I was injured when I made my escape. A man in the woods helped bring me to your keep, but I was so badly sick that a man—I think it must have been your father—said I was good as dead and ordered his men to bury me."

"My father?" Sonia laughed. "My father is many leagues from here, in his own keep. You must mean my husband."

"Your husband? But...he was so old."

"Thrice my age, tis true. I am nineteen now and married these long five years."

Villem didn't know how to respond. It seemed monstrous to marry a child to an old man. He knew such things were common, but not that the age difference could be so vast.

She stroked his forehead. "I see you are shocked. Worry not. He plans to put me aside soon. I'm barren he says, so he has no heir. The witch tells me it's as like to be he who is barren, so I may yet dream of having a family one day."

"Are you unhappy?"

She tilted her head in thought. "I worry whether my father will take me back in after I'm set aside. He's a harsh man, and likely will blame me for my misfortune." She frowned. "Perhaps he'll see a use for me in marrying me off again to another old man."

"You should not be treated so, my lady," Villem said.

She shrugged. "It's the lot of any girl child. Our value lies in what alliances we can bring to our fathers."

Villem had no sister, so he hadn't been forced to consider such things. He had overheard his mother once, speaking to his father about arranging a marriage for his younger brother, Vonn. At the time, Villem had only wondered what they had planned for himself; he hadn't thought for a moment what such marriages must be like for the young woman forced into it without any consideration of her own desires. Not that his desires were taken into account either. "I recently came of age, and I wondered if my parents would marry me off soon. I don't think I would have been given a say in it. I could only hope it would be someone as kind as you."

"You are sweet to say so." Sonia bent and kissed his cheek. "Hmm, I'll need to get the razor and shave you. Though perhaps a beard would suit you. Are you hungry?"

Duchess whuffed, making Villem laugh. "I think Duchess is. If it's not too much trouble, I could have some soup."

"No trouble at all. I'll return shortly."

A short while later, with Duchess happily gnawing on a large bone in one corner of the room, Sonia set down the spoon in the now-empty soup bowl and set the bowl on the small table. She turned to Villem and gave him an inscrutable look. She put a hand to her cheek and flushed red. "I...I wonder if you would turn me away?"

"What do you mean, my lady?"

She pulled up his blanket and slid into bed beside him. Villem was suddenly overwhelmed with confusion, his body responding immediately to the soft warmth of her body next to his. He had never been touched by a pretty woman before, and the desires of his body overruled any thoughts his mind tried to dredge up or any lingering aches from his wounds. He felt he needed to say something but could think of nothing to say, and her mouth covered his and all further thoughts of resistance fled.

15
IMRIC

The next couple of days were filled with dull plodding along a dusty road, alleviated only by the beauty of the endless inland sea to their left and the massive wall of snow-capped mountains to their right. Necks began to ache from the constant act of looking over one's shoulder to see if the dragon had come. One time there was a cry of terror that sent everyone scurrying for whatever shelter they could find. It turned out to be merely an eagle drifting on the breeze.

Imric had never been around so much suffering and sadness before, and it dampened his spirits. The old lady who kept baking them bread in the mornings had lost her husband, though she wasn't certain he was dead. Many others were worse off. They had seen their loved ones die or knew for certain the part of the city where they had once lived had been drenched by the dragon's acid clouds.

He had never had to walk so much, and without the heartening magic of the spire to add strength to his steps it added to the misery. Broken blisters covered the soles of his feet.

As the refugees paused to rest and eat a meagre lunch, shouts from the road ahead drew their attention. Soldiers on horseback led two large wagons drawn by mules. They were forcing people off the road, roughly using the butts of their spears at times. Xax and Livia stood in the center of the road and tried to halt the men. They were nearly run down and had to leap aside to avoid being crushed by a team of mules and their wagon. A soldier pointed his spear at Xax and shouted, "Out of the way, old timer!"

"Is this the way to treat people?" Xax called back to the man vainly as the soldier rode on without stopping.

"What do you think they're doing?" Imric asked. "Going to help the injured?"

Livia shrugged. "It would be nice to think that, but I doubt it."

Xax shook his fist at the cavalcade. "My bet is Duke Erol sent them to retrieve the treasury, if it hasn't already been looted."

"That sounds right," Livia said. "Money before people, though I'd like to think better of my uncle."

The refugees returned to the drudgery of the march and were rewarded at dusk by reaching the point where the sea began to curve away to the west, signaling they were drawing near at last to Valandiria.

"How much longer before we reach the city?" asked Azer, who seemed to be the leader of the six nomads who had attached themselves to the group.

"We'll camp soon at the northernmost tip of the sea, at the junction where the road heads north toward East Gate or west to Valandiria," Xax said. "If all goes well, we should arrive in the city by this time tomorrow."

Another long slog the next day brought the weary column within sight of the city walls. A small harbor snuggled into a curve of the sea below the spot where the land began to rise dramatically into sheer cliffs, with the duke's castle nestled high above the calm waters, its towers seeming to jut into the clouds.

"It's beautiful," Imric said. "So different from Tolgaria."

"I keep forgetting you never got to travel with us when we visited Uncle Erol," Livia said. "The city isn't nearly as large, but it is pretty.

The townsfolk all live below the slopes of the mount, with only the castle dominating the heights."

"Those cliffs look so steep," Imric said, "as if the walls of the castle drop directly down into the sea."

"You can't see it from here," Xax said, "but there is one balcony off the great hall that juts out over the water enough that one foolish young nobleman a few centuries ago actually leapt from it into the sea. He even lived to tell the tale."

"Jumped?" asked Balmar, who trailed after Livia.

"He must have been crazy," Imric said. "Why would he do such a thing?"

Xax smiled. "It was a sweltering hot summer. Hot enough to drive a man mad."

"How did they rescue him?"

"That was easy. There's a stone jetty at the base of the cliff not far from there, ostensibly to allow the castle to receive supply by water in the event of a siege."

It was beginning to grow too dark to see details of the city, but lights became visible from lamps and torches and added their own beauty to the night. Though everyone was exhausted, no one wished to spend another night camped beside the road.

All three moons were out tonight—the large white one and the small, and the tiny red moon that the superstitious believed was a sign of bad luck. Imric was surprised at the size of the crowd before the huge city gate, and he detected an angry buzz in the air.

"What's this?" Xax said and began elbowing his way forward. Livia had her hand on Xax's tunic to keep from losing him in the crowd, so Imric snatched Livia's hand and followed.

"They won't let us in." This was the refrain passing through the crowd, said angrily by some, fatalistically by others. "They aren't going to let us in."

The big oaken gates were closed. Xax glared up at a sergeant-in-arms. He had to shout to be heard over the noise. "These people are refugees. Why aren't you letting them in?"

The guard waved his hands downward toward the crowd as if to settle them down. He shouted, "Follow the road west! There will be a camp! Safety! Food! Blankets! Follow the others!"

Some did as the guard suggested, turned and trudged away to follow the road west. Xax shouted up at the guard again, waving his walking stick with the green crystal at him to catch his attention. "We have the royal family here! Let us in!"

The sergeant stared at Xax. Then his eyes widened when he noticed Livia standing next to him. "Princess! Are you all right? Where is the king?"

The crowd that remained became hushed, waiting to see what would happen. Livia only had to raise her voice a little to be heard. "Prince Balmar is here with us. Prince Imric as well. The wizard Xaxanakis. The king is dead. Please let us in."

Noise swelled again as people in the crowd began to talk all at once. The sergeant waved his arms to try to shush everyone. When he could speak at last, he said, "Everyone back up so we can open the gate."

Xax looked around to be sure everyone was with him. "Where's Balmar?"

"I think he's with the nomads," Livia said. "He doesn't like crowds."

"Let's go find him."

The crowd was shuffling back from the gate as Xax led Livia and Imric through to where the six nomads were grouped about Balmar. Xax put his hand on Balmar's shoulder. "They're going to let us in. Come."

One door of the gate groaned open just enough to let four

guardsmen pile out, gripping their spears with white knuckles. The sergeant pointed down from the wall to where the remaining royal family stood. "There! Those ones only!"

"What?" Livia cried. "They can't take us in and leave everyone else behind!"

"I'm afraid that's exactly what they'll do," Xax said.

Livia shook her head. "I won't go. These people need help."

"I'm not sure they'll give us a choice," Xax said.

"They can take Balmar. He's better off here with Uncle Erol. Imric, too, if he wishes. But it was you, Xax; you taught me that a real leader must do what's best for his people, not what's best for himself. I'm staying with them. I'll take them to this camp. Once I see them safely there, I may be able to return, or you can find me there."

"I don't think they'll let you go, so if that's your wish, you'd better slip away quickly now. I'll follow you once I am able. But don't be surprised if the duke sends riders to fetch you back."

"Wait, no!" Imric cried. "I want to stay with you!"

Livia had a pleading look in her eyes. "We'll be back as soon as we can, Imric. I promise. But you're better off here. And Balmar will need someone familiar with him. He'll be confused. Stay with him."

Imric felt torn. Part of him wanted to stop the endless march. To sleep in a comfortable bed and have real food again. Hot food. He wanted to see Valandiria and the castle. But Livia was the only person left he truly loved. He didn't want to let her go.

Livia bent forward and kissed his cheek. "Please stay. I'll see you soon." With that she ducked into the midst of the nomads, and the seven of them moved off into the crowd.

Xax gripped Balmar by the arm and reached out to grasp Imric's hand. "Here we are," he said to the approaching guardsmen. "Here are the princes."

The first guard to reach them looked confused. "Where's the other? The princess?"

"You must be mistaken, young man," Xax said. "These are the royal heirs. Get them inside to safety."

The guard looked unhappy, but he waved them to follow, and his fellows took up spots around the two princes and Xax. They gently pushed Imric through the gate ahead of Balmar, but Xax halted.

"You can go in as well wizard," said the guard who had led the squad. "But no one else."

Xax grunted and nodded his head. "Where is this camp your sergeant mentioned? For the refugees."

The guard pointed. "The route along the Skendris River to the junction with the road to Brelyn. Milord has men there setting up pavilions for all the refugees. He's sending food, water, supplies, everything."

"Why there?" Xax asked.

"Milord says it's not safe here. Says the dragon will likely come. And there's the army from East Gate."

"Darus? He marches already?"

"Aye. Our scouts say he has near three thousand men with him. The duke says he marches to claim the kingship."

Xax looked bewildered. "How can Darus know the king is dead? The news couldn't have traveled that far so quickly."

The guard shrugged. "I don't think Darus cared whether his father was alive or not. With the magic gone, he came to claim the throne. Leastways that's what I hear."

"Lead on, young man," Xax said to the guard.

Imric took Balmar's hand and led him after the guards as they trooped through the city toward the castle.

The buildings looked so different here, made from stone and wood rather than marble. They were painted with bright colors, as opposed to the austere look of Tolgaria. And dominating the view, towering into the sky, the duke's castle upon its mount. It was smaller than the castle Imric grew up in, yet it looked more majestic. Excitement built in his belly to explore this new realm.

Balmar's grip tightened until it hurt, and Imric used his other hand to pry his fingers loose. "It's all right, Balmar. Don't worry."

When they reached a crossroads, Imric saw down to the docks in the small harbor, crowded with fishing boats and small trading vessels. The road began to rise, at first gradually but then steeply as it neared the castle gates. The portcullis creaked upward, and Imric was surprised to see that the courtyard was bustling with soldiers and men carrying supplies and arms to and fro. Preparing for a siege, he supposed. He wondered how worried he should be, though he still found it absurd to think of his brother Darus going to war against his own people.

The guards hustled them up some stone steps and into an entrance hall lined with tapestries and statues of the previous dukes, going all the way back to the time of the first king, Aronis Kaldarion. Legends from the history books Livia loved so much. It struck Imric with a sense of wonder that these were his own ancestors. The guards turned them over to a steward, who led them through a maze of hallways and staircases before at last depositing them in a large chamber with an astonishing floor. And standing in the middle of that floor was his uncle, Duke Erol Kaldarion, looking stout, heavily bearded, and much taller than his brother the king. He was staring down at the floor, which was made of large colored tiles that spread the entirety of the room and formed a fabulous, detailed map of the realm. Imric had seen crude maps of the Greatlands before in books, but nothing remotely as grand as this.

The steward coughed softly, and the duke looked up. "Ah, what's this? Oh, Balmar!" Erol rushed over and grasped Balmar's arm in greeting. "You're safe! Wonderful! Where is everyone else? Your father?"

Balmar looked bewildered, his mouth hanging open.

"Greetings, Duke Erol," Xax said. "I'm very sorry to inform you that your brother was slain by the dragon."

Erol nodded in greeting but did not extend his arm to Xax. "I might have expected to see you turn up during times like this, wizard. Have another vision?"

Xax nodded. "They do seem to happen when times become fraught."

Duke Erol looked sideways down at Imric, then wagged a finger at him. "You…must be Imric. I have seen you before, did you know? My brother never wanted me to. Wanted to pretend you didn't exist. When I visited him once, Livia made a secret rendezvous with me to show me the babe that had been the cause of so much trouble. All grown up now, I see. How old are you now?"

"Th- thirteen, almost fourteen, Uncle," Imric said.

Erol threw an arm around Balmar's shoulders. "I'm very sorry about your father. There were rumors from some of the refugees, so I was prepared for the worst." He walked them over to the part of the floor map he had been studying. Imric saw that it was their own part of the realm, the inland Sea of Alia and its three great cities, the vast wall of mountains just to the east. Markers were set on various tiles, depicting knights on horseback with varying coats of arms.

"What's this, Uncle?"

Erol pointed north to the pass through the mountains that led to East Gate. A marker was there with a coat of arms Imric didn't recognize. "That is your brother Darus's army. So far it's camped just outside the mouth of the pass, readying supply wagons and such." He waved a hand at the other markers. "These others are the troops of my lords. I sent out a call to arms, and these are the ones whose riders have arrived to announce their march."

"Will they arrive in time?"

Erol shrugged. "Too soon to say. It depends on when Darus begins his own march. Forgive me, you must be tired and hungry. Let's get you situated. Where's Livia? Don't tell me she's lost as well?"

"Livia is fine. She's helping settle the refugees, then she plans to come here."

"That's a relief. She's a wonder. Just like her magnificent mother, at least when it comes to smarts."

Xax had been wandering about the room, examining the map. "Duke Erol, your coastline is remarkably accurate, though there are many flaws with other parts of the map."

"I have men bring copies of the map with them when they go on embassies or trade expeditions to see if they can gain more detail from local experts. An elf trader once laughed at the map and insisted on fixing the coastline. As for the flaws, I defer to your extensive travels and would be happy to have you give my men corrections so new tiles can be painted."

Erol snapped a finger to the steward. "Yarus, find good rooms for my nephews and the wizard. Let them wash and rest and we'll have an early supper."

"Yes, milord. Come, young princes. Milord Xaxanakis."

The steward led them away, Imric glancing back over his shoulder to see that his uncle was once again studying the grand map. Only one staircase later, Steward Yarus placed them in adjacent rooms and gave a flurry of orders to various servants. Imric had barely had time to take in the details of his new room before he was plunged into a steaming bath of soapy water. He was mortified when a maid entered the room and began laying out fresh clothing on the bed, paying no heed to the naked young man trying desperately to hide himself beneath the few remaining bubbles of his bath.

"There you are, young prince." The maid turned and looked

directly into his blushing face. "Do you require anything else?"

"N- n- no, thank you."

"Very well. If you need help dressing, just ring that bell there on the nightstand."

Imric dunked himself down into the water.

While drying off later, he noticed something interesting that he hadn't seen during his cursory look around the room. A large wardrobe had been hidden from his view by the canopy bed, and though it looked to be made from a different kind of wood than the ones back home, the shape was the same. And it was built into the wall, just like most of the wardrobes in Tolgaria. His first thought was that this castle must have been built or designed by the same people who built the other. He grew excited at the idea that there may be secret passageways here to discover and explore. Part of him wanted to start right away, but he was freshly washed and the steward had said supper would begin shortly, so he pushed aside the desire to go exploring and finished dressing.

He didn't have to wait long before a servant fetched him to join the others in the hall, where they then proceeded to a small dining room with two trestle tables. A thick burgundy carpet covered most of the floor, and tapestries on the wall depicted hunting scenes. Duke Erol stood up from one of the tables and beckoned them over. Only two others sat at his table, while the other table was nearly full with what seemed to Imric to be younger people and children.

"Xax and Balmar, please sit. You already know my family, but young Imric has never been introduced. This is my wife Bora." Erol indicated the stout woman with kind eyes seated to his left. "And this is my eldest son Istvan." His arm swept to the young man to his right, who looked about the age of Darus or Balmar. He had a twinkle in his eye and a flashing smile, and Imric wanted to like him immediately. "Imric, perhaps you would more enjoy the other table?

Those are our seven other children."

Imric glanced over at the table where seven boys and girls of varying ages were poking and prodding one another while maintaining a flurry of whispered conversation. "Th- thank you, milord, but if I could, I'd prefer to remain here with my brother and Xax."

"As you will." Duke Erol indicated to them to sit and ordered a servant to begin serving the meal.

"I'm very sorry that Livia did not arrive with you," Istvan said, flashing another smile. "She has always been good company. I hope she will arrive shortly."

"She said she would come as soon as she was able," Xax said. "She's helping the refugees."

"It's noble of her, of course," Erol said, "but I already have many men there to help. I've sent riders to fetch her, so she should join us in no more than a day or two, I should imagine."

"I warned her you would probably do so," Xax said.

"We need all of the surviving royal family here now," Erol said. "We must crown the new king as quickly as possible. In these perilous times—a dragon and an invading army—the realm needs assurances that the Kaldarion line is unbroken."

"I'm guessing you have a plan in mind," Xax said.

"There should be no question, I would think. Balmar is the heir. He must be crowned king."

Balmar straightened from his slouch and grinned. "I am king!"

Xax stared into Erol's eyes. "You know full well that he has not the capacity to rule. Though Varun failed to name Darus as his heir, we all know that he intended to."

"You would have a traitor sit the throne? A boy who would invade the realm and slaughter its people? The boy has shown his stripes. He isn't fit for anything but a noose or the headsman's block."

"He only wants what he believes is his, even if he is unwise in how he is going about getting it. You could avoid much bloodshed and heartbreak for our people by choosing to support Darus."

"Xax," Erol said, shaking his head, "do you honestly believe Darus would be a wise king? I do not. I believe he would be one of our worst. He has always been hot tempered and a bit of a bully. His mother doted on him to the point of spoiling him."

Xax sighed. "You may be right, though my long experience tells me that you cannot always judge how a person will turn out. People do sometimes change with time and responsibility. I share your worries about Darus, but we both know Balmar cannot rule. I know you won't see it my way, but the true eldest child of Varun would make for the wisest and best ruler of the realm."

Erol shook his head and chuckled, and was about to reply when Istvan broke in. "Livia's a girl. She can't be king. I adore her and she is smarter than anyone I know, but the people wouldn't accept her."

Erol clapped a hand to Istvan's shoulder. "My son is impetuous but correct. Only the tribes beyond East Gate, and only some of them mind you, accept women as leaders. Our people would rise up against such a move."

"I believe you underestimate the people," Xax said. "You draw on limited, local experience, while I have seen with my own eyes women ruling far larger realms than this and brilliantly at that. Believe it or not, women often make for better, wiser rulers than men."

"We have debated this many times in the past," Erol said, looking exasperated. "Never have we agreed, so there is no point to this. Balmar will be king, and I will serve as regent and rule in his name. Tell me, wizard, do you see in me the qualities of a bad ruler?"

Xax looked down at the table. "I suspected this was your solution. And no, I don't believe you would be a bad ruler, but this way leads to bloodshed. Terrible bloodshed that could be avoided."

"The army Darus leads is small. My forces will outnumber his once we gather our strength."

"Size matters little, and you know it," Xax said. "The soldiers of East Gate are blooded veterans, while most of ours have experience only of the practice field or perhaps chasing the odd pack of goblins raiding chicken coops. I tell you, Darus will sweep through your army like a scythe. Your only hope is to hold out in the castle and hope he is unsuccessful in his siege, but in the meantime his roving bands will lay waste to the surrounding countryside."

"How would it be different with Livia as queen?"

"At least there would be a chance. Darus adores Livia. He wouldn't be happy, but I also believe he could be talked around to it. He wouldn't wish to war against a sister he dearly loves."

"You haven't heard the reports I have had," Erol said. "His raiders are already slaughtering people and burning their properties. He is not going to stand down now, even for his dear sister."

Xax turned to address Erol's wife. "Lady Bora, please forgive this inappropriate dinner conversation. Your husband and I can take it up again later in private, so we can turn to more pleasant subjects now."

The rest of the supper was remarkably subdued, and Imric never found a way to broach a conversation with Istvan. The boy was older, true, but he seemed friendly. Imric wished to question him about secret passages, but he didn't want to bring that subject up around the adults, as they would likely forbid him from exploring. When the meal ended, Duke Erol briefly introduced Imric to his small horde of children, far too many for Imric to remember all their names, and then Imric accompanied Xax and Balmar back to their rooms.

After saying good night to Balmar, Xax paused outside Imric's door. "I'm very worried, Imric. I feel that terrible times approach and I am unable to do anything to prevent this from happening."

Imric didn't know how to reply. "I wish Livia was here."

Xax nodded. "Me, too, though it wouldn't change what is coming. Please keep this between us, but I worry that the duke wishes to ensure Istvan eventually takes the throne. I may be wrong, but I can't help but feel I'm correct in this. Erol has long been ambitious. He loved his brother but he always believed he would be the superior ruler."

"But…" Imric began. "But Istvan could never be ruler. After Balmar there is Darus. And…and though my father never recognized me, I am also in the line before Istvan, or at least I think so." Imric felt uncomfortable speaking these thoughts aloud, as he had never before allowed himself to consider the idea of being an heir.

"You are not wrong," Xax said, "but that may not stop Erol from doing what he must to place Istvan on the throne at some point. It's a moot point, as he'd have to defeat Darus first, and I don't believe he can do that."

"I thought the magic of the spire drove out those who could do great evil," Imric said. "If my uncle had such deceit in his heart, shouldn't he have been driven out of the realm?"

"Magic is complex and far from perfect. It could not read the changes that might happen inside a person. Erol has always been a decent man, but he has his weaknesses, as do all of us, and I fear his particular weaknesses can germinate into something terrible. I hope I'm wrong."

Imric stared gloomily down at the floor. "Xax? If we have no hope against Darus, shouldn't we try to leave here before his army arrives?"

"You're a smart lad. Erol would never allow us to depart. We'd have to try to slip away, and he would certainly send men out to search for us. It's best we remain here for now, though it would not be a bad idea for you, if you get the chance, to figure out how to reach that small jetty at the base of the cliff I mentioned earlier. Just in case." Xax winked at Imric.

That gave Imric a frisson of excitement. "That will give me something to do."

"Good night, young man," Xax said, and turned toward his own room.

"Good night, Xax." After shutting the door, Imric dropped the bar so he would be undisturbed. He was too excited to think about sleep just yet. He approached the wardrobe, intent on discovering the secret passages of this new castle. He wished Livia was here to explore with him. Soot as well. He suddenly felt bad that he hadn't thought about Soot in so long. He missed her terribly and hoped she was safe.

16
SOOT

Soot could not believe she was about to give up on her own mother, but she could think of nothing else to do. Her mother's corpse lay bloated and fetid outside the doorway to the castle kitchens, a butcher knife on the floor near her outstretched hand. The dragon had not killed her. A terrible gash in her chest, likely from a spear, had slicked the floor with a wide pool of blood. Looters, Soot figured, probably using a spear from one of the guards who had fled after the king's death. Or perhaps a guard had done it, turned looter himself.

Soot had tried everything she could think of to move her mother, but her corpse was too heavy. Now all she could think to do was to cover her with a thick bedspread, taken from one of the bedrooms upstairs. Tenderly she kissed her fingertips and touched them to her mother's forehead, then spread the cover over her. She wished she could weep some more, but she was out of tears. She understood why no one had come with her to help, yet she was still angry with Imric and Livia. This was her mother. She could not go off to Valandiria and not try to help her.

With a sigh, Soot picked up the bag of foodstuffs she had rescued from the rats in the kitchen. "I love you, Mama," she said, then turned toward the passage that led toward the outside doors. As she trudged along the hall, she thought back to when she had slipped away from her friends to go look for her mother. She had been terrified, but there was no helping it. Meri was all she had and she couldn't leave her behind.

The city had seemed mostly deserted as she crept through it. Corpses lined the streets, sometimes in singles or pairs, and other times in greater numbers, as if the acid clouds had swept down on an entire crowd all at once. The smell was horrific, and she dared not look too closely at the bodies. Even from her peripheral vision they looked like charred meat. Every now and then she saw looters carrying things from a house. She didn't know if they would be dangerous, but she hid from them regardless, sometimes sliding into alleyways and taking a longer route. Luckily there was no more sign of the dragon.

The castle gates had been deserted, just a scattering of corpses to show that the guards had died at their posts, looking like they had been cooked alive by the deadly acid clouds. Cautiously moving through the corridors toward the kitchens, she had heard the sounds of people calling out excitedly, and once through an archway she glimpsed a band of them tearing down tapestries in order to pile expensive silverware and other treasures onto them. Looters, she had thought with disgust. The city and its people were dying, and all these people could think about was their greed. Wasn't the magic of the spire supposed to have driven such people out of the realm? Or did they turn to wickedness only due to the circumstances?

During the days while she had mourned over her mother's body, Soot had heard noises several more times, but no one had come near her. Now, turning into the large hall that led to the gates, she heard sounds ahead. She jumped back just in time. The voices of several men echoed from the entrance hall. She heard one commanding voice ring out: "You two stay here and guard the wagons. We'll return quick as we can."

Soot crept further back down the hall so she could catch a glimpse of them once they passed the intersection. It appeared she was trapped for a while, at least until the looters took their wagons and departed. A troop of men entered the intersection and Soot was surprised to see they were guardsmen, though their livery was blue and silver, so they were not the king's guards. This made her curious, so when she felt she had given them enough lead time, she followed them as quietly as she could. They seemed to know where they were going—they passed through a maze of corridors and stairwells without hesitation. As they kept going up, it struck her where they must be heading. The treasury! She wondered if it had already been looted.

She grew tired as they climbed higher and higher, the magic of the spire no longer lending its strengthening energy to her sore muscles. She sighed with relief as the men reached the top of the king's tower and turned into the short hallway to where the treasury was kept. She dared not move close enough to watch, so she crouched at the base of the final staircase and listened. She figured they would begin cursing once they found the treasury empty.

The commanding voice rang out again. "Look at this mess! So much blood!"

Then the shouts and screams began. One word her ears caught multiple times: "Dragon!" No, no, no, no, no, she thought. It can't be. The dragon can't be inside the castle, can it? She thought of huge rats she had seen squeeze through tiny holes and understood that it was indeed possible. Ice seemed to run down her spine and settle in her bowels. Fleeing soldiers appeared on the stairs, pelting downward so fast Soot didn't have time to flee herself. Instead, she stumbled backward down the corridor on this level and sought refuge in a doorway. Her entire body shook, and her teeth chattered so hard her jaw began to ache. She tried to get her breathing under control, but it was impossible as she watched screaming guards arrive on the landing and continue down the next set of stairs. One guard had not even made the first step when a vast black blur filled the passage and huge jaws snapped shut on the man, his scream cut off instantly.

Soot pulled herself as deeply into the sheltering arch of the doorway as she could and tried to hold her breath. She was certain the dragon would turn down her passageway and come for her. She consoled herself with the thought that she would be with her mother again.

But the sounds began to fade down the stairwell. Soot panted several times before peering down the hall to see a deserted landing, only a dark smear of blood marring the white marble.

What should I do? Taking the stairs was out of the question now. And if she waited too long, the dragon might return and catch her scent. An idea struck her. She reached for the handle of the door and found it locked. On trembling legs she wobbled down the hallway to the next door and almost cried out in relief when it opened. She closed the door as quietly as she could, then turned to examine the room. The builders had often used wardrobes as their entrances to the network of secret passages in the castle, but there was no wardrobe in this room. It appeared to be a study. There was an oaken desk and padded chair. A lamp hung above the desk, and there was a candelabra as well. A small shelf of books was the only other furnishing and was the likeliest place to begin the search.

Though her heart continued to pound, Soot found the panic receding as her mind set to work on the puzzle of whether there was a catch that would allow the shelf to slide to the side or swing out from the wall. Her fingers swept along the outer sides of the shelf, though she didn't expect to find anything there. The catches were usually hidden on the insides. She began carefully pulling the books from their places and setting them in piles on the carpet. When she finished, she began feeling along the inner panels. Perhaps there was no secret passage in this room. She had just about despaired of finding anything when her finger encountered an obstruction. She pressed it and nothing happened. Next, she began shoving it in different directions, and on her second try it moved and she heard a click. She paused to breathe for a few moments, then put her weight into the shelf to see if it would slide to the side. It didn't, but she felt a slight give that gave her hope, and she moved to the opposite side and began to push from that end. The shelf slid slowly aside, catching for a moment on the thin carpet before scraping over it. Several more hard shoves produced an opening large enough for Soot to squeeze through.

Was it her imagination or did she hear a distant roar? She needed light, so she searched the desk and found flint and steel. She had to climb onto the desk to reach the lamp and lift it down. It seemed to take forever to finally get the wick to light. Grasping the handle on the lamp, she looked around for her bag of food and realized she had no idea where she had left it. It might be in the corridor, but she was too afraid to open the door. Instead, she slipped into the secret passage. She set the lamp down so she could use all her strength to pull the shelf back into place. She didn't think it was necessary, but something inside her wanted as many walls between her and the dragon as possible.

She picked up the lamp and examined the passage. It ran only a short way before it began sloping downward, as she had hoped. Passages on the lower levels where she and Imric played often had similar chutes that ran between the different floors. She didn't like the chutes because for some reason spiders seemed to favor them for making their webs, but this time she had no alternative. She held the lamp high and peered into the dark, and indeed, cobwebs filled the chute. At least she didn't see any spiders. She hoped the webs were old. Holding the lamp out in front of her, she began to ease down the slope on her bottom, her feet catching on the cracks in the marble to keep her from sliding too fast. Webs wrapped about her hands and caught in her hair. She had to resist the impulse to drop the lamp and scrape her fingers through her hair to fling off the arachnids she imagined were crawling all over her. Imric never seemed bothered by this horror. He liked to take a candle and burn away the cobwebs, and he would slide quickly down the chutes as if it were a game. She wished he were here with her now.

At last she reached the bottom, where she placed the lamp on the ground and scrubbed at her head and body, hoping to dislodge any spiders that may have taken up residence. When she calmed down, she took up the lamp and started down the passageway until she came to the end and another chute. In this painstaking manner, she went down level after level, counting as she went, until she was fairly certain she had reached the ground floor. Now to find a way out.

These lower floors were familiar from her explorations with Imric, so it didn't take long for Soot to find an exit. After clambering out of a wardrobe in a deserted bed chamber, she remained still for a long time, listening for any sounds. There was only silence.

At last she worked up the nerve to open the chamber door and stalk down the hallway, heading toward the main entrance. At each intersection she paused to listen, but still she heard nothing. Approaching the grand hall near the exit, she encountered a body, that of some courtier, bloated and long dead. Like her mother, the courtier had likely been slain by looters. Soot held her breath and passed the body to enter the grand hall. There were more corpses here, though she had seen them before when she had first returned to the castle. All were long dead. The large double-doors at the end of the hall were flung wide. Soot thought she recalled them being only slightly ajar when she passed through them last, so she slowed even further as she approached them.

The entry hall beyond was a mess, with the carpet slashed to ribbons by the passage of clawed feet, and vases and other decorative objects smashed and scattered about. The huge entrance doors also stood open, and what Soot saw beyond them horrified her.

The castle steps led down to a courtyard scene worse than any nightmare. The pieces of two wagons were so badly smashed as to be nearly unrecognizable. Freshly dead horses and men lay scattered about as if a young girl had thrown a tantrum with her play dolls. Heads were wrenched from bodies slashed to ribbons. There was so much blood.

Soot's first instinct was to flee back inside, yet that thought horrified her even more. She needed to escape. She needed to find her friends. To do so, she had no choice but to walk through the carnage. She couldn't make her feet move. Where was the dragon? She saw no sign of it other than the destruction it had wrought, and she heard no sounds on the faint summer breeze.

Her eyes tried to pick out the clearest path through the puddles and runnels of blood and gore. She began picking her way down the steps to the right side, turning her eyes from the worst of the sights. It seemed to take forever to make her way across the courtyard to the gates that led out into the city. With the worst of it behind her, Soot gave a sigh of relief and picked up the pace, wishing she still had the bag of food for the journey ahead. A scraping sound made her heart skip a beat and she froze in her tracks.

Slowly turning her head, she looked up toward the source of the sound. High up above her, the great black dragon clung to the side of one of the towers. Soot's heart began racing in her chest. The beast's head was turned away from her, but she worried if she made any move, it might notice her. Moving only her eyes, she searched for the nearest cover. She saw that if she made it past the gate just a few steps away, the wall would shield her from the monster's eyes. She wondered how good the dragon's hearing was. Knowing she couldn't stay where she was, she forced herself to draw in a shuddering breath, then darted quickly behind the wall and flung her back up against it, panting for air as quietly as she could manage. She listened for any sign that the dragon had reacted to her movement, but she heard nothing.

It was several minutes before she could build up the courage to move again. She followed the castle wall as long as she could to remain out of sight. There was no way into the city proper without passing into view, but she found an alleyway that was a mere twenty paces away from the wall and chose that as her point of escape. Twenty paces in view of the dragon. It felt like the entrance to the alley was miles away. She couldn't see the dragon from here, but she imagined it gazing directly down upon the spot where she needed to cross. She told herself to run, but her legs would not respond. She thought, why not just stay here out of sight for a while? She was about the slide down into a crouch against the wall when a terrible screech rent the air. Looking up in terror, she saw the dragon take flight. Its wings spread wide and began to beat the air as it plunged from the tower. It dipped and then soared upward. Soot thought it meant to dive upon her, but instead the dragon roared and passed over her spot and vanished beyond the rooftops of the city.

Soot shuddered and shook, her skin covered in goosebumps, and she realized she had soiled herself. No matter, she was alive for now. There were plenty of deserted houses in the city where she could search for fresh clothing and some food to tide her over for the long walk north to Valandiria.

17
DINARA

"A wagon!" Miranvel cried. "Perhaps more than one."

Dinara sat up and listened, rubbing her neck where the collar had spent years chafing it. Faintly she heard the creak and squeal of wagon wheels, and the neigh of a horse.

Orderic called his remaining warriors together. So few remained. Miranvel held himself apart, as usual, staring down the road where there would have been a cloud of dust if the recent rain had not dampened the ground. Other than the elf and Orderic, the only other men in fighting form were Eiric and the scout Tevin. And Weevil, if you could count the boy, though he had never yet been allowed to participate in any fighting.

"Tevin, get a look at them and see if there are soldiers," Orderic said. "If so, we'll leave Willa here. She's a woman, so they'll most likely render aid. We can find a way to get her back later."

"If no soldiers?" Tevin asked.

"We'll commandeer a wagon so we can move Willa."

"Kill them all," Miranvel said with a low growl.

"If it is one wagon and a few people, be my guest. Otherwise hold your temper, Miranvel. I don't need to lose any more of you now. We've few enough left to be of any help to Darus. We'll load Willa in the wagon and head to Valandiria."

The elf hissed and scowled at Orderic as Tevin hurried off to spy on the approaching strangers.

"Eiric, finish packing the tent and tarps and help Meldon get ready," Orderic said. "Weevil, prepare the horses. We may need to leave quickly. What's wrong, Dinara?"

"You should go now," Dinara said. "At least hide yourselves beyond that ridge. Let me go with Willa and these people. It will make it easier for us to return to you once she's recovered."

Orderic stared into her eyes, and Dinara felt as if he could read her thoughts. He scratched at the stubble on his cheek. "Perhaps," he murmured.

"No," Miranvel said. "The girl means to leave us. Don't trust her."

"Is that true, Dinara? I see you removed the collar."

Dinara rubbed at her neck again. "I'm tired of being viewed as a plaything. I can help Willa now. That's all I meant by it. I've nowhere to go and no one else but Willa."

"You all hide," Miranvel said. "I will handle the wagon myself."

Orderic shook his head. "You'll do as you're told, elf, whatever I decide. Let's get the horses and be ready to move once Tevin returns."

Weevil handed reins to each of the men in turn, then hopped up onto his pony. It wasn't long before they saw Tevin racing back toward them. Even before he reached his horse he was already shouting: "It's an entire train of them. Dozens of wagons. Hundreds of people."

"Soldiers?" Orderic asked.

"I saw some, couldn't tell how many."

Orderic pursed his lips and looked back at Dinara. "We'll try it your way. See to Willa's health, then meet us at Valandiria, if possible. If not, we'll come for you when we can. Brelyn's their most likely destination, but we'll find you. If you try to disappear, we'll find you as well, and you'll lose whatever reward Darus would have offered after our victory."

Dinara felt relief flood through her. This was the chance she needed. She stood up and moved toward her pony.

"No," Orderic said, plucking the reins of Dinara's pony from Weevil's hand. "We'll keep her for you. Those folks are more likely to help you if you appear stranded. Come, men, let's move!"

The four men, the elf, and the boy spun their mounts and headed for the ridgeline. Dinara turned to watch for the wagons. She seated herself next to Willa and used the damp cloth to mop her brow. "You'll be all right," she whispered.

The sounds of the approaching train grew loud, and Dinara saw the lead wagon. So many people followed on foot that they overflowed the small road. A few men on horseback carried spears or crossbows. Some began to point in her direction once they noticed Willa's huge form. Two soldiers trotted ahead and drew up a few paces away.

"That's one big woman," the first soldier said.

"What happened?" asked the other.

Dinara pointed at the scatter of bodies under the trees. "Raiders. They've been burning farms nearby. You can see a few of them here, and the soldiers they slew. They injured my friend. Can you help us? I have no way to move her to find a healer."

The soldiers stared down at Willa for a few moments. "She looks in a bad way," one of them said.

"She'll live if she gets aid."

Both soldiers looked at Dinara and passed a glance between them, the type of look Dinara was used to when men noted how attractive she was. "No room in the wagons 'less we dump something," one said. "We'll see if someone's willing."

The wagons were drawing near and the two men trotted up to meet them. Dinara couldn't hear what was said, but she saw them pointing and talking to wagon drivers. The first shook his head, and the second and the next as well. The wagons and the crowd of ragged people began to pass by her now, everyone staring curiously.

Dinara wondered what had caused these people to flee, as they had so obviously done. Was it Darus already? If so, he had moved faster than Orderic expected. The fourth wagon pulled to the side of the road. Two women sat on the driving board and looked down at her with pity in their eyes.

One of the soldiers had dismounted and approached Dinara. "These women have bolts of cloth in their wain. They've a couple of blankets as well, so you don't get blood on their wares."

"Thank you," Dinara said. "How can we get her up?"

"Good question," the soldier said. "I'll fetch some men."

It took four men, grunting and straining, to lift Willa up into the wagon and lay her on a pair of blankets spread out over the bolts of cloth. Dinara thanked them before clambering in to sit next to Willa. She glanced at the two women, who smiled warmly at her. They looked like mother and daughter, the elder with graying hair and the younger in her early twenties. The older woman made introductions and Dinara gave her name along with Willa's. She had to repeat the story about the raiders, and both women clucked their sympathies.

"What happened to you?" Dinara asked. "It looks like a column of refugees."

"Tis what we are," the older woman said. "We come out of Andiria. Many here come from Tolgaria as well. The dragon that attacked us destroyed their city not two days later."

Dinara's eyes widened. "A dragon? Are you certain?" She had only heard of dragons in tales. That they might exist in real life was a terrifying thought.

"Oh, aye. Didn't want to believe it ourselves, but once you see it, you can't help but believe."

The soldiers helped get the wagon back into line, and it began to slowly creak along the dusty track.

"Are you headed for Brelyn?" Dinara asked.

The old woman shook her head. "We're not sure. Most are taking the road along the river to a camp being set up by the duke. We decided to go our own way. Might be Brelyn or might be elsewhere. Depends on who's willing to take us." She pointed at a corner of the wagon. "There's a tarp there in case the rain starts up again. Keep our cloth dry, as well as you and your friend."

Dinara nodded and returned her attention to Willa. Sweat slicked her brow and she mumbled incoherently as her head turned from side to side. Dinara changed the bandage on Willa's side and grew more worried when she saw the angry red puckered look of the flesh around the wound. She squeezed as much pus as she could from it before layering on clean cloth and binding it. She hoped someone on the wagon train had some healing arts. Willa wouldn't likely make it another day without help.

18
VILLEM

When Villem awoke he was alone in the bed. Memories of what had happened last night washed over him, along with a cascade of emotions. He felt guilty for sleeping with a married woman, but he also felt the wonder of how he had felt with her. It was beyond any of his adolescent imaginings.

He sat up and immediately regretted it. Dizziness swept over him and the back of his head ached. When he could open his eyes again, he saw that Lady Sonia was not in the room. He had so much he wished to say to her. And he wanted to feel her kisses again.

He was about to roll over to try to get out of bed when the maid Marta entered bearing a tray. She swept over to the bed and set the tray on the bed stand.

"Here's your breakfast, sir. Do you need help with it?"

"Where's Lady Sonia?"

"Still in her room, last I checked."

"Thank you. I can feed myself."

"As you wish." The maid departed as swiftly as she had come.

Villem thought he didn't feel hungry, but the moment he moved the tray onto his lap, he suddenly felt ravenous. There was enough bread, cheese, apples, and milk for two people, but when he had finished, Villem still wished for more. He set the tray back on the stand and slowly swiveled his feet out to allow him to sit up on the edge of the bed. The brief dizziness passed and he felt as if he might be able to stand. Unfortunately, he could see no sign of his clothing. With an impatient sigh, he lay down again, hoping someone would come soon.

He wished Duchess was there to keep him company. The dogs back home never much interested him, so he was surprised at how much he had begun to care for the scrawny mutt.

Sleep had nearly overcome him again when someone finally entered the room. It was the maid Lidia, holding a bundle of clothing and some boots. Behind her came the witch, Marianna.

"Ah, you're looking so much better," Marianna said. "I think you'll be well enough to leave today."

Leave? The idea of departing hadn't entered Villem's mind. He kept thinking about how Lady Sonia's husband meant to put her aside, and he dared dream that perhaps his father would allow him to marry her. He knew his mother would see it as an insult to have him marry a sullied woman, but Villem didn't care. His memories of last night were too vivid. "Do I have to go?" he asked Marianna.

Lidia set the clothing on the stand near the bed and departed.

Marianna watched her go before she turned to sit on the stool beside the bed. "It's best if you do. If you find you are still too weak, I think we should move you to my cabin until you regain your strength."

"Have...have I offended Lady Sonia?"

Marianna shook her head. "She is ashamed to face you. I think she feels she misused you."

Villem wondered if Marianna could possibly know about what had happened. Surely Sonia wouldn't tell anyone. "I don't understand."

Marianna leaned in close. "She is with child now," she whispered. "Her lord will be very happy with her."

Villem's mouth worked but nothing would come out.

Marianna put a warm hand on his cheek. "I'm sorry if you feel hurt, and I apologize for my role. Milady ordered me to create the potion."

Villem felt his face redden. "How…how can you know she is with child?"

Marianna chuckled. "I have my ways. And it was a potent potion."

"I thought you said you had no magic."

"Tis no magic. Merely the right herbs, and knowing the right time of month to use them."

"She said she was barren, or maybe her husband…"

"I knew it was more likely him than her. And now we know."

"But…then it's *my* child."

Marianna put a finger to his lips. "On your honor, you can never say that to anyone. She has a chance for a contented marriage now. Don't take that from her."

Villem felt a tear trickle down one cheek, and his face flushed again. "I'm such a fool to think she could want me."

"Want has nothing to do with it," Marianna said. "She likes you very much, but she is duty bound."

Villem tried to think of something to say that might change things for the better.

"Shush now," Marianna said. "Let's see if you are well enough to ride, or if we must move you to my place." She began unfolding the clothing.

"I'd like to dress myself please," he said. "Everyone has seen far too much of me for my liking."

Marianna laughed. "As you wish. I'll await you outside the door."

It took longer than he would have liked, but Villem finally managed to dress himself. He wondered who the clothing had belonged to. The clothes were not too fancy, but they were well made and clean. The boots were slightly large, but they would do.

He joined Marianna outside the room. "May I at least say goodbye to Sonia?"

She put a hand on his arm. "I'm sorry. I tried to convince her, but she is so mortified. She says she can't do it."

He nodded curtly and scowled.

"You're looking well, at least. I bet you can ride. Milady prepared provisions for you. They are packed on your pony."

"How did she know it was my pony?"

"You raved about many things when you were delirious. The pony came up several times. And that dog. You really must love it."

"She saved my life. More than once, I think."

"Then treat her well," the witch said.

"They should not call you a witch. You are not much like the stories."

When they exited the keep, Duchess bounded up the steps, yelping, and began to lick Villem all over. He couldn't help but laugh. "Good girl, Duchess. Let's go for a ride."

He imagined even the pony seemed glad to see him. She pawed at the ground with one hoof. Villem put one foot in the stirrup and looked around. No one was there to see him off, except for Marianna. He could see the guard Akun up on the wall near the gate, but no one else.

Villem took a deep breath and hauled himself into the saddle. He steadied himself from a spell of dizziness, then looked down at Marianna. "I owe you my life as well. You have my everlasting gratitude."

She smiled and reached forth to grip his hand. "Go slowly. You need to take it easy. Get lots of sleep, if you can."

He gave a quick salute to her. "Come on, Duchess!" As he rode forth through the gate, Villem turned for a final look back at the witch. He waved, then noticed a shadowy form standing in the highest window of the keep and waved to that person as well. He was pretty sure he knew who it was.

The road went off in three directions. Villem stopped the pony in the middle of the intersection and considered his options. He had no business north, so that left two possibilities. Go west and see if his family would take him back. He thought that they might, but the loss of his father's warhorse made him wonder. Then there was the road heading toward the heart of the kingdom around the Sea of Alia. The capital of Tolgaria and the other great cities he had always dreamed of one day seeing. In the end it was a simple choice. He whistled to Duchess and turned his pony along the track heading southeast, away from home.

19
KATHKALAN

When Kathkalan at last came down from the hills and found a small hamlet near the Skendris River, he was aghast to see an endless line of refugees streaming westward on the road across the river. He had taken this longer route because he had wished to avoid the refugees he had expected would pack the road to Andiria, but clearly he had miscalculated.

There was no help for it now. It would take too long to retrace his route. He nudged his horse forward and soon found the ferry landing. The two men who operated the ferry looked at him with awe. He held up a silver coin and the men scrambled to pull aside the rope and let Kathkalan lead his horse onto the ferry.

Once across, the elf rode up to the stream of refugees, prepared to wait impatiently for a chance to cross the road. He needn't have worried; the first wagon to spot him jerked its team to a halt, and everyone stared at him as he trotted across. Hearing shouts from the west, he saw that the road was becoming even more chaotic. A large troop of soldiers and knights, along with their wagon train, was heading the opposite direction and were trying to force the refugees from the road. Where the way was flatter, it wouldn't have been so bad, but at that point, the northern side of the road was marshy, and the south had only a small strip of land before hitting the river.

Kathkalan shook his head at the logistical nightmare and continued past the road, skirting the bog until he was out of sight before turning east. The city of Valandiria couldn't be too far away, but Kathkalan had no desire to spend the night in a city of man. With so much of the land under cultivation, he would need to find a nice copse of trees to camp under.

He noticed movement ahead of him; others heading east off the road, just as he was doing. They were too far away to make out details, but he thought it looked like six or seven horsemen. They were traveling a bit slower than Kathkalan, so he began to draw closer to them, and as dusk approached, he saw that it was five men and one boy, leading some spare horses.

A large grove of trees stood ahead and he hoped to camp there, but he had no wish to settle down for the night next to these other travelers. He kicked his horse into a trot, hoping to put the men behind him as he searched for another suitable camping spot.

The men spotted him just as he was able to make out some details. A small shiver ran down his spine when he noted the skinny figure with one arm. Could it be? After so many centuries? He hadn't thought to run into any trouble in this peaceable land, yet if Miranvel was traveling with these men, they were unlikely to be men of good heart. Bandits more likely, or marauders, preying on the refugees. That seemed like something the fallen elf would be likely to do.

Miranvel would love to settle the old score, Kathkalan imagined, though he would be too much of a coward to try it without aid. Would these men help him? Kathkalan knew he could handle Miranvel, but a group of men together could spell trouble, even for a warrior of his prowess. He loosened his sword in its scabbard. He was preparing to face a dragon; six on one would be a good warm up.

The men had stopped their horses and turned to await his

approach. Kathkalan drew his horse up fifty paces from the men. Miranvel urged his horse forward two paces and halted.

"You," Miranvel said. "After all this time."

"Exile," Kathkalan said. "You were warned never to return to these lands."

Miranvel turned to one of the men. "We can take him."

He saw uneasy looks on the faces of the men. They had their hands on their weapons, but then the man with whom Miranvel had spoken pulled his hand back and shook his head.

"No," said the man. "This is no fight of ours, unless he makes it so." He raised his voice. "We want no trouble with you, elf. Go your own way."

"Cowards!" Miranvel cried.

"Come, Exile," Kathkalan said. "Let's settle this." He urged his horse forward at a walk.

Miranvel addressed the men behind him. "He means to assault me. Will you aid me?"

The man who Kathkalan assumed must be the leader of the band spoke. "Stop, elf, or you'll force us to defend our comrade."

Kathkalan never paused, and now he unsheathed his black blade and pointed it at Miranvel. "The exile has forfeited his right to life. I care not how many bodies I must leave to rot. Do as you will."

With a strangled cry, Miranvel whipped his horse around and kicked it into a gallop. His comrades looked startled, then turned their own steeds to follow the fleeing elf.

Kathkalan considered whether it was worth trying to run them down. As his heart had begun to beat faster in anticipation of battle, the magic of the crystal shard had poured strength and resolve into his body. But he shook his head. He felt certain he would have another encounter with Miranvel soon enough. It was good to let the exile stew in his cowardice.

Kathkalan sheathed his blade, then urged his horse onward. He would have to bypass the grove of trees and look elsewhere in order to camp. He had no desire to be ambushed in his sleep.

20
IMRIC

It was back into the secret passages again for Imric. The design of the passages left no doubt in his mind that the castle architect was the same as for the king's castle in Tolgaria. He felt right at home. Bearing a small lamp to light the way, he was working his way downward, hoping to locate the closest exit to where the jetty would be. It was a laborious process, because many exits had no peepholes, and he didn't want anyone to notice him opening exit doors. One time he had slid aside a panel that was inside a wardrobe, like the one in his room, only to have a person open the wardrobe door at that precise moment. Luckily there were long dresses filling the cabinet, hiding him from view, so he had silently slid the panel back into place and breathed a sigh of relief.

He came to another of the chutes leading to the next level down. It had worried him that by going down too far, it might make it impossible to return in time for lunch. He found it irritating that he was expected to attend every mealtime with the duke's family. It seemed he was forever being forced to cut short his explorations to return and clean up for another meal. After agonizing over it for a time, he had chosen to tell Xax that he wasn't feeling well and would lie abed and take no lunch. He didn't like lying to the wizard, but he was keen to explore, and after all, wasn't it Xax who had all but ordered him to find a route to the jetty?

Carefully he crouched and slid slowly down the stone incline, ignoring the cobwebs that stuck in his hair. He halted when he reached the bottom and listened. It was probably only his imagination, but he thought he had heard the scuff of leather on stone somewhere ahead. After listening carefully for several moments, he shook his head and continued on. One more level down should bring him level with the sea, he thought.

There it was again! He was certain he had heard it this time. It didn't sound like rats to him. His imagination ran wild. Perhaps there were goblins hiding in the castle walls, stealing out at night to feast on servants or young children. It was silly to think such things, he knew, but who could be inside the passage with him?

As silently as he could, he crept forward. If he knew the passages as well as he did back home, he could shutter his lantern, but he had no choice here. Whoever it was would see him coming. He decided to be bold. "Who's there?" he said in a loud whisper.

There was silence for a minute, but then the sounds resumed, coming his way. He saw a dark form take shape ahead. His heart pounded. Perhaps it's an assassin, he thought. "Wh-who is it?"

The figure drew close enough for him to make out eyes glittering in the light of his lamp. A hand rose and drew back the hood of a cloak, revealing the face of a young girl with dark, mousy hair. "Who are you?" she asked.

Imric felt relief flood through him. He couldn't be afraid of a girl no older than ten. "I asked you first," he said.

"Maisie," she said. "Never seen you afore. Never seen anyone in the passages afore."

"We arrived here a couple days ago. I'm Imric."

"If you're new here, how did you know about the passages?"

"They're just like the ones back home in Tolgaria."

Maisie's eyes widened. "You came from the king's castle?"

"Aye. I'm his youngest son."

The eyes grew even wider. "You're a prince!"

Imric shrugged. He had sure never felt like one. "Who are you, Maisie?"

"Please don't get me in trouble, milord," she said. "I know I'm not supposed to be here."

"I won't," Imric said. "I'm just curious who you are, that's all."

"I-I'm just a scullery maid, milord. I do my work fast so I can have time to myself."

"When we're alone, you don't need to call me milord. Just Imric will do. You remind me of a friend back home."

She smiled, though he thought she still looked nervous. "It would be funny to be friends with a prince."

"What do you do in here?"

"I was going to my secret place. Would you like to see?"

He nodded. "I would. And later, maybe you can help me."

"Help you? Milor— uh, Imric, how could I possibly help you?"

"I'm supposed to find a way to the jetty near the sea."

Maisie grinned. "Oh, that's easy. It's not far from my secret place. Come on!"

She turned and began shuffling forward through the gloom.

"You never use any light?" Imric asked.

"I used to," she said, "but now I know the way, plus my eyes get used to the dark."

"I do that back home," Imric said, "but here I don't know the passages well enough yet."

Soon enough they came to another slope and slid down. A few more turns and Maisie showed Imric a hidden latch to open a panel behind an overturned rowboat. A pile of tarps lay beneath the boat, smelling of mildew.

"People don't come here often," Maisie whispered. She pointed to the wan sunlight off to the left. "That's the way to the jetty."

"Thanks for showing me," Imric said.

She nodded and slid the panel shut, then returned the way they had come and took a different passage. Shortly they came to a blank stone wall.

"I came upon this by accident last year," she said. "I used to pretend this dead end was my own little secret room." She motioned to the pile of blankets and other bric-a-brac against one wall. "Once I grew sleepy and lay down to take a short nap, and my foot kicked against this spot here, see?" She knelt down and pressed her hand against a corner of the stone wall. A click sounded loud in the confined space, and with a low rumble, a section of the wall slid in and to the side. Light flooded in.

"That's amazing," Imric whispered. "I never found anything like this back home. What's in there?"

"Come see." Maisie crawled through the opening, and Imric followed, his hands encountering hard packed dirt as he went.

Maisie gave him a hand to help him to his feet, and he grinned at what he saw. They seemed to be inside a deep well with a square opening far up at the top, dim sunlight filtering down. Ivy blanketed the walls. Here at the bottom was a square of earth about five paces to a side.

"What is this place?" Imric asked. "Why would they build this here?"

Maisie shook her head. "No idea. But I love it. I wanted to plant my own little garden here, but it doesn't get enough sunlight. Also, it gets too mushy when it rains."

In the dim light, Imric could see Maisie clearly for the first time and saw she was a scrawny girl of perhaps nine summers with dark brown hair that looked like it could use a wash. He had been imagining her much like Soot, but her face was too round and her nose too flat compared to Soot's.

Imric gazed upward. "Have you ever climbed up there?"

She looked shocked. "You could fall and kill yourself!"

"So, what do you do here?"

She looked abashed.

"Go on," he said. "I won't make fun."

She hesitated, then said, "I pretend I'm a princess and everyone has to do whatever I say."

"My friend Soot gets tired of being ordered around all the time," Imric said.

Maisie's eyes gleamed. "What's it like being a prince?"

"I've never felt like a prince. My father pretended I didn't exist. Only my sister took care of me."

She tilted her head at him. "Well, you are a real prince." She waved a hand at her secret place. "And in here you can pretend to be a king, if you like."

"I'll come again when I can," Imric said with a smile. "Thanks for sharing your secret place with me."

Maisie grinned. "I'll go back with you at least up to my level."

After returning to the passage, Maisie showed him how to close the stone door. He retrieved his lantern and they retraced their steps upward through the maze of passages. Maisie showed him the panel where she always entered, in the back of a large fireplace in an unused guestroom.

"How did you first discover the passages?" Imric asked.

"Twas an accident. A kitchen boy was chasing me. I went into a room and climbed into a big wardrobe to hide. My hand felt something funny on the back of the wardrobe, something that moved, and when I slid it to one side, the panel opened."

Imric smiled. "Pretty much how it happened for me, except being chased by a kitchen boy."

"Thank you for being nice, Imric. I hope I see you again." With that, Maisie clicked something and the brick wall closed up with a low rumble.

Feeling happy, but also tired and hungry, Imric headed back to his room. When he finally reached it and opened the cabinet door, he was shocked to find Xax seated on his bed, glaring at him.

"Sick, eh?" the wizard said.

"M-my door was barred," he said.

Xax held up his walking stick with the green crystal knob. "You really think that could stop me?"

"I'm sorry I lied," Imric said. "I just wanted time to explore. And anyhow, I was doing what you ordered—I found the way to the jetty."

"You need to be careful, Imric," Xax said. "Events are moving quickly now; times are dangerous. Do you know what has happened in the time you've been roaming your secret passages?"

Imric shook his head.

Xax patted the bed next to him, and Imric sat down near the wizard.

"Well, scouts reported to your uncle that your brother's army began marching yesterday morning. They expect it will be here in three days. Your uncle threw all tradition out the window and had your brother Balmar crowned king in a hasty ceremony not one hour ago. And he had himself officially anointed regent."

"Darus is marching to war," Imric murmured. "We should escape while we still can."

"I don't know if that's an option," Xax said. "I don't like the idea of leaving Balmar behind."

Imric tried to hide his scowl. He had never much cared for Balmar, so the thought of deserting him did not seem so terrible, though he immediately felt ashamed for having such thoughts. "But no one needs me here. I can go try to find Livia."

"I'll discuss matters with Duke Erol during supper," Xax said. "Perhaps he'll see wisdom in removing at least one heir from danger."

21
LIVIA

Though Livia believed it was her family's responsibility to take care of the refugees, she did not feel like a leader. She had studied enough history to know what leadership meant, but she did not believe these people would look to her for guidance. Still, she did not regret her decision to accompany them.

Many of the folks nearby had been with her since fleeing Tolgaria, so there was a fatalistic sense of shared misfortune between them. The six nomads gave a feeling of comfort to her, though she still knew so little about them. They were a quiet group who kept to themselves, communicating in an odd tongue, except for the rare times Azer spoke with her.

The road alongside the Skendris River was chaotic. Her uncle had clearly sent out a call to gather his banner men, so large troops of soldiers and their accompanying baggage trains kept forcing the refugees to the side of the road. This took much time and caused a terrible backup, and it grew worse whenever the area beside the road became impassable. At those times, the refugees came to a full stop and piled up in droves until the soldiers finally passed. At a spot where a small dirt track led north, many refugees chose that route, hoping it might be better, though Livia suspected troops would be coming from that direction as well.

Livia believed Xax was right that her uncle would send soldiers to fetch her back to Valandiria, so she constantly looked back over her shoulder, trying to see if anyone on horseback was following them. She got lucky—her uncle's guards rode by during one of the times she had stepped off the road for a call of nature. The guards had called out to the refugees, asking if they had seen the princess, but they all shook their heads, and the guardsmen rode on. She was relieved. She had feared someone would tell the guards about her presence, but they had remained loyal. A fierce sense of affection filled her breast. These poor folks had lost everything. She was doing nothing special for them other than sharing their misery. Yet they clung to some form of love for her despite everything. She didn't know who would become king, but she meant to ensure the king would do everything in his power to help all the refugees. She would devote her life to this cause, if she must.

She remained in the bushes until the men had vanished from sight. Being returned to her uncle's keep might not be a terrible thing, but she would still feel like a failure, as if she were being treated like a small child and not a grown woman of twenty summers who could take care of herself.

When she caught up to the slow-moving column, people called out to her and told jokes at the guardsmen's expense. Azer looked worried, though, and drew near.

"They will return at some point, lady," he whispered.

She put a hand out to squeeze his shoulder, but he stepped back and looked embarrassed.

"Forgive me, lady. I mean no disrespect. It's only that in our lands, a woman does not touch a man who is not her husband."

Livia was taken aback. "I apologize. I-I wish I knew more of your customs," she stammered. "The books that have mentioned the Arid

Lands say so little about your clans."

Azer smiled. "We have no books, but we have storytellers who know all the histories of our people. Perhaps one day I may return to your lands and bring one of them with me."

Livia inclined her head slightly. "I would like that very much."

Azer seemed to want to say something else, but appeared hesitant. "What is it?" Livia asked.

Azer gave a small shrug. "Your people around us here. I hear them speak as if they consider us to be your, how do you say, bodyguards. It's an honor if it were true, to be sure…but, great lady, we are simple merchants. None of us are warriors."

Livia smiled. "Don't worry yourself over this. I consider you to be companions who have shared our misfortunes together. I hope that we are friends."

Azer bowed his head. "You are most kind, lady. We are honored to be your friends."

It had grown late, so the refugees made their way to any relatively flat ground they could find to make their camps for the night. Luckily, as the line of people had left Valandiria behind, a group of her uncle's men had passed out bundles of food and flasks of water. It wasn't much, but at least they had something to survive on until they could reach the camp her uncle was setting up.

The old woman who baked bread for her each morning shooed some men away from the best plot of ground to ensure that Livia and her escort of nomads could lay out their blankets in some comfort. Livia worried what would happen if the rains came. Only a slight drizzle had come so far, and that was during the day. Almost no one had any shelter, though a few were fortunate enough to have wagons under which they could seek some respite. Luckily, the sky looked clear, with all three moons visible. Livia was thankful this tragedy had happened during summer.

While eating a small supper, Livia watched the trains of soldiers passing along the road. Apparently, their lords decided that having a road free of traffic was more important than allowing their men to sleep. When Livia rolled herself up in her blanket, she lulled herself to sleep to the sounds of wagon wheels, neighing horses, and clanking steel.

22
SOOT

Soot stared up at the guard on the wall above the gate into Valandiria. "But you must let me in! Everyone I know is in there!"

The guard cackled at her. "Away with you, runt. No one gets through these gates without the duke's say so."

Soot thought about her friends, or at least those she hoped were her friends. She had spent a considerable amount of time on the long trek from Tolgaria wondering about her place in this vastly changed world. Her mother, the only relative she knew about, was dead. Princess Livia seemed friendly enough, though only Imric had ever truly seemed like her friend for as long as she could remember. With all that had happened, she wondered if Imric would still think of her that way. After all, she was only a servant. One of the lowest of servants at that. She looked up at the guard again. "Prince Imric would want to know I'm here. Please ask him."

The guard laughed harder. "You get funnier by the moment. As if a prince could have a care in the world for a guttersnipe like you."

"Laugh all you want," Soot yelled. "I remember your face. You won't be laughing so hard when the prince has your head on a spike."

"Off with you, rat, before I stick my spear in you!"

Soot scampered off into the shadows. It had not been easy even to approach the city gates. Camps of soldiers were everywhere, and the guards kept shooing her away anytime she got too close. It looked to her like the realm was preparing for war, though what good all these soldiers would do against a dragon was a mystery. At least the light of their campfires and the calls and shouts of half-drunken men lent a cheerful quality to the cool night air.

Perhaps she would have better luck at a different gate, she decided, so she began skirting the city walls, sticking to the shadows to avoid further confrontations. She was glad there was no moat, but sometimes the piles of earth grew large and forced her away from the wall. When she could, she trailed her fingers along the cold stone to help guide her way in the darkness.

It was a very long walk to reach the western gate, and Soot had already been exhausted by the long hike from her home city. Several times she considered lying down in a clump of grass to sleep, but something kept her feet moving one after the other until she saw the torches lighting up the battlements above the second gate.

As she slipped nearer, still hiding in the lee of the wall, she saw an amazing sight. The most gorgeously accoutered horse rider she had ever seen was approaching the gate. A warrior dressed in black from head to toe, on a magnificent black horse. They would have been difficult to see in the darkness if not for the torchlight glittering off the scales of the man's armor.

Soot slipped in as close to the gate as she dared while remaining hidden. The only thing not black about the rider was his pale face, and she gasped when the rider drew near enough to make out details. It was an elf! She had seen only a few elves in her life—mostly emissaries to see the king, though there had been a few merchants as well—but none of those elves had looked as noble as this one. She thought he must be the king of the elves. She held her breath as the elf halted his horse and looked up at the guards atop the gate.

"I am Kathkalan, here to see Duke Erol," the elf said.

There was no immediate response from the guards, and when Soot glanced upward, she saw three of them conferring with each other. One of the guards eventually leaned over the parapet. "We have orders to allow no one through the gates, unless they be the banner men of Duke Erol. I will send a runner to the castle to inquire whether we may let you pass, but what may I say is your purpose in seeing the duke?"

Soot saw a look of irritation flash upon the face of Kathkalan before it turned smooth again and he looked up to respond to the guard.

"I had not thought to come to your city until I saw your army gathering. I believe I may be of some service to Duke Erol in the coming battle."

"My apologies, sir," the guard said, "but it may be some time before we receive a response from the duke. You may, of course wait here, if you wish, or if you prefer to make camp nearby, we can call on you should the duke decide to grant you entrance."

Irritation again showed on the elf's face, but he nodded and then sat so still in his saddle that he reminded Soot of the statue of King Aronis back in Tolgaria. Soot's blood suddenly froze when the elf's eyes slid over to stare at the spot where she was hiding. There was no change of expression on the elf's face, but after a few moments of gazing, Kathkalan dismounted and drew his horse to the side of the gate near where Soot was crouching.

From the moment her heart had started pounding in her chest, Soot had felt the return of the vanished magic of the spire. The familiar feel of strength and confidence filled her for the first time since the spire had fallen, and she was struck with wonder at how this could be. Was Kathkalan magical himself?

"Why do you hide here, child?" Kathkalan asked.

"I-I've been trying to gain entrance to the city, milord. My friends are all inside the castle."

"From the looks of you, that seems doubtful."

"I know how I look, milord," Soot said. "I worked the kitchens in the castle at Tolgaria, but my best friend is Prince Imric, and he's in there now."

A small smile crept onto the elf's face as he said, "Do you believe this Prince Imric would care that you are stranded outside the gate?"

Soot was not at all certain of this, but she nodded. "Yes."

Kathkalan's eyes bored into hers for what seemed an eternity. "I will bring you in with me. Not out of kindness. I wish to see if you speak the truth. It will not go well with you if you are lying to me."

"I'm not lying," Soot said. She licked her lips before adding, "I don't think I'm lying."

The elf turned to his saddle bags and rummaged until he found a brush. He loosened the buckles on the saddle and began brushing down the horse.

The wait was clearly going to be a long one, and Soot was nervous about interrupting the elf, but her curiosity overcame her fear. "I feel the old magic since you came. From the spire."

Kathkalan glanced at her, then resumed rubbing down his mount. "I have a fragment with me."

Soot was confused. "A fragment of what?"

"The crystal that sat atop the spire."

She was about to ask whether the fragment still contained some of the magic, but then it seemed a stupid question—obviously it did. It must be wonderful to have a bit of the magic that you could carry around with you, she thought. Running up staircases would be easy again. And long treks across the countryside would not be so exhausting. "Are you the king of the elves?"

The elf did not pause his brush strokes. "The elves have always had a queen."

She could think of nothing more to say, so she fell silent and watched Kathkalan as he finished grooming his horse. Afterward, the elf stood like stone again for a very long time, until at last the gate began to creak open.

Kathkalan held out a hand. "To me, girl, quickly now."

Soot stepped out into the torchlight and grasped the elf's hand.

The gate stopped once it was wide enough to admit the horse. One of the guards poked his head through. "You may— What's this, sir?"

"The girl's with me," Kathkalan responded, and pushed Soot through the gate ahead of him as he began leading his horse through.

The guard began to stammer, but the elf cut him off. "I take responsibility for her," he said.

The guard looked unhappy, but he nodded and indicated that Kathkalan should follow him. The elf's grip on Soot's hand hardened, and she understood it was his silent way of telling her she would not be slipping off into the town.

The walk through the small city was long, and Soot thought the exhaustion of the long day would have become overwhelming if not for the frisson of additional energy the fragment lent her. She noticed that the guard felt it as well. She saw his eyes widen and he kept glancing around at the elf lord. They walked in silence all the way up the long rise to the castle gates, where a groomsman took the elf's horse, and the guard turned the pair over to a steward, who gave them an appraising look before leading them up some stone steps and through an oaken entrance door. There the steward halted and turned to the elf.

"Sir, the duke is in chambers for the night. The chief steward said I should provide you with a room, and the duke will see you in the morning." He glanced at Soot. "However, I was not made aware of this…young lady. Is she your…servant?"

Kathkalan seemed to consider this for a few moments, then nodded. "Yes, she is. She may share my quarters. Tell me, is there a Prince Imric here?"

The steward looked startled by the question. "Why yes, sir. The young prince is also in chambers for the night. Do you wish a meeting with him as well in the morning?"

"It would be good to see him before my meeting with Duke Erol, if possible."

The steward gave a bow. "I'll see what I can arrange, sir. Now if you'll please follow me to your rooms."

23
VILLEM

Sir Villem Tathis knew that he should be depressed about his lot in life, yet he felt happy and carefree instead. He knew he looked a sorry excuse for a knight—no armor, no weapons other than a small knife, no warhorse, and he thought he had no money either until he came across a purse in the saddle bag on his pony. His newfound best friend Duchess seemed happy as well, scampering about sniffing everything. He had plenty of food and water for the both of them, thanks to the guilty conscious of Lady Sonia.

Though Sonia's husband had a huge head start, Villem had hopes about catching up to him and somehow retrieving his father's warhorse. He kept coming across crossroads until he had no idea which way the lord might have gone.

He began to daydream. Perhaps he could meet a lord from the sunny south, someone who would take him on as a knight and let him build a fresh life. Or maybe he could fight gloriously against the invading East Gate army and earn honors from the king himself. The king might see so much promise in the young man that he would offer his daughter's hand in marriage. Did King Varun have a daughter? He couldn't quite recall. He had a vague idea that he had heard about a princess, but it might just be his recently fevered mind playing tricks on him.

Duchess's barking snapped him out of his reverie, and he noticed what looked like a caravan ahead of him on the road. There were many wagons and riders and even people marching on foot. There could be two or three hundred of them, he thought. He drew up his pony on the side of the road to wait for the train to pass.

Two riders rode out to meet him. Both were men-at-arms with blue and silver livery. Villem didn't know who owned such colors.

"Greetings, traveler," one of the soldiers said. He had a bushy beard and unsettling gray eyes. "Is this the road to Brelyn?"

Villem glanced back the way he had come. "I suspect one of these roads leads to Brelyn, though I can't say which one. If you keep going north, you should find your way there eventually."

"Beautiful farmlands out here," the man said. "Never been out this way before."

Villem took a good look around. He supposed many would find the view beautiful. So much green. Sheep grazing in the pastures, surrounded by walls of piled stones. Compared to his home of Iskimir, however, with its crystal clear lake and its rolling hills, he found this land dull. Flat for as far as the eye could see.

"The breadbasket of the Known Lands, from what I'm told," he responded.

"You're not from around here then?"

Villem shook his head. "I'm from Iskimir. Just trying to make my way to join the king's army."

The two soldiers chuckled. "Taking an odd route to get there," the bearded soldier said.

Villem nodded ruefully. "I got waylaid by bandits. Lost everything. What you see here is just the kindness of Lady Sonia from a small keep back that way."

"Sorry to hear that. Hopefully she'll show kindness to us as well, let us camp on her lands."

"Aye," Villem said. "She probably will. Tell her Sir Villem sends his regards."

"A knight, is it? You really did lose everything."

The first wagon had caught up to them and began to pass. He was about to speak again when he heard a shout from one of the following wagons.

"Villem! Is that truly you?"

It was a voice he recognized. Over the shoulders of the guards, he saw a lithe, raven-haired figure standing in the bed of a cart, waving at him. "Dinara?" He knew he must look a fool with his mouth hanging open, but he could think of no reason why she would be here with this wagon train.

Dinara hopped down from the wagon and jogged over to him. "I'm so happy to see you!"

"And I you," Villem said. "Wh-why are you here? Where are the others?"

"Far away from here, I hope," she said. "I never wish to look upon them again."

"I thought…" He scratched at his cheek. He couldn't help but notice the collar was gone from her neck. "What about Willa?"

Dinara stuck a thumb at the wagon in which she had been riding, which was just passing them now. "She's here, in the back of the cart. She's hurt bad. I don't know if she'll live."

Villem's spirits fell. An irrational thought had made him hope she had left her lover behind, but no, they were still together. "Well," he said, "if you find the keep of Lady Sonia, down that way, there's a healer named Marianna. She saved my life, and she'd do her best to save Willa's, I'm certain."

Dinara's face brightened. "Is it far?"

Villem shook his head. "A half day's ride. A little longer with your wagons. When you hit crossroads, just keep taking the north roads."

Dinara glanced at the two soldiers, then drew closer to Villem. He got the idea she wished to say something without them hearing, so he slid from his pony.

"What is it?"

She leaned in close so she could whisper. "Could...could I go with you?"

He was surprised at her words, but his heart warmed. "You would leave Willa?"

Her face reddened. "I'm not a bad person. I only wanted to see her safely to a healer, and you say there's one nearby. I can't be with her anymore, not after what she did."

Villem did not need to ask what she meant. The moment she said the words, he pictured the farmhouse with all the kids, and Willa laughing as she helped murder them. He reached down to pet Duchess.

Dinara seemed to notice the dog for the first time and was startled. "Isn't that...?"

Villem nodded. "Aye, from that very day. See the scar from Simon's crossbow?"

"How did you...?"

"It's a long story. One I'll be happy to tell you on our journey, if you still wish to come."

"Thank you," she said. "I wonder if these folk will think me terrible for abandoning my charge."

"They don't know you," Villem said. "As long as they help Willa, don't worry what they think."

"I'm going to slow you down," she said. "I don't think your pony can carry both of us."

"It's all right. I feel like walking anyway. Zora can use the rest." He stroked the pony's nose.

"Let me run and fetch my bag from the cart. I...I need to kiss

Willa goodbye and say thanks to the women who helped us. Wait here."

Villem nodded and watched her run after the wagon that was now a good hundred paces past them. He absentmindedly scratched Duchess behind her ears.

The bearded soldier drew closer again. "Your luck's turning if you know that lass."

"Aye," Villem said. "That it is."

When Dinara returned, Villem tied her bag onto Zora and then helped her up into the saddle. He began leading the pony along the side of the road until at last they passed the wagon train. No one spoke until the rumble of the wagons was far behind them.

"I'm sorry," Dinara said.

Villem looked up at her. "What do you mean? You've no need to be sorry."

"It's just…" Dinara stared at her hands. "I'd been dreaming of escape for so long. Ever since that day at the farm. It seemed impossible. Then when Willa was hurt, I felt responsible for her. I had to see her safely to a place where she could be healed. But once I saw you, the need to escape washed over me all of a sudden like a rainstorm."

"You needn't be ashamed of that," Villem said. "You did what you could for Willa. Now you need to help yourself."

"In this realm, women don't set out to help themselves," she said.

Villem plodded along for a few moments, revisiting the recent revelations he'd had about the unfairness of women's lives. "It's not right," he said at last. "But now with all these refugees it won't seem so unusual for a woman to come to a new city or town and seek aid or employment."

"It can be dangerous," Dinara said.

Villem glanced back at her again. She was truly the loveliest woman he had ever seen, and he suddenly understood why she would feel the way she did. Most men who saw her, even lords, would wish to possess her beauty. His face reddened and he turned it away from her. "I will help if I can," he said. "Do you know where you wish to go?"

"No," she replied. "South, I suppose. Where were you heading?"

He fidgeted with the reins of the pony. "I had thought to join the king's army. Not sure what else I can do."

"Going that way, you may run into Orderic again," Dinara said. "And Miranvel. Anyway, the king is dead; you hadn't heard?"

Villem jerked to a stop so suddenly that Duchess barked at him. "Truly? He's dead?"

She nodded. "Why do you think there are so many refugees?"

He shook his head. "Those are the first I've seen. I thought they were fleeing Orderic's depredations. I-I can't believe the king's dead. Did Darus attack already?"

"No, it was the dragon."

Villem twisted his mouth into a rueful grin. "I see, you are having fun at my expense."

Dinara laughed. "You haven't heard of anything! I'm not joking with you."

"But...there are no dragons. They're just tales to scare little children."

She stared at him, and he found it hard to hold her gaze, so he turned to stroke a hand down Zora's muzzle.

"What do you think happened to the Spire of Peace?" she said, then answered her own question. "Dragons are real, and one destroyed the spire. Everyone says so. And then it went on to attack Andiria and Tolgaria, where it slew the king."

Villem felt overwhelmed. He didn't want to think Dinara was having him on or lying to him, but it all seemed so impossible. How could dragons be real? No one in his entire life had suggested they were anything other than myths.

"It's all right, Villem," Dinara said. "I know how you feel. I didn't believe in them either. I had a conversation much like this one with the women on the wagon."

From the muddle of thoughts coursing through his head, Villem tried to pick out one. "Who will be king now? Darus? Maybe now there's no need for him to invade."

"I don't know," Dinara said.

"I don't know what to do now," he said. "I don't want either of us to run into Orderic. I could take you to Iskimir. I'm sure my father would take you in."

"Do you think I would be treated well there?"

"I wouldn't leave you there unless I was certain you would be," he said. "It's a large town. There must be something there for you."

"I'm not so sure," she said. "Life at East Gate didn't prepare me well for a normal life. I don't think I have any skills to offer. My mother taught me to sew, of course, but I was never very good."

"You could easily marry, I'm sure. Any man would want you."

"Something's wrong with me, I know." She stared down at her hands. "I don't want marriage. I don't want children. I never have. Even as a child something didn't seem right. My mother, the other children, all acted as if getting married was all one should ever hope for. The thought of marrying a man always filled me with dread."

That threw water on Villem's idea that perhaps Dinara liked him. He tried to think whether he knew of women who never married. The witch Marianna was the only one who came to mind, and that didn't strike him as a good example. "There must be work for women alone. Perhaps in larger cities."

They came to a fork in the road. Dinara indicated the direction from which the refugees had come. With no good ideas in mind yet, and wishing to avoid Orderic's band, Villem guided the pony onto the other road, which was heading more toward the southwest. It was strange to be wandering lost and taking random roads in the heart of the realm, yet with Dinara as a companion, Villem didn't mind.

24

IMRIC

Imric had just finished dressing in preparation for breakfast when there was a knock at his door. When he opened it, he was greeted with a wonderful surprise.

"Soot!" he cried, and without being able to help himself he flung his arms about her and hugged her tight. "I'm so happy to see you!"

"You're hurting my ribs," she said in a strained voice.

He let go and examined her. "I've never seen you so clean. And with such clothes."

Soot scowled and pointed a thumb over her shoulder. "He made me take a bath and put on this fancy stuff. It itches."

Imric's jaw dropped when he saw who stood behind his best friend—the most glorious looking elf he had ever seen, resplendent in shining black, which made his skin seem all the more pale in contrast.

"My name is Kathkalan, young lord," the elf said. His voice was as melodious as the few elves Imric had seen before, but there was a hard edge to it as well. "You have interesting friends."

"Thank you for bringing Soot back to me, my lord," Imric said.

"Just Kathkalan. My people have no lords. I beg forgiveness, but I have an urgent meeting." He gave a curt nod of his head, then turned and stalked down the hall with quick, sure strides.

"How did you meet him?" Imric said.

"At the gate," Soot replied. "He acts stern, but he helped me." Her face grew more animated. "He has a fragment from the spire! Did you feel it?"

Now that she mentioned it, he had felt the familiar flow of magic the moment he had recognized Soot outside the door, but he had ignored it, thinking it just the excitement of reuniting with her. "The fragment holds some of the magic?"

She nodded. "It's much less powerful than when it was whole, but it's wonderful to feel it."

"What's wonderful is having you back," he said. He wanted to hug her again, but he suddenly felt bashful. She looked good. He had never seen her sharp features so clearly. Usually, they were streaked with dirt. Her hazel eyes seemed to shine in the lamplight. She looked awkward in a lady's dress, and he wondered if she had ever worn a dress before. He had certainly never seen her in one.

She glanced at the dress when she noticed him staring. "I need to change. I feel ridiculous."

"You look…nice," Imric murmured, then felt his face flush.

"You're silly," she said, giggling.

"I…uh…let's get breakfast."

"I *am* starving," she said.

"Come on then," he said, and took her hand to lead her the same way Kathkalan had gone. "You must tell me everything that happened to you. Did you find your mother?"

She plunged to a halt, and Imric realized he had been so overjoyed to see Soot again that he had overlooked the obvious. Her face said it all.

"I-I-I'm sorry," he stammered.

She shook her head. "Not your fault. I'm not ready to talk about it yet." She urged him to continue on.

Imric's thoughts turned to the disappointing news he had from Xax that morning. "It's funny that you came here just when I had hoped to escape. We're about to be besieged. Xax asked Duke Erol if we could go west to find my sister, but the duke refused to let us leave."

"Why would he insist on keeping you here?"

"I don't know," Imric said.

When they reached the dining hall and heard the bustle from the two large tables, Soot halted again. "I can't go in there," she said, shaking her head. "So many people. Lords and ladies. Imric, I'm a serving girl."

"Not to me, you aren't," Imric said. "If I'm really a prince, as they keep insisting, I should get to have some things my way. Come. If anyone tries to shame you, we'll leave and break our fast elsewhere." He took her arm and tried to lead her into the room, but she resisted.

"I don't have proper manners, Imric," she whispered, her face pale. "They'll know me for what I am."

Imric wanted to say he didn't care what anyone thought of her, but he saw how frightened his friend was and relented. "All right, wait here. I'll explain to Xax and we can eat in my room."

She looked relieved and gave a small smile.

Imric hurriedly explained the situation to Xax, and the wizard understood. He smiled and waved to Soot, and told Imric he would speak with him later. Imric was glad to see Duke Erol was not yet in the room, since he didn't feel he needed to explain to him as well. On the way out the door, Imric stopped near a servant.

He indicated Soot with his hand. "We'll be taking breakfast in my chambers. Please have something sent."

"Yes, milord," the servant said, and hurried off to do as he was bidden.

Imric smiled to Soot, took her hand, and led her back toward his rooms. "Some of the clothes in my wardrobe might suit you better. I have so much to show you. Are you tired?"

She nodded. "The bed was too soft. I couldn't sleep until I got down onto the carpet. The journey was tiring."

"I remember. Well, I can show you the passages later, once you are rested."

"You've found them here? Like back home?"

He grinned. "You'll love it."

25
KATHKALAN

Duke Erol Kaldarion was the first man Kathkalan had met who did not look impressed by the elf's appearance.

"Have I seen you before?" the duke said.

"No," Kathkalan replied. "I tend to avoid your people whenever possible."

"Then why are you here?"

"I'm hunting the dragon."

The duke quirked one eyebrow. "The dragon isn't here."

"It will be."

"How can you be so certain?"

Kathkalan stood as rigid and still as a statue. "I know dragons. They don't begin establishing the boundaries of a new hunting ground only to stop half finished."

"You expect it to attack soon?"

"It's likely."

Duke Erol grunted. "A besieging army and a dragon at the same time. What do you want from me?"

"I propose an exchange of aid."

"Go on."

"I'd like to examine your castle, especially the upper reaches and the roof."

"Why?"

"From questioning refugees, the dragon has so far done what they typically do when they attack a city. At some point it settles onto a promontory or other great height to rest and survey its handiwork. When it attacks here it will surely pick a point atop this castle, as it did in your other two cities. I wish to devise a trap and attempt to slay the beast."

"I'm not keen on anyone wandering my castle unescorted," the duke said.

"You do not wish the dragon slain?"

"Of course I do." Erol began to pace along the carpeting. "But I'm not sure it can be done. Our weapons do no harm. I was told a soldier fired a scorpion bolt into the beast from short range and it could not pierce its hide."

"You're right," Kathkalan said. "No weapon of man can harm the dragon. But my sword can."

"You mentioned an exchange of aid."

Kathkalan nodded. "An army marches toward you. I will help you against your rival."

Duke Erol chuckled. "Forgive me, but as potent a warrior as I imagine you are, how does a single elf help me win this coming battle?"

Kathkalan hated having to pretend courtesy with the man, as if they were equals. This man whose entire existence was but a single grain of sand to the vast beach of Kathkalan's life. That the man understood nothing of what an elven warrior could do was not surprising. But he bit back the replies that sprang to his tongue and concentrated on the task at hand. "What do you *feel*, Duke Erol?"

"I don't understand what you are playing at."

"Your heart is not beating fast, so it would be very faint, but you should still be able to feel it."

Duke Erol glared at the elf, then stopped pacing and seemed to concentrate for a moment. His eyes widened. "Just a small tingle, as of the old magic that is lost. Is that it?"

Kathkalan pulled forth the shard of crystal on its chain. "This came from your spire after it was destroyed. The area it affects is not large, but it may be greatly beneficial in battle. Your opponents are those who were driven away by the magic. They will be weakened when they draw near, just as your warriors will be strengthened."

Duke Erol took a step closer, then hesitated. He held a hand up near the crystal. "May I?"

Kathkalan removed the chain from around his neck and held it out. The duke took it and walked over to an arrow slit to examine the crystal in the sunlight. He looked long and hard before turning back to the elf. "I apologize if I was brusque earlier. This would be very helpful indeed. If we may use this in the coming fight, I give you leave to look over my castle. If you need help building your trap, don't hesitate to ask."

Kathkalan gave a tiny bow of his head to Duke Erol and reached out for the shard. The duke hesitated for a moment and took another look at the crystal before handing it back.

"Have you broken your fast?" the duke asked. "Perhaps you would join my family?"

Kathkalan smiled grimly. "I thank you for your gracious offer, my lord. However, I wish to begin as soon as possible. The dragon will come when it comes, and I must be ready for it."

26
LIVIA

Another long, dreary day of slogging along the dusty road was drawing to a close, the sun edging down close to the horizon. Rumor had spread among the refugees that the camp was not far off now. A commotion caused Livia and her companions to turn to look what was happening behind them.

A horseman wearing the blue and silver of Duke Erol was shouting something to the refugees on the road, but he was too far away for Livia to hear what he was saying. But the man trotted forward a hundred paces and began shouting again in a hoarse voice, and this time she could make it out.

"We have a new king! Long live King Balmar! As the king is unable to rule, Duke Erol Kaldarion has been named Regent. Long live King Regent Erol! Darus Kaldarion has been named traitor and has forfeited all claim to the throne. He is banished forever and condemned to death! Long live the Known Lands!"

The herald nudged his horse forward again to repeat the message farther down the line of refugees. A buzz of excitement went up from everyone around Livia, and she paused in her walking to consider what this news meant for her family. If Darus was officially out of the line of succession, that meant her little brother Imric was the new heir, at least until Balmar ever conceived a son. She tried to imagine Imric as king, and it brought a smile to her face. How ironic that the child her father had rejected could end up king, though he had never been raised to know such duties as came with being monarch of the Known Lands. Anyhow, she thought, Balmar will likely live a long time, so Uncle Erol will rule.

She was not sure what she felt about Erol ruling the realm. She had met him several times throughout her life, either when he visited his brother in the capital or on the rare occasions her father had taken her with him to Valandiria. He had always treated her warmly, but she knew so little about him in truth. Would he rule wisely? Assuming he beat Darus in the coming conflict, could he unite the realm? She had no idea.

The coming of the dragon would change everything. From what Xax had taught her about dragons, it would likely take the former heartland around the Sea of Alia as its new territory, meaning the realm would need an entirely new seat of power. So many thousands of people had been displaced and needed new homes and livelihoods. The nobles of the southlands had always been difficult to keep in line—she could imagine them taking this opportunity to rebel. The Known Lands needed a strong king now more than ever.

As her feet trudged forward once more, her eyes were drawn to a large, fallow field off to the right side of the road. It was unusual enough to see a horse standing alone in an unfenced field, but now that she drew closer, she saw that the horse appeared to be loaded down with packs.

Azer must have noticed the horse as well, for he drew near and said, "Something is wrong there, lady. Perhaps I should go check it out."

"No," Livia said. "I'm so bored with all this walking. I need the distraction. We shall go together."

All six of the nomads fell in place around her as she left the road and approached the horse. The beast's head was down, not to graze, but out of exhaustion, and she saw that while the horse did have saddle bags, it also carried a rider, though the man was lying down across the horse's neck. Neither horse nor rider moved as they approached. Livia drew to a halt several paces away. Clearly the man was a soldier—he wore chain mail armor and a well-worn sword dangled from a scabbard at his side.

"Hello? Are you well, sir?" she asked.

The man remained motionless, his head hidden behind his steed's neck. Could he be dead, she wondered, or merely unconscious? She began to take a step forward, but Azer held up a hand.

"Let me, lady." He stalked slowly around the horse, keeping several paces away. He stopped and examined the man for a few moments, then edged closer. The other five nomads took up defensive positions in a circle around the exhausted beast. "Can we help you, sir?" Azer asked.

The horse gave a pitiful whinny, but the man did not stir. Azer walked around to Livia.

"We could lead the horse to the road, where we may find more help," he said.

Livia nodded. "What do you think is wrong with him?"

Azer shook his head. "He has been in a fight. His helm is badly dented. I'm surprised he is still alive."

He spoke something in his native tongue to Ragif, who stood nearest the horse's head. Ragif stepped forward and took the horse's reins. When he tried to lead the horse toward the road, the beast gamely stumbled forward a few steps before collapsing to its haunches. Its rider began to scream. Horrible, soul-wrenching screams. Everyone stepped back in fright at first, but then Livia ran forward, and the nomads hurried to assist her.

"Quickly!" Livia cried. "Pull him free before the horse collapses."

Babak and Samir got their hands under the man's arms and dragged him from the horse. The man stopped screaming and began to pant heavily. The two nomads laid him out on the soft ground.

"My head!" the man screamed. "Kill me!"

"He's in terrible pain," Azer said. "It's the helmet."

"Can we do something?" she asked.

"I'm not sure," Azer replied. "He's a big man. He might hurt us if we get too close."

Livia walked up to the man, who was thrashing and moaning on the ground. She knelt in front of him and reached a hand out to lay it on his chest. "Sir, let us help you."

"Aaaaaagh! Kill me, you bitch!"

Livia blinked several times and shook off the insult. She saw where the man's helm had been crushed against the side of his head by a powerful blow. She turned to Azer and pointed to the man's arms. He nodded and spoke several words to his companions. Fuad and Zaur nervously approached on either side of the man, then pounced down to pin his arms down. The man began to thrash harder and yelled curses such as Livia had never heard. He tried to kick at the men holding him, until Babak and Samir grabbed hold of his legs. Livia beckoned Ragif to come closer.

"Azer, have him place his foot on this part of the helm. You'll pry up on the other side. If it works, Babak and Samir might be able to pull him free."

Azer looked doubtful. "It's steel, my lady. I'm not sure I have the strength."

"We must try."

He sighed and nodded.

Ragif pressed his foot down hard on the cheek piece of the helm. The soldier continued to yell and tried to bite him, but Ragif's boots were of sturdy leather. Azer gathered himself and pulled hard on the opposite cheek piece. He grunted and strained, and it looked to Livia as if the helm bent outwards a little. The soldier screamed louder than ever, and Livia clapped her hands to her ears. She nodded to Babak and Samir, and they began to pull the man's legs.

It wasn't working. Zaur let go of the arm he had been holding and jumped up to help Azer pull on the helm. The soldier began to beat at them with his fist. With two men pulling, the helm bent further, and suddenly the man slid free. Fortunately, the soldier lost consciousness and silence fell.

When Livia stood up and peered back toward the road, she saw that a good number of refugees had stopped to watch. "My thanks to all of you," Livia said to the nomads. "There's a wagon approaching on the road. Let's see if it has room to carry this man."

"Yes, lady," Azer said. "The horse must be put down. It is too far gone."

Livia nodded sadly. "Pull the packs and put them in the wagon as well please."

The owner of the wagon complained but relented once he saw how badly injured the man was. The side of his head was swollen, and his whole face was red and slicked with the sweat of fever. "He doesn't look likely to live, milady."

"We'll seek help for him when we can," Livia said. "Thank you for your kindness."

The driver knuckled his forehead and flicked the reins at his mules to get the wagon rolling again.

27
IMRIC

Imric entered the makeshift throne room and stared around curiously. Two large, ornately-carved wooden chairs stood on one end of the chamber, a large balcony behind them. His brother, the new King Balmar Kaldarion, looked pitiful and bored, slumped in the leftmost chair with a petulant look on his face. His uncle, Regent Erol Kaldarion, sat straight and proud in the other chair. He nodded to Imric and smiled.

Situated about the room, but leaving an empty path to the thrones, were a scattering of noblemen, all armed and armored, each bearing a different coat of arms. Imric recognized only a few of them. Of more interest to him was the opposite end of the room. Sunlight shone brightly through another large balcony. The wizard Xax stood on the balcony and looked out at whatever panorama it showed, ignoring the proceedings in the room. Imric badly wished to walk to the balcony and see what Xax was seeing. He had not been this high up in the castle, and he was sure the view would be far more interesting than this ceremony he had been required to attend.

A flash of movement in his peripheral vision returned his attention to the thrones, where his uncle had stood to address the assembly.

"This is a momentous day for the Known Lands," he began. "Our kingdom has suffered much in these past weeks. We have lost our beloved king, my brother; had two of our greatest cities destroyed by a monstrous dragon; and now the traitor Darus marches at the head of an army to begin a civil war. Yet today is great, for we have a new king." He paused to sweep an arm toward Balmar. "All of you have answered the call to arms. Already we have more than double the number of men that Darus has, and more troops continue to arrive. We shall smash the traitor, let there be no doubt. Once peace has been restored, we can make plans for how to deal with the dragon. Losing the magic of the Spire of Peace has made many of our people fearful for our future. We will show them that our future is not to be feared, but rather to be welcomed. Come forward, lords. Kneel to your new king and swear your fealty!"

The gathered lords began to move as directed, and Imric moved with them until he saw Uncle Erol wave him off. For the first time, Balmar perked up and he even grinned as the assembled lords swore their oaths to him. When the ceremony finished and the lords returned to their places, Uncle Erol beckoned Imric forward.

Imric had not been told why he was being summoned, so he felt unsure of himself, and awkward at having to march forward alone before the eyes of everyone in the room. He didn't know what was expected of him, so he slowed and halted at the spot where the lords had knelt down to his brother.

"Kneel, young Prince Imric," Erol said.

Imric knelt to one knee and gazed down at the burgundy carpet. He saw the felt boots of his uncle and a strong hand was placed upon his head.

"I, Regent Erol Kaldarion, in the name of our good King Balmar, anoint thee, Prince Imric Kaldarion, as heir to the throne of the Known Lands." In a whisper, his uncle added, "You may rise."

Imric stood up and awkwardly accepted the polite applause of the gathered nobles. Uncle Erol bent down to whisper in his ear. "Go join Xax. The ceremony won't last much longer."

With relief, Imric scurried over to the balcony, where Xax smiled and clasped his arm to congratulate him. Imric looked out over the balcony and the view took his breath away. The Sea of Alia rippled and glistened in the sun for as far as the eye could see. Off to the right, he saw the mouth of the Skendris River. To the left, a scattering of fishing vessels bobbed on the small waves.

Behind him, the voice of his uncle rose once more, but Imric ignored it, grateful that his part in the ceremony was over. He had to pull himself up so he could peer down over the edge of the balcony. It was a dizzying sight. The cliff face seemed scooped out in this spot, so if he were to leap, he would fall directly into the water far below. He turned to Xax excitedly.

"This is the place where the prince jumped in your story!"

Xax nodded. "Aye, though don't get any ideas. He was lucky to survive such a fall."

Imric shuddered. "I wouldn't dream of it." He peered down again and couldn't imagine how anyone could be insane enough to make the jump on purpose. The water seemed so far away.

"Your brother seemed taken with the story after he heard it. He stared down there a long time and said he could make the jump. I talked him out of it, but he worries me. He's so unhappy these days."

"You don't think he would do it, do you?"

Xax shook his head. "I wish I had the means to get him away from here, though. You as well."

"You're worried about me?"

"I'm probably being paranoid, but your uncle keeps saying things that make me nervous."

They remained silent for a while, taking in the view.

"Do you see the river over there?" Xax asked.

Imric turned his attention back to the Skendris. "Yes."

Xax went into lecture mode, which was becoming more and more familiar to Imric of late. He got the feeling that Xax missed having someone to teach. The wizard waved an arm out towards the expanse of water. "Our people have always called this a sea, but in truth it's simply an enormous lake. You've seen the one large river that flows into it, where Tolgaria stands, but there are several other rivers and many streams that empty into the lake as well. The Skendris River is the only outflow, at the lake's lowest point. It runs all the way to the ocean, far to the west."

The view was so spectacular, Imric felt he could stand here for hours and never get bored. It seemed so peaceful that the talk of war and the dragon felt almost unreal. Almost. He had seen the dragon. He knew firsthand the terror and destruction it could wreak. "Xax, why hasn't the dragon attacked us here?"

"I have a guess, though I can't be certain."

"What's your guess?"

"When a dragon establishes a new territory, it always seeks out a lair. Somewhere it will feel safe and comfortable. Usually in a cave of some sort, deep beneath a mountain. In my opinion, the most logical such place in these parts is the city of Kaldorn."

"Where the dwarves live?" Imric had always known the capital city of the dwarves lay close to Tolgaria, directly to the east in the vast mountain range that blocked off the eastern horizon. He had dreamed of getting to see it one day, though he knew it was unlikely. The dwarves had little to do with men other than a bit of trade. Livia had taught him that their father had only once visited Kaldorn. "I always heard the dwarves were fierce warriors. Wouldn't the dragon fear them? Aren't there lots of small tunnels in their city? It couldn't possibly root them all out, could it?"

"Fierce and mighty warriors they are, aye, but even they would have trouble to slay a dragon, especially one as large as this one. The dragon would be wary, but it would not fear them, and the dwarven great hall would make a superb lair for the beast. As for the labyrinth of corridors, there's a reason dragons are also called wyrms. They can squeeze themselves into cracks and holes you might deem impossible, much like mice or rats, and if a hall became too tiny, the dragon can pour clouds of death through it with its breath."

"I feel sorry for them," Imric said.

Xax squeezed his shoulder. "I do as well, young man. If that is what has happened. The dragon may be doing something else entirely. We must count ourselves lucky each day that passes without seeing the monster."

Imric's mind filled with images of the terrible black dragon burrowing through tiny tunnels in the dark, blasting clouds of acid through each small corridor it encountered. He shuddered and tried to turn his attention back to the beauty of the view in front of him. For the rest of the ceremony, he picked out new details from the panorama, but his thoughts kept creeping back to death beneath the mountains.

That night Imric awakened suddenly. At first he thought he was woken by nightmares about the dragon, but then he heard it again—a scuffling sound from the side of the bed where the wardrobe stood. It was too dark to see, so he concentrated on listening. There was a creak, and then the sound of the wardrobe door opening, and light burst forth and blinded Imric. He covered his eyes with his hands until his vision adjusted to the light.

"Who-who's there?" he stuttered. Part of him was afraid, but he assumed it must be Soot. Who else could it be?

"Don't be alarmed," came a whisper. "It's me, your cousin Istvan."

This was a surprise. His cousin, the eldest son of Uncle Erol, had sat at the meals every day but had never spoken a word to Imric. He seemed nice enough, but Imric knew older boys often couldn't be bothered with younger ones. Why would he sneak into his room in the middle of the night?

"Why are you here?" he whispered.

Istvan scrambled out of the wardrobe and placed his lantern on the end table near Imric's bed. He brushed off his clothes with his hands. "I haven't been through the tunnels in ages. Forgot how dirty they are."

"I didn't know you knew about them," Imric said.

Istvan chuckled. "I doubt many boys growing up in this castle would fail to discover them. They aren't that hard to find. I don't much like crawling around in the dark. And I hate spiders. Sorry to surprise you like this."

"You've never spoken to me before."

Istvan shrugged. "Sorry. My father ordered me not to talk to you."

"Why would he do that?"

"I wasn't sure, at first. Now I think I understand, and I've come to warn you."

"Warn me?"

"I think you're in danger. And your wizard friend as well. You should escape while you can."

"I don't understand."

Istvan stared down at the floor for a few moments. "I don't want to speak ill of my father, but…but I don't want my own cousin to be hurt either. I knew Father was proud to become regent and get a chance to rule the realm. But I never thought he could do something bad. Something wrong. He came to my bedroom tonight and sat with me. Told me I was going to be king one day. He swore it. I asked him what he meant. That you were the heir. He shushed me and said I wasn't to worry about that. Our side of the family was meant to rule, he said. He said you were a kindly boy, but that you were never raised to be king. King Varun had disowned you and ignored you. You were never taught how to rule. Never even taught to be a knight. He said having you as king would be the downfall of our realm, and he would…he would ensure that never happened."

Imric's mind whirled. Too many differing thoughts collided with one another in his head, and he could not seem to sort them out. Would his own uncle do something to him? To Balmar? "Why are you telling me this?"

Istvan shook his head. "You're my own cousin. My blood. I don't wish harm to you or the king. I wouldn't want to be king if it meant doing evil to my own family."

"Why did he go to the trouble of naming me heir?"

"He needed all the lords on his side to defeat Darus. They had to see that he intends to do the right thing. However, once Darus is gone, none of that will matter."

"If we try to escape, won't Uncle Erol hunt us down?"

"I'm sure he'll try, but I don't know what else you can do. Maybe the upcoming battle will distract him."

Imric found it hard to breathe. "I'll go to Xax. He'll know what to do."

Istvan nodded. "He's a wizard. Surely he can help hide you."

Imric wasn't so sure about that. Xax did not seem anything like the wizards from the tales. He almost never did magic, and when he did, it seemed to sap all the energy out of him. He saw no reason to tell this to Istvan, though. "Thank you, Cousin. I wish I could have known you better."

Istvan smiled. "Who knows? Perhaps one day that can still happen." He sighed and grimaced. "It's back through the tunnels for me now. Please, make Xax understand. The danger is real, I believe. Good luck, Cousin."

With that, Istvan picked up the lantern and crawled back into the wardrobe. The door swung shut, leaving Imric in darkness again. Creaks and sliding sounds came from the wardrobe, but Imric ignored them and tried to think what to do. Should he wait until morning to see Xax? He had a feeling he wouldn't be able to fall asleep with this new worry filling his head. He decided he had to go now. His first thought was that he should creep through the tunnels like Istvan had, but then it seemed silly. No one would care if they saw him visiting the wizard, even in the middle of the night. So, he crawled out of bed and quickly dressed, then unbarred the door and crept down the hall to Xax's room. He knocked twice, waited a few moments, and knocked twice more. He heard Xax's voice grumbling and presently the door swung open.

"What's this?" the wizard asked. "What could be so important you have to wake me in the middle of the night?"

"Can I come in?"

Xax heaved a sigh and stepped aside to let Imric enter. He did something to make the green crystal on the top of his walking stick emit a soft light. "Sit down. Sit down. Tell me what simply cannot wait until morning."

When they were situated, Imric related everything Istvan had told him. The wizard remained still and silent for a long time after he was finished.

"What do you think we should do?" Imric asked at last, unable to bear waiting any longer.

"I don't know," Xax said. "I'm perplexed Erol would go ahead with yesterday's ceremony to make you heir if he meant to turn right around and have you murdered. It isn't logical. I don't believe he intends to act quickly. We're likely safe for now."

"How can you be sure?"

The wizard shrugged. "I can't. But if we flee now, Erol will scour the countryside looking for us. It wouldn't be easy to hide."

"Livia has managed it so far," Imric pointed out.

"He only sent a few men to search for her. He'd send far more after you."

"So we just stay here?" Imric tried to imagine what meal times would be like, sitting there with his uncle and Istvan as if nothing were wrong.

"I need time to consider this," Xax said. "Darus's army should arrive tomorrow. If we decide to make a run for it, that may be a good time, when Erol is distracted. You said you met a girl from the kitchens. Have her bundle up some supplies for us. Food that's good for travel. It won't hurt to prepare."

It was a relief to have something to do, even if they would not be departing immediately. Imric bade good night to Xax and returned to his room to toss and turn for the remainder of the night.

28

KATHKALAN

Sweat slicked Kathkalan's brow as he worked in the hot sun. He drove another spike through the iron strut and pressed down upon it to test its strength. It would do. That was the last of the support pieces, so now he could begin laying out wooden crossbeams to form a walkway across the stone well.

He climbed out to stand upon the castle's roof and used a rag to wipe the sweat away. It seemed a waste of time to expend such effort on something that held little chance of success, but he had nothing better to try. If he had the resources and the time, he would have fashioned a strong steel mesh to drape over each of the towers that surrounded the rooftop. They would not hold the dragon, of course, but they might snag in its claws and irritate it long enough to allow Kathkalan to get in close and deal a killing blow. There was too little time, however, and when he had examined the castle's forge and its supplies, he had seen that there was no chance of manufacturing what was needed.

The well drew his attention. The roof was flat between the towers, except for one spot where a square hole about five paces across dropped into darkness. He had no idea why the castle's builders had placed it here. The well was overgrown with ivy so thick, Kathkalan could easily have climbed down to the bottom if he wished. Instead, he decided to bridge the gap, about a pace and a half down from the rim. It was the only plan he could come up with. Lure the beast across the roof so that it passed over the well. If he could manage to do that while he waited hidden on the bridge, he could strike at the beast's belly from below as it passed overhead. He smirked at himself for thinking this idea had any chance of success, but dragons were known for their cunning, not for intelligence.

He had put the smiths and their apprentices to work making rows of tall iron spikes that he could place to either side of the roof, forming a crude path leading to the well. Carpenters had already built two pens on either side of the well to hold small flocks of sheep. Even with plenty of food and water, the sheep bleated their unhappiness at being cooped up on a hot rooftop under a blazing sun. He hoped they would be enough to lure the hungry dragon across the rooftop to pass over the well and enable him to strike.

Kathkalan took a long swig from his water skin. He heard someone approaching and looked around.

"My pardon, sir elf," said a nervous-looking steward. "Regent Erol asks you to attend him."

Kathkalan glared at the man until he lowered his gaze. "I'm very busy at the moment. Did he say why?"

"He did not tell me, sir, but I'm certain it must be because the traitor's army has arrived."

Kathkalan perked up at that news and began walking toward the eastern edge of the roof. The steward hastened after him. Kathkalan stopped at the edge and took in the view. A dark wall of mountains formed the horizon. The elf had good eyes, but he could barely make out the distant shapes of tents being erected. *There they are*, he thought. If Erol were smart, he would remain behind his walls and force Darus to besiege him. He did not expect Erol to be smart, especially with the magic of the crystal shard to aid him. He glanced over at the sweating steward. "You see those stacks of wood over there?"

"Sir?"

"Get a team of carpenters up here. I'll show you what must be done. I'll go meet the regent, but if you fail to do what I need, you'll answer to me."

The man gulped and nodded.

When Kathkalan entered the room, the regent stood with a group of his nobles examining a vast map of the realm. Kathkalan glanced at his home, the forest of Laithtaris, and was surprised to see how accurate it was. Regent Erol noticed his entrance and strode forward to meet him.

"I'm glad to see you, elf," Erol said. "It's time you upheld your promise to me."

"So, you plan to attack, I assume."

"You think I'm wrong? Darus has fewer than three thousand soldiers. I now have more than seven thousand. He has no knights, and I have more than three hundred. Even without your bit of magic we should have little trouble defeating him. With your bauble, it should be a rout."

Kathkalan shrugged. "I will keep my promise."

Erol nodded. "Very good. We will attack in the morning."

Kathkalan thought the evening would be better, when the sun would be in the eyes of Darus's army, but he said nothing, merely nodded and took his leave. He wanted to be certain the wooden platform in the rooftop well would be completed properly.

29
VILLEM

Villem had never walked such long distances before, and his leg muscles burned. He wished they had more than one pony. What had started out as a pleasant journey over flat farmlands had become much harder as the sun turned hotter and the ground rose into a series of small hills.

They had met few travelers on the road, and most they had met had been refugees. Near the top of the rise ahead of them, Villem saw a small, brightly-colored carriage standing in the middle of the dirt track. A stocky man in peasant garb walked around from the front of the carriage to watch at them as they approached.

Villem drew Zora to a halt and looked up at Dinara. "Wait here. Perhaps he needs help."

"Be careful," Dinara said. She clucked at Duchess to keep the dog close.

Villem walked forward alone and stopped a few paces short of the man. "Did you break a wheel?"

The man shook his head. "Our mule came up lame. I had to put her down."

"I'm sorry to hear that."

The man nodded toward Dinara. "That pony could help."

Villem studied the carriage, which was designed to hold two people, and just one driver. It looked like something he had once seen at a fair in Iskimir. "It doesn't look like your carriage could hold us all, unless you have no passengers."

"I have a passenger. The greatest troubadour in the realm."

Villem had seen a number of entertainers pass through his father's castle. A number had called themselves minstrels or troubadours, but none had ever claimed to be the greatest in the realm. "Who is this famous troubadour, if I may ask?"

The stocky man chuckled. "Surely you have heard of Tristopher? His honeyed tongue can win the heart of any woman."

Villem looked around at Dinara, then back at the man. "We could put that to the test. Looks as good a place to camp for the night as any. I am Sir Villem Tathis of Iskimir. May I ask your name, good man?"

"I am Othar. You are far from home...sir." The man had a skeptical look on his face, reminding Villem that he looked nothing at all like a knight at the moment.

"I am. Have you been to Iskimir? I don't recall a Tristopher passing through."

"Nay. We have spent the past few seasons around the great sea, not the west lands. The money is far better in the great cities."

Villem nodded. "What brings you this far out now?"

"The lord of Brelyn hired Tristopher for a summer festival. We meant to head back to Valandiria after, but we heard about the dragon. A rider from Duke Erol came to ask for supplies and men from the lord of Brelyn. Said they were building a new city south of here for all the refugees. Tristopher thought the refugees might need some good cheer."

"That's where we're headed as well," Villem said. "My pony has never drawn a carriage. Not sure how well she'd do, but we might give it a try, assuming we can all fit."

Othar knuckled his forehead. "We appreciate your aid. You sure you want to camp now? Still a couple hours of daylight left."

"I've been walking all day. My legs can use the rest. And there are shade trees here."

Othar nodded. "All right. Help me push the carriage off the road and we can unpack the pavilion."

As they worked, Villem wondered why Tristopher remained hidden away in the carriage. With the curtains drawn, he had yet to see the man.

"He doesn't like the sun when it's this hot," Othar explained. "And he won't do anything that might damage his hands. They are worth more than their weight in gold."

"What does he play?" Villem asked.

"He knows many instruments, but his favorite is the gittern."

"Will he play for us?"

Othar quirked a brow in at Dinara, who was brushing down the pony under the trees. "With a lady as fair as that, he just might favor us with a tune or two."

"Her name is Dinara," Villem said.

"Is she your wife?"

"Let's just get this pavilion up."

When the camp was prepared and a small fire going, Othar knocked on the door of the carriage and helped Tristopher out. Villem had never seen such a man. Tristopher was gaunter than any man he had ever seen, and his hands and fingers were long and thin.

"He looks deathly ill," Dinara whispered to Villem as she pulled provisions from the saddlebags.

Othar spread two blankets and a bear skin inside the pavilion, and Tristopher sat on the blankets and let Othar wrap the bear skin around his narrow shoulders. The troubadour gave Villem the barest of glances before settling his eyes on Dinara.

Villem passed cheese, bread, and apples to Othar, and in return, Othar uncorked a small flask of ale and brought forth some wooden cups.

"Dinara is a lovely name," Tristopher said, in a startlingly deep and mellifluous voice. "And unusual."

Dinara swallowed what she had been chewing and replied, "It's common up north."

"I see. May I ask where you are from?"

"The town of Ulfoss on Frozen Lake."

"Ah. I've heard of the lake, but I've never been so far north."

"Sane people don't travel there if they can help it," Dinara said.

Quiet fell for a few minutes while people ate. Dinara tossed some food to Duchess, who pounced on it greedily.

Villem set down his ale mug and said, "I'm not sure we can all fit in the carriage. It's very small."

Othar nodded. "It will be awkward."

"The lady might sit in someone's lap," Tristopher said, a mischievous smile on his lips.

Villem and Dinara glanced at each other before Dinara replied, "I'd rather lie atop the baggage on the roof."

All three men were aghast at the thought.

"A-a-a lady cannot lie on a carriage roof," Tristopher sputtered.

"Well, I'm no lady," Dinara said, "and I think I could manage fine."

"If someone must ride atop the baggage, it should be me," Villem said.

Dinara glared at him and Villem wondered why she seemed upset. Would not riding in the carriage be more comfortable for her?

"Let's get some sleep and discuss it in the morning," she said.

"Will you not let me play for you, my lady?" Tristopher said.

"Do as you will," she replied. "Perhaps it will soothe me to sleep. First I need a short walk." She stood up and walked from the pavilion, Duchess following at her heels.

Tristopher had Othar bring him his gittern and then began to tune it. Villem had wished to follow Dinara so he could talk with her, but she was likely attending to bodily functions, so it wasn't appropriate. He supposed he would not get the chance to learn what was wrong, so he settled himself in his own blanket and listened to the melody the troubadour began to pick out with his spindly fingers. The man was truly very good.

Villem's eyes began to grow heavy, but he forced himself to remain awake until Dinara returned and settled into her own blankets. Duchess cuddled up near Villem. He let himself be lulled to sleep by the soft music.

A loud clanging noise woke Villem from a deep sleep. He sat up, rubbing at his eyes. Duchess was barking and growling.

"I knew it," Dinara screeched, and gave a vicious kick to something on the ground near Villem.

Villem shook his head, trying to clear the cobwebs. "Dinara? What's happening?"

"Wha-what is this?" Tristopher added, sitting up still wrapped in his bear skin.

"Your man tried to murder Villem. Look!" She pointed at something on the ground.

The word 'murder' snapped Villem wide awake. He saw the form of Othar huddled on the ground, groaning and holding his head. Where Dinara was pointing lay a dagger. He noticed that Dinara had a frying pan in one hand just in time to see her whack Othar in the head again, likely breaking some of his fingers. Othar cried out and began to weep.

Villem snatched up the dagger. "Dinara, stop hitting him!"

"He meant to kill us, Villem!" She kicked Othar in the ribs. Duchess lunged in and snapped at the man's leg.

Tristopher huddled deeper into his bear skin, eyes wide.

Villem stood up and held his hands out to Dinara. "You're going to kill him if you keep it up. Let me get some straps and bind him up. Duchess! Go on!"

"What's wrong with killing him?" Dinara said. "Keep him alive and he's like to try again."

"No!" Othar howled. "N-never would have hurt you, l-lady!"

Villem tried to wrap his mind around the idea of someone trying to kill him. No one in this realm had needed to worry about such a thing for thousands of years, because the magic had always driven such people away. Could a person live their entire life within the dictates of the magic, and then change so drastically once the magic was gone?

"Why were you trying to kill me?"

Othar's hands still cradled his wounded head, blood seeping from between the fingers. "No." He groaned loudly. "No, you're mistaken. I-i-it was a joke. A bad joke. I had too much to drink."

Dinara was shaking her head. "I know what I saw."

"Where are you really from?" Villem asked. "You can't be from the realm. You couldn't have lived here with such evil in you."

"We're from Coldhaven," Tristopher said. "I was born there. Never even been to the realm until now. I am sorry about my man. I had no idea he meant to do you harm."

Othar glared at his boss with shock apparent on his face. "You're the one who suggested it! 'The woman and pony will be ours once he's out of the way.' Remember?"

Tristopher spread his hands wide and smiled. "You're not injured, sir knight. The damage is all ours. Your lady is fierce as well as beautiful."

Villem kept his eyes on Othar, the dagger held at the ready. "Dinara, get the tethers from their dead mule and tie this man up."

"What are you planning to do to us?" Tristopher asked.

"I won't murder you unless you try something stupid."

Dinara returned, prodded Othar into a sitting position, and began wrapping tethers about his middle, pinning his arms to his torso. "What will we do, Villem?"

Villem shook his head. "We can't let men bring evil into our lands."

Tristopher began to cackle.

Villem's face reddened. "What is so funny?"

The troubadour fought to get his laughter under control. "Your pitcher has shattered into a thousand pieces, and you still think it can hold water!" He began laughing again.

Othar said, "Do you know how many live in exile outside your realm? Not just here in the north. Mitinya in the west. Miradis and Tibria in the south. Tens of thousands of men have dreamed of the day they could enter the realm and exact revenge. I heard there's even an army marching from East Gate. Your realm is a barely warm corpse, ready for burial."

Villem wanted to lash out at both men, but in his heart he had the feeling they understood the truth better than he did. "The realm isn't dead yet, not as long as there are men to defend it." The words rang hollow to his ears, but he forced himself to believe them.

"So, what will we do?" Dinara asked again.

"Take them to the nearest keep and turn them over to the lord. He can decide their fate."

"That's my carriage," Tristopher said. "You can't keep my carriage."

"I don't want your carriage," Villem said. "I wish we had never met."

He checked the bindings on Othar, then fought off Tristopher's feeble protests and tied him up as well. Crouching by Dinara, he whispered, "You saved my life. Thank you."

"I knew something was wrong," she murmured. "I could smell it."

"They fooled me," Villem replied.

As they lay down to try to get some sleep, Villem scratched Duchess behind the ears. "Good girl, Duchess. If either of these men moves, you wake me up."

Duchess licked his hand.

"I can't sleep tied up like this," Tristopher whined.

"Then lie there quietly. If you keep me awake, I'm going to start breaking things, starting with your little lute."

"It's not a—"

"Not another word!"

Othar kept groaning about his head. Villem decided to try to ignore the pitiful cries, since the only other option was to bash the man into unconsciousness with the frying pan.

He wrapped himself in his blanket and tried to convince himself he could still fall asleep. His mind kept turning over and over with images of tens of thousands of bad men pouring across the borders into the Known Lands.

30
LIVIA

The long line of refugees began to slow and then came to a halt. Livia clambered from the wagon holding the wounded soldier and walked along the side of the road toward the rise ahead. The six nomads followed her, as they usually did, behaving as if they had become some sort of royal guard. Livia didn't mind. They had never given her reason to doubt their friendship, despite some of the whispers and glares thrown at them by some of her folk. It embarrassed her that her people automatically treated outsiders with suspicion, though the nomads seemed to have been accepted by the people who had been with them all the way from Tolgaria.

When she reached the top of the rise, Livia caught her breath. The road ran down the slope to a crossroads. One road turned northeast toward Brelyn. The river forked here, the greater part continuing west while a smaller branch turned southwest. Livia recalled reading about the grand engineering project that had created this unnatural fork in the great river, so it was interesting to see it in person. Roads followed each fork, and a small ferry sat unused at a tiny dock. The jam of refugees was caused by soldiers giving instructions. But it was the fields off the road beyond the tiny hamlet at the crossroads that brought Livia up short. They teemed with many thousands of refugees, more than Livia had believed possible. Tents and pavilions dotted the dusty pastures, but not nearly enough for so many people. Some had turned wagons into makeshift shelters, and still more simply milled about or sat in the yellowed grass.

Livia looked at Azer and shook her head in consternation. "Come," she said, and began walking down the small slope toward the soldiers at the crossroads.

The hamlet consisted of about a dozen wooden huts with shingle roofs. The only well in the village had a long line of refugees, waiting their turn to trample through the mud to fetch water. A couple of unhappy villagers stood in doorways, glaring helplessly at the chaos.

Three men-at-arms stood at the crossroads, speaking to each group of refugees in turn before passing them on to a pair of men near a stack of crates who handed each refugee a small bundle before herding them off toward the pasture camps.

Livia strode up to the three soldiers and halted, chin held high. The men ignored her and continued telling the refugees about the camp, how more tents would soon be arriving, and that carpenters would begin building shelter for everyone if they would just be patient. Livia cleared her throat loudly, and one of the soldiers looked at her, a scowl on his face.

"Wait your turn like everyone else," the soldier said.

"Who is in charge of this…this mess?" Livia asked.

The man's face reddened in irritation. "Woman, the line moves slow enough without people trying to cut in front. Move back to your place, else we'll place you under arrest."

Livia's mouth hung open for several moments while she collected her thoughts. "I am not cutting the line, soldier. I am Princess Livia Kaldarion, and these refugees are my charge. I'm asking you politely, who is in charge here? I wish to speak with them."

The soldier looked more closely at the dirty, road-worn finery she wore. His face took on a wary look, and his partners stopped talking and looked her over as well.

"How are we to know you are who you say you are?" the first soldier said.

Livia looked along the line of refugees and saw many familiar faces. She pointed toward the crowd. "Most of these have been with me since we left the capital. Ask any of them who I am."

The soldier glanced at the ground before meeting her gaze again. "Our orders are from the regent, milady. We weren't told the command had been given to you."

"I'm here to help," Livia said. "I'd like to speak with the commanding lord, so I may offer assistance."

One of the other soldiers pointed at the nomads. "Who are these foreigners? They should move along. We have enough problems here."

Livia's cheeks flushed, but she fought to hold her temper. "These men are ambassadors from the south. They have been of great service during our time of need. They deserve respect."

The soldier glared suspiciously at the nomads before turning back to Livia. He pointed to the nearest house. "Lord Sewell is there, unless he's out planning how the city will be built. He's in charge."

"One more thing. We have an injured man. Where are the healers?"

The soldier pointed along the road toward Brelyn. "There's a pavilion set up outside the fence line." With that he turned away and resumed giving instructions to the line of refugees.

Livia turned to Azer. "Let's pull the wagon out of line."

Azer nodded and turned to his fellows.

The wagon's owner was annoyed. He insisted on getting his share of the packages being handed out to the refugees. Though Livia did not like taking more time than necessary to get aid for the wounded soldier, she knew it wasn't fair to press too hard on the man, so she and the nomads also collected the small packages when their turn came. She tossed her package in beside the wounded man and helped turn the cart onto the northeast road. Other than the line of people getting water from the well, this road was empty of traffic. Livia and the nomads helped push the cart through the crowd, then hit open road and were able to move faster. She saw the pavilion the soldier had mentioned about two hundred paces beyond the edge of the hamlet.

As she trudged alongside the cart, Livia studied the mass of people inside the fences. She shook her head to see such a mess, but was grateful it wasn't winter or raining. It was a logistical nightmare. She wondered how long it would take before disease started spreading like wildfire through the camp. The nearest city of any size was Brelyn, and she knew it couldn't cope with so many people and would resist any attempt to send the refugees there. She could only hope whoever was in charge here had the foresight to press for more supplies from the lords in the vicinity.

They were drawing close to the pavilion when she saw an unusual sight. A tiny carriage drawn by a dappled gray pony was making its way slowly down the sloping road in front of them. A man sat on the driving board and a woman lay atop the baggage on the carriage's roof. Carriages were rare, typically only used by the nobility in large cities. This one was smaller than any she had previously seen, and was painted in pastel colors, making it seem as if it were part of a circus troupe. This road wasn't as wide as the river road, so Livia indicated to the driver that he should ease off to the edge. The pavilion stood to the left of the road and not much farther, so it made sense to give way to the carriage.

The man driving the carriage nodded his thanks and glanced into the wagon as they began to pass each other. He did a double-take and looked shocked, then pulled the pony to a stop. "He's alive! I don't believe it!" He jumped down from the driving board and walked to the cart, which had also stopped.

"You know this man?" Livia asked. She saw that the carriage driver was young, probably not far off from his coming-of-age day. He had deep blue eyes and mussy brown hair and had the fitness of a seasoned soldier, though she saw no weapons on him. Then she looked at the woman on the carriage roof and caught her breath. It was the loveliest woman she had ever seen, with long raven tresses, high cheekbones, and a wide, expressive mouth. The woman smiled down at her, and she felt goosebumps rise on her arms.

"He's a knight," the young man said, peering over the rim of the cart to study the wounded man. "I saw the battle where he was hurt. Didn't think he could survive. He took on an entire band of marauders almost singlehanded."

"You only watched?" Livia asked, reluctantly pulling her gaze away from the astonishing woman.

"I wasn't in a position to help. I was tied up, a prisoner of those marauders." He nodded down at the man. "His fight gave me the chance I needed to escape."

Livia's mind was in a turmoil. Until this moment, she had intended to turn the wounded knight over to the healers, then find the lord in charge of the refugees and learn how she could help. Now she found herself wanting to know more about these newcomers, especially the woman. Each time she caught a glimpse of her another little shock ran through her body. She had never reacted that way to a woman before, and her feelings confused her. "I…I still don't understand. Are you his friend?"

"I owe him my life, I suppose, but I couldn't say we know each other well. I saw him once at my father's keep, and then at the fight where I made my escape. Forgive my manners, I should introduce us.

I am Sir Villem Tathis, from Iskimir." He pointed up at the woman on the roof. "She's Dinara, originally from Ulfoss."

Livia nodded to both of them. "You may call me Livia, and these are my companions, merchants from the Arid Lands far to the south."

The nomads each gave their name, touching a hand to their foreheads and bowing slightly. Livia saw Azer's questioning glance; clearly he wanted to let the young couple know they were addressing a princess. Livia gave a small shake of her head. She didn't want the friendliness of the pair to turn into the usual formality that accompanied royal titles. She noticed Sir Villem studying her clothing.

"Forgive my appearance," she said. "I haven't had a change of clothes in a fortnight, not since we fled from Tolgaria."

"Not at all," Villem said. "I was in much worse shape myself recently until I lucked into a bath."

The wagon driver cleared his throat impatiently. Livia gave him a tight-lipped smile and turned back to the knight. "We're bringing the knight to this pavilion. It was very nice to meet you, Sir Villem."

"It was our pleasure," Villem said. "Perhaps we shall meet again, soon I hope." He had a wry, dimpled smile.

Livia nodded and gave a final glance at Dinara before turning back to the wagon to lead it on toward the pavilion.

Azer leaned toward her. "I think that young man was smitten with you, lady."

Livia coughed several times into a fist. "Don't be silly," she finally managed to say. Young men never paid attention to her, except for the young nobles hoping for the prestige that went along with her title. She was well aware that her crooked teeth and mousy hair, even with its unusual silver coloring, made her more homely than most women her age. If the young knight had reacted unusually toward her, she hadn't noticed, her attention drawn to his traveling companion. All she could think to say was, "He's much too young."

Azer gave her a sly smile. "He's a good-looking boy. But forgive me, lady; perhaps a simple knight is not highborn enough for a princess."

Livia rolled her eyes. "Let's get him down from the wagon and inside. The poor wagon master has things to do."

The wounded knight groaned as they carefully lifted him from the wagon and carried him into the pavilion. Given everything else Livia had seen since arriving at the refugee camp, she expected to find more chaos here, so she was surprised to find orderly rows of blankets laid out, most with a patient being attended by what she supposed must be healers. Livia knew from her studies with Xax that the healers of the realm relied upon a mixture of knowledge garnered from the wizards, the elves, and the dwarves when they practiced their art. There was no magic involved, just ages of experience and experimentation in herbology, minor surgery, and other pragmatic solutions, from stitching to cleansing. With only two known wizards remaining and the elves and dwarves being so insular, there were few masters of the craft among men. And there were many charlatans.

As the nomads laid the knight on a blanket, Livia studied the healers and was relieved to see they seemed competent. At least one thing was working well for the refugees. A short man in brown robes approached.

"Is he your man?" he asked, indicating the injured knight.

"No," Livia said, "merely someone we came across during our journey. His head is injured from a battle."

"You were kind to bring him. Worry not, we'll take good care of him."

Livia made introductions, and the man told them his name was Keenan.

"Has disease struck the camp yet?" Livia asked.

"We've been fortunate so far," Keenan said, "but with conditions what they are, it is only a matter of time."

Livia nodded, thanked Keenan, and they began the walk back toward the hamlet. The line for the well only seemed to have grown longer, and Livia wondered if there were no other sources of water. The river wasn't far, so why were they not exploiting it to make water more readily available? She knocked on the door of the hut that the soldier had indicated belonged to Lord Sewell. There was no response. Livia stopped a soldier who was passing by.

"My pardon, but do you know where I may find Lord Sewell?"

The soldier looked impatient and flung an arm out toward the camp. "If he's not here, he's most likely on the plateau."

Livia examined the camp and saw no sign of a plateau. "Where?"

"Just go that way and you'll find it."

Weariness stole over Livia as she watched the tens of thousands of people in the camp. Did she really want to wade through all of that right now? What she really wanted was to find a place to sleep for a week. Her feet ached and were covered with popped blisters. Her knees and back hurt as well. When she turned to speak to Azer, a familiar splash of color caught her eye, and she saw the small carriage drawn up near another of the hamlet's houses. She latched onto the excuse to avoid wading through the masses of refugees and headed toward the carriage. A soldier stood guard outside the door of the hut.

"Greetings, soldier," Livia said. "May we enter?"

"No." The soldier looked over her dirty finery. "Milady."

"I'm looking for the couple who own this carriage."

The guard shrugged. "They'll be out soon."

"Why is this house off limits?"

"It's our gaol. Until we get a better one built."

Just as Livia was wondering why the couple would be in a gaol, the door opened and they exited.

Villem's dimpled smile creased his face when he saw her. "Livia! Fortune favors me this day."

Dinara stood silently behind Villem and smirked at him while rubbing a hand across some old scars on her neck. Livia longed to ask her how she got them. Instead, she studied Sir Villem. Could Azer truly be right? Was the boy taken with her? She thought it more likely that he was acting that way in order to poke fun at her plainness. Or perhaps he was so polite and eager with every woman he met?

"It's nice to see you both again," Livia said. "Why the gaol, may I ask?"

"A pair of scoundrels we encountered on the road yesterday," Villem said. "Tried to murder me in my sleep."

"That's..." Livia was at a loss for words. Murder was all but unheard of within the realm. It reminded her that the magic that had protected the lands for so long was gone. "That's horrible."

"Aye," Villem said. "I think it will happen more often now that all the undesirables can return. It will be a flood, I believe."

Her brother's army marching from East Gate seemed bad enough, but it had never even entered Livia's mind that a horde of other vengeance seekers would pour into the realm. "Life will never be the same," she murmured, to herself more than Villem.

"Were you visiting the gaol?" Villem asked.

Livia felt her cheeks flush. "No, I...I saw the carriage and wondered if you were staying in the town. We hadn't decided what to do ourselves."

Several barks came from the carriage.

"It's my dog," Villem explained. "She doesn't like being cooped up in there. Um, we were just about to discuss what to do next. We had thought to remain here until we saw how bad it was. I suppose it's up to Dinara. I had thought maybe to head for Iskimir."

"That's on the southwest road, isn't it?" Livia asked.

Villem nodded. "No more than three or four days."

Dinara spoke for the first time. "May I ask you something, Livia?"

Livia felt a tiny thrill when she said her name. I'm acting like a silly little girl, she thought, gazing into Dinara's brown eyes. "Of...of course," she stammered.

"How does a woman come to travel alone with an escort of foreign merchants?"

Livia was perplexed by the question. "Why do you ask?"

Dinara flicked her eyes off into the distance before returning them to Livia. "I've recently found myself a lone woman without family in a strange land. I've been wondering what such a woman can do to make a life. Villem said there will be many like me now, with all the refugees."

"I hadn't thought about it," Livia said. She looked toward the refugee camp and understood that Villem was surely correct. What had once been almost unheard of would suddenly be quite common with many orphan girls and widows seeking some means of living their lives. "In the past a woman who found herself alone would seek a husband."

Dinara made a sour face. "That's what Villem said as well."

"Trust me," Livia said, "you would have no trouble finding a husband. You could have your pick of men."

Dinara looked away and rubbed harder at the scars on her neck. The dog in the carriage began barking again.

"I think we'll find a place to camp for the night," Villem said. "Would you join us?"

"We will, thank you."

"I dislike the idea of being herded into that field," Villem said. "Not sure there's much choice, though, unless we wish to travel some distance away from here. The guards told us they promised the villagers to keep everyone on that side of the road to prevent them from destroying all their lands."

Livia studied the mass of humanity sharing the pastures on the far side of the road. "You're right, it won't be pleasant. But I'm too exhausted to travel farther today."

It took more than an hour to force their way through the crowd to find a place to park the carriage. More than once men tried to pick a fight when they saw the dark skin of the tribesmen, but Sir Villem made them back down, or in some cases the presence of the two women calmed the tensions. When they settled on a place to camp, Livia dropped her bag and collapsed on top of it.

"Lady," Azer said. "I'll take Fuad and Babak and go for water."

Livia looked up at the kind nomad and felt her eyes fill with water. These men showed so much kindness and she wasn't sure why she deserved it. "You must be exhausted, Azer. You should rest."

Azer looked away, though a small smile creased his face. "I am well, lady. We need the water."

"Be careful," Livia said. "When people are miserable, they find ways to take it out on others."

Azer flipped the hood of his robe over his head. "We shall keep our heads down." He nodded to his men and they huddled close together and shuffled off toward the distant well.

The three remaining nomads set about making camp. Sir Villem opened the door of the carriage and a dark form barked and leaped into his arms, tail wagging frantically. Dinara laughed and scratched the dog behind the ears as it licked Villem's face.

"Who's this?" Livia asked, grinning.

Villem set the dog on the ground, and it approached Livia and began sniffing the fingers she held out. "I call her Duchess. She has saved my life more than once."

The dog was getting old, Livia saw. It was black but liberally streaked with gray. A livid scar ran along one flank. "Duchess? Don't let any nobles hear you calling your dog that." She said it with a laugh, but she knew some nobles would indeed take offense.

"She's worthy of the name," Villem said.

Duchess licked her hand and she patted the dog's neck. When she looked up, she realized a lot of people were watching the new arrivals. There was no place to find privacy in the crowded pasture, and more and more refugees were pushing in every moment. Livia sighed. There would surely be trouble here. More soldiers were needed to keep the peace. Conditions were going to get much worse before they got better.

Livia stood up and tried to see what the soldier had called a plateau. She saw that the back fence of the pasture abutted a small rise of perhaps five paces before it levelled off. It wasn't what she would have called a plateau, but she supposed it could be viewed that way. A miniature plateau. She wondered what Lord Sewell would be doing up there. So far there were no refugees there that she could see. Evening was approaching, and she was too tired to push her way through the crowds to search out Lord Sewell, so she decided that was a task for tomorrow. For tonight, she would help settle into camp and try to get to know these interesting new friends better.

31
IMRIC

Breakfast was a grim affair, and much earlier than usual, Imric having been shaken awake long before sunrise. His uncle was absent at the meal, as was his cousin Istvan, and no one spoke as they ate. Soot adamantly refused to join them for meals and took them in her room instead. Imric had noticed that his brother Balmar had grown more sullen over the past week, and this morning he stared into his porridge without eating. Imric shuffled himself closer and nudged Balmar in the arm.

"Are you well, Brother?" he whispered.

Balmar lifted his head enough to give Imric a miserable glance before letting it hang again. "Don't want to be king," he murmured.

Imric glanced at Xax, who seemed lost in thought. A nervous tension ran through Imric's body, and he wondered if it was only the upcoming battle or if his cousin Istvan's warning was part of it.

As the meal drew to a close, Steward Yarus entered the room, clapped his hands, and ushered the rest of the regent's family out of the room before approaching the main table. "Your majesty, a great event is upon us. Allow me to lead you to the balcony where you may watch the battle."

When they all stood up, the steward shook his head at Xax and

Imric. "My apologies. The regent asked that you remain in your rooms for now. He will see you shortly." He beckoned to a pair of guardsmen, who stepped forward and indicated that the pair should follow them. Imric wanted to protest, but Xax gave him a hand signal to remain calm. When they reached their chambers, the wizard asked the guards if they could wait together in one room. The guards apparently had not been given explicit instructions and seemed confused for a moment, but relented and left them in Imric's room.

"This is for the best, I think," Xax said.

"Why wouldn't he send us with Balmar?" Imric asked. "This doesn't feel right."

"I agree. And I think it's time we made our escape. Did your friend gather the bundles as I asked?"

"Her name is Maisie," Imric said, feeling irritated that the wizard was willing to put his friend in danger but not willing to learn her name. "She has everything stashed beneath one of the boats."

"Good. If you need anything here, gather it quickly and let's go get Soot."

"What about Balmar? We can't leave him here."

The wizard's eyes widened. "We certainly can't kidnap the king. We wouldn't get in much trouble if we were caught fleeing ourselves, but if we took the king, Erol would have us executed."

"Uncle is going to murder Balmar," Imric said. "He's my brother. I can't desert him."

Xax put his hands on his hips. "And just how do you expect to be able to bring him with us? You'll stroll onto his balcony and the guards and the steward will simply let the two of you leave?"

"I don't know. But I'll think of something. I have to try."

Xax sighed and shook his head in defeat. "It's going to take me a long while to make my way through your miserable tunnels. Go take a look if you must, but be honest with yourself. If it's impossible to get Balmar out of there, as I expect, at least allow me to save you."

Imric was relieved Xax was giving him a chance, so he nodded and helped the wizard open the secret door in the wardrobe. They each took a lantern before climbing into the tunnel.

"Remind me how to get there," the wizard said.

Imric had taken him through the tunnels two nights ago, showing him how to reach the room with the boats. He went over the route in a hurried whisper, and they went to get Soot. Imric had visited her via the tunnels a couple of times before, so they didn't startle her, though she was surprised to see the wizard clamber out of her wardrobe.

"Come, child," Xax said as he brushed dust from his knees. "We must hurry."

She didn't argue. Imric had told her a quick escape might become necessary. She grabbed the bread from her breakfast tray and followed the pair back into the tunnel. When they came to the first fork, Imric told her what he needed to do and said he'd join them as soon as he could, then he took the way that led to the climb up to the next floor.

It took more than half an hour for Imric to make his way upward to the nearest exit that would take him close to the throne room. When the bookcase slid aside, a maid yelped and dropped the duster she had been using. She held her hands out in front of her pale face, and Imric felt bad for frightening her.

"It's just me, Prince Imric," he said.

"M-m-m-milord," she stuttered. "I thought you were a haunt. F-forgive me, milord!" She was out the door before he could apologize.

He set down the lamp, headed for the throne room, and when he came to the archway leading inside, he hesitated and snuck a peek. Beyond the two tall chairs that served as makeshift thrones, Balmar stood on the balcony that overlooked the northern side of the city. No one was with him. In fact, other than two guardsmen inside the throne room, they were all alone. Luck is with me, Imric thought.

He hurried across the room to join Balmar on the balcony. Though he wanted to get his brother out of there in a hurry, he was curious how the battle was going, so the first thing he did was look out at the breathtaking scene before him. He had seen the gorgeous view across the room looking out over the Sea of Alia, but this panorama was no less spectacular. The castle was high up on its hill above the city, so the buildings and streets far below looked like fabulous toys. Few people moved about, and he saw why—most were lining the city walls, trying to catch a view of the battle that would decide their fate. Imric couldn't imagine that they could actually see much from down there. After all, he could barely see details of the armies even from his high perch. Lining the horizon were the imposing Hellisgaard Mountains. Below them at the very edge of his vision, he saw movement, but it was too far away to make out details. He looked over at his brother and noticed he was not even trying to watch the battle. He was staring down at the city, a deep scowl on his face.

"Balmar," Imric said. "Come with me."

Balmar seemed to snap out of a daze as he looked at Imric. "Why?"

"Please, Brother. We're in danger. Follow me and we'll be safe."

"Don't want to be king anymore," Balmar said.

"You won't if you come with me. We'll go find Livia."

Balmar's face brightened at that. He nodded. "Find our sister."

Imric held out a hand and Balmar took it. Imric turned to lead him to the escape tunnel, then stopped short as several figures entered the throne room. The first was Steward Yarus. He was followed by Uncle Erol, Cousin Istvan, and two more guards.

"You were supposed to be in your room, Imric," Erol said. "Why are you here?"

"We were watching the battle, Uncle," Imric said. "I thought you were there."

"I wish I could be there," Erol said. "The fate of the realm rests on today's events, but the fate of my family rests on what happens here. Lord Mitinya has long claimed to be the best general we have, so he will lead our troops to victory."

"Victory is so certain?"

Erol nodded. "Not only do we outnumber Darus's men, we have a secret weapon, one that will leach the courage from their hearts and the strength from their arms. Where were you taking the king?"

Imric glanced up at his brother. "We couldn't see the battle from here. I thought we might find a better view from one of the towers."

"Not likely," Erol said. "Yarus can bring some spyglasses that can help us with the view."

"Certainly, milord," Steward Yarus said, and headed out the archway.

Regent Erol waited for the steward to depart before flicking a sign to his guards. "Now!"

"Father," Istvan said, his eyes wide and sweat trickling down his face. "Let me take Cousin Imric back to his room."

"Too late for that, Son. Leave the room, now!"

"No, Father! I don't want this!"

"It's not your choice to make," Erol said. He pointed to the nearest guard. "You! Take him out of here."

The guard headed toward Istvan, who began backpedaling to keep away. Erol ignored them and looked at the other guards.

"Crossbows," he commanded, and the guards snapped to the ready.

"W-what is this, Uncle?" Imric asked.

Erol stalked toward the two young men. "I loved my brother, but he's gone, and none of his children are fit to be king. Without a strong leader, the realm will have civil war. I am meant to rule, and my son after me."

"You can't mean to murder your own kin," Imric said. He tried to estimate his chances of fleeing. He hated the thought of leaving his brother behind. He saw three guards pointing cocked crossbows at him, and another trying to chase down his cousin. A strong arm pressed into his chest, and Balmar pushed himself in front of Imric.

"I am king," Balmar said and pointed at the guards. "Put down the bows."

The guards hesitated, half lowering the crossbows.

"Balmar, run!" Imric yelled, and took off to the right, trying to burst past Erol.

Erol snatched a war hammer from the wall and lunged toward Imric. Imric thought he would make it past, but suddenly he tripped and sprawled on the carpet. He looked around in time to see Erol swing again. In a panic, Imric scrabbled forward on his hands and knees.

The hammer crashed down onto Imric's left foot with a sickening crunching sound. He screamed as his world exploded with excruciating pain. Suddenly Balmar was there, scooping Imric up in his powerful arms.

"Don't hurt my brother!" Balmar bellowed as he rushed toward the archway.

"Shoot! Now!" Erol screamed.

Through the white-hot wall of pain, Imric still felt the thudding impact of two crossbow bolts slamming into Balmar's back. His brother staggered forward and somehow found the strength to keep going, though he swerved away from the archway.

Screams came from all around, but Imric could make no sense of them through his pain and terror. Was that Istvan? His uncle? Another bolt struck Balmar and he nearly fell. Despite the overwhelming pain, Imric felt the wetness of tears dripping from Balmar's face. His brother groaned loudly, staggered on two more paces, and tossed Imric over the balcony.

The pain that had seemed like Imric's entire world suddenly gave way to sickening vertigo. He was falling, plunging downward, and his stomach twisted in knots. He wanted to scream but his throat seized up. Then he struck something hard, and it gave way before him. Cold enveloped him. *Am I dead?* Yet he still felt pain radiating from his foot. He tried to breathe and sucked in ice cold water. He panicked and began thrashing his arms about. *I'm underwater*, he realized. He couldn't breathe. Water filled his lungs. *This is it*, he thought. *The end.*

Something seized his arm and yanked him upward. He couldn't think through all the pain and fear. Then the top half of his body was lying over the side of a boat and he was coughing out an endless stream of water. Someone was pounding on his back.

He kept coughing out water, and someone kept repeating over and over that they couldn't believe it, they couldn't believe it. It sounded like Soot, though Imric told himself he was hallucinating. A strong arm pulled him fully into the boat onto a blanket, and Soot was there, pulling the blanket around his shoulders.

"I can't believe he survived that fall," Soot said.

Imric felt consciousness slipping away, but Xax's voice boomed out, "He needs help, but right now I have to row. We have to get away from here."

Then everything went black.

32
KATHKALAN

Kathkalan left his horse behind in the castle, not wanting to chance losing her in the coming battle. In his countless years, he had never fought in a battle with men, and he was not happy to start now, but a promise was a promise. Men would pose little danger to him, he knew, though there was always the chance of an ill-fated arrow striking through the eye holes of his helm. He reminded himself to keep his head down. The weapons of men could not pierce his armor.

And he had the crystal with the remnants of the great magic. His secret weapon. He was well aware that the soldiers with whom he marched forth from the city were inexperienced, while their opponents were veterans. In a normal battle that experience would count far more than numbers. But he had the crystal shard.

In the early morning darkness, the soldiers marched in separate columns, each for their separate lord, which Kathkalan felt was stupid. The army should work together as one, not fight as distinct units.

Kathkalan walked alone, and he hurried to catch up with Lord Urith Mitinya, who was in command of the field. He had no real desire to speak with the man, but he felt duty-bound to point out a glaring mistake the man was making.

"Mitinya," he said as he drew near.

The lord glared at him as he continued walking, disliking the elf for not treating him with the respect he felt he deserved. But Regent Erol had made clear that the elf was key to his battle plan, so he suffered his presence. "What do you want?"

"Your foes have almost no horsemen. It's their great weakness. You have them, but they are scattered throughout your units."

"They are knights," Lord Mitinya said as if speaking the obvious to a child. "They belong to their lords and they fight for them."

"They would serve you far better as a united cavalry. Group them together and swing them around to the rear of the enemy at the right time. They can wreak havoc on the archers, and eventually strike the main force in the flank or rear. Even against veterans it could be enough to turn the battle your way."

"The lords would never allow it. Nor would the knights. Our numbers will tell in this fight."

Kathkalan saw little point in continuing to argue with this man who had no experience in a pitched battle, but he had little else to do at the moment. "So, no strategy other than to march right into them. The sun will glare into your men's eyes as soon as it tops the mountains."

"Leave be, elf," Mitinya growled. "The regent ordered me to suffer your presence, but I don't need to listen to you yap."

Kathkalan grimaced and took a different angle of march so that he drew away from the commander. He almost wished he could allow the man to suffer the defeat he so clearly wanted.

Ahead, lords were beginning to draw their men up into battle formation. Kathkalan could see the enemy now, drawn up in clean ranks on a slight rise three hundred paces ahead. The first light of the sun broke over the mountains and set the enemy's spear tips to glittering.

The enemy force looked tiny compared to the men of the Known Lands. Less than three thousand facing off against seven. But they were seven thousand raw men with the rising sun shining in their eyes and fear lurking in their hearts. Without the crystal fragment, Kathkalan thought the battle would be a disaster. As it was, he would need to force himself to the forefront of the melee in order to lend the shard's magic to his side. It would be enough, or it wouldn't. Either way, Kathkalan had no intention of dying this day.

He made his way to the far-left side of the army. The center might be more logical, but that is where Lord Mitinya would fight, and Kathkalan hoped the man might be humbled early. I'll turn the enemy's right flank, he thought, and keep my shield toward their archers.

The small East Gate army stood silent and still, ready to form their shield wall when the time came. Mitinya apparently wanted to wait for the sun to blaze fully into his troops' eyes before he sounded the call to advance. There were enough men in the army that they could have been spread further to threaten to envelop the flanks of the enemy, but Mitinya kept his lines compact.

Kathkalan sought out the lord in command of the leftmost unit of soldiers, a group of about seventy men, most of them with spears and shields, though a few had crossbows. He saw three knights on horseback, one of them the lord in charge of the group. "You! Man!" Kathkalan called out as he drew near.

The lord stared down at him from atop his steed but said nothing.

Kathkalan tugged the chain holding the crystal shard out from beneath his scale hauberk and held it forth to gleam in the sunlight. "Do you feel this?" Of course, Kathkalan knew he could. The harder a man's heart pounded, the more effective the magic was, and no man would have a steady heart before a battle.

"Aye, I feel it." The man held his horse tight to keep it steady. "I heard about it, but I didn't truly believe until now. I'm glad you're on this flank."

Kathkalan held the crystal higher. "This can win this fight for us. Follow my lead and I'll remain with you, else I'll move on to find someone willing to listen."

"What do you want me to do?" the lord asked.

"Your infantry will march with me to strike at the end of their line and turn it. I'd like you and your two horsemen to linger just behind us. Convince that lord over there to lend you his knights as well, if you can. The only danger we have right now are their archers. They have the high ground and can hit us from the side as we sweep around their shield wall. I'd like your horsemen to go after their archers. Can you do that?"

"The men expect me to lead them."

"That's for me to do now, and I have this." He dangled the shard once more. "Do you want to win this battle?"

The lord's helm tilted his assent.

Kathkalan said, "Good" at the very moment the horns blared from the center. A great shout went up from the army, and the enemy hefted their shields and firmed up their line. Kathkalan walked to stand in front of the line of soldiers and turned to face them. He held up the crystal shard. The eyes of every soldier nearby turned to him.

"Do you see this?" he shouted. "I know you feel it!" He dropped the shard back beneath his hauberk, then drew his black longsword and held it high. "Follow me!"

With another shout, the line moved forward, and Kathkalan held his shield high, lowered his helm, and stalked forward. He looked to his right to see the entire long battle line moving forward. Arrows and quarrels began to hiss in both directions, a few finding their mark. A crossbow bolt caromed off Kathkalan's shield and clanged off the helm of the man next to him. Hearts pounded harder, and the magic surged. Kathkalan was calm, but even he felt it—strength and courage flowed through him. They were close enough to the enemy now that Kathkalan saw their grim, determined faces turn pale as the stomach-churning fear and weakness from the magic struck their line.

"Charge!" Kathkalan yelled, and ran forward at an angle to swerve around the end of the wavering shield wall. As veteran as the enemy troops were, they had never had to fight with the effects of the magic inflicted upon them. The nearest troops panicked and turned to flee.

Kathkalan caught up to his first man and hamstrung him from behind. Another man found the courage to stand his ground, shield up and spear wavering in front of him, eyes wide behind the holes in his helm. Kathkalan swatted aside the spear with his blade and kicked the shield, sending the man stumbling backward. He paused a moment to see that the entire line in this area had crumbled away like wheat chaff in a strong wind. Even better, six knights had burst around the flank and were charging into the ranks of archers.

Don't get too confident, Kathkalan thought. Things may be going badly down the line. He sliced the arm of another fleeing soldier, then turned to shout encouragement to the men around him. He meant to urge them to press forward along the flank of the enemy army and roll them up, but instead he caught sight of something that froze his tongue.

A dark speck moved through the sky, almost lazily, but Kathkalan knew what it was. It had to come now, of all times, he thought. The dragon.

The men around him had not noticed the new arrival. Kathkalan allowed them to press forward around him. He turned and pushed through the men behind until he broke free. Then he began to run. He felt no remorse at deserting these men; aiding them had been an expedience. On open ground, the dragon was unstoppable. Kathkalan had to get to the castle, where the beast was likely to settle once it tired of the slaughter.

The roar of battle beat upon his ears, and no one had yet noticed his departure. He saw a squire holding a spare horse and headed toward him. Before the boy could protest, he yanked the reins from him, leapt into the saddle, and kicked the horse to a gallop in the direction of the city.

He spared a glance at the dragon as it dived. The creature cared nothing for sides. It would devastate both armies. Kathkalan heard the first screams go up from the masses of soldiers as they noticed the dragon for the first time. The beast pulled out of its dive and soared over the ranks of soldiers, blasting a cloud of black acid as it flew.

Kathkalan turned away, his mouth grim, and kicked the horse again, though it needed no urging to run faster from the black death billowing in the sky behind it.

33
DARUS

Darus Kaldarion gazed over the dark ranks of his soldiers and smiled grimly. He could not believe his Uncle Erol had been stupid enough to sally forth from the city to face him on the field of battle. Had he remained behind his ramparts, Darus had no means of taking the city, and his men had not the patience for a protracted siege. The best he could have done was pillage the countryside and try to force more nobles to his cause. Darus knew he wasn't a bright man—not smart like his sister Livia—but he was wise enough to know he was unlikely to win a long war. He had much superior troops, but there were not so many of them, and attrition would tell in the end. So he smiled at his uncle's blunder.

The sun tipped the mountains behind him and glinted from spear tips and helms. He saw the greater numbers of Erol's forces, but it did not worry him. His only concern was his right flank. His left was planted firmly against rock outcroppings of the foothills, but the right was on a bare rise with no natural protection. He had placed his best troops there and prepared them for what was likely to come. They knew when to swing around to meet a flanking maneuver and they knew help would arrive, for Darus had laid a trap. He had little in the way of cavalry, but what he did have he planned to use. Twenty men on horses or ponies, led by Orderic and his crazy one-armed elf, lay hidden in a stand of trees out beyond his right wing. A boy had shimmied up a tree to yell down to Orderic when the time was right. When the enemy pressed hard upon the right flank and believed victory was imminent, Orderic's small band would take them in the rear. Inexperienced troops like his uncle's would almost surely break.

Darus could see it as clearly as if it were already happening in front of him. He would be king, as he was meant to be. As his father had failed to acknowledge. And the people would pay for the suffering Darus had endured. Not just the fear and weakness the magic of the Spire of Peace had sent churning through his innards, but the months of bloody beatings and worse before he finally proved himself to the vicious men of East Gate.

A horn sounded from Erol's lines, followed by several more, and his uncle's troops began their slow march forward. Darus's men were disciplined and would not move until the time was right to press an advantage. They set themselves in a solid shield wall and readied their spears. Behind them, farther up the rise, a line of archers and crossbowmen shuffled impatiently, waiting for the signal.

A roar went up from Erol's men, while Darus's remained silent. The first clash of arms sounded from the right flank, though the roar of battle quickly spread along the entire line. Darus watched the center. His spearmen had honed their craft in countless battles against the barbarian tribes beyond the mountains. These men had better armor, but the barbarians were fiercer and more battle hardened. Darus knew his lines would hold easily, and if anyone panicked, it would be the Greatlanders. Not his men. He only wished he had more horses, so he could run down the enemy more easily once the rout started.

Arrows and bolts took up their deadly hissing, followed by the thump and crack as they slammed into shields and skidded off helms.

Cries of panic came from the right. Too soon, Darus thought. It's far too soon for Orderic to have had time to strike.

Darus vaulted onto his pony and turned it along the ranks of archers to see what was happening to his right. He signaled to Captain Guiron to bring his small troop of reserves. Something wasn't right. He saw his own veterans throwing down their arms and fleeing in terror. He saw men he had campaigned with for years running as if they were unblooded youths. This cannot be happening, he thought.

He twisted in the saddle to shout at Guiron, sword pointed to the right flank. "At the run! Now! Hold the flank or I'll skin you alive!"

Darus planned to join them, but he first glanced at his center and left to ensure the panic was not spreading. Pride filled his breast as he saw those ranks scything down enemy troops like ripe grain. That's how the battle was meant to go.

What in the name of Aronis is that? Darus saw an ink black stain in the sky growing quickly larger. He might have thought it an eagle if not for its size, and suddenly he knew, and his heart fell. It was the dragon, and Darus felt all hopes of kingship fading away. It had to come now. The worst possible moment. He gave one last, sad look over his troops, then turned his pony through the line of archers and kicked his steed into a gallop. Find Orderic, he thought. Get as many troops out alive as possible.

"Back to East Gate, you bloody fools!" he shouted. "Retreat!"

He didn't pause to see how his men would react, nor did he watch the dragon. Eyes fixed straight ahead, he galloped as if demons were at his back. The wind of the dragon's first pass slapped at him, and he heard the blast of its deadly breath. He had heard enough of this dragon to know it was not a flame drake. It was worse. If he could not outrun the clouds of acid, he would die screaming and clawing at his eyes and throat.

He looked for horsemen. Had Orderic charged? No, he saw only a pair of enemy knights, now turning their mounts to escape the dragon. Orderic must still be in the grove. Darus plowed by the knights and aimed for the trees. Only a hundred paces away, but it felt much farther. Screams rose up behind him, and Darus's back tingled as he imagined the acid washing over him. He would never make it. No, he thought, I'm meant to be king; this cannot be the way I end. But as fresh screams rose up not far behind him, the thought returned: I'll never make it. And then the trees were growing larger, and he risked a glance over his shoulder. He saw devastation. Black clouds roiling across the ground, hundreds of bodies flopping and writhing in agony. The dragon lazily swooping by in another pass, spitting out another dark cloud as it went. But Darus breathed a sigh of relief, for the dark cloud had not reached him yet.

He plunged into the tree line and began to shout for Orderic. No one was there. He passed through the grove and saw his men, their mounts fleeing north toward home. Darus nodded to himself. Perhaps he could salvage something from this after all. Let the dragon destroy Uncle Erol's army. Let it destroy Valandiria. If enough of Darus's troops escaped, he might yet be king.

34

KATHKALAN

Kathkalan glared up at the guard atop the wall. "I repeat, open the gate! You want that dragon dead? I'm the only one who can do it."

Another guard, eyes wide with fear, joined the first and pointed out toward the battlefield. "The dragon's there. You want to slay it, there you go."

"Your regent had an agreement with me. You must let me in!"

"Regent Erol told us nothing about you."

Kathkalan was at a loss. Perhaps his one chance to get close to the beast where it was very likely to land, and it was going to be ruined by the idiocy of men.

"Open the gate!" one of the guards shouted.

Kathkalan looked up, happy that the man had finally seen sense, until he noticed the guard was pointing toward the battle, not looking down at him. He twisted in the saddle and saw the leading pack of fleeing soldiers—those who had mounts—had caught up to him. The gate began to creak open. Kathkalan planted his horse in front of it to ensure he would be the first through. Three men on horses were the first to arrive behind the elf. He didn't look around at them, but he couldn't help but overhearing.

"Do you think it wise to enter the city?" one of the knights panted. "The dragon will surely come here next."

"I'm going to find the regent and get him to safety," said another knight.

"Well, I'm with Jon," said the third. "You go on in there. I'm heading west."

With that, one of the men kicked his horse into action, and the second man followed, leaving the last to curse the both of them.

The gate opened enough to allow Kathkalan to enter, and he urged his horse to a gallop. The cobbled streets were nearly deserted. The few men he did see were scurrying about like rats on a sinking ship. Kathkalan worried he would run into a stubborn gate guard when he reached the castle, so he was relieved to find the gate already open when he arrived. He cantered to the stable, dropped from the horse, and tossed the reins to a wide-eyed stable boy, then took off running toward the entrance door.

He ran through the castle, ignoring the shouts of surprised stewards and servants. Running up several sets of stairs, he was grateful again for the energy the magic of the crystal lent his legs. His lungs heaved by the time he burst onto the roof. Seeing no sign of the dragon yet, he paused to catch his breath. Swiping an arm across his sweaty forehead, he stared toward the scene of the battle but saw no sign of the dragon other than wisps of rapidly dissipating black clouds.

Kathkalan walked over to the well and looked down to see that the carpenters had done as he had asked—the wooden platform was complete. Large iron spikes jutted from the roof along two sides, allowing a clear path that ran directly over the well. Kathkalan moved to the first sheep pen and pulled away the loose boards that hid the sheep from sight, then went to the second pen and did the same. He felt like a silly youth, hoping against hope that his obvious, amateurish plan—never mind that it was the only one he could come up with—might actually work. He had a premonition that he would be standing on this rooftop looking stupid for the rest of the day.

A flash of movement hit his peripheral vision. The dragon flew by and spewed a cloud of acid into the city. Faintly he heard screams from far below. He had nothing to do but wait now. He pulled the black sword from its scabbard and sat on the edge of the well to watch and listen as the dragon destroyed the city.

Three towers jutted up above the castle roof, two of them about twenty paces higher and the other even taller, their conical roofs tiled in gray slate. Dragons liked to survey their work from the highest spot, so Kathkalan hoped it would be one of these towers.

Time passed and Kathkalan could only wait impatiently as the dragon rampaged throughout the city. He heard the distant crackle of burning acid, the pitiful screaming of men and animals, and the frightened bleating of the sheep. He caught only rare glimpses of the dragon, as it mostly flew low over the city it was destroying. One time he felt a shudder run through the stone of the roof. The dragon must have landed on the castle, somewhere below roof level. He gave thanks that the clouds of acid tended to fall rather than rise through the air. He fought the urge to get up and peer over the edge of the roof to see what the dragon was doing. Keep your patience, he thought. It will come or it won't.

The dragon screeched from far away, so he knew it had taken flight again. Kathkalan picked away drying blood that had spotted the scale armor of his right arm, then looked up again just in time to see the dragon loom large over the rooftop as it swooped in and landed with a crash on the tallest tower. With his spine tingling, Kathkalan leapt down to the wooden platform inside the well. He took up the rope that led to the door of the pen on the side where the dragon had landed. The sheep were bleating louder than ever in their panic. He jerked the rope hard enough to pull open the door to their pen and listened as the sheep poured out and stampeded around the well to run to the far side of the roof. He wondered if they would run right off the edge. Would their bleats, along with their brethren still in the other pen, be enough to draw the dragon? The beast should be hungry after its work, and dragons disliked the taste of men. Sheep were far more to their liking. *Come, beast! Come and feast!*

Another roar from the dragon made Kathkalan duck further to be sure he would not be seen. The arm holding his sword at the ready was taut, and the magic of the crystal shard poured more strength into him as his heart thundered in his chest. *How long must I wait?* Then he heard it—the swooping sound and thud of the dragon landing on the rooftop, followed by the scraping of its claws on the rough marble blocks.

Kathkalan had lived for so long he had lost track of the years ages ago. It had been long since he had felt a true threat to his life. It struck him that he could be drawing his final breaths; that he might actually die in the next few moments. He felt so alive, and though he desired to remain undetected, a laugh burst unbidden from his throat.

The great black head of the dragon burst into view over his head, the sinuous movement of its neck swinging it like a snake swimming in a swamp. One wing appeared, pulling the bulk of the beast's body over the well. It was so fast! Kathkalan feared the dragon would be across before he could strike, so he lunged before gathering all the power in his legs. His black sword pierced the dragon's belly, but the speed of the drake was such that it pulled away before the blade could bite deep. Blood from the wound pattered onto the platform next to Kathkalan and began hissing and smoking. And the dragon screamed its rage and pain. Kathkalan looked up to see the dragon rearing backward, its neck raised, its eyes blazing down at him. Never had Kathkalan felt his own death so near. Would it blast him with acid?

The neck plunged downward like an eagle diving for fish in a river. Kathkalan dove aside and the dragon's snout struck the platform where he had been standing a moment before. With a great cracking sound, the platform shattered, and Kathkalan felt himself falling. He let go of his sword and frantically reached for the ivy growing along the sides of the well. The vines burned his palms and tore away from the wall as he plummeted downward. His body twisted so that his arms could no longer use the ivy to slow his fall. He kicked out with his feet and one of them snagged a larger vine. It caught and swung Kathkalan's body into the side of the well so hard he felt ribs cracking just before his helm struck and all went black.

35
SOOT

Xax kept rowing frantically but wasn't making much headway against the choppy waves. The sleek boat had four banks of oars, but Soot was too small to be able to help, so she sat at the stern of the boat, alternately staring miserably at the pale form of Imric, bundled in a blanket near her feet, and watching over her shoulder for any sign of pursuit. The small mast had not been raised, and Soot had never been in a boat before.

"Xax, maybe we'd go faster if you got the sail up?"

"Soon," he replied. "It takes time, and I want to be out of view first."

"I'm worried about Imric. He needs help now."

"I know." It was turning into a hot day, and the wizard's brow was dripping with sweat. "If they catch up to us, they will kill him. Kill us all, actually."

Soot knew what she was about to say was unfair, but she couldn't help herself. "I thought you were a wizard. Can't you do anything?"

Xax's face turned even redder than from the exertion alone. "Magic isn't like in the tales. There are no magic wands. No fantastical spells to save the world. It's hard and it's weak. It has limited uses."

Soot stared down at Imric. "I'm just afraid for him is all," she whispered.

"Take the tiller back there. When you see the mouth of the river, steer us toward it. Once we catch the outflow, I can help Imric."

Soot looked around and found what must be the tiller. She wanted to say she didn't know how it worked, but it didn't look like it should be difficult to figure out. She turned the handle in one direction and watched how the boat veered slightly to one side. She looked past Xax and was pleased to see the mouth of the river in plain view about half a league away. "I see it."

The wizard nodded. "Perhaps it's my imagination, but I think I feel its pull. Anyhow, Imric can't wait any longer." He seated the oars and crawled forward to kneel next to the boy. He pulled aside the blanket and began lightly probing various parts of Imric's body.

"Is he all right?" Soot asked.

"I haven't checked everything yet. I'm worried about internal injuries. I don't know how he hit the water."

"Did you see his foot?"

The wizard nodded. "Just a glimpse. It's a mess, but it's not likely to kill him like other injuries could."

Soot adjusted the tiller slightly. "Please don't let him die." She looked away so Xax wouldn't see her eyes fill with tears.

After several more minutes of probing, Xax seemed to relax a bit. "I think he got lucky. Let's see the foot now." He carefully lifted Imric's leg and laid it across one of the benches. With the knife from his belt, he carefully cut away the boot.

The foot looked horrible to Soot. It was bent far out of shape and had swollen badly and turned different colors, some nearly black.

Xax tenderly placed his hands atop the foot and closed his eyes. He began murmuring to himself. This went on for a long time, and Soot saw no sign of magic. The mouth of the river drew near, and the boat picked up speed. Soot had to adjust the tiller more and more often to keep the boat steady. She became nervous that she would do something wrong, but she did not want to complain to the wizard and break his concentration. The boat gained more speed and seemed to get sucked into the river like it was being swallowed. When the boat steadied again in the middle of the river, Soot took several deep breaths and tried to relax.

"It's the best I could do," Xax said, suddenly looking sickly and exhausted. "I was never good with healing. I wish Zoya was still alive."

Soot looked at Imric's foot and saw that the swelling had gone down and the awful colors had nearly vanished. But the foot looked as deformed as it had before. "It doesn't look right at all."

"It never will, sadly. But I've relieved the pain and knitted the bones together. He'll live."

"He won't…" Soot had to pause to gasp in a deep breath. "He won't be able to walk right."

"Better to hobble than to crawl."

Soot let the tears flow freely now. Through the blur of tears, she saw the wizard stiffen and lurch upward to peer back toward the distant city.

"The dragon," he said. "It came."

Soot shook her head. She didn't want to think about anything else right now. Imric coughed, and when Soot rubbed her eyes clear, she saw his eyes were open. She let go of the tiller and dropped down to cradle his head. "Imric!"

"I'm…alive?" he croaked.

The wizard dropped heavily onto the bench next to him. "Lucky for you we had taken the boat out already, or we'd never have reached you in time."

Tears filled Imric's eyes. "Balmar," he said in a voice that was nearly a groan.

"What happened?" Soot asked.

"He's dead. He saved me."

"Your uncle?"

Imric nodded. "I still can't believe it. He…" Imric dug his elbows into the bottom of the boat to push himself up slightly as he tried to see his foot. "My foot!"

Xax shook his head. "I'm sorry. It was the best I could do."

Imric stared at his foot for a long time. "You should have let me drown," he whispered at last.

36
DINARA

Tempers were flaring throughout the refugee camp by nightfall, and it was clear to Dinara that more space was needed soon. The newly-arrived folks had been pushed into a crowded corner of the pasture, but there simply was not enough room. It was too crowded even to put up the small pavilion from the carriage. The stench of the nearby latrines did not help the situation. Fights broke out a number of times and had to be quelled by guards. One time the soldiers had to spear a man whose rage at the encroachment of the newcomers grew too great. A nervous tension simmered as people laid out their blankets in crowded rows to try to get some sleep for the night.

Dinara sat with her back against a carriage wheel, watching her newfound friends. Friends. That was a word she had not used much in her life. Certainly not in the past few years at East Gate among the rough soldiers. What was the young Sir Villem to her? Was he a friend? She knew he was attracted to her, yet he seemed to accept the fact that she could not return the attraction, and in her experience few men were able to do that. As far as she could tell, he seemed to genuinely wish to help her. Then again, he seemed smitten with Livia, the intriguing woman with road-worn but rich-looking clothes, who surrounded herself with a bodyguard of foreigners.

Who was this woman? Dinara did not believe she was a tradeswoman. She had the bearing of someone used to deference from those around her, even if she seemed to genuinely care about the misfortunes of the refugees. And the way Livia stared at her. Dinara had spent her life with men staring at her good looks, and women resenting her for them, so she recognized the way Livia looked at her. But there was a confusion there as well, as if Livia had never known a woman could be attracted to another.

Dinara could not deny her own attraction to the young woman. She was not a beauty, but then Willa had been anything but pretty. Livia had something in the eyes. An intensity…an intelligence that Dinara was not used to seeing in people. She needed a chance to get to know her better, but there had been no opportunity so far.

Livia sat huddled in a blanket near the six nomads, talking softly with the leader Azer. Dinara could not hear what they were saying, but she heard the tone of sadness in their voices.

Villem sat apart, scratching Duchess behind the ears. He clearly wished to honor the privacy of the conversation going on. Dinara thought she might have hurt his feelings when she moved over to the carriage wheel to have time to herself to gather her thoughts. She needed the time, though.

What do I want? Villem seemed to think going to Iskimir and helping her find a new life there was the best option, though he harbored deep resentment of his family. She enjoyed Villem's company, but did she really want to throw herself on the good will of his father? Having lived with nothing but cold her whole life, a part of her was curious to head farther south and see what that part of the realm was like. But women did not simply travel alone through the lands. And then there was Livia. Would she still be intrigued by this woman if she got to know her better?

Dinara did not know the answers to her questions, and she was not sure she would get answers anytime soon. She did not like the idea of passively going along whatever route seemed easiest, like a stick pulled along by river rapids. She wanted to choose her own path, yet each path she looked at seemed murky. She let her mind drift briefly to Willa, wondering how she was doing, but she dismissed the thoughts quickly. That part of her life was over. She rubbed at the scars on her neck from years of wearing Willa's collar. She had done what she had to do to survive, and part of her had even enjoyed certain moments, but now she felt relief at putting that in the past, even if the unknown was frightening. She sighed and got up to return to her blanket, laid out near Villem. Duchess panted happily at her, and she patted the dog's haunch. Villem gave her a questioning look.

"We can't stay here," she said. "It's bad now and will only get worse."

He nodded. "Should we continue to Iskimir tomorrow?"

She stared down at her travel-worn boots. "I…I'm not sure. It's something to consider, but the way you speak about your mother and father, is it really a good idea?"

Villem pulled a wry face. "Iskimir's the only place I've ever really known. It's hard to make choices when you know so little about everything else."

"What do you think about going south? Just to see, I mean. It's warm there, and most of the danger seems to be here in the north."

Villem peered up into the starry sky, where all three moons were making the night bright. "It's hard without coin. We have next to nothing. If we pass through Iskimir, I may be able to convince my father to give me some. He might be happy to if he knew I wasn't staying." He shook his head. "Then again, perhaps he would want me to stay. I really don't know."

"And her?" Dinara asked, nodding toward Livia.

"What about her?"

"You like her."

He shrugged. "I don't know her. She seems to want to stay here and help with the refugees."

"I think she's a lady. Not sure why she's hiding it."

"Is she hiding it? I like it that she seems humble. Not lording her title over everyone, whatever her title might be."

"You'd leave her behind so readily?"

"Like I said, I don't know her. I know you, and I want to see you settled somewhere before I worry about anything else."

"You don't owe me anything."

He gazed into her eyes. "It's easy to say that. Even if I weren't a knight, I wouldn't believe I didn't owe it to you to see you safe."

Dinara felt mixed emotions at his words. She did not like him taking any sense of ownership over her future, yet at the same time she knew the goodness of his intentions and that warmed her heart. "Perhaps we should talk to Livia before we decide where to go," she whispered, then lay down and began tugging the blanket about her. "Sleep well, Villem."

Duchess licked her cheek.

"Yes, you too, Duchess."

37

VILLEM

Villem watched the dark shape of Dinara toss around under her blanket until she finally fell asleep. Her questions had only made him more confused. It's funny, he thought, a couple years ago I felt I was so grown up and ready for people to take me seriously. Now I feel more and more like a child who has no idea what to do with himself.

He felt movement behind him, and when he turned, Livia was laying out a blanket nearby. She glanced at him as she sat down. He noticed the nomads bedding down for the night.

"You looked thoughtful," Livia said in a low voice to keep from waking Dinara. "Do you want to be left alone?"

He shook his head. "I'm happy to talk. You sure you aren't too tired?"

"I'm exhausted. But I won't be able to fall asleep just yet."

"You look…sad."

She glanced away, and moonlight cast a sheen on her eyes. "My friends are departing tomorrow. We've been together for weeks. I've grown fond of them."

"I'm sorry. How did you come to travel together?"

"Simple chance. We happened to be near each other when the dragon attacked Tolgaria. Been together ever since, taking care of each other."

"They're from the far south?"

"The Arid Lands, yes. They came seeking a trade deal for their people. Their timing couldn't have been worse."

Villem began scratching Duchess's fur again. "Hard times for everyone."

"I'm afraid it may only get worse," Livia said.

Villem glanced around at the crowded, slumbering camp. "You plan to stay here?"

"I think I must. These people need help."

"They do. How can you help them?"

Livia blew out her breath. "I haven't told you everything yet. Didn't want you to treat me differently."

"I figured you for a noblewoman. Your clothes. The way you speak and act."

"You've never heard the name Livia before?"

Villem thought for a moment. "Well, I have, but only the…" It suddenly crashed home for him, and he felt stupid. "You're…you're the princess. Livia Kaldarion."

She smiled ruefully. "And now you'll never act normal around me ever again."

Villem had no idea what to say. He looked at Duchess and rubbed harder at her fur. It did not feel real that he was sitting here in the dark with a member of the royal family, someone so far above his station that he never imagined he would even see them in his lifetime, let alone speak with one. How could she possibly expect him not to treat her with reverence? Then his face reddened when it struck him that her father, the king, had just died, and here he was worrying about how he should treat her.

"You don't have to be awkward around me now," Livia said. "Even in the moonlight I can see you blushing."

Villem shook his head. "I-I don't…"

Livia sighed. "Let me tell you about the last few years of my life. I never was a typical princess. I had a wizard as a tutor. I told him once that he had ruined me. Half-joking of course, but in some ways it's true. I'm twenty and unmarried. Do you know how rare that is for a princess? My father began bringing around suitors four years ago, pressing me harder and harder to accept one. I refused and he grew angry. He grew more insistent, and I found it difficult to fend him off. I knew he was going to force it this year, whether I found someone acceptable or not. Of course, that won't happen now."

"I'm so sorry, your highness, about your father."

She tilted her head at him. "Don't call me that. Call me Livia."

Villem gasped in exasperation. "How? How can I? You are roy—"

"I don't care. It's the one order I'm going to give you. Call me Livia, at least in private. Please."

He hung his head but nodded. "May I ask why you couldn't marry?"

"I'm too well educated."

"I don't know that word."

She nodded. "It's what the wizard called it. Educated. It means my eyes were opened too wide. I learned too much. Far more than any noblemen learn. It really did ruin me for marriage. My father sent a parade of handsome, muscle-bound oafs to me and expected I could be content with one. Not one of them could converse about anything deeper than how to best polish their armor." She threw a hand to her mouth. "Forgive me! I'm being insulting. And unfair as well. I know the boys really aren't as bad as I'm saying. Some of them have some learning. They can even hold a conversation. Sort of." She shook her head. "It's just that…I need more. Maybe something is wrong with me. None of them interest me." She laughed. "And here I am speaking so forthrightly to a young man I don't even know. I'm sorry."

"Please don't apologize to me," Villem said.

"I haven't had anyone to really talk to since leaving Xax behind in Valandiria. My nomad friends are wonderful, but not much for talking."

"I'm not so well read myself," Villem said. "I may not be good at conversation either."

Livia laughed softly. "You're a good listener, which is just as important to me right now."

"Forgive me for stating the obvious, my lady, but you should be sleeping in one of those houses, not out here on the ground."

She was shaking her head long before he finished the sentence. "I'm here to be with all those who are suffering. The last thing I want is special treatment."

"You have no guards. Aren't you afraid of what might happen? There were fights tonight, and I expect it will get worse."

"I must find a way to prevent it from getting worse. Tomorrow I'll speak with Lord Sewell and see how I may help. If I must have guards, he'll assign some to me."

Villem nodded. "I'm sure you will succeed."

Livia placed a hand on his arm. "I'd love to have your help. You and Dinara."

Villem felt miserable. He really wished he could stay and get to know this most unusual princess. "I...I wish I could, my lady. I think we have to go. Dinara talked about going south tomorrow."

Livia frowned.

"If you order it, we would remain, of course," Villem said.

"I told you the only order I would ever give you," Livia said. "Go if you must. You are fortunate to have such a remarkable woman."

Villem felt his face flush. "She's not my woman. I'm only helping her."

"How a knight from Iskimir came to be aiding a woman from the icy north. That's a story I would love to hear someday. Anyhow, get some sleep, Sir Villem."

As Villem rolled himself into his blanket and snuggled up next to Duchess, he pondered the strange twists and turns life could take.

38

KATHKALAN

As awareness slowly returned, so came the pain. A giant seemed to have wrapped a hand around Kathkalan's chest and was squeezing so hard it hurt to breathe. It felt as if a spike had been driven into his forehead where it had cracked into the wall. His entire body felt like one enormous bruise. With tremendous effort he forced his eyes open.

He was staring down a long tunnel leading to a bright light. I recognize this, he thought. Some of his kindred, having been revived when on the brink of death, had described seeing such a tunnel of light. They said nothing about the pain, though. His eyes adjusted more to the brightness, and he saw the lines of marble blocks and the tangles of ivy and realized he lay at the bottom of the well. I'm not dead after all.

It was a long fall, he thought. I should be dead. Perhaps every bone in my body is broken. This will be a strange, lonely place to die.

Faintly he felt the touch of magic from the crystal shard, lending a bit of strength to his body and mind, making him feel that perhaps all was not hopeless.

It suddenly occurred to him that his head was pillowed on something soft. Out of the corner of his eye, he saw his sheathed sword leaning against the wall of the well. My sword was unsheathed. I stabbed the dragon. Not well enough, but I wounded it. Someone has been here. Sheathed my blade. Put something beneath my head.

He heard the rasp of moving stone. A gasp of someone surprised. "You're awake!" The sound of a girl's voice. Soot?

He tried to turn his head toward the sound of the voice, but his head was too heavy and throbbed with too much pain. Stringy brown hair and wide eyes appeared above him, a forehead creased with worry lines. The face was not Soot's.

"I've brung water, milord," the girl said in a voice just above a whisper. "Can you drink?"

Now that she mentioned it, his mouth and throat felt like the parched lands far to the south. He opened his mouth a crack and put the tip of his tongue to his lips. The girl dropped to her knees beside him. He couldn't see what she was doing, but soon she held a cloth above his mouth and squeezed drops of water from it into his mouth. It tasted sweet as nectar. He stuck his tongue out further, and she wrung more water from the cloth.

"I seen you afore, great lord," the girl said. The next she said in a murmur so low he barely heard her: "All in black." Then louder: "Never seen an elf afore."

"Water. More," he rasped.

He heard her dip the cloth, then she brought it back to his mouth and dribbled more water on his tongue. His throat felt better, and he thought he might be able to speak. "The…dragon."

The girl's eyes grew even wider. "Dragon?" She shuddered and glanced up the well before turning back to Kathkalan. "It flew away."

So, he had failed to slay it. He had figured as much. *Didn't strike deeply enough. I'll likely never get as good a chance again.* It was rare in his long life to feel a sense of failure, but he felt it now. He felt tired. He wanted to slip away into nothingness.

"I don't know how to help you, milord," the girl said. She sounded close to tears.

Kathkalan opened his eyes again. "What is your name?"

"Maisie, milord."

"Maisie. Can you…bring men to help me?"

She looked down and her cheeks flushed. "I…I didn't want them to know about my secret place. They'll never let me come here again."

"Secret place?"

She lifted her hands to indicate the ivy-covered walls around her. "I'm the only one who knows of it. Well, and the young prince, but he's dead now. The king as well. All dead."

"Dead? The king?"

Maisie nodded, then leaned closer to whisper conspiratorially. "The steward said it was the dragon. But I know a maid married to a guard who said it was the duke who done it."

"Why?"

Maisie shrugged. Her face brightened. "When I cleaned your sword, the cloth I used burned up."

"Blood. As dangerous as the breath. Did you get any on you?"

"No. But I found this." Maisie held up a black, shiny object bigger than her hand. "Thought it was part of your armor at first, but it doesn't fit nowhere."

"Hold onto that. It's rare and valuable. You can tell your grandchildren about it one day."

Maisie's eyes grew wide with wonder. "What is it?"

"A scale from the dragon."

Maisie looked awestruck.

Kathkalan tried to understand how badly he was hurt. First he tried to pull his legs up, bent at the knees, and was surprised when they complied. Perhaps they aren't broken after all, he thought.

"You can move," Maisie said. "I thought you was dying."

"I may be," Kathkalan said. "Too soon to tell."

He lifted his hands and placed them on his stomach. One arm hurt terribly, though he wasn't certain it was broken. He worried about his head and torso, but so far he had been luckier than he deserved. He must have been more successful at slowing his fall than he had imagined. He drew a deep breath, and pain enveloped his chest.

He panted awhile before he was able to speak again. "Girl. Maisie. You need to bring help. Move me to a bed."

Maisie frowned, then sadly looked around the walls of the well as if seeing them for the last time. She stood up and gazed down at him. "I'll come back soon." She turned and vanished from sight. He heard her scuffling grow fainter.

The sunlight over the well dimmed. It was hard to see clearly, but he thought clouds were passing overhead. He wondered how much time had passed since he had fallen. Was it the same day? The next? He did not feel he could have lain there much more than a day.

He did not even realize he was falling asleep until the sounds of scuffling on stone woke him.

"Here, see?" It was Maisie's voice. "The great elf lord, just like I said."

He heard grunting, and then the face of a man appeared above him, joined soon after by another.

"I don't believe it," the first man said.

The other man stared up the well. "He fell down this? And lived?"

The first man looked up as well. "Never knew this was here."

"Can you help him?" Maisie asked. She picked up his sword and cradled it in her arms.

The men stared down at Kathkalan. By their clothing, he thought they must be from the kitchens.

"Depends on how badly hurt he is," the first man said.

"Won't be easy dragging him through those tunnels," said the second man.

"Please," Kathkalan murmured.

The men looked startled, as if they had not realized the elf could speak. A few drops of rain began to patter down, and the men looked up the well again.

"Might as well get going," the second man said. "Coran, get his feet."

"Aye," Coran said.

The two men grunted and heaved Kathkalan up, Coran holding his calves and the other gripping him under his arm pits. Pain bloomed through his chest, but Kathkalan stifled a groan. Coran led the way, following Maisie as she led them through a square hole in the marble wall into a dark tunnel. She held a lamp that provided a bit of flickering light in the gloom. The men grunted and cursed as they struggled to carry him. At times his bottom dragged on the stone floor. The pain was bad enough that he lost consciousness a few times, though never for long.

"Here," Maisie said. There was the sound of sliding wood, followed by more light entering the tunnel.

The men staggered out through a hole in the back of a large cupboard and into what looked like a storage room full of crates and sacks.

Kathkalan lost consciousness again. When he awoke, he was lying in a bed. The blankets were rough, so he knew it was not the bed of his own room. A plump woman stood over him, her deeply-lined face creased with what looked like a permanent scowl.

"You'll live," she growled.

She sat next to the bed, then held a cup to his lips. He sipped tepid water, coughed painfully, sipped some more.

"There's soup when you feel like it," she said.

"Name?" he whispered in a raspy voice.

She glared at him a moment. "Call me Cookie. S'all you need to know. You may be a great lord out there, but this kitchen's mine."

He grunted assent. It occurred to him that he did not feel the magic of the crystal. He grasped at his chest. Nothing. His armor was gone. So was the necklace holding the shard.

Cookie smirked at him. "It's all back there." Vague hand wave over her shoulder. "Maisie's seeing to your clothing and such."

He nodded. "The castle…dragon?"

"Dragon's gone. Kilt most of the town. King's dead. The beast's breath burnt through many a door. Good thing the kitchens be so deep inside."

She let him sip more water, then stood to go.

Kathkalan lifted a hand. "How…badly am I hurt?"

Her scowl deepened. "You were lucky. Heard that fall was a long one. Three cracked ribs. Dislocated shoulder. Bad bruise up here." She pointed to her forehead. "Lucky you had that helm or your head would have cracked like an egg. Healer set your shoulder 'fore you woke up." She shrugged and left.

Kathkalan felt relieved. He had been hurt far worse than this during his life. He would mend. He thought, *I have unfinished business with you, dragon.*

39
LIVIA

Livia rose early to see the nomads off. She wished she could hug them. In the wan light, each man in turn came before her to bow his head, touch fingers to forehead, and mumble something in their tongue. Azer was the last.

"I'm sorry to leave you, great lady."

"I hope we will meet again one day," she replied. "And I'm sorry for the man you lost."

"Teymur," he said and put a hand over his eyes for a moment. "We all would have joined him if not for your Xax. Please, thank him once more for us when you meet him again."

"I will. I would give you all the coin I have, if I had only had any on me when I went into the city that day."

"Do not worry yourself. We will make do with the kindness of strangers."

"Have a safe journey home, Azer."

He bowed his head again, hefted his small pack, and turned away to join his comrades as they picked their way out of the camp.

Though they would not see it, Livia lifted a hand in farewell. She sighed, thinking about what to do next. Try to coax more food from the guards, she supposed. She had insisted the nomads take everything they had for their journey. It was too dark to see whether the soldiers were at their station near the crossroads yet. Carefully she began making her way through the camp, stepping over snoring bodies, ignoring the curses when a dog barked at her. She detoured to a woman's latrine, since the line was not yet so long as it had been last night. Inside the small tent, she nearly vomited from the stench. They cannot go on like this, she thought. We must do better for all these people.

More people were rousing by the time she drew near the crossroads. The line for the well was growing long, but it was nothing compared to the line of refugees on the main road. The soldiers were busy, pointing folks to a new pasture farther along the side road.

Livia found the rear of the line waiting for food bundles. The sun had risen by the time she reached the front. She asked if she could have more for her friends, but the soldier shook his head and gave her one small sack.

"Is Lord Sewell here?" she asked the soldier, indicating the hut they had pointed out yesterday.

"Don't think so," the soldier said. "Thought I saw him and the builders heading for the plateau already."

It took half an hour to make her way back to the carriage. She felt alone now, with the nomads gone, even though many of the people nearby had accompanied her all the way from Tolgaria.

Duchess thumped her tail and panted at her. Villem sat in his blanket and grinned. Having pulled off a chunk of bread for herself, she passed him the sack of food.

"We each have to go if we want more," she said. "Where's Dinara?"

"In line for the latrine, my lady." Villem fetched a wrinkled apple from the bag and took a bite.

"Call me Livia," she said, though she knew it was a lost cause. She pointed toward the rear of the pasture. "I'm going to the plateau to find Lord Sewell. Do you plan to leave soon?"

"I can't say yet, my...Livia," he said. "Asked Dinara that question, and she didn't answer me. Just grumbled and walked off. I'd go with you to find this lord, but I'm afraid someone might steal my pony."

"You should be here when she returns."

He nodded and tossed the rest of his apple to Duchess.

It took more than an hour for Livia to skirt the camp and reach a rough ramp leading up to the top of the small plateau. She glanced down at her dirty clothing, wishing she could look more presentable. Looking like this, Lord Sewell might not take her seriously. Livia paused to catch her breath when she reached the top. Men in several small groups worked in the distance. The plateau was rocky and had not been used by the villagers. Long yellow grass and dandelions grew in patches. Livia headed for the nearest group of men. When she drew near, she saw the men were laborers, sweaty bare torsos, wide-brimmed hats, resting in the bit of shade thrown by a young plane tree.

"Where might I find Lord Sewell?"

The men seemed inclined to ignore her, though one, perhaps hoping to be rid of her as quickly as possible so he could get back to his rest, pointed toward a pair of men in the distance.

As she approached the two men, she found them deep in conversation, one of them pointing here and there to show how he wanted something done. One man noticed her drawing near, and the two of them turned in her direction. She examined them as she took the last few steps before halting. One was a thin older man, nearly bald, and by his dress she took him for an engineer. The other was only a few years older than Livia herself, pleasantly plump, an unruly mop of blond hair, and ruddy cheeks. She nodded to the second man.

"Lord Sewell?"

The man got an expression on his face as if he wanted to show irritation, but he had such a habit of being good natured couldn't pull it off. "Aye." He took in her road-worn but expensive clothing. "My…lady?"

She disliked using her royal rank, but she felt she had no choice if she wanted to accomplish anything with this man. "I know I haven't had a change of clothes since fleeing Tolgaria. Forgive my appearance. I'm Princess Livia Kaldarion."

The eyes of both men widened.

Lord Sewell scratched the back of his neck, looking perplexed. "Are you? Your pardon, my lady. I've never been to the capital. Never seen anyone from the royal family, except for Darus and the duke. I mean the regent."

Livia pointed back toward the camp. "Many there know who I am. They've trekked alongside me."

"You do have the famous silver hair, and you look a little like Darus," Sewell said. "And the regent said you were missing. Do you know he sent word to have you sent back to Valandiria if we found you?"

"I'm not surprised. My uncle has no right to command me. I'm here to help the refugees."

"And how might you do that? We're doing everything we can for them already."

"You most certainly are not. I've lived among them. I see how bad it is. You'll be lucky if plague doesn't sweep the camp within the fortnight. They need more wells. Better latrines. And there are too many of them. They need a lot more room."

Sewell's face had turned different shades of red as she spoke. He looked both angry and nonplussed at the same time. "I don't have the resources, my lady. What do you think I'm doing up here now? Planning a new city, yes, but first I'm having these men build barracks to house the refugees more comfortably." He pointed to groups of men busy digging foundations not far away.

"That's admirable," Livia said. "For the long term. But something must be done now to help these people, or you will see riots soon. And death. Please, Lord Sewell, let me help you."

"How exactly would you help me, my lady?"

"Put me in charge of the people down there. You concentrate on building up here."

Sewell kicked at a clod of dirt. "Even if I wanted your help, the regent would have my head if I ignored his orders to return you to him."

"I heard the talk in the camp last night," Livia said. "Darus's army was nigh. The city could be under siege as we speak. It would do no good to send me back now. At least wait until you know what has happened."

"Blasted courier," Sewell said. "I told him to keep the news to himself." He glanced at the engineer, who shrugged his shoulders. Sewell sighed. "I can let you stay a day or two, until we hear more news. I'll tell my soldiers to obey your orders concerning the refugees…within reason. Speak to the townsfolk so you don't break any promises I made to them."

"Thank you, Lord Sewell. I'm grateful. Can you send a man with me now to pass along your orders? I'd like to get started immediately."

"Aye." He turned to the engineer. "Savinyon, detail one of your men to bring my command back to the captain in charge. Have him detail two guards at all times for the princess."

When the engineer made ready to accompany her, Livia began to turn away, then stopped. "Lord Sewell? If I understand the markers correctly, you aren't thinking big enough for the city."

Sewell's jaw dropped, and he glared at her without responding.

"We've lost Andiria and the capital, and perhaps we'll lose

Valandiria as well. It's not often a man gets to design an entire city from scratch. This will be a new capital, I expect. Think big. Much bigger."

"How would we pay for such a thing?" he asked, frowning.

Livia paused for a moment, imagining just how much turmoil the realm would face in the coming years. Where had the treasuries of Tolgaria and Andiria gone? Still locked away in their vaults? Stolen by scavengers? Carried off in some fashion by the dragon? She had no idea, but regardless, so many refugees from cities that had been destroyed meant that at least one new city was desperately needed. "Don't worry about costs for now," she finally said. "It will be a long, slow process. The lords of the realm will donate much of what is needed, because the realm requires it. And when the new king settles into place, he will find the gold."

She knew he wasn't taking her advice happily, so she turned away without waiting for a reply, beckoning to Savinyon. She hoped she had not angered the young lord too much. He seemed a friendly sort, and she liked the thought of discussing the design of the city with him, if he would only allow it. Perhaps in the evening. For now, her mind began to fill with plans for helping improve the lot of the refugees. First off, see the captain, then meet with the villagers.

40
DINARA

When Villem told Dinara that Livia was a member of the royal family, she got the impression he felt it would help make up her mind about departing. As far as she was concerned, it only made things more confusing.

Dinara knew her experiences at East Gate had not prepared her for life in the realm. The people there were harder, harsher, yet somehow more practical than the Greatlanders. A woman loving another woman. It had been a constant source of jokes at the fortress, but on some level it was also accepted. In the realm, few even acknowledge it as a possibility. And this young woman—this princess apparently—had noticed her in a way that suggested attraction. If true, could Livia admit to such a thing? Probably not. Would a princess be allowed to consort with a girl of low birth, or even of high, had she been such? Perhaps if it were kept hidden away, locked behind closed doors. Could either of them accept such a thing? As bad as it sounded, was it worse than living without love at all? Did love between two women always mean having to hide it from society?

The fact that Livia was royal meant little to Dinara. She had almost no experience with nobility, other than seeing Lord Darus at a distance a few times. Strange to think that Darus was Livia's younger brother.

Villem wanted to head south. Dinara wanted a chance to talk with Livia before deciding. Villem tried to hide his unhappiness, but he was not very good at it. He was going to rub the fur off Duchess before much longer.

They had both walked separately to get food packages, since one needed to stay to watch the pony and carriage. The supplies had to last the day, so breakfast had been meagre and both remained hungry. Besides the ever-present stench of the latrines and of sweaty, dirty people packed far too close together, life in the camp seemed to consist of waiting in long lines. A line for water. A line for the latrine. A line for food. It was tempting for Dinara to give in and agree to leave. But the thought of departing without seeing Livia rankled. She had to know. *Is there any chance at all?*

And then she saw her. While standing in the line to get more water, Dinara spotted Livia walking with a thin man toward one of the houses of the village. She thought about going to her immediately, but she had waited in line so long and was getting close. Plus, Livia would be inside the house. It wasn't like she could vanish. Impatiently, Dinara continued to wait in line with her two empty water skins.

She had just drawn up the bucket and begun to fill them when Livia exited the house alongside the thin man. She almost lost hold of the bucket in her hurry to finish filling the skins. Livia stopped to talk with the man, which gave Dinara time to finish her chore and pass the bucket on to the woman behind her before rushing toward the house.

The thin man dipped his head and walked off the way they had originally come, while Livia turned to survey the camp and saw Dinara. A smile lit up her face, and Dinara stopped rushing and smiled back.

"Hey there!" Livia called out. "I thought you would be gone."

Dinara shook her head. "Couldn't leave without saying goodbye, especially now that I know what a high and mighty lady you are." Holding the two water skins, she gave an awkward curtsy.

Both of them laughed.

"Like I told Villem, I don't want you treating me special. Call me Livia, please."

"Livia," Dinara said, rolling it slowly off her tongue like it was something exotic. "Have you found what you were after?"

"I think so. The captain in there is going to pass word along to his men to obey my orders. Should allow me to do what's needed. I spoke with a village elder as well. He's not happy, but he understands the current pastures simply won't hold so many people. I promised not to use their croplands, so that means spreading out farther up the road there."

"That's wonderful."

Livia nodded. "I need to get teams organized to start digging new wells and latrines. More to set up the new pastures and get people moving."

"Sounds like you'll be busy," Dinara said, her heart sinking as she realized she was unlikely to get any time alone with this remarkable young woman.

An odd look passed over Livia's face. She glanced away and then stared directly into Dinara's eyes. Her cheeks flushed. "I...wish you luck in your travels. I hope you find what you're looking for."

Dinara looked around to see if anyone was paying attention to them. No one seemed to be. She stepped toward Livia and leaned her face in closer to whisper in her ear. "You sure you don't want me to stay?"

Livia lurched back a step, her face flushing red. "I-I...I don't know what to say."

"Say you'd like me to stay." Dinara felt her heart thudding in her chest, wondering if she had pushed too hard too fast.

Livia put a hand to her cheek. She was having trouble meeting Dinara's gaze now. "You…must do what is best." Then very softly. "But I do wish you could stay."

Dinara felt herself trembling. She had never been an aggressor before. Never imagined doing such a thing. She flashed what she knew was her most dazzling smile. "Then I shall stay." She glanced over her shoulder toward the camp. "Let me bring the water to Villem. Would you like me to help with your work?"

Livia chewed her lip. "How about we get your carriage out of that mess and move it to one of the new pastures?"

Dinara grinned at Livia and passed her one of the water skins. "Come on, your royalness!"

41
SOOT

Soot worried about Imric, naturally, but now she was starting to worry about Xax. The wizard looked ready to collapse, with dark bags under his eyes and a trembling in his hands. He had not been able to manage the mast on his own, and he had refused to stop the boat for the night, instead taking the tiller and continuing to steer the boat all night while Soot got some restless sleep.

Soot had never been on a boat before, so she had been terrified of hitting rapids or waterfalls, but fortunately the Skendris River seemed to hold no such terrors. She checked Imric for the hundredth time that morning. He snored away, sometimes thrashing and groaning in pain that was more remembered than real, since Xax had healed him. His bones may have been knit together, but his mind still needed healing.

"You're pushing yourself too hard," she said to Xax. "You won't help Imric by collapsing."

The wizard rowed on without seeming to have heard her words. She was about to repeat herself when he finally spoke. "I'm afraid for all of us. His uncle was willing to murder his own nephews for power. He won't stop now." He rowed silently for a bit. "What could change a man so? He was not always like that before, else the magic would have driven him away. Something corrupted him. The promise of power, I suppose. There was a saying about that back where I came from."

Soot didn't care about such things. She just wanted the wizard to stop the boat somewhere safe and get some rest. "It doesn't matter. Imric and I need you to take care of yourself. You're all we have right now."

Xax stared hard at her for a minute. "You're wise for a kitchen girl." He yawned widely. "I'll look for a place to tie up. Promise."

Not entirely believing him, Soot began watching out for a likely place. The only other boats they had seen had been when they passed a couple of small villages. The river often paralleled the road, and each time it came into sight they saw lines of refugees. Xax certainly would not want to tie up on that side of the river.

"Xax," she said, hesitantly.

"Mmm?"

"You said magic was weak. How could you build the Spire of Peace if it's weak?"

Xax chuckled. "Where do I even begin with that one?" He rowed silently for a long while.

"You see, the spire was something unique. It was the first—and only—time that all the wizards came together to spend years working with a single goal in mind. Not only that, but we had both the elves and dwarves working alongside us. Without them, I'm certain it would not have been so powerful. Those races don't see the energy we call magic. They don't bend it to their will. But they do, in their unique ways, somehow incorporate it into whatever they craft, which is why dwarven and elven goods are far superior to anything crafted by mankind. They built the spire itself, and they experimented until they figured out how to create the great crystal. We spent our time trying to work out the logic behind the magic we would meld into the crystal. How it turned out…" Xax shook his head. "…we'd never be able to duplicate it. There are no guidebooks. We fumble around and try to figure out what works and what doesn't. Perhaps magic isn't weak, and it's just our knowledge of it that is. It sure is taxing to use, though."

"What about that crystal?" Soot asked, pointing at the walking stick. "Is it magical?"

The wizard stared at the green crystal atop the walking stick for a moment. "You know, this was gifted to me by a dwarven king long, long ago. He called it an amplifier."

"I don't know what that means."

"Well, let's see. Say I wanted to create a gust of wind, or a bit of fire. On my own, I could do that, but what I created would be small. When I focus all my energy through this crystal, the wind can become a gale, and the flame can become a conflagration. It helps me make magic more powerful than I could otherwise manage."

Soot could not wrap her mind around so many words thrown at her all at once, but she saw buildings ahead on the southern bank. "There!" she cried. "A village."

When they drifted closer, Soot noticed a small pier alongside a ferry. She looked at the wizard, and he grunted and nodded. They tied the boat up across from the ferry barge. Xax negotiated with the ferryman and paid him a couple bits of copper, then led Soot to a cottage the ferryman had recommended. The woman who answered the wizard's knock seemed kindly and agreed to put them up for the night.

"Poor child," she said as Xax carried Imric through the door and laid him tenderly on a thick blanket near the pot-bellied stove.

Imric was awake but not speaking to anyone. He stared around the room, at the woman and her grown daughter, then closed his eyes and fell asleep. Xax talked softly with the woman for a while, but he kept yawning and soon excused himself to roll up in a blanket and join Imric.

Soot was not very tired herself, so she promised the woman she wouldn't wander far and went for a walk around the tiny village. There were only eleven buildings, one of them a tiny trading post. How can people be happy living in such a boring place? she wondered. She sat on the pier and tossed rocks into the river, watching the refugees crawl along the road on the other side like a line of ants. The ferryman asked her a few questions, but her grunts and one-word responses soon convinced him she was not in the mood for conversation.

Assuming they could escape the regent's wrath, what would her life be like now? She supposed she was better off than most of those poor folks on the other side of the river, though on the other hand, those people were not being hunted by soldiers. She still wasn't used to thinking of her friend Imric as a prince, but the fact was that he was. Being with him, as well as with a wizard, likely meant they could find a place of refuge somewhere. Would she be returned to the kitchens once that happened?

She missed her mother. It was terrible that she had not had a chance to properly grieve for her. Her eyes became blurry with tears just thinking it. She had no one now except Imric. Maybe Livia, wherever she was. She wished Livia was with them now. She would feel better. The wizard might be as smart as Livia, but he lacked her warmth.

Dark clouds started covering the sky, and once they dimmed the sun, Soot decided it was best to return to the small hut. When she opened the door, she saw Imric was awake. The woman's daughter was seated nearby, spooning soup into his mouth and chattering away at him.

"Are you hungry, young miss?" the older woman asked.

Soot nodded and gratefully accepted a bowl of soup before sitting near Imric. "Did I hear you mention an elf?" she asked the daughter.

The woman grinned. "I was just telling the young lord here that he isn't the only interesting person to pass through of late. Why just last week a king of the elves passed through. All in black, even his horse. Asked to be ferried across the river. Paid in silver."

Soot thought about telling the young woman that the elves did not have kings, but decided it wasn't important. It was interesting that Kathkalan had passed this way. She sipped at her soup, thinking it wasn't bad but needed a little more salt. She kept glancing at Imric, hoping he would perk up and start talking again. She missed her friend. True, what had happened to his brother and to his foot was horrible, but it wasn't like him to remain gloomy for so long.

"He doesn't talk much, does he?" asked the young woman.

"He's been through a lot," Soot said. "He'll talk when he's ready."

Xax woke briefly in the evening, as rain pattered on the roof. He took a bowl of soup, then bedded down again. Soot was relieved and slept much better that night. She almost looked forward to another day of floating down the river tomorrow.

42

DARUS

Darus sat his mount on the small rise and stared at the distant walls of Valandiria. A horse whickered behind him, one of the thirty mounted men he had managed to scrape together after the disaster. Orderic had dismounted and stood nearby, his stocky form rigid, blond hair blowing in the slight breeze.

"City doesn't look bad from here," Orderic said. "Might be the dragon left it alone."

Those few who survived the battle had been too busy fleeing for their lives to watch what the dragon did once it grew bored of slaughtering the two armies. Darus had spent three days gathering survivors, sending all those on foot back to East Gate to lick their wounds and prepare for further action. Thirty mounted men. That's what he had that remained useful to him for the moment.

He had surveyed the battlefield earlier, trying to estimate how many enemy soldiers might have survived the slaughter. It was the worst sight he had ever seen. Thousands upon thousands of dead, their skin sloughed off or burned almost as if by fire, yet different, worse. Melted. Their armor and weapons twisted or pitted beyond use. The horses were the worst. He shuddered to think back on it.

Was the city alive, or had the dragon slain it, too? That could make all the difference. Was his uncle alive or dead?

Darus looked over at Orderic. "Let's go in for a closer look."

The ride took a couple of hours. A rain squall blew through and then away just as quickly as it arrived. Their spirits were soaked more than their clothes.

There was no sign of movement around the city as they approached. Darus called a halt just outside arrow range. All looked quiet and empty. The gate had been burned away by acid, so the dragon had indeed attacked.

"Slowly," Darus said, and eased his mount forward.

More corpses. No signs of life. They passed through the gate and could not help but gasp at what they saw. Where marble or stone had been used, the buildings still stood but were badly scarred and pitted. Everything else was gone.

Darus walked his mount forward again. He avoided looking at the corpses until he saw one his eyes refused to pass over. A child of less than ten, probably a girl, lying beneath what had likely been its mother. The pair had been melted together into one puddled form with two blackened heads, the mother's arms embracing the child, hopelessly trying to shield it. The worst thing was the smell, the fact that besides the corruption, in some ways it smelled good, like well-cooked bacon.

Darus was not a sentimental man, but even he fought horror and grief at seeing what had been done to all these innocent townsfolk. When he had sent bands out to terrorize the countryside, he had known it was horrible, but it had its purpose. The ends justified the means. Not to mention, his men had centuries of pent-up rage at their unwanted exile from the realm; at those who got to live comfortable lives in peace, while the men of East Gate lived dreary lives in the cold, windy pass, shielding the realm they loathed from the barbarian hordes who would have gladly raped the kingdom if they had the chance.

But this. A few killings was one thing, but this was a charnel house of horrors. Darus heard men retching behind him. He couldn't blame them. Then he heard laughter, starting low and growing stronger. He looked around and saw the crazy elf, Miranvel, eyes wide, cackling with glee. He had an urge to plant his sword in the elf's gut, but he was not certain he could manage it. Miranvel was insane, but he was also the best swordsman they had. With a shield, and the elf unable to use one, Darus might pull it off, but he didn't kid himself that the odds were good.

"Stow it!" he growled. "Get your dog to heel, Orderic."

The laughter faded, but Darus could feel the elf's eyes boring into the back of his head. Have to get rid of him soon, he thought. Too bad I need every man I can get right now.

The only sound was the hollow ringing of hooves on the pitted cobblestones. They had yet to see a living soul.

"There!" cried Tevin. Orderic's scout was pointing up the long rise toward the gate of the castle.

Darus saw movement there. Guards atop the battlements. So there is life here after all. He scowled his disappointment. If the castle survived, his uncle was likely still a problem. Darus threw up a hand to halt his small band and turned to look them over. The boy, Weevil, caught his eye. He had wanted him to give his mount to a more useful soldier, but Orderic had argued the boy stay with them. Now Darus was happy he had not insisted. He crooked a finger at Weevil.

The boy looked nervous but nudged his pony closer.

"Boy, ride up to that gate and ask how things stand."

Weevil's eyes widened. "They'll put a bolt in me."

"I doubt they've spotted us. You don't look a soldier. As far as they know, you're one of them. Act like it. Say you rode in from one of the nearby farms. Just get the news we need."

The boy looked pale, but he nodded and urged his pony onward.

Darus and his men waited impatiently for what felt like an hour before the boy returned.

"They heard our horses," Weevil said. "I told them a group of us came to the city. That the others were searching for family. The sergeant told me to beat it, but another guard said a few things. Said the king is dead. Said the old duke is king now."

"So my uncle lives," Darus said. He gave a momentary thought to his brother Balmar. He would never admit to loving the dolt, but he had a certain grudging brotherly affection for him. Now he was almost certainly dead. He wasn't sure how he felt about it, though at least it was one fewer obstacle to the throne. "What else?"

Weevil shrugged. "Just that they plan to go west soon. Get away from the dragon. Guess they're building a new city somewheres."

Darus scratched at the stubble on his cheek. "West, eh?" Erol must have men out there, planning out this new city. How many? If I get to them first... "West it is."

He turned his mount and headed back the way they had come.

43
LIVIA

Life was improving for the refugees, just not as fast as Livia would like. Enough pasture land had been found to spread the people out in a bearable manner, and even better, the number of new refugees had slowed to a trickle. Wells took time to dig, and she had teams working hard on several new ones, but in the meantime, she had taken Villem's advice and sent a request to Lady Sonia for aid. The lady had kindly agreed to use empty wine tuns to ship potable water to the camp, not just from her estate, but from several of her neighbors as well. New and better-designed latrines had been dug, in better locations. Since there were few tents, simple lean-tos were being constructed to provide shelter. Food was the biggest remaining problem, for there was not nearly enough coming in to feed everyone.

Livia watched as a small wagon train of food, tents, and blankets rolled in from the western sea port of Langaria. Too small, she thought. Better than nothing, but we need far more.

"My lady?"

She turned to see Lord Sewell approaching. She had not seen him since that first meeting on the plateau. "Yes, my lord?"

"Before I get to the bad news, let me just say that I'm grateful for what you have done. Not only have you helped far more than I imagined possible, but the truth is, I'm far happier concentrating on designing the new city. I think taking care of people is not one of my strengths."

Livia was pleased at his words, but her heart sank at the mention of bad news. "I'm happy to help any way I can. I take it you are sending me to my uncle now?"

"A handful of riders came in. They say more soldiers will be following on foot. The battle was a disaster. The soldiers claim they were already losing the fight, but then they were attacked by the dragon. The battle turned into a slaughter. The soldiers say we'll be lucky if a thousand men escaped with their lives. The dragon moved on to the city." Sewell looked at the ground and shook his head. "I don't see any point in sending you anywhere right now."

Livia's hand had flown to her mouth the moment he started speaking. "This is horrible! Those poor men. My...my brothers! And Xax! Did...did the soldiers say anything about what happened at the castle?"

"These men fled while the dragon still raged. I'm afraid we'll need to wait for more news to learn about your family and friends. I'm sorry. I have a couple of cousins who live in Valandiria. I'm afraid for them myself."

Livia put a hand to Lord Sewell's shoulder. "I wish there was something we could do."

"I'll send riders to pick up what news they can. As for us, it's probably best we continue our work. Do something useful to take our minds from our troubles."

Livia nodded. "Thank you for bringing me this news, Lord Sewell, however sorrowful it is."

He gave a slight bow and walked back toward the village. Livia wasn't sure anything would take her mind off the worry for her brothers and her old mentor. How silly now to think that all morning she had spent her time worrying about whether Dinara really liked her or whether it was just because of her royal blood. How inconsequential and selfish it seemed now. Her feelings about the woman were so muddled. She was not supposed to have feelings like this for a woman, yet she could not deny what her body told her each time she saw Dinara. She had tried searching her memories, trying to understand if she had always felt like this, but had just not consciously known it. She had found only one memory that seemed pertinent. Long ago, when she was twelve or thirteen, there had been a pretty chambermaid who started coming every day to clean her rooms. Livia had no idea why this particular maid had seemed unusual to her, yet she had learned the time of day when the maid usually came, and she had begun making excuses to always be there. A couple of times she had even got bold enough to ask the maid to draw her a hot bath, and she had felt an unusual thrill at disrobing in front of the maid to get into the bath. She had been too young to read anything into her actions at the time. All she knew was that she had never felt any such feelings about any of the boys her father had tried to pair her up with.

She was about to go search for Dinara, when a man came running up to her, panting heavily.

"My…lady!"

"Calm down, please. How can I help?"

"I've come from the healers' tent. A man…a-a-a knight is there. My boss said you wanted to be alerted the moment he awoke."

"I did. But it wasn't so urgent you needed to give yourself a heart attack. Breathe!"

"Th-thank you, milady. It's just…well, he's very angry."

"Oh, dear. I'll come immediately."

The man nodded gratefully and dropped his hands to his knees, still panting. Livia gave him a pat on the back as she passed him, headed for the healers' pavilion, the pair of ever-present guards trailing after her. She had a feeling she knew why the knight would be so angry. It was a long walk, and when she drew near, she heard shouting. She picked up her pace.

"Thieves!" came a deep growl of rage.

Livia entered the pavilion to find a scene of chaos. The injured knight was staggering through the cots in the tent stark naked, trying to catch the chief healer.

"Please, sir!" said the healer. "You're going to hurt someone."

The knight's head was swathed in bandages, but his wound no longer looked swollen, and his color was much better than the last time she had visited him. "Sir!" she cried out. "I have your belongings."

The knight halted and turned his glare on her. The pair of guards flanked her as protection.

"No one has robbed you," she continued. "I took them for safekeeping until you were well enough to reclaim them."

He stood silently for several moments, breathing heavily, then put his hands to his bandaged head. "Agh! It hurts!"

The sick and wounded in the tent—those who were awake anyhow—looked relieved that the knight had stopped his rampage.

Livia motioned to a nearby healer. "Get him back in bed, please."

The woman nodded and nervously tried to do as Livia asked. Fortunately, the knight seemed docile now and gave no more trouble. Livia took a stool and sat near him.

"I'm sorry your head still pains you."

The man groaned and closed his eyes.

"What is your name, sir?"

He stayed silent long enough that she thought he wouldn't answer, but at last he did. "Kogan."

"Sir Kogan, let me assure you. Your arms and armor are safely stored in the building nearby where the commander of this camp sleeps."

She saw no reason to mention that she herself was sleeping in a room there as well, at Lord Sewell's insistence. He had been aghast at the thought of a princess sleeping on the ground with the rest of the refugees. Livia had not argued too hard with him; to be honest, she was grateful for the straw pallet, as well as for the change of clothing Sewell had scrounged up for her. Nothing fancy, but it was far better than the expensive rags she had been wearing for weeks.

Kogan slitted his eyes open. "My horse," he croaked.

Livia worried he might explode again, but she drew in a deep breath and told him the truth. "I'm very sorry, but your horse had to be put down."

Kogan opened his eyes further and studied her. "Who are you?"

"I found you and brought you here. Please, call me Livia."

Kogan nodded faintly and closed his eyes again. She sat with him until his breathing became regular, then she thanked the healers and left to resume her work.

She walked past the village well, intending to speak with the quartermaster about rationing the food stores and about sending more riders to beg various lords to send supplies, when she heard distant shouting and saw a rider approaching at a gallop along the river road. She had a premonition she wouldn't like the news he bore, so she walked in a daze to the crossroads to await his arrival.

The rider kept shouting something over and over to anyone in earshot as he whipped on his exhausted steed.

"The king! The king is dead! Long live King Erol!" the man cried, pulling the frothing horse to a halt in front of the other soldiers.

Livia had expected it, but having it confirmed that Balmar was dead made her sway and drop to her knees in the dirt. *No! No! No!* her thoughts repeated as the tears came.

44
AZER

Azer rolled himself out of his blanket and stared into the cold ashes of the fire. It was still dark, and the others remained asleep. Through the branches of the trees—it was still difficult for him to imagine how a land could have so much green—Azer looked at the red moon and tried to understand why he was growing more and more miserable.

He was headed home. He should be happy, as the others seemed to be, despite the difficulties of the road. Some people they met treated them kindly. Others looked upon them as if they were lepers. The ferryman who got them across the Skendris River had refused to help them without payment, and the only item he would accept was a beautiful dagger belonging to Fuad that was easily worth several hundred times the cost of the crossing. The poor treatment they sometimes got as foreigners was not the reason for his unhappiness, though.

"You look so sad, brother. Is all well?"

Azer looked over and saw Babak had risen and now knelt nearby. "My body is fine. It is my mind that aches."

"What troubles you?"

Azer shook his head. "I'm concerned about the lady Livia. Danger is coming for her; I can feel it. I can't help but feel that I deserted her when she needed me."

"What can we do, brother? We are not warriors."

"To the people of our tribe, we are not. But all people of our tribe learn the spear, bow, and sword. We have all had to fight off raiders who would have robbed our caravans. We are warriors compared to most of the people of this land."

"We have no weapons or armor. Just a few knives, and Fuad no longer has even that."

"You are right, brother," Azer said. "And you should return home with the others. I must follow my conscience and return to the lady."

Babak remained silent for a long time, until the first faint light of the new dawn touched his face. "I wish to go home," he said at last, "but I will not let you return alone. Honor demands I go with you."

"You are too kind, brother, but I absolve you of any honor in this. Lead the others home. I will be happier knowing you will reunite with your families."

"The others can decide on their own. I am going with you."

Azer clasped a hand to Babak's shoulder and squeezed gently. "Of course I am pleased to have you as my companion."

"At breakfast we can put it to them. I am certain Samir will go on. He is terribly homesick. Zaur probably as well. I don't know about Ragif."

"It matters not," whispered Azer. "I will feel better, knowing that I return to help the lady."

45

VILLEM

Villem felt like a mosquito preserved in amber, stuck in a situation that seemed all but unbearable, yet unable to compel himself to leave without some form of closure. He imagined himself taking Zora and traveling alone to Iskimir, and it seemed pathetic. Yet this camp, despite the improvements, was miserable. He liked Dinara and wished he could get to know Livia better, yet both women worked themselves to exhaustion each day and had little time for conversation. What little spark of interest they showed seemed reserved for each other.

The past few weeks had changed Villem. He had developed a live and let live sensibility alien to his younger self. But he had to admit the idea of romance between Dinara and Livia bothered him somewhat. He could not see the point—they could not give each other children, and why else would one have a romance? It seemed dangerous as well. He knew most people in the realm would frown on such a relationship at best. He did not want to think about the worst consequences. He kept kicking himself for such thoughts, telling himself he was being jealous. He kept meeting fascinating women and none of them desired him.

He was seated inside the tent Livia had wrangled for him, large enough to keep his pony inside. The carriage stood next to the tent, though he had no idea why they were keeping it. Duchess lay at his feet, napping, while he sipped water and tried to convince himself it was time to move on. He could not even help out the teams working to improve the camp, because he worried someone would steal Zora. His neighbor—the old woman who had helped so often with small bits of food during their trek from Tolgaria—had offered to watch the pony for him, but he knew she lacked the strength to prevent someone from taking the beast and he did not want to place such responsibility on her.

Hearing shouts in the distance, he stood up and walked outside to see if anything was amiss. There had been nothing but bad news of late. The new king was dead and the dragon had massacred the army and destroyed Valandiria. Rumors from the south said none of the lords had sent any aid, and there were whispers that the south meant to break away and form their own kingdom. The sea lords to the west had apparently already done so. Would a new king let those parts of the realm go peacefully? Would there be civil war? It already felt like ages ago that the realm had known nothing but relative peace for its entire existence.

The shouts came from the direction of the small town and crossroads. Villem wanted to walk over and see what was happening, but he felt tied down to his pony. He looked back at his tent. Could he leave her alone for half an hour? He sighed. Probably not.

Making a sudden decision, he reentered the tent, saddled Zora, and gathered his few belongings to tie them behind the saddle. He felt bad about not saying goodbye to Dinara and Livia, but would they truly be sorry to have him gone? He whistled for Duchess to follow and walked Zora toward the crossroads, picking his way carefully between the tents and lean-tos. When he drew closer, he saw what had caused the shouting. A ragged band of soldiers was straggling into camp from the highway. Remnants of the decimated army, he assumed.

He reached the road and climbed into the saddle, then began walking Zora toward the nearest clump of newcomers. The men looked exhausted and half-starved. Most had lost their weapons. A couple had ugly wounds that had begun to fester.

Villem was shocked to spot the colors of Iskimir on the shield of one soldier. His father had been in the battle! He dismounted and hurried toward the man, a broad-shouldered fellow perhaps a decade older than Villem. He recognized the man, though he did not know his name. He had seen him a few times, pulling guard duty around his father's keep. Now he felt embarrassed that he could not properly address him.

He was fumbling around for a way to catch the soldier's attention, when the man looked directly at him and his eyes widened.

"Young Villem!" the soldier exclaimed. "You look…well."

Villem understood that the man did not really mean the last word but had not known what else to say. He wondered just how much his travails had changed his appearance over the past few weeks. "You as well," Villem said, for lack of a way of addressing the man. "What news of my father?"

The soldier paled and his eyes darted about before returning to meet Villem's. "I'm sorry, milord. I have no idea. After…after the dragon, I ran, like everyone else. Since then I haven't met any of our boys from Iskimir."

Villem sensed there was something more. "But…"

The soldier lowered his eyes. "Your brother Vonn. I-I saw him fall during the battle. A spear…" The man trailed off, his face flushing.

My brother, Villem thought. Vonn. Slain in battle. It did not seem possible. Vonn was only thirteen. Father would not have allowed him to fight, would he? He had usually gotten along well with Vonn, regardless of how much his mother—well, stepmother—favored the boy. He tried to picture the round, freckled face with lifeless eyes and he simply could not imagine it. "Perhaps you're mistaken," he murmured. "He may have only been wounded."

"Aye," the soldier said, looking relieved. "Perhaps only wounded."

That could explain why his father had not arrived, either with the horsemen who had come through days ago, or with these men on foot. He would have searched for the wounded Vonn on the battlefield and taken him into the city to get aid. That must be it.

Absently he clapped a hand to the man's shoulder. "I must go there. Help them."

The man looked hesitant. "Should I accompany you, milord?"

Villem examined the man and saw the deep lines of fatigue, the patina of fear. "No, you go on home."

The soldier looked like he wanted to say something, then dropped his gaze to the ground and shook his head. "Luck be with you, young lord."

Villem nodded to the man and climbed into his saddle. He turned the pony in a slow circle, hoping to spot Dinara or Livia, but neither was in sight. Calling for Duchess to follow, Villem weaved his way through the soldiers and took the road east toward Valandiria.

46
IMRIC

"Look at that! So many people!" Soot cried out, pointing ahead and to the right.

Imric could not see where she was pointing, since he still lay swaddled in a blanket in the bottom of the boat. Xax had made it clear there was no reason Imric couldn't join them on the benches. His foot may have been ruined, but it was healed. Imric would have to learn to deal with his crippling the best he could. Naturally, he had petulantly refused to deal with it in any way, regardless of how exasperated it made the others.

"I hope Livia is here," Xax said.

"Over there. Aim for that dock," Soot said.

"You're at the tiller. You aim for it. I'm rowing." Xax's gaze met Imric's and his voice took on a grumpy tone. "The only one who's been rowing for days now."

Imric had been wallowing in self-pity the entire voyage, but now for the first time he felt a glimmer of hope. "Could Livia really be here?"

"Looks like every refugee in the kingdom is here," Xax replied. "This is where she would want to be."

After tying up the boat to the ferry dock, Soot and Xax climbed out and turned to look down at Imric.

There was nothing Imric wanted more than to see Livia. "Well! Help me!"

Xax shook his head. "You need no help, young man. Now climb up here and join us."

Imric was aghast. He stared down at the horror that was his foot. He could not believe it was part of his own body. "I can't walk with this. And I have no boot. People can't see…this."

"I'll wrap it for you, if you like," Soot said.

Why were his friends picking on him? Couldn't they see his life was ruined? A tear rolled down Imric's cheek as he shook his head. "Can't you bring Livia here?"

Xax rummaged in the small pack he had taken from the boat and pulled out a strip of cloth. He handed it to Soot. "Here, go ahead and wrap it. We're not going anywhere without him."

As Soot clambered back into the boat, Imric thought about pulling his foot away, but he knew it meant acting like a baby and he didn't like Soot seeing him that way. Her tender touch on his foot was comforting as well. She glanced at him when she thought it might be hurting him as she wrapped the cloth about him, but he shook his head to indicate he was fine. She gave him a shy smile. His spirits lifted a tiny bit and he managed a small smile in return.

When finished, Soot stood and held an arm out to him. "Let's go, lazy bones."

He was too embarrassed to refuse, so he gripped her forearm tightly and allowed her to ease him up onto a bench. He felt dizzy at first, but it passed. With her encouragement, he put his good foot beneath him and wobbled to a standing position.

"Put some weight on the other foot," Xax said. "It won't hurt."

Tentatively, Imric touched his lame foot to the wooden deck. He imagined pain coursing through him, but he knew it wasn't real.

What was real, however, was that the foot did not feel like a foot at all. It did not press flat to the deck. It felt as if both his sole and the instep of his foot were touching the planks at the same time, and that side of his body felt uneven, as if it were slightly shorter. He leaned heavily on Soot as she helped him step up onto the dock, where he would have fallen if Xax had not caught him. The foot that felt so wrong also felt like it did not want to bear his weight.

"It will take you some time to get used to walking again," Xax said.

Imric had been able to run and crawl through his secret tunnels with a good bit of agility throughout his life, so the thought of being crippled for the rest of his life was horrifying. Soot helped him take a few tentative steps, and he hobbled badly, lurching like a zombie from the scary tales Darus used to tell sometimes when he was still around.

He looked at all the people milling about in the near distance. "I don't want people to see me like this."

"You can't just hide yourself away," Soot said.

"They'll stare at me and call me a cripple."

"Aye, some might," Xax said. "There are always people who take pleasure in the unhappiness of others. But those who love you will always love you."

Imric did not think that was very helpful, but he allowed Soot to keep helping him hobble onward. To be honest, he had never gotten to be so physically close to her, and the part of him that wasn't grumbling about his fate was intoxicated by her warmth and how wonderful her arm felt around him.

"I'm not going to do this forever," Soot murmured to him. "You can walk on your own if you set your mind to it."

They were drawing close to a crossroads near a tiny village, but there were thousands of people living in tents and hovels spread out across a line of pastures stretching off along the northbound road.

"How will we ever find my sister in all this?" Imric asked.

"We'll check the village," Xax said. "She's nobility, so if she's here, someone will know where she is."

Imric need not have worried about people staring at him—there were enough injured soldiers and refugees that he was not the only person limping about. They passed through a line of people receiving small packages of food and came to the nearest small house. A soldier stood guard outside the oak door.

Xax held up his walking stick, the green crystal knob sparkling in the sunlight. "Young man, can you please tell me where I may find Princess Livia Kaldarion?"

The soldier seemed entranced by the glittering jewel and it took him a few moments before he responded. "Lady Livia? She's a princess? No one told me that. I was told she was in charge of the refugees and we were to obey her orders."

"And where is she?"

"She's inside," the guard said, jerking his thumb at the door behind him.

"May we enter?"

"I'm here to keep people out. She's not to be disturbed."

Xax looked exasperated. "She'll want to be disturbed by us." He pointed at Imric. "This is her brother, Prince Imric. I'm the wizard Xaxanakis, her tutor. Perhaps you've heard of me?"

The guard looked doubtfully at the hobbled Imric, but then his eyes widened when he heard the word 'wizard'. "You're the wizard? Don't much look like one, but hold on and let me check."

The guard opened the door just wide enough to stick his head inside to speak inaudibly with someone. Then he swung the door wider and waved them in. It was very dark inside after the glare of the sun, and it took a while for Imric's eyes to adjust to the lamplight.

Another soldier sat at a table, shuffling through a pile of parchments. Imric was not an expert on insignia, but he knew enough to know this was a captain. He looked them over with a doubtful expression on his face.

"You're a wizard?" the captain asked Xax.

"Yes. More importantly, this is Prince Imric Kaldarion, the rightful heir to the throne, here to see his sister."

Imric felt more shock than the captain. Not once during the boat voyage had Xax mentioned him being heir to the throne. The thought had not even entered his head, but now that the wizard said it, he realized Balmar was dead, and that made him the next in line. The first thought he had after it hit home was that this was the last thing he wanted.

The captain stared hard at Imric for a minute, multiple expressions flitting over his face. He scratched at the stubble on his face. "Rightful heir. That will surprise King Erol. I think I heard you were dead."

Imric's face flushed. "My uncle murdered my brother Balmar. He tried to kill me and gave me this." He pointed at his ruined foot.

The captain looked a little pale. "Those are...terrible things to say. Why? Why would Erol murder his own family?"

"It should be plain," Xax said. "He wanted power. First for himself, and later for his son."

The captain kept shaking his head. "No one does such a thing. No one."

Xax shuffled forward a few steps and smiled kindly. "I understand how hard it is to believe. The people of this realm have always lived within the protective magic of the spire. But it's gone now. We'll all have to grow used to people making their own decisions, unswayed by how the magic makes them feel."

"Lord Sewell must be informed at once," the captain said. "I suspect there will be trouble." He sighed. "But let me see if Lady Livia is awake. She's been grieving since learning of the death of the king."

The captain walked to the farther of the two other doors in the room and knocked gently. He waited for a response, then knocked a little harder. He must have heard something, for he opened the door and spoke to someone inside. Then he stumbled to move out of the way as Livia brushed by him into the main room.

"Imric! Xax!" Livia threw herself at them, trying to crush all three in an embrace. "And Soot as well. I'm so happy you're alive." Tears streamed down her face.

Imric didn't know why she was crying, but it made his own eyes tear up, and he hugged her fiercely in return. He barely noticed the captain slipping out of the house.

"We're in grave danger," Xax said. "We can't stay here."

Livia looked panicked at the wizard's words. "What do you mean? I'm not letting you go."

"Livia," Xax said in a gentle voice. "Your uncle murdered Balmar and very nearly succeeded in killing Imric. He won't give up the kingship now that he believes he has it. It's likely he has soldiers searching for us as we speak."

Livia looked sick and held her hand out toward the table. She staggered toward it and sat down hard in the chair. "I can't believe it. Erol was always good to me."

Imric shuffled forward. "I was there. Look what he did to my foot."

Livia sniffed and followed Imric's pointing finger. Her eyes widened as she took in the misshapen, heavily-wrapped appendage. "No," she whispered. "My poor Imric."

Imric had the impression she would have embraced him again if only she had the strength to stand. It scared him to see his sister like this. She had always been so strong.

"You should come with us," Xax said. "Gather some supplies and we can use the boat."

Livia shook her head vehemently. "No, I-I can't. I have much too much work to do here still. The people…"

"Imric needs you more than they do right now. You're all he has left. We must find a lord powerful enough to shelter us. If you remain here, Erol will execute us all."

"He can't do that," Livia cried. "Imric is the rightful heir."

"I taught you not to play the fool," Xax said. "People care about stability. They will care more for the idea of Erol being king than for a boy few have even heard of."

"They won't want a lame king anyhow," Imric muttered. "I say let him be king. I just want to live in peace somewhere."

Xax and Livia both looked at him with horrified expressions.

Soot punched him lightly on the arm. "Don't be stupid, Imric. You don't get to choose."

"How can you think such a thing?" Xax asked. "Erol would never allow you to live."

Imric felt like shriveling up into a tiny ball. "What can we do? We don't have an army to stop him."

Xax knelt in front of him and grasped his shoulders. "Listen to me. We can find support. The only thing that held the realm together was the magic, along with the stability of the Kaldarion kings. Now there will be powerful lords who will want nothing more than to declare their independence. We can go south, or even to the sea lords of the west. Someone will take us in."

Imric glanced at Soot, who looked as miserable as he felt. "I wish we could run away somewhere where no one knows who we are."

Soot shrugged helplessly.

"Getting away and hiding isn't a bad idea for now," Xax said. "We must get to the boat and go before it's too late."

Livia stood up, a determined look on her face. "I'll pack some food for you. But I must stay here. Erol won't hurt me, and I can persuade him to leave you alone."

"You're smarter than this, Livia," Xax said. "Erol may not hurt you, but he cannot allow Imric to live or there will always be a threat to his power."

The door opened, letting sunlight fill half the room. Four men trooped into the room. One was the captain, and two looked like guards.

"Lord Sewell," Livia said to the fourth man. "I'm so glad you're here."

Lord Sewell studied Imric and Xax for a few moments, his face grim. "This is an unfortunate turn of events, my lady."

"How dare you say that?" Livia cried. "Imric's my brother. There's nothing unfortunate about him being alive."

Sewell's face reddened. "That's not what I meant. I meant that King Erol will have all our heads for this if I don't hold you until he arrives."

"Erol is not the rightful king," Xax said.

"I'm not sure that matters to all the soldiers out there," Sewell said, scowling. "I'm not happy about it, but I must hold you. Give no trouble and we'll treat you as kindly as we can."

Xax tried to protest that there was no reason to detain Soot or himself, but Lord Sewell would not be deterred. His guards and the captain marched all four of them to the next house over. Xax made a point of hobbling along using his walking stick. This house was smaller than the first, with only two rooms. Lord Sewell's men took Xax's belt knife, but left him his walking stick, then rousted a pair of prisoners out of the smaller room.

"This room is for the ladies," the captain said. "You four will take the great room. I'll have more pallets brought in so you can sleep. Blankets as well."

Imric thought his friends were as deeply in shock as he felt, so no one put up any resistance. Becoming a prisoner with his sister was about the last thing he had expected could happen. Soot still held his hand, and he was suddenly grateful she was there with him, even if she would have been better off free.

The soldiers departed, leaving the group alone with the two other prisoners.

The stockier one grinned at the newcomers and held his arms wide. "Welcome, friends. You have the honor to be in the presence of Tristopher, the greatest troubadour in all the lands." The man swept an arm out to indicate his companion, a pale man so emaciated it looked like a stiff wind could blow him away. "And you may call me Othar."

"Our pardon, Othar," Xax said. "None of us are in the mood for introductions just now."

Othar bowed. "Certainly understandable. I'll just pull our pallets over from the other room. The ladies will want fresh ones, not these flea-ridden ones we've been using."

Livia glared at the two men. "You're the ones who tried to murder my friends!"

Othar held his hands up defensively. "Whoa, milady! I assure you the tale has been exaggerated. Tristopher wouldn't hurt a gnat, and I'm just a poor servant."

Livia turned to Xax. "These men are vile creatures. Keep a close eye on them." She turned back to Othar and pointed to Xax. "This man is a great wizard. He can turn you into a rat if he wishes."

Tristopher spoke for the first time, his deep, melodious voice belying his deathly pallor. "My lady, I swear to you we shall do no harm to you or your companions."

Livia began pacing the room, while Othar went to bring the sleeping pallets from the other room.

Imric slumped down against the wall, and Soot slid down next to him. He had finally been perking up a little after the gloom of the boat, but now everything seemed worse than ever.

Soot squeezed his hand and leaned in to whisper in his ear. "I'm happy we found Livia."

He nodded but remained silent.

"Do you really think your uncle will hang us all?"

Imric scowled. Soot wasn't doing a good job of making him feel any better. "Very likely."

47
DINARA

Dinara returned to the pavilion after helping to organize some newly-arrived food supplies as Livia had asked. Villem was gone, as were Duchess and the pony. That was unusual, but she supposed the young man was growing so bored that he had decided to take a ride. She sat on her blanket and swigged some water. Such heat. She had never experienced it up north or at East Gate.

Patience had never been one of Dinara's virtues, and she was growing irritable that nothing further was happening with Livia. After that initial heady excitement, Livia had thrown herself into her work so hard that Dinara suspected the girl was trying to avoid further romantic encounters. Even worse, Lord Whatshisname had insisted Livia live in one of the houses, while Dinara was stuck in this tent with the sullen Villem. And now Livia was in mourning over her brothers. Dinara knew that was how Livia should be feeling, but it didn't help that Dinara was stuck doing chores in a camp full of people for whom she had little care, suffering through stifling heat, terrible smells, and meagre food.

She took a short nap, and when Villem still had not returned, she decided to search for him. She figured he would return to the tent as soon as she left, but she couldn't sit around all day feeling irritable. If only Livia would finish her mourning. It would help Dinara's spirits considerably just to catch a glimpse of her again.

There were fewer soldiers now, which thinned out the crowding some. For a couple of days it had felt like the soldiers were everywhere, many of them wounded, but now they were starting to head out toward whichever keeps or castles they had come from. It struck Dinara, not for the first time, how much grief there would be throughout these Northern provinces that had supplied the army for Regent Erol. How many towns had sent all their able-bodied men, only to get back one or two of them, and those wounded in body or mind, or both? How many of their lords had been lost alongside their men?

Dinara pulled her scarf tighter about her head and walked faster. She had taken to wearing one of late, since so many of the men—soldiers and refugees both—stared at her or made lewd comments. She couldn't hide the shape of her body, though, so the scarf helped only a little. She envied Livia for getting to have a pair of bodyguards with her when she moved about. Dinara's head often ached from the stress of constantly having to keep an eye out for trouble.

She reached the village without seeing anyone she recognized, so she headed for Livia's hut and stopped in front of the single guard. "May I please visit with Princess Livia? I'm her friend Dinara."

The guard was a grizzled, middle-aged man with graying whiskers on his deeply-lined face. "Go away," he said.

Dinara's mouth dropped open at his rudeness, and she wasn't certain how to proceed. After a moment, she asked, "May I please speak with the captain?"

The guard shook his head.

Dinara glared at the man. She was about to give up and head back to the pavilion, when the door opened and another guard stepped out, this one much younger. When he saw Dinara, he grinned.

"Hey! It's the pretty one," he exclaimed.

Dinara usually shut down such advances quickly, but at the moment she was desperate, so she tried a smile instead. "Is the captain about? Or Lord Sewell?"

"Captain's here, but he's upset about something. Don't want to be disturbed, he says."

"Shut your trap, Elbert," the older guard said.

Dinara widened her eyes and batted her lashes at the young guard. "How about Lady Livia?"

The guard pointed at the next hut. "Oh, she's being held there now."

The older guard socked Elbert in the arm.

"Ow! Why'd you do that?"

"I warned you to shut up."

Dinara left the men to their bickering and approached the two guards at the next house. She remembered it was being used as a temporary gaol, so it was worrying that Livia would be there. Had they cleared out the prisoners to give the princess more privacy?

"May I please speak with Princess Livia?" she asked the guards.

"Sorry, miss," one said. "No one can visit the prisoners without Lord Sewell or the captain's say so."

"Prisoners? How can the princess be a prisoner?"

"You'll have to ask the captain or Lord Sewell."

Nothing about this made any sense to Dinara. Lord Sewell had seemed to like Livia as far as Dinara could tell. Livia had mentioned that he might have to send her back to her uncle at some point, so perhaps that was what was happening.

Dinara cinched the scarf tightly about her head and walked back toward her tent. She hoped Villem had returned.

48
VILLEM

The sun shone directly overhead as Villem trotted his pony along the road. He had encountered a handful of soldiers, some alone, others in pairs, all of them left behind by their comrades due to injuries that slowed them down. The only man who had interested Villem was one wearing the livery of Lady Sonia's husband. He had questioned the man, but the man had been hurt badly enough to be uninterested in helping. All he had said was, "Dead. They're all dead."

Now in the scorching heat, Villem saw a lone figure ahead, stumbling along the road. As he drew near the stumbling man, Villem was shocked by what he saw. The man did not look over at Villem, but the part of the man's face that he could see was horrifically burned. His left arm hung uselessly at his side. The eye on that side was a dark, empty socket. The remaining skin of his forehead was pale and slicked with sweat. Duchess barked twice at the man, who ignored them both and kept lurching onward. How can this man not just give up and die? Villem thought.

Zora had already trotted past the man when it dawned on Villem that he knew the shape of the man's nose. It can't be, he thought, before dropping out of the saddle and running back toward the man. Duchess began to bark excitedly, chasing after him. He ran around in front of the man, who ignored him until Villem grabbed the arm that looked uninjured.

"Father!" Villem cried.

The man stopped walking, his one good eye centered on Villem's chest. His voice came out as a weak, frightened rasp. "Vonn? Have you returned to haunt me?"

"Father, it's Villem." He wanted to pull his father into an embrace, but his injuries were too much.

"Leave me be, spirit," Lord Artur Tathis whispered. "Villem is long gone. Gone forever, like his brother."

Duchess barked again and circled around to Artur's uninjured side.

Tears were streaming down Villem's cheeks now. "It's truly me, Father. Villem. I'm here."

Artur's eye rose to examine Villem, fear and perplexity warring in his gaze. His good arm rose and he cupped Villem's cheek with his hand. "Son?"

"Yes, it's me." Villem was openly weeping now.

Artur stumbled to his knees, and Villem rushed to prop him up by his good shoulder. "For-forgive me, Villem. Never…never should have…told you."

"You're going to be all right, Father," Villem cried, though he knew it wasn't true.

"Lay…me down," his father said so softly Villem could barely make out the words.

Villem wished he had a blanket as he softly laid his father's head down, cradling it with his hands.

Artur's breathing sped up and his body arched with pain. "Looks—looks like you're the lord of Iskimir after all…my son."

Villem dropped his head onto his father's good shoulder and wept uncontrollably, as Artur's breathing became erratic and eventually stopped. It felt to Villem as if his presence had stripped away the only thing that had been keeping his father going. Duchess whined and darted in to lick Villem's cheek.

Villem couldn't move. He couldn't think. Even after he stopped weeping, he held onto his father's corpse as it grew cold.

Duchess began to bark insistently.

"Stop it, girl." Villem was irritated that the dog wouldn't leave him in peace while he mourned.

Duchess growled, then started barking again.

Villem snapped his head up to look at Duchess and saw she was staring down the road as she barked. He followed her gaze and saw a large band of horsemen approaching. He couldn't tell the numbers. Thirty? Forty? Fear tingled along his spine. The men would either belong to King Erol or to the enemy army. If the latter, Villem had to act fast. The men were drawing too near.

He raced to Zora and leapt into the saddle. He kicked her to turn her around, glancing over at the approaching riders. Now his blood froze throughout his body. While he could not yet make out the features or colors of the men, he saw that one slender figure had but one arm.

No! No! No! No! No! he thought, and kicked Zora into a gallop. *Not them again!*

He had to make it back to camp and warn them what was coming. Even as panic coursed through his body, Villem looked down at his father's corpse as he rode past. *I'm so sorry, Father,* he whispered. He promised he would return to give his father a proper pyre.

49
DARUS

Darus stared at the retreating horseman, surprised that Orderic had called off the crossbowmen.

"Leave be," Orderic repeated.

"It's him," hissed Miranvel, clearly wanting to give chase. "The boy."

"You think I don't know that?" Orderic growled. "I said stay."

Darus coughed into his hand. He was feeling under the weather the past two days. He nudged his horse up close to Orderic's. "We've slaughtered every straggler we've passed so far. What's special about this one?"

"Long story," Orderic said, "but he's a good kid. I like him." He fingered his jaw where Villem had punched him, what seemed like years ago.

They had reached the spot where the boy had been kneeling on the ground. The corpse of a man lay stretched out in the middle of the road. Darus gave the man a cursory glance as they ambled by him. Suddenly he sneezed, then twice more in quick succession.

Orderic stared at him. "Perhaps we should call a halt until you feel better."

Darus shook his head. "My only chance is to reach the remains of their army before Erol does. Can't let them reform. I may even be able to talk them over to my side."

"If that was your aim, why kill all these others?"

Darus waved a hand as if swatting away a fly. "These men were all injured. No use to anyone."

Orderic shrugged. "Might not be far off now."

Darus coughed again. "Send word around to the men not to do anything foolish once we get there." He pointed at Orderic. "Especially your elf! I want a chance to make my case."

"They may outnumber us."

"I doubt they do. If so, I'll be bold. They're beaten, frightened men just looking for a way to restore their courage. These people loved me, before that blasted magic drove me away to East Gate. They can love me again."

Darus saw the look of doubt that flashed over Orderic's face, but the man nodded and turned to pass word among his men. Darus shrugged his cloak closer about his shoulders to fend off the shivering that racked his body despite the bright, sunny day. *I'm the rightful king*, he thought, a mantra he had been repeating to himself for years now. *I'll either rule this realm or I'll destroy it.*

"Rider!" came a shout from behind.

Darus tugged his mare to a halt and waited.

Orderic ambled his horse over to him. "It's Tevin."

"I figured." Darus had ordered the man to keep watch behind for signs of Erol.

Tevin galloped up and came directly to Darus. "Good news, sire. Erol's three leagues behind us with no more than a dozen knights. He has a wagon train and perhaps four hundred more men, but he's left them far behind."

"Does he know we're here?" Orderic asked.

"I doubt it. He hasn't even sent out any scouts. He must think we went back to East Gate."

"A dozen knights," Darus said. "Any archers?"

"Not with Erol. He left a few guarding the wagons."

Darus grinned. He might feel sick enough to want to lie down and not get up for two weeks, but this was too good to pass up. He scanned the road in both directions and saw what he wanted. Pointing in the direction the boy had fled, he said, "That grove beside the road there. We'll set an ambush. Quick, let's get moving! We can end this all in one blow."

When they reached the trees—tall oaks mixed with a few birches—Darus had Orderic arrange the ambush. Darus's bowels were grumbling ominously, so he sought some privacy deeper into the woods. He found a rill and dropped to his knees to splash water on his face. He had been ill a few times in his life, but always before he had been in a castle with healers, comfortable beds, and decent food. His stomach lurched hard, so he desperately worked the knots holding his breeches up.

A good half hour passed before he felt well enough to return to his men.

"You all right?" Orderic asked.

"How have you arranged it?" Darus asked, ignoring the query.

"Weevil will hold the mounts out of sight back there. Eight men have crossbows, so I have them up in trees ready to snipe. I ordered them to be patient, let the riders start to pass by before they fire. A handful of men with spears will defend the tree line. The rest will be divided into two mounted groups over there and back there. When the time's right, they'll sweep in from front and rear to finish it up."

"Everyone in their armor?"

"It's bloody hot, but yeah, everyone but the bowmen."

"The enemy won't be armored. Not in this heat. Not if they aren't expecting us. This could really be it, Orderic."

Orderic grinned and held an arm up, which Darus clasped. "King Darus Kaldarion, the second of his name."

"And here I am on the day of victory, sick as a dog and shitting my breeches."

"The histories don't need to mention that part."

The wait seemed interminable. Darus silently hoped that Erol had not turned his men around. Another couple of hours like this and Darus's men would all be cooked in their armor, even with the shade of the trees.

"Here they come!" called out one of the crossbowmen from his perch up in an oak tree.

Orderic walked along the lines of his men, reminding them to stay quiet.

Darus wanted to mount up and join one of the bands that would sweep in after the initial ambush, but he did not trust his stomach. So he hid behind the trunk of a large oak, alongside one of the spearmen. Distantly he heard the faint clopping of many hooves on the hard-packed dirt road. *Don't attack too soon*, he thought. *Don't allow Erol to get away.*

The sounds of hooves and jangling metal grew louder, then louder still. Darus quietly slid his longsword from its sheath. Finally it came—the cracking sound of crossbows loosing their quarrels. Screams and shouts rose from the highway. A horse shrieked in pain louder than any man. The spearman next to Darus darted around the trunk toward the road. Darus heaved two great breaths and followed.

Ten steps brought him close to the highway. Crossbows snapped out their quarrels again, and more screams followed. Darus glared out into the bright sunshine and smiled grimly. It could not have gone better. Only two men remained on their horses, and one of those steeds was listing from a bolt in its haunch. Several men were flat on the ground, either unmoving or barely so. Three men stood upright with swords drawn. One charged toward the trees. Another was shouting at the third. With a pounding of hooves and loud shouts, the rest of Darus's band charged in from both flanks.

The swordsman who had attacked into the woods had no armor, just fine clothes and a broad sword. He managed to swat aside the spear of the first man he encountered and then run the man through. However, he could not free his blade quickly enough, and Orderic lunged in from the side and skewered the man.

It was all over. The few men still alive had thrown down their weapons and yielded. Darus waited for Orderic to clean his blade, then walked with him onto the road where his riders surrounded the prisoners.

Darus shielded his eyes from the sun and examined the four panting men who still stood. A few others lived but were hurt too badly to do more than lie moaning in the dirt. Darus recognized two of the standing men as knights or minor nobles that he had seen before, though he could not recall their names. The next was Erol, a hand held to the quarrel stuck through his left arm, his eyes glaring murderously at Darus.

I should feel triumphant, Darus thought, yet all I feel is tired. He heard a groan turn to a gurgle, and saw the one-armed elf slicing the throats of the wounded.

"Butcher," Erol said, still glaring at Darus. "You were my favorite nephew once, you know. Now nothing but a butcher."

"A king actually," Orderic said. "You should try kneeling. Perhaps it might save your life."

Erol sneered at Orderic. "A lie. You scum would never let me live." He turned back to Darus, and his eyes softened. He held his hands up as best he could and dropped to his knees. "I will kneel to you, nephew, but not to plead for my life." He indicated the fourth standing figure, which Darus saw looked a bit like Erol. "I ask only that you show mercy for my son, Istvan. He's a good lad, nothing like you or me. Kill us all if you must, but he doesn't deserve it. He's no threat to you, I swear."

Darus studied the young man. He had seen Istvan before, naturally. Funny that he thought of him as a boy, when Istvan was a year or two older than Darus. Experience changes everything so much, he thought. Istvan still looked a boy, and a frightened one at that. Darus made a beckoning motion. "Come here, Cousin."

Tentatively, Istvan approached, then halted just out of reach. He couldn't meet Darus's gaze.

"Pity we didn't know each other better growing up," Darus said. "Are you truly the sweet boy your father claims?"

Istvan's eyes dropped to the ground and he shrugged pitifully.

Darus stepped closer and put a finger under Istvan's chin, then lifted his head up so their eyes could meet. "Would you bend the knee to me, Cousin?"

Istvan tried to look back at his father, but Darus gripped his chin so he could not look away.

"Say yes, boy," hissed Erol.

Slowly Istvan nodded, though tears brimmed in his eyes.

Darus stepped in and threw an arm around Istvan's shoulders, turning him toward his father. "You do understand that your father is a traitor and has to die?"

Istvan's body stiffened.

Erol was staring hard at his son. "Be strong, Son. I'll go gladly if I know you'll live."

Beneath Darus's arm, Istvan's body began to shake as he broke down in tears. Darus let him go and stepped back, then held forth his longsword to Istvan. "I swear you will live, but you must execute the traitor."

Istvan's head snapped up and his astonished eyes met Darus's. "Y-you can't mean it."

"Fail to do this, and you will join them."

Any remaining color in Istvan's face drained away.

"Don't think, Son, just do it!" cried Erol. He flung himself onto all fours and lowered his head to offer up his neck.

Slowly Istvan raised his hand toward the hilt of Darus's sword. His fingers inched forward, then stopped, and he let drop his hand. "No," he whispered. "I cannot."

Darus met Miranvel's eyes and he gave a small nod.

With a gleeful cackle, the elf leapt forward and brought his blade down on Erol's neck, nearly severing it. Istvan thrust his arms out as if he could somehow prevent what was happening.

Darus let his sword drop, then pulling the dagger from his belt, he stepped forward and thrust it into Istvan's lower back, aiming for the kidney. Warm blood gushed over Darus's hand. Istvan gave a gasping grunt as he turned toward his cousin. Darus let go of the dagger and caught Istvan in his arms as he began to drop. "There, there, Cousin," he whispered in his ear. "There, there."

Slowly he laid Istvan out on the dirt road. He retrieved his dagger and wiped it on Istvan's tunic before sheathing it. Picking up his sword, he nodded to Orderic. "Slay the rest of them. Put the heads of these two in the crook of a tree to drain, then throw their bodies in the river. Leave the rest of the bodies here."

"Aye, sire," Orderic said.

Darus held a hand up. "I'm feeling worse. There's a brook back in the woods. We'll make camp here. Send a fresh scout to keep an eye on the wagon train."

50
DINARA

Villem still had not returned by the time Dinara reached the tent. She noticed for the first time that all of his possessions were gone. Her worry about Livia had her nerves stretched taut already, and now she felt hollowed out. It's my fault, she thought. He wanted to go south and I ignored his wishes because of my faerie tale dreams about a princess I'll never be able to have. She felt as if she had betrayed and lost her only friend. True, they did not know each other deeply, but Villem had treated her well even when it was clear she did not reciprocate his interest.

She had hoped he might have some idea of how to help Livia. Perhaps steal her away from the gaol during the night. Dinara collapsed onto her blanket and tried to figure out what she should do next. Should she forget Livia and follow Villem to Iskimir? That seemed silly. She could never love him in the way he wanted, so what was the purpose other than him being the only friend she had in the realm? But then again, what could she possibly hope for with Livia? A princess would never be allowed to have a forbidden relationship. Even if Livia was interested, would Dinara be content to be hidden away as a scullery maid or some such and meet only in secret?

"Are you feeling well, young miss?"

Dinara looked up to see the kindly face of the old woman who was their neighbor. "Did…did you see where Sir Villem went?"

The old woman's face took on a sad look. "Saw him ride out a few hours agone. All packed up like he didn't mean to return. Took the dog as well. Can't imagine why he'd leave you behind, pretty thing like you."

Dinara nodded numbly.

"He rode toward the village," the woman said.

"Iskimir," Dinara murmured. "Probably gone home to Iskimir."

"Ears aren't so good nowadays. Could nae hear you."

Dinara tried to smile at the woman. "Thank you. You're always so kind."

The woman waved a hand. As she was ducking back out of the tent, she said, "If you're still here, I'll cook you something special tonight."

Dinara stared around the nearly empty tent. Don't just sit here, she thought. Get up and do something. The problem was she could not think of anything to do other than try to seek out Lord Sewell. And he was a noble, while she was no one. Why should he give her a moment of his time, let alone listen to what she had to say?

It suddenly felt sweltering in the tent. There was no breeze and the sun was relentless. Dinara got to her feet, though it felt as though it drained most of her remaining strength to do so. She wished it would rain again, even just a little. She stumbled out of the tent and looked around the camp. Where would Lord Sewell be now? The plateau, where he seemed to spend most of his time, or back in the tiny village? She had to skirt the camp anyway, so she started walking toward the crossroads.

As she drew near, she glared at the guard outside the house where they were keeping Livia. Why would Lord Sewell treat her in such a manner? She supposed he owed fealty to the new king, but it still felt wrong. She headed for Lord Sewell's hut to see if he might have returned. The guard who had treated her rudely was still there. She did not expect better from him, but she had to try. "Is Lord Sewell in?"

"Told you before to bugger off."

"Was it your mother taught you to be so rude? Or mayhap you were dropped on your head as a babe?"

The guard swiveled his spear around in the dirt. "I'd stick you with this if I thought I'd catch no trouble. Now piss off."

Dinara stalked away in a huff, incredulous that any person could treat another in such a manner. She had encountered a few men like this at East Gate, but that was to be expected at such a rough outpost. She headed around the camp toward the plateau, hoping to find Lord Sewell there. Before she had gone twenty paces, she heard galloping hooves. When she turned, she saw Villem riding toward her, his pony in a lather. She had no time to feel happy at seeing him—the wide-eyed look on his face told her something was dreadfully wrong.

Villem pulled his pony to a halt and looked down with surprise. "Dinara? Didn't expect you'd be the first person I saw. We're in grave danger. Get Livia if you must, but we need to go now!"

"What is it?"

Villem shook his head as if he did not want to take the time to explain. "Orderic is coming. I saw Miranvel as well as thirty or forty others."

Dinara had to force herself to take a couple of deep breaths to quell the panic that wanted to clench her throat. She pointed to the gaol hut. "They've locked Livia up in there. Can you get her out?"

Villem slid down from his pony. Duchess jogged up, panting heavily and too tired to do more than drop to the ground near Villem's feet. He handed the reins to Dinara. "Here. Let her rest. I'll warn the others and try to get Livia."

Villem sprinted toward the gaol. Dinara rubbed her hand down Zora's flank and felt how the pony was shaking with exhaustion. "Good girl, Zora."

She heard Villem shouting out to the soldiers who began to gather around, but he was too far away to hear his words. She hoped they would listen to him. She had always liked Orderic, but she wasn't sure he would treat her well now. And Miranvel…just thinking of the elf sent a shiver down her spine. She wondered if Darus might be with them as well. She knew he was young, perhaps only seventeen or so, but he had always seemed much older, like a grizzled veteran of multiple campaigns. He was a hard man. If he was coming, she wanted to be far away.

Villem ran back to her, shaking his head. "They're like hens when a fox has entered the coop. Even the captain doesn't want to believe me. They won't free Livia."

"What should we do?" Dinara felt horrible for hoping he would decide they should just leave the camp to its fate, especially since that meant abandoning Livia as well.

"Lord Sewell's the last hope, I suppose. The captain said he's up there." Villem pointed toward the plateau.

At least heading toward the plateau meant putting some distance between them and the approaching enemy. The pony was too blown to ride, so Villem walked her as quickly as he dared, Duchess trailing at his heels. Dinara's mind felt like it was whirling too fast to think, so she marched silently by Villem's side, sweating profusely in the heat and trying to keep up with his long strides.

The walk was a long one, so Dinara's mind finally settled enough to make her wonder what Villem had been doing riding east instead of south to Iskimir. "I thought you had left for good," she said.

He looked at her for a few moments. "I went to look for my father and brother. They were in the battle."

Dinara wondered how he could know, then realized one of the retreating soldiers must have told him. "So, you ran into Orderic."

He nodded. "Not before I found my father, though. Wounded unto death. Told me before he died that my brother was killed in the battle."

Dinara looked at Villem, saw his hardened eyes, and her own eyes brimmed with sudden tears in place of the ones he was not shedding. "I'm so sorry, Villem."

He shrugged. "My brother was a good kid. Too young. Father should never have taken him along."

Dinara did not know what else to say. She realized this meant Villem was the heir to Iskimir. His step-mother would be doubly miserable.

They had not yet reached the plateau when they ran into Lord Sewell, heading back toward the village. He looked tired and was mopping sweat from his brow with a stained kerchief.

Villem drew Zora to a halt. "My lord?"

Sewell looked irritated by the distraction. "Hmm? Do I know you?"

"We are Princess Livia's companions. This is Dinara, and I'm Sir Villem Tathis."

"Lord Villem Tathis now actually," Dinara added, and noted how Villem looked dazed at her words, as if he had not considered the meaning of his father's death.

Lord Sewell studied both of them more carefully. "I know Lord Artur Tathis. Does…does this mean he has passed on?"

Villem pointed his thumb behind him. "He was mortally wounded in the battle, along with my brother Vonn."

Sewell inclined his head. "Grave news. I'm very sorry for your loss."

"My lord." Villem hesitated a moment. "Raiders belonging to

Darus Kaldarion—thirty or forty horsemen—were on my heels as I rode here. I tried telling your captain, but he seemed disinclined to believe me."

Beneath skin reddened by the sun, Sewell turned pale. "Darus's men? You sure it wasn't King Erol? I've been expecting his arrival."

"Sorry, my lord. It was most definitely Orderic, one of Darus's lieutenants. Raiders."

"Thirty or forty," Sewell murmured, as if to himself. "Was Darus with them?"

"I saw them only at a distance, so I can't be sure. I recognized the one-armed elf."

Sewell shook his head. "The king will expect me to defend the camp, but I have perhaps eighty men. None of them horsemen, and no crossbows either. They'll ride right over us."

Dinara felt foolish to speak up, but she could not help herself. "Perhaps you could arm enough refugees to frighten them off?"

"I-I'm not sure," Sewell stuttered. "You know, I met Darus once. Just a young man of thirteen or so, but already strong and fierce even then. He seemed so angry all the time. I don't think he scares easily, so neither will his men."

"You have spears, my lord," Villem said. "Some high ground with that plateau. You could make a stand there."

Sewell looked around at the plateau, as if assessing the chances of Villem's idea. "I couldn't simply abandon the refugees. They would slaughter them. No. No, we must defend them."

"There is little time, my lord," Villem said. "Whatever you decide must be done quickly."

"Right." Sewell drew in a deep breath, squared his shoulders, and began marching toward the town. "You'll help us, Lord Tathis?"

Again Villem looked startled to be addressed as a lord. "I...I have no armor or weapons, my lord."

"We'll find you something. Many of the wounded soldiers did not make it. Some of their arms will work for you, I'm certain."

As they neared the hamlet, Lord Sewell gathered the captain and the nearest solders. "Captain, I want you to gather every solder we have, and be quick about it. Have them fully armed and prepared for battle."

The captain glared at Villem before responding. "What about men on duty, milord?"

Sewell shook his head. "Pull them off. We need every body we have for what's coming." He turned to Villem and Dinara. "You are friends of the princess. Free her, and if you would be so kind, convince her to organize the refugees as best as possible. There may be fighters among them, archers as well. Even a few hunting bows might make a difference. Any who are willing to help should gather near that small ferry landing. We'll anchor ourselves against the river."

Dinara was relieved that she would be able to free Livia.

Villem asked, "Where are the spare arms, my lord?"

Sewell pointed north. "Check the healers' pavilion. They would keep the arms of any wounded who died."

As Sewell continued to pass out orders to his men, Villem turned to Dinara. "I'm going to try to arm myself. You'll be with Livia?"

Dinara nodded, then gripped Villem by the arm. "We shouldn't stay here to fight. You've seen Miranvel and the rest. It will be a slaughter. Best we make our escape while we have the chance."

Villem thought for a few moments. "I cannot run from this, but you should take Livia to safety. If there is time, she can pass word to the refugees as Sewell asked, but then you should take her away."

"I wish you would go with us. I'm afraid for you. If you survive the battle, where will we meet?"

Villem thought a moment. He looked far older than he had mere days ago. "Iskimir. If I live, that's where I'll go once I can." He pressed a hand over Dinara's, then turned and strode off toward the distant pavilion, leading Zora with Duchess following on his heels.

Dinara watched him for a moment, then headed for the gaol. The guard was already gone from the door, so she pulled it open and entered. Her eyes took a bit to adjust to the gloom. She heard Livia's voice.

"Dinara! What's happening out there? We hear such excitement."

Dinara was happy to see Livia again. She was surprised at how many prisoners were in the room. She noted with dismay the troubadour Tristopher and his murderous companion Othar. Three others were in the room—a middle-aged man holding a walking stick, and a boy and girl, holding each other's hands. The way Livia stood near the three strangers made Dinara believe that she knew them or at least had become friendly with them. Dinara tried to think of a way to get Livia out of there without being burdened with the criminals. "Livia, the lord has freed you. Come quickly."

"This is my brother, Imric," Livia said, pointing at the young boy. "His friend, Soot, and my mentor, Xax. I cannot leave them here."

"Lord Sewell said you were free with your companions, so they may come as well. I didn't know you had another brother."

"He's the youngest."

"What about us, my lady," Tristopher said in his melodious voice. "Surely you don't mean to leave us here?"

"Lord Sewell did not free you," Dinara said. She held open the door to allow Livia and her companions to exit, then hurriedly closed it behind her to shut in the two scoundrels.

"It's a relief to have fresh air again," Xax said. Dinara examined him in the daylight and saw a dark-haired man in his middle thirties, with a bland face extraordinary only for the piercing brown eyes and expressive eyebrows. He held a walking stick with a green crystal knob on the end.

Dinara pointed toward the medical pavilion. "Sir Villem has gone there to arm himself. Raiders belonging to Darus are coming. I'm afraid it will be a slaughter."

"My brother is coming?" Livia asked.

"I don't know that Darus is with them. Villem saw Orderic and his raiders, perhaps forty men on horses. Lord Sewell doesn't have the means to beat them. He has no archers and no horses of his own." Dinara paused. She did not really wish to tell Livia what Lord Sewell wanted her to do. She wanted to escape immediately while there was still time. Guilt won out in the end. "Lord Sewell asked if you could speak to the refugees. Maybe find any who can help in the coming fight, especially any who have bows."

They had passed around the corner of the small house and could see Sewell and his captain organizing the soldiers.

"This is no good place for battle. Not without archers to defend against cavalry," Xax said.

Livia looked pale. "The refugees are in grave danger." She began walking toward the nearest of the camps.

Xax looked at Imric and Soot. "Come, don't get separated or we may never find each other again."

As they began following Livia, Dinara looked toward the medical pavilion, hoping to see Villem, but there was no sign of him. Dinara took in a deep breath and followed the others.

51
VILLEM

Villem loosely tied Zora outside the pavilion and told Duchess to stay. He paused inside the tent and looked around. It was a large tent, so there were about fifty cots, most of them occupied with injured or sick soldiers and refugees. Six men and women in white robes were attending to the patients. One man noticed Villem and walked over to greet him.

"May I help you?"

"Lord Sewell told me I should find arms and armor here. An attack is coming."

The man blanched. "Will we be in danger?"

"Quite possibly. We need as many men as possible to arm themselves for the defense."

"There's a pile over here. We put all clothing and belongings here. I don't know which belong to soldiers who have passed away and which belong to those still living."

"It matters not," Villem said. "Should I survive the coming fight, I shall return what I borrow."

A large man with naught but a sheet wrapped about his shoulders stood up from his cot and approached, apparently having overheard the conversation. Villem glanced at him, and then realized who he was.

"You're the knight from the battle at the stream."

The knight had an angry-looking wound on the side of his head, and Villem remembered how he had been struck there by Willa's maul. His helm must have saved his life. "You're the one sat his pony across the stream and watched," the knight said in a gravelly voice.

"I was a prisoner of those marauders. I've seen you before at my father's keep in Iskimir."

The knight's eyebrows rose. "I was there with Lord Kamron. Don't remember you."

"I recall your fellow knight being thrown out for drunkenness."

The knight shrugged. "He was always a mean drunk."

"You took on the raiders almost single-handedly. I never saw such bravery."

The knight sneered. "Foolishness more like. I got pissed enough to refuse to retreat when I should have."

"Yet you lived. You're hard to bring down."

The man looked slightly embarrassed, as if unused to compliments. "Aye, perhaps. I was nearly away when some scrawny fellow with one arm showed up and nearly skewered me. I was lucky his horse brought him in too close and I managed to sock him a few times in the jaw."

"That's the elf, Miranvel. He's on his way here now with even more of those raiders. It's why I'm here to arm myself."

"Haven't seen too many healthy soldiers around here," the knight said. "You'd do better to run off, like I should have."

"Are you going to run?"

The knight stared at the pile of equipment for half a minute before responding. "I suppose not. I'd like another chance at that elf. Besides, if a little sprat like you isn't running, how can I?"

The two grinned at each other, then began picking through the piles of equipment to find pieces that suited them.

"I'm Villem, by the way," Villem said while buckling on some greaves.

"Kogan." The huge knight was struggling to find armor that would fit him.

"Your head wound looks nasty. Does it still hurt?"

"Keep getting terrible headaches. Makes me want to kill myself."

"Don't say that!" Villem was shocked at the very idea. "I'm sure you'll get better."

"Perhaps. That healer there says maybe or maybe not. No telling with a head wound."

They continued arming themselves in silence for a few moments, until Kogan threw a hauberk to the floor in disgust. "My own armor is around here somewhere! That noble lady took it from me."

"You mean Livia? She probably brought it to the commander's hut. I can take you there, if the raiders haven't shown up yet."

"Let's not waste time then," Kogan said, and headed for the exit.

Villem snatched up a shield and followed. Duchess was barking at something, but paused to whine at Villem before she turned about and started barking again.

"What is it, girl?" Villem saw that a line of six mule-drawn carts stood in the road ahead. Leading the procession was a small carriage, drawn by a piebald mare. Two men-at-arms on ponies guarded the small caravan. "You barking at them, Duchess?"

As if he had given her permission, Duchess took off running, barking furiously. Villem shrugged at Kogan. "The house is that way anyhow." He took Zora's reins and led her down the road.

Duchess stopped near the carriage at the head of the caravan, wagging her tail and yapping. One of the men-at-arms was trying to shoo her off with his spear.

"Don't stab her, please," Villem cried as he drew near. "She's my dog."

"Well get it away from my lady's carriage," the soldier growled.

"Come, Duchess! Stop that!"

The door of the carriage opened and a slender form lowered herself onto the step to descend. "I know that dog," came a voice Villem instantly recognized.

"Lady Sonia! What are you doing here?"

"Sir Villem! I was hoping I would find you here. I didn't expect it would prove so easily done."

Sir Kogan broke in impatiently. "Where's my stuff?"

"Sorry," Villem said. He pointed to the small house where Livia had been living with Lord Sewell. "It should be in there." As Kogan strode off, Villem turned back to Sonia. She looked as pretty as he remembered. "You brought more supplies? You needn't have come yourself."

Sonia made to step down, so Villem dropped Zora's reins and hurried forward to give her a hand.

"I…I was hoping to have a chance to speak with you, Villem."

"Why?"

Sonia looked around, as if she wished to find a better place to speak. When she looked at Villem again, her face flushed. "Did you mean what you said…when you said I should leave my husband and come with you?"

Villem felt the bitterness creep back into his mind. She had used him and had only wanted to bear a son to make her husband happy. "I-I'm sorry. I was foolish and not thinking right. Anyhow, you made it clear what you wanted."

Sonia reached out a hand toward Villem's face, but he took a half-step back. "It is I who must apologize. The witch…I mean Marianna…told me you felt badly used by me. I was selfish. Only thinking what would make my life with my husband better. I didn't realize you would feel the way you did."

"So, what does this mean?" Villem asked. "You've changed your mind and want to leave your husband now?"

Sonia looked down at the ground. When she looked up again, she had trouble meeting Villem's eyes. When she spoke, her voice was barely more than a whisper. "It seems...I am a widow now."

It dawned on Villem what she meant. Her husband had gone to the terrible battle where the dragon had attacked. He shouldn't have been surprised that the lord was among the slain. Now he felt even worse, not because Sonia's husband was dead, but because she may have only come to him because of her husband's death. He knew he should tell her how sorry he was for the tragedy, but his bitterness burst forth instead. "So, I'm just the next best."

Sonia put both hands to her belly, and tears crept into her eyes. "I'm sorry you feel that way. I can understand why. But I do like you very much."

"Not enough to leave an unloving husband."

She stared at the ground again. "No."

Villem was at a loss as to what to think. He did not like the idea that she wanted him only because her husband had died. And he really didn't know her very well; he had simply been smitten with her due to his lack of romantic experience. Not that marriages needed the couples to know one another. Most marriages were arranged, and often the intended pair had never even spoken to one another. Did he want to marry this woman? As much as he hesitated to think it, he was lord of Iskimir now. His step-mother had always been cold toward him. There was no telling what she would be like now. Having a pretty, noble-born wife might help in regards to his relationship with the woman he had always thought was his mother. And Sonia was bearing his child. Could he say no to her, knowing it meant he was abandoning his own baby? The greatest blow in Villem's life had been learning he was a bastard and would not gain the inheritance he had always believed was his. How could he allow his own child to be a bastard?

He thought about Dinara and Livia. He liked and was attracted to both of them. But they seemed to like each other more than him, no matter how strange that thought seemed.

"I…don't think I can make a decision so easily," he said at last.

Sonia nodded. "Can we spend some time together? See how we get along?"

"I'm not sure we'll get that time. You see me armed because we are about to be attacked here. I may very well not survive what is coming. You should return to your keep for now."

Sonia's lovely face paled. "Attacked? Why must you fight? Come away with me and you will be safe."

Villem shook his head. "I cannot do that. There are thousands of innocents here. They need all the help they can get. I wish you had more soldiers with you. We could sure use them."

Sonia looked over at the nearest man-at-arms. "They aren't mine to command anymore. My husband's younger brother has inherited the castle. His wife dislikes me. I…I must find somewhere else to live."

"What about your parents? Was your father at the battle?"

Sonia shook her head. "He's too old. My brother Havlin took the troops. He's well. He stopped by the keep on the way back. Told me they were lucky. They were in reserve when the dragon attacked, so they were able to flee. I can return home, of course, but then my father will just marry me off to some other lord I don't know. That is, if there are any lords left in the area. So many widows now."

"I have friends here. We'll find them and you can stay with them until the battle is over. I have an idea about your wagons."

Villem walked over to the driver of the lead wagon. "I'll lead you to where the wagons are needed. Follow me." Villem took up Zora's reins again and whistled to Duchess. He nodded to Lady Sonia to accompany him.

"Where are we going?" she asked.

"We're commandeering your wagons for the coming battle. Lord Sewell is using the river to anchor his right flank. We can use the wagons to curve around from his left back to the river so the cavalry cannot easily flank him. Perhaps I can talk your two soldiers into staying to help as well."

As he was speaking, Villem noticed a large gathering of people in the refugee camp. He pointed toward the crowd. "That has to be my friend Livia speaking to those people. You should go find her, so I can concentrate on the coming fight."

Sonia looked panic-stricken. "No, no! I'll stay with you."

"The danger grows every moment. You'll be far safer with Livia and my other friends."

"I'll go when I must, but for now I'm staying."

"You mentioned Marianna before. Did a large woman with a wound in her side ever arrive at your keep?"

"Aye, she came with a train of refugees. I would have turned them away if they had not mentioned your name." She shook her head. "I'm sorry. Marianna tried her best, but the woman's wound had soured beyond help."

"I see," Villem said, wondering if he should ever tell Dinara the news about her former lover.

They were passing the village well when Villem saw Sir Kogan emerge from the last hut. He was fully armed and armored, and he grinned at Villem and pounded a fist to his chest.

"Found it! Now that fucking elf is going to die!"

52
IMRIC

Imric grew more and more amazed at his sister as he listened to her speak so confidently to the growing crowd of refugees. She had always seemed so studious in the past, preferring to be alone with her reading than to be around any gatherings of people. This was a side of her he had never seen before. He recalled the conversation with Xax about why Livia could never be queen of the realm. It saddened him that the people would refuse to be ruled by the one person who truly seemed to be the best to lead them, just because she was a woman.

These people, at least, seemed willing to listen. Several men stepped forward when she called for volunteers to aid in the defense. Three of them had hunting bows, and a handful more had some training in one weapon or another. Livia told those men to go to the healers' pavilion to find armor and weapons. She told the rest of the refugees to arm themselves with whatever they could find. If Darus's men attacked, she said, it could be a slaughter, but the refugees vastly outnumbered them. If they were willing to fight back, the raiders would be overwhelmed.

"Livia is wonderful," Soot whispered in Imric's ear.

Imric shivered at the feel of Soot's lips so close to his skin. Whatever happens, he promised himself, I'm never going to part with

Soot ever again. Then he remembered his hideously disfigured foot, and his mood soured. *Perhaps she will not want to be with me*, he thought.

When Livia finished her speech, a man stepped from the crowd and shouted a question. "Will there be civil war? Who will rule us?"

Livia looked unsure of herself for the first time. Xax was standing near her, and he stepped forward.

"We cannot know for certain what will happen. However, by the rule of tradition, we know who the rightful heir is."

There were shouts from the crowd, some crying Erol's name and others calling out for Darus. Imric was shocked people were still willing to support his brother after he had invaded the realm.

Xax held up his hands to quiet the crowd. "Neither of those men is worthy. Darus is a traitor who has slaughtered thousands of your countrymen and even now threatens us here. Erol slew his own nephew Balmar and very nearly succeeded in murdering young Imric here as well, all for the sake of trying to claim power that he was not entitled to. You may not have heard his name, but this young man, Imric Kaldarion is the rightful heir to the throne."

As murmuring spread through the crowd and they all tried to catch a glimpse of him, Imric wished he was a turtle and could draw his neck into his shell. He wanted to cry out that he did not want to be king. That they should take Livia as queen instead. But he was afraid to speak to all these people. Soot suddenly kissed him on the cheek, and it made him feel a little better and he straightened his posture.

"You all remember beloved Queen Elinor," Xax continued. "You know she died in childbirth, but what many of you never were told is that the child lived. That child is Imric. You have shown yourselves willing to listen to the Princess Livia Kaldarion. Know that she will always be there to help guide King Imric. Unite together behind the rightful king, and we can restore peace to the realm."

There were ragged cheers from the crowd, but too many people seemed uncertain what to hope for. The man who had called out the question now cried out again. "Let us see this Imric better. Hold him up!"

There were murmurs and cries of assent from the crowd, and a growing number began to take up the chant: "Hold him up!"

Again Imric wanted to hide, but there was nowhere to go. Xax and Livia were both beckoning to him, and Soot began to tug him forward by the hand. Dinara took his other hand and helped lead him forward. Imric was still in awe of Dinara. He had seen any number of women considered to be beauties during his time in his father's castle, but none of those women compared favorably to Dinara. Reluctantly, Imric allowed Xax to lift him up onto his shoulders.

"Wave to them, Imric," Livia said.

His face burning with embarrassment, Imric hesitantly waved to the crowd. The nearest people seemed to like what they saw, for they began to chant again: "Imric! Imric!"

Livia stepped forward again and held up her arms. The crowd slowly grew quiet again. "Remember, we may not have much time. Arm yourselves any way you can. If the raiders attack you, fight back. Run and you are defenseless. You outnumber them a thousand to one!"

"Where will you be, princess? And the young Imric?" cried an elderly woman.

"We shall be right here with you," Livia replied. "Your fate is ours as well."

Imric forced Xax to set him down, then huddled with Soot behind everyone else.

"You're shaking," Soot said, and put an arm around his shoulders. "Are you all right?"

"I hate this," Imric replied. "I don't want *any* of this."

53

VILLEM

"I thought you said they were on your heels?" Lord Sewell shouted.

Villem shrugged. "When I saw them, they were. I've no idea what they're up to."

Against the wishes of the drivers, the soldiers had commandeered a dozen wagons and formed them into a rough, semi-circular wall to shore up the left flank. It was growing dark, and only one of the moons was out, so men were lighting lamps and torches.

Lady Sonia's small carriage was parked behind the line of wagons. She had tried gamely to remain awake, but had finally succumbed to exhaustion and fallen asleep inside her carriage. Her wagon drivers had chosen to remain and were taking turns guarding her carriage. Villem had spoken to one as he rubbed down her horse, asking the man to ensure he got her out of there quickly if the raiders showed up.

Sir Kogan had gone silent when he had been introduced to Lady Sonia. Now he snored soundly, wrapped in a blanket by one of the wheels of her carriage.

"Sitting here waiting is almost worse than if they showed," Sewell said.

"Let the men sleep in shifts," Villem said. "They may attack at night, or they may not come until the morrow."

"Aye, nothing for it. I wish we could rid ourselves of all those refugees. I'm worried the raiders will ignore us and massacre them."

"At least we're not completely helpless now," Villem said. Besides three men with hunting bows, they now had ten horses they could use, though none of them were warhorses. "If we only knew how much time we had, we could withdraw everyone to the plateau and use its natural defenses. There aren't many pathways up."

"There's too much to move," Sewell said. "All those supplies and tents, and we don't have any wells up there."

"Still better than this. Want me to take my pony and scout them out?"

"And ride right into them in the dark? I'd rather keep all fighting men close."

"I need a walk," Villem said. "I'm going to check on my friends."

Villem was tired of the endless waiting for the enemy to arrive, so he was happy for a chance to look for Livia and Dinara. He left Zora behind and tried to get Duchess to stay as well, but the dog refused and followed him toward the vast refugee camp.

"I'm going to have to teach you how to stay when you're told, girl," he grumbled, though really he was happy for her company.

It did not take as long as he had imagined to find his friends. He asked the first people he met where they were, and they pointed toward a large bonfire at the rear of the camp, not far from the base of the plateau. It took half an hour to wend his way through the dark, crowded field before he finally reached the fire. Duchess began barking and ran ahead to leap onto a laughing Dinara.

"It's Villem!" Dinara cried. "Come join us!"

A large group of refugees encircled the bonfire, with Dinara, Livia and the rest of their friends huddled near each other on the west side. Dinara scooted over to make room for Villem on a blanket between herself and Soot. Soot still held tightly to Imric's hand. Livia sat next to Imric, while Xax stood before the fire.

"Xax has been telling the most fantastical stories," Dinara said. "I don't believe a word of them, but they are good for taking our minds off the danger."

Villem sat down. "How can anyone laugh and tell stories at a time like this?"

"What else are we going to do?" Dinara asked.

"I don't know. I just find it strange. How is Livia doing?"

He had no sooner spoken her name than Livia appeared, standing over him. She got Dinara to move over so she could sit between her and Villem. "Is everything all right?" she asked once she was settled. Duchess planted herself in front of the trio, tongue lolling happily.

"The soldiers are tense from the wait."

Livia sighed and then took both Villem's and Dinara's hands in her own. "I wish we had more time to get to know each other. I finally find some new friends, and we may all perish soon."

"Don't speak like that," Villem said, squeezing her hand lightly. He was thrilled she had called them friends. "I do wish you could lead all these people away from here, though."

"Some people are going, but most can't. People need food, water, and shelter. It isn't easy moving it all, especially since you took most of the wagons."

"What happened to our tent and the carriage?"

Dinara laughed. "Those two criminals finally realized no one was guarding their door. They've taken up residence in the carriage, probably hoping they can steal a mule or pony."

Xax had begun speaking to his audience again, though Villem had been concentrating too much on his friends to hear what the man was saying. When he heard the name Aronis, however, he began to pay attention.

"So, the wizards led your tribe on a long, treacherous journey through the barbarian lands, until at last they came to the great mountain pass where East Gate now stands and into what you now call the Known Lands. Thus it was that Aronis became your first king, and your tribe began to call themselves Greatlanders. Since the Spire of Peace already stood, you Greatlanders have known peace ever since, only needing to guard the single pass that breaches the Hellisgaard Mountains."

Dinara leaned over Livia to whisper to Villem. "Can you believe he said our people were a barbarian tribe, no different than any of the others? He said we changed because we took in the wizards and they taught us their language and much of their knowledge, so we became different."

Livia laughed. "It is true, though, however silly you think it sounds. Xax taught me most of what I know. He's the wisest man in the world."

"How can he know so much?" Villem asked.

"He's a wizard," Livia replied. "I know he doesn't look it, but he has been alive for thousands of years."

"Is he part elf?" The elves were the only people Villem had heard of who lived impossibly long lives.

"No," Livia said. "But the wizards have that in common with the elves. Here at least. I never could understand everything he told me. He said that where he came from, their lives were no longer than any others. Only when they came here did they begin to age so slowly."

"Xax is a wizard. It's hard to believe. But then I didn't believe in dragons either. Where are all the other wizards?"

"Most have been killed over the centuries. According to Xax, only two others may still be alive. He believes one of them is responsible for the dragon coming and destroying the spire."

"I thought the wizards were good?"

"All except the one called Bilach. He's the one who tricked the elves and dwarves into going to war with each other, many thousands of years before we came to these lands."

"Just our luck," Villem said. "Only the good wizards die off, leaving us with the bad one." Exhaustion was catching up to him and he was having trouble keeping his eyes open. Livia's warm presence next to him was the only thing keeping him from lying down to sleep. Xax had continued his story for the crowd, but Villem cared only for being with Livia and Dinara. After all, it could very well be their last night together.

"Do you miss the magic?" Livia suddenly asked.

"I certainly don't," Dinara said. "I've never even felt it. I lived my entire life beyond the influence of your magic."

"It's strange to imagine that," Livia said.

"I miss it," Villem said. "I never realized how hard it is to practice with the sword or lance, to run, or even to climb stairs until the magic deserted me. We grew up with it. Never knew what it did for us until it was gone."

"There's more," Livia said. "I think some people—perhaps many—behaved well only because they feared the magic turning on them. What will happen now when people can choose to do whatever they wish?"

Villem couldn't help himself and yawned hugely.

Livia yawned as well. "Looks like we all should get some sleep."

Villem was a little disappointed when Livia released his hand so she could roll herself in her blanket, but was happy to be among friends. Duchess snuggled up between Villem and Livia. Villem fell asleep to the soothing sound of the wizard's words before the crackling bonfire.

54
DARUS

"Pass me the heads," Darus said.

The boy Weevil was leading the extra mounts, and one skittish mare had the honor of carrying the two sacks holding the heads of Darus's uncle and cousin. Weevil untied the sacks and passed them over to Darus, who tied them together and slung them across his saddle pommel.

"You remain here with the horses," Darus said to Weevil. "I'll send someone to fetch you once this is done."

Darus led the rest of the men onward along the road. In the near distance, they could see the smoke of many fires, so they knew they were close.

That morning Orderic had tried to convince Darus to confront the convoy of foot soldiers coming from Valandiria. Without their leader, he had argued, they could do no better than to bend the knee to Darus and accept him as their new king. Darus, who was feeling a bit better, had hacked and coughed and spat up phlegm, then told Orderic they were moving onward. The wagon train was slow. They could deal with it any time.

They topped a final rise and saw a small hamlet at the crossroads ahead. Off to the right, lining the road that headed north, a string of refugee camps held perhaps twenty thousand people. Probably more, Darus thought after looking more closely. *This is where I need to be. These people loved me once. They will love me again.*

Miranvel began to laugh, until Darus glared at Orderic and Orderic told the elf to desist.

"You see that?" Orderic asked.

Darus did not bother to respond, as it was obvious that they all could see the pitiful defensive arrangement that faced them a little beyond the crossroads. No more than a hundred foot soldiers. No knights that he could see. If they had any archers, Darus saw no sign of them. A small line of wagons to try to hold the flank not covered by the river. Darus almost felt sorry for these men.

"Slow and steady," Darus said. "Keep behind me, and don't let your elf do anything stupid."

The soldiers saw them coming and began forming up into a shield wall, spears thrust outward to deter any charging horses.

Darus called a halt just outside of arrow range. "See anyone with bows?"

"Not sure," Orderic said. "Maybe a couple behind the line."

"What is that, nine, ten horses?"

"Looks like."

"They're helpless. Pass me a shield."

Orderic ordered Eiric to hand his shield over to Darus.

"Wait here," Darus said. Hefting the shield, he walked his horse toward the defensive line. He watched carefully for any movement from bowmen. Last thing he needed was to reach the brink of victory only to be taken out by some huntsman with a long bow.

He got to within shouting distance and reined in his mount. "Who's in charge here?" His voice sounded raspy from too much coughing.

A man standing in the center of the shield wall responded. "That would be me. You're Darus."

"King Darus. And who are you?"

"Lord Sewell."

"Never heard of you. Where you from?"

"A tiny province north of Vimar Keep."

Darus grunted. Slowly he untied the sacks from his pommel. He opened one to check its contents, then opened the other one and drew forth the head of Erol Kaldarion. He held it up by the hair so all could see its features, then tossed it so it rolled on the ground. "Your loyalty is admirable, but the reason for it is gone." He reached into the other sack, drew forth his cousin's head, and tossed it so it landed near the other. "All reasons for it are gone. We'll have peace now. The realm will be restored. Just bend the knee."

Lord Sewell spat. "You traitorous butcher! This land deserves better than you."

"Be that as it may, I'm what it's got. Bend the knee. Any of you men who come forth and take a knee will be forgiven."

Darus watched as the shield wall shifted, the low rumble of the soldiers' voices barely audible.

"Hold firm, men!" Lord Sewell cried. "You'll not bow to this monster!"

"What's your alternative?" Darus called out. "Do you plan to call yourself king in my place?"

"Imric Kaldarion is the rightful heir," Sewell replied.

That took Darus by surprise. "Heard he was dead, he and Balmar both."

"Imric lives."

"Huh," Darus grunted, then coughed and spat. "Where is my little brother?"

"He's safe."

"You notice I said *little* brother. Meaning I'm the heir."

"You forfeited any rights to the throne when you turned traitor," Sewell said.

"You really want the blood of these men on your hands? How about all those people out there?" Darus pointed toward the refugee camps.

"We know you're a monster. You'll merely prove how unfit you are to rule."

A twang sounded loudly in the still air. Darus brought up the shield and an arrow caromed off. Lord Sewell cursed at one of his men.

Darus nudged his steed, turned it about, and headed back toward his men. He refused to hurry, but listened carefully for the snap of another bowstring. It never came.

"That went well," Orderic said when Darus drew near.

"Ignore the soldiers for now. Let's go speak to the people. Leave the elf here. He'll only make things worse."

Miranvel was less than pleased to be left behind. Darus could feel his glare boring holes in his head as he led his men toward the camps.

The refugees had begun to congregate, and more were crowding in by the moment. Darus was amused to see many of them carrying makeshift weapons—hay forks, sharpened pieces of wood, eating knives, and more. *Perhaps they don't love me as much as I remembered,* he thought. He raised a hand to halt his men.

"Do you have anyone to speak for you?" he called out to the teeming masses.

The crowd began to part as several people pushed through to the front. Darus saw the flash of long silver hair and had a premonition of what was coming.

55
LIVIA

"They're really coming." Livia heard the fear in her own voice. She looked at Imric and knew she needed to get him away as fast as possible. She turned to Villem.

"Please, Villem. Take Dinara and Imric and Soot and get them away from here. I can't do what needs doing unless I know you're all safe."

Villem looked pale but determined. "I'm not leaving you. You need more protection than anyone."

"I have Xax!"

"He's not enough. Not with Orderic and that insane elf and the rest." Villem looked at Dinara. The fear on her face made her lovelier than ever; it tore his heart to send her away. "Dinara, if you take the north road quickly, you may catch the carriage of Lady Sonia. I told her drivers to head that way when trouble came. Once in the clear, make for Iskimir. Tell my mother that Sonia is carrying my child. The baby's the heir if…if I don't make it."

"Don't say that," Dinara said. "You shouldn't stay here. None of you. There's no reason to let Orderic murder you."

"I can't leave," Livia said. "These people depend on me."

"And I can't let Livia go unprotected," Villem said.

Xax stepped forward. "I do have *some* small power to protect her, you know."

"We're wasting time!" Livia cried. She stepped toward Imric and took his shoulders in her hands. "Take Soot and go, Brother. Follow Dinara and do as she says." She leaned in and kissed his cheek before turning to Soot. "You take care of him now."

Soot nodded and gripped Imric's hand harder.

"I'll go," Dinara said, "but I expect to see you both by this evening. Up the north road somewhere."

Dinara stepped up to Villem and gave him a quick peck on the cheek. Then she turned to Livia.

They stared into each other's eyes and Livia felt a shiver run through her body. She had been avoiding having to deal with the strange feelings she had for this woman. Now there may never be time to try to understand them. She held her arms open so Dinara could hug her. Dinara stepped into the hug, but then she kissed Livia full on the mouth. Livia was shocked, but she could not help but be excited at the same time. She had never experienced anything like this. The kiss seemed to go on for an eternity. Livia pressed harder into the hug and kissed Dinara back. When it finally ended, they held each other at arm's length and just stared at one another.

"By the evening," Dinara whispered. "Promise."

Livia nodded. "I promise."

Dinara turned, grabbed Imric's free hand, and began tugging the two youngsters along as she strode away.

"Wait," Villem cried. "Take Duchess with you."

Dinara nodded and paused to allow Villem to encourage the dog to go. It took some coaxing, but finally Duchess followed Imric and Soot, looking back at Villem only once.

Livia watched them go. She knew Villem and Xax were watching her, and her cheeks flushed. "Let's get this over with," she said, whirling about and stalking off through the camp without looking at either of the men.

People in the crowd saw her coming and began to form an escort around her and her two companions. Livia breathed deeply, trying to control the pounding of her heart. Up ahead, the crowd grew thick. They were watching something happening at the crossroads. It seemed to take forever to slowly press their way through the vast throng. They were finally drawing near the front of the crowd when Livia heard the unmistakable sound of her brother's voice.

"Do you have anyone to speak for you?" Darus called out.

"Let us through," Livia said to the refugees blocking her way.

They melted aside, many of them touching hands to their foreheads and dipping their heads and murmuring her name. Livia broke free of the press and saw her brother Darus for the first time in three years. She was shocked by how much he had changed. Gone was the red-cheeked young knight so proud of his accomplishments in the practice yard. Sitting astride his mare as if born in the saddle, this was a hardened warrior, the skin of his face weathered and lines deeply-etched in his forehead.

"Little brother." She had always called him that, and it escaped her lips before she realized he might take offense at having it used in front of so many of the people he wished to have as his subjects.

There was surprise written on his face now. It was clear he had not expected to find her here. "Sister. You're speaking for these folks?"

"As much as anyone can, I suppose."

"I'm sorry about Father."

She had not expected to hear an apology. "Darus," she began, then hesitated. "You can still do what is right. There's no need for any more bloodshed."

"That's exactly right," he said. He looked over the crowd and raised his voice. "As my sister said, there's no need for more blood to be spilled. It's time to bring peace back to the realm. You all know me. You know I'm the rightful heir to my father's throne. I swear to you all, I can reunite our lands once more." He held his arms—one bearing a scarred shield—high, aiming them out at the crowd. "Give me your loyalty and the Known Lands will be greater than they've ever been!"

There was a smattering of cheers and a few voices called out Darus's name, but mostly there was silence.

Then a rock flew from the crowd and nearly struck Darus. It whizzed by his head and struck the horse of one of his men. The horse bucked and the man crashed to the ground.

Darus looked enraged. He drew his sword and held his shield up to cover his body.

"Stop!" Livia shouted. "Stop this!"

The crowd behind Livia felt like an ocean wave suspended in the air, ready to crash down. Livia was terrified that these defenseless, innocent people could not take the onslaught of heavily armored, experienced soldiers. She looked at Xax, silently pleading for him to do something.

The wizard leaned in toward her. "Spread the word to everyone to cover their ears. Then put this in your ears. I hope this works." He handed her some sort of gummy substance. She noted that he kept some for himself. He gripped his walking stick hard, holding it vertically in front of his chest with the green crystal on top, and began edging forward.

Darus had turned away and was speaking calmly to one of his men. Livia assumed it must be Orderic, the man she had heard so much about from Villem and Dinara. She looked for the one-armed elf but could not see him.

Livia turned to Villem. "Tell everyone to cover their ears. Hurry!"

Villem nodded and pushed into the crowd, crying out the order over and over again.

Livia was horrified to hear what her brother said to Orderic.

"Have the men gather up some women and children and be quick about it. Lord Sewell will surrender right quick when he sees what we're willing to do."

He can't mean it, she thought. Not my little brother.

Then she saw Xax. The wizard looked so small and frail compared to the group of armored warriors on their steeds, yet he strode up to them without hesitation. Darus turned to look at him.

"I remember you, old man. Always getting my sister to read books."

"This is your last chance, Darus," Xax said in a voice that shook only slightly. He lifted his hands to push something into his ears. "Surrender yourselves and you'll be treated with more mercy than you have shown to others."

Darus's mouth dropped open. Then he began to roar with laughter, though it was quickly cut off by a coughing fit.

The man Livia assumed was Orderic drew his sword and kicked his horse toward Xax, followed by the rest of his men. Livia's heart skipped a beat, and an icy hand seemed to take hold of her throat. As if from a distance, she heard voices calling out to 'cover your ears'. The horsemen were about to ride down Xax. She saw the wizard lift the green crystal to his mouth. Just in time, she stuffed the gummy substance into her ears.

An incredible blast of noise, louder than ten thunder blasts put together, shook the ground beneath her feet. Even with her hands covering them, her ears pained her. The effect on the horsemen was astonishing.

Horses screamed and fell to the ground, where they kicked and flailed, often crushing their riders beneath them. Blood poured from their ears. The soldiers were in even worse shape. Those not trapped beneath their steeds were flopping on the ground like fish on dry land, most of them weeping, hands clasped about their heads.

Somehow, incredibly, Darus had won free of his falling horse and was staggering away as fast as he could go. He dropped the shield and pressed his hands to his bleeding ears.

Livia's eyes were drawn to the wizard. He stood straight for a moment, then collapsed to the ground. A silence fell but for the groaning of the soldiers and the screams of the horses. The crowd seemed to be in shock at what had happened. Livia ran to Xax and cradled his head in her arms. She feared he might be dead, but she heard his ragged breathing and was relieved. She looked up to see Darus still swaying and staggering onwards, making his escape.

Suddenly the crowd gave out a tremendous roar and surged forward. People who had never harmed another person in their lives found themselves venting their fears and anger on the fallen soldiers, pounding them with sticks and rocks and anything else they happened to have.

"Is it really over?" Livia whispered. She suddenly thought of Villem and tried to pick him out in the crowd, but it was too chaotic. Then he was there beside her, his hands still pressed to his ears.

"I can't believe it," he said. "Is he all right? He really is a wizard."

"Take care of him, will you? I must find Darus."

Villem caught her arm as she stood up. "Don't do it. Don't give him a chance to do more harm. He's done. Leave it be."

Livia gazed into his eyes and knew what he said made sense. Then she jerked her arm free and ran after Darus.

56
KOGAN

Sir Kogan could not take any more of this standing around waiting for something to happen.

He had stood near Lord Sewell, preparing to meet the charge of the enemy cavalry. It never came. Instead the enemy leader took his men and headed for the refugee camps.

Then Kogan saw something that warmed his heart. The one-armed elf had remained behind.

"Let me through," Kogan yelled at the spearmen formed up in their shield wall. "Now!"

He pushed men aside and headed straight for the elf, who was watching his companions trot away. As if in slow motion, the elf turned and saw Kogan coming.

"You're mine now, you bastard!" Kogan screamed.

The elf grinned widely and slipped down from his pony. He drew his sword and waited.

Kogan halted about five paces away. "Still feel my fist on your jaw?"

The elf cackled. "This will be a pleasure."

An arrow whipped by the elf's ear. Kogan turned about and screamed at the archers behind the shield wall. "Don't you fucking dare! He's mine!"

He turned back quickly to his opponent, but it was too late. The elf had rushed him while his back was turned. As he came around, the elf's blade punched into his gut.

"Ooof," Kogan said, pain jagging through his body worse than he had ever felt before. No! he thought. I. Will. Not. Let. This. Happen!

Time seemed to slow. The elf was about to yank his sword free. Kogan ignored the raging pain and pushed his body further onto the blade, his hands reaching out toward the elf. Too late, the elf realized what Kogan intended and tried to pull away. Kogan's fingers wrapped about the narrow neck and squeezed.

He could feel his strength draining from him, as if the blood spurting from his belly was stealing it from him. Kogan squeezed harder. He rode himself up the blade until he was face to face with the elf, whose eyes were bulging from his head. Kogan held on with the last of his fading strength, watching through dimming eyes as the elf's face turned purple.

"I got you," he panted. "Fucker."

57
AZER

The return journey had seemed to take forever. When they had finally reached the ferry, the man had refused to come across and take them. Azer had railed at the man in vain before finally giving up and heading south. He remembered seeing villages on that side of the river, some of them with ferries of their own.

Their party had split in half. Fuad had taken Vugar and Samir and headed for home. Babak and Ragif had come with Azer. Three men. Azer had no idea if they could make any difference for the lady Livia. He only knew that he could not live with himself if he did not try.

They were half-starved. Few people offered the ragged foreigners food or lodging. The more desperate they became, the more seldom such kindness occurred. When they had finally reached a village with a ferry, they had had nothing to offer the ferryman. He didn't want an eating knife. Nothing they had interested him. Then the man's wife showed up, bringing the ferryman his lunch, and she cursed her husband out when she saw how pathetic the huddled men looked. She said he needed to show kindness to strangers. The man turned beet red, and grumbling under his breath, he ferried them across the river.

Two more days they had stumbled north, growing ever hungrier, wondering why they had made such an accursed decision. Now they would die in this far off land, and their families would never know what had happened.

They had been lucky last evening. They threw themselves down to sleep beneath a willow tree. A plowed field was nearby, and a boy saw them and ran off as if frightened. But then he returned with his father, bearing a basket of foodstuffs. Azer and his companions wept at such kindness.

This morning they felt stronger as they walked on. They had made it off the road in time to allow a large band of soldiers on horses go trotting by. An hour later, they topped a rise and saw the familiar refugee camps and tiny town spread out in front of them. They passed a boy holding a string of mounts. He stared at them with a scowl on his face as they passed by.

They were nearing the town when a blast of sound reached them, so loud they could not imagine what could have caused it. They felt the ground shake, and a few moments later, a blast of warm air brushed their faces.

Azer heard the rumblings of a crowd beyond the houses. "Hurry," he rasped. "The lady may need our help."

They came around the last house and were confronted with a strange sight. A large man, wrapped in steel from head to toe, staggered toward them, his hands pressed to his ears, which were bleeding.

He did not appear to see them. He seemed to be raving mad, repeating the same line again and again. "I am the king! I am the king!"

Azer had no idea if the man finally saw him or not, but as the man neared him, he stumbled and fell into Azer's arms. The man was heavy, and they both crashed to the ground.

Babak and Ragif scurried to pull the man off Azer.

"Lay him down," Azer said. "He is badly injured."

"It hurts so much," the man muttered. "So much. My head."

With a surge of strength, the man pushed the nomads away and staggered to his feet. He turned back the way he had come and strode forward several steps before halting.

"I will kill you wizard!" the man screamed. "And you Sister! I loved you most of all, yet you betrayed me!"

Azer heard the tears in the man's voice as he raged and screamed. He saw how the man's face reminded him of Livia, and he understood that this was her younger brother, Darus, the man who led the invasion. Darus seemed nigh unto death, as far as Azer could tell, but he seemed dangerous still, and Azer feared what he might yet be capable of doing.

"Darus!" Azer called out, and when there was no response, he cried it again. There was still no response, and he realized Darus must be unable to hear from the wounds to his ears. Azer motioned to his comrades to move to either side of the madman. Loosening his dagger in its sheath, Azer slowly walked around Darus, trying to draw his attention.

But another figure appeared. Livia, walking directly toward Darus with compassion shining from her eyes. Her brother continued to scream, as if he were blind as well as deaf. When she drew near, Livia held out her arms as if wishing to embrace Darus.

"Little Brother," she said. "Calm yourself and let us tend to your wounds. You need aid."

"No, lady!" Azer cried. "He will harm you!"

Livia seemed to notice Azer for the first time. She smiled. "Azer, you have returned."

Any thought of further reunion was cut off by more screams from Darus. "Sister! I cannot see you!"

Livia drew within two paces of Darus. "I'm here, Brother."

Darus took his hands from his ears and rubbed at his eyes. His breathing became ragged. "Is…is that you, Sister?"

"Yes, it's me." Livia still held her arms wide, wanting to embrace Darus but hesitating. She glanced from her brother to Azer, as if seeking a sign of hope.

Azer shook his head, hoping desperately to warn her away. He noticed Darus's right hand gripping the hilt of the dagger still sheathed at his side.

"He intends you harm, lady," Azer said. "Madness has claimed him."

Livia shook her head. "No, he…he's confused is all." She took another step forward.

"Sister," Darus said, then lunged toward Livia, drawing forth the dagger at the same time.

Azer darted to intercept him, and Babak and Ragif charged in as well. Livia gave a shriek as she saw the flash of the blade in her brother's hand, and she stumbled backward. Darus was upon her, his right arm plunging forward with the blade. Azer slammed into him from the side. As they struck the ground and rolled, Darus tried to turn the blade on Azer.

Ragif grabbed hold of Darus's arm before he could strike, and Babak threw himself onto Darus's legs to help pin him to the ground.

"I am the king, you bastards," Darus moaned. He let go of the dagger and tried to put his hand to his face. "My head, it hurts!"

Azer uncapped his water bottle and held it to Darus's lips. Darus sputtered and choked some down. He shook his head.

"No. No. My head!"

His ears had been bleeding, but now blood erupted from his nose and mouth. He began coughing, trying to say something.

"I am so sorry, brother," Azer said to the man.

"I want…want my mother," Darus gurgled, and then his breathing shuddered to a stop.

Livia rushed forward and dropped to her knees next to them. Her face looked stricken.

Azer looked at her. "I wanted to help you. I'm sorry we arrived too late."

"Oh, no. Not too late," Livia cried, sobbing. She put one arm on her brother's body and encircled Azer's neck with the other.

He had not the energy to tell her it was inappropriate, and a part of him was very glad to feel her touch and the wetness of her tears on his face.

58

DINARA

Lady Sonia had been glad when Dinara insisted they stop.

"Livia and Villem will come for us here," Dinara said.

Sonia called for the driver to halt the carriage beneath a large plane tree near a stream.

Dinara had not thought she could catch up with the noblewoman, since she was in a carriage, but she had found her parked not far up the road. Sonia had been standing atop the carriage, watching events unfold. When Dinara's small group arrived and told Sonia that Villem had sent them to her, they had mutually decided it was time to put some distance between them and the unfolding dangers.

They had all been too worried to speak much during their short journey from the camps. Dinara wished she could go back, but she knew she could not leave Imric and Soot alone. Now the pair were playing with Duchess in the stream, laughing and splashing water at one another.

How quickly the young heal, Dinara thought. Such a terrifying day, and yet they can laugh and play.

"How do you know Sir Villem?" Lady Sonia asked.

Dinara did not really want to talk to the woman. She had been shocked when Villem said she was carrying his child. How could he know that? How could such a thing have happened in the short time between him fleeing from captivity until they met again on the road? She surreptitiously studied the lady, begrudgingly admitting that she might be somewhat pretty, in a pale, delicate sort of way. "It…it's a long story."

"We may have a long wait."

"Villem told me you are carrying his child."

Sonia blushed and she put her hands to her belly. "He…he didn't tell me about you."

"We aren't lovers," Dinara said. "Just…friends."

Sonia tilted her head at Dinara. "I've never heard of men being just friends with a woman. At least not with one as lovely as you."

"Well," Dinara muttered. "It's possible."

"Yes, well. It's true. About his child."

"How can you know? You have the morning sickness?"

Sonia shook her head. "The witch told me. Well, I am getting sick in the mornings now as well, but I already knew."

"Witch? Are they real as well? I guess nothing should surprise me now."

"Marianna isn't really a witch. Everyone just calls her that. She's a healer."

"Oh. But doesn't it seem like magic if she can know you are with child before there are signs?"

Sonia thought about it for a moment. "I suppose. She says it isn't magic. Just the herbs she chooses."

They silently watched the youngsters play for a while. Imric found a short stick and began throwing it for Duchess to chase and bring back.

"Are they siblings?" Sonia asked.

Dinara thought it an odd question. Imric had silver hair and Soot was dark all over. They looked nothing alike. "No, just friends."

Three of Sonia's men had accompanied them, two on horses. They were busy preparing a camp in case they needed to remain there for the night.

"You rule your own castle?" Dinara asked.

"What? Oh…no. After my husband died, I no longer have a home."

"I'm sorry about your husband. Was it recent?"

"It was the big battle. With Duke Erol. I mean King Erol. Sorry, it's hard to know who holds what title these days."

Dinara tried to calculate in her head. She wasn't good at it, but she figured Sonia must have taken Villem to her bed before knowing she had lost her husband. She thought Villem should have been better than to sleep with a married woman.

"Don't be angry with Villem."

"How can you—?"

"I see it in your face. It wasn't his fault. He wasn't well. I…I took advantage of him." Sonia's face reddened again and she stared at her hands.

Dinara could think of nothing to say. She wanted to dislike this woman, yet her honesty was somehow disarming. After an uncomfortable silence, she asked, "What will you do now?"

"I don't know. These men belong to the new Lord Wotton. They were kind enough to stay with me during these troubles, but they'll surely head home soon. I'm hoping they might be willing to take me to Iskimir."

"Where Villem is now lord."

"Is he? I knew he was a knight, but I had no idea…"

"His father and brother both died at that same battle."

Sonia flung a hand to her mouth. "Oh, dear. How terrible."

"Anyhow, we're heading the wrong way if you want to go to Iskimir, at least from what Villem told me. You have to get across the river and go south."

Sonia nodded.

"Villem will come," Dinara said. "I'm sure of it. He can take you to Iskimir."

Sonia nodded again.

"I know nothing about men," Dinara said.

"What do you mean?"

Dinara laughed. "I thought Villem fancied me. I kept trying to think of a way to let him down gently. It's embarrassing to find out how wrong I was."

"Maybe you weren't wrong," Sonia said.

Dinara shrugged. It didn't matter, she supposed. She had felt Livia's reaction during the kiss and knew that was real. Dinara bit her lip. Would a princess be able to have such a relationship? The same questions she had had for the past several days roiled through her mind. She didn't want a secret love. But that may be all that was possible with Livia. *If she'll even have me*, she thought.

59
IMRIC

Soot took her turn to throw the stick for Duchess, but the old dog was beginning to tire. She still eagerly chased after the stick, but she was panting hard now.

"Maybe we should stop," Imric said.

Soot nodded.

"Look, bees," Imric said, pointing. He followed their flights and saw some heading up into the branches of the nearby tree. "I think their hive may be up there."

"Want to climb up?" Soot asked.

"No. We might get stung."

Soot nodded. "Do you think Livia and Xax will be all right?"

"I don't want to think about it. I'm afraid if I do then something bad will happen." He had had enough terrible days of late. He thought back to the day the dragon had attacked Tolgaria. Then later when his uncle had murdered Balmar and smashed Imric's foot. He hated that he would never be able to run or jump again. They had removed their boots to play in the stream, and now Imric felt self-conscious about his hideously-deformed foot again. He hurried to seat himself under the tree and begin to pull on his boots. Xax had cut and re-stitched one so it would fit over his foot. Soot sat next to him and watched as he tied the thongs. When he finished, Imric stared miserably at his foot. Duchess came panting up and plopped down in the grass, still holding the stick in her mouth.

"Soot?"

"Hmm?"

"Do you think anyone will ever want to marry me?"

She giggled. "As ugly as you are, who would want to?"

Imric felt tears well up in his eyes.

Soot put a hand on his knee. "Hey! You know I'm only joking, don't you?"

Imric looked away so she wouldn't see his puffy eyes.

"Anyhow," Soot went on, "since when have princes ever had a choice who they marry? Their marriages are always arranged."

Imric sniffed and wiped a finger under his nose. "I don't want an arranged marriage."

"Maybe Livia will help you find someone you like?"

"You're the only one I like," Imric whispered, afraid she might hear him, yet unable to help himself.

"Don't be silly," Soot said. "You aren't allowed to marry a kitchen scullion."

Imric wanted to look at her, but he simply couldn't do it. "Would you?" he asked. "If you could, I mean?"

"Any girl would be lucky to have a prince."

"But would you *want* to, if you had a choice?"

The silence stretched out so long, Imric thought he might go mad.

"Of course I would, silly," she said at last. "But…but I never allowed myself to dream it."

Relief flooded through Imric. She did like him. More than just as friends. "What about my foot?"

"What do you mean?"

"It's so ugly." Imric turned to look at her.

Soot shrugged. "Is that what you're worried about? You should worry more what Livia will think of your crazy schemes."

Imric smiled. "Maybe I'll be king. Then it won't matter what anyone thinks."

"I thought you didn't want to be king?"

"I don't. But if it's the only way I could marry you, I'd do it."

Soot tilted her head onto his shoulder. "We're too young, anyhow."

"A couple more years and we won't be."

"I miss my mamma," Soot said.

Imric hesitated, then put his arm around Soot's shoulders.

Duchess let the stick go and barked at them.

60
VILLEM

The sun was still well above the horizon when Villem rode Zora to find Dinara and the rest. *It's not a good sign*, he thought, *that when I think of Sonia and Dinara, it's still Dinara that fills my mind first. She loves Livia. I'd better get used to that idea. And Sonia bears my child.*

Villem had to keep reminding himself of that last fact, because it did not seem real yet to him. *A child of my own blood. A boy, if Marianna is correct.* He thought about playing with a baby. Of teaching a growing boy how to fight with a sword or shoot a bow. How to ride a horse. He thought he had little idea how to raise a child, but it seemed it might be fun, at least when the baby wasn't crying. He had vague memories of his brother Vonn crying as a baby, and he had hated it.

He spotted the carriage ahead, parked beneath a large tree. *So they didn't ride very far*, he thought. A man gathering kindling saw him coming and shouted to the others, and soon the two women, Imric, and the girl Soot had all gathered to await his approach. Duchess barked like mad and ran to meet him. Villem slowed Zora's gait so he could have more time to study the two women who were most often occupying his mind of late. *It isn't fair to compare any woman's* beauty to Dinara's, he thought, but Sonia is quite pretty. Not all marriages start with love. He thought back to that sweet night he had spent with her. *We might be happy together. Or else we may never love each other, and we'll bicker and grow more and more unhappy over time. And the baby…*

He thought briefly of his step-mother. He dreaded seeing her again, especially with the terrible news he would bring. Likely she would have heard already from the soldier he had met. But Villem knew for a certainty that his father was dead. She would be unhappy to see Villem again, he was pretty sure, but what about Sonia and the baby? Perhaps his mother might soften toward them once the baby came?

"You kept your promise," Dinara said as he dismounted and petted Duchess.

"What happened?" Imric added, fear etched onto his face.

"Livia is fine," he said, to set Imric's mind at ease. "Most everyone is fine."

"Why do you look so unhappy then?" Dinara asked.

"Do I?" Villem tried to think what would make him look unhappy. He had been so afraid to face Orderic and his men, especially the crazed elf Miranvel. He had thought it unlikely he could survive a fight with these veterans, given that Villem himself had no experience with fighting other than on the practice field. Yet he had told himself he had to remain and face the danger, else he could not live with himself. "I think I'm just disappointed a bit. I thought I might die, but at least I would prove to myself that I could be brave. Then it all ended so fast, and I got to prove nothing."

"Silly," Dinara said, smiling beautifully. "You are one of the bravest men I have met, and I've lived among many warriors."

Villem wondered if she was just trying to make him feel better. He glanced at Lady Sonia and saw the way she cringed, as if she feared anything he might say to her. If he was as brave as Dinara insisted, he should do something to calm her. He walked closer and waited until her eyes met his. "Sonia, would you…would you come to Iskimir with me?"

He saw confusion and hope battle on her face. "You would have me?" she said, barely above a whisper.

Villem was uncertain what he truly wanted, but he felt any hesitation on his part would only deepen her nervousness. "Aye." He let their gaze linger for a few moments before he turned to Dinara. "And Livia suggests it may be best for all of you to come with me to Iskimir. For a while at least. Until things are settled."

Dinara looked surprised. "Will Livia join us?"

"She may. She has lots of work to do. With the fall of Valandiria and her uncle, there cannot be enough support for so many refugees in one place. Livia says they need to be broken up into smaller groups, and temporary homes must be found for them. It will be years before the new city is ready."

Dinara turned to Sonia. "Would you like company in your new home?"

"I would be delighted," Sonia replied, a shy smile on her face.

"How about you Imric? Soot?" Dinara asked.

Imric shrugged. "I don't know anything about Iskimir."

Villem grinned. "It's a smaller city than you're used to, but it has the most beautiful lake. I think you'll like it."

"Does the castle have any secret passageways?" Soot asked.

Villem was nonplussed by this strange question. "I…I never found any there. I don't think so."

"We'll just have to look for them then," Soot said, and she and Imric gave each other sly looks.

The journey back to the refugee camp was uneventful, except for Sonia's three men informing her that they were sorry, but they had to return with the carriage to their new master. Sonia had nodded and thanked them, though she looked a little pale.

The sun was setting as they rode past the plateau and saw the muted celebrations in the camps. Bonfires were already lit in several places, but the camps seemed too calm after such a huge victory. Villem guessed people were ashamed of the bloodlust that had consumed them when they attacked the fallen soldiers. Villem had been shocked to see it, though a small part of him had wanted to join them.

They halted at the crossroads and Villem pointed to the former gaol. "Livia said you will sleep there. I'll join you later. I promised to return this armor I borrowed." He whistled for Duchess to follow and turned Zora toward the medical pavilion.

As he passed the spot where they had once camped, he noticed the small carriage was still there, and he dared to hope the two ruffians might have departed. He could use the carriage for the trip to Iskimir. But then Othar appeared from behind the carriage, and Villem's hopes were dashed. Othar noticed Villem and glared at him. Probably still wants Zora to pull his carriage, Villem thought. He realized he had better be quick at the medical tent, so the man did not get a chance to steal the pony.

When he reached the pavilion, he tethered Zora's reins to a guy rope and bent down to scratch Duchess behind the ear. "Wait out here, girl. Bark if anyone comes close."

Duchess stared blankly at him and licked his arm.

Villem looked back to see if he could still see Othar, but it was growing too dark. All he saw now were the bright bonfires. "Stay!" he repeated to Duchess, then ducked into the pavilion.

Inside nothing had changed. The same healer that had spoken with him before approached him, though this time he smiled. "We were worried," he said. "Instead, we had only two minor casualties."

"Thank you for lending me the equipment I needed."

The man nodded and moved off to help a patient. Villem dropped the shield onto the stack and shrugged off the hauberk, then sat down to unlace the greaves. He was nearly finished when Duchess began to bark. Villem hurriedly doffed the rest of the armor. He decided to keep the sword and poked his head through the exit. No sign of Othar that he could see. Duchess had stopped barking and now stared up at Villem expectantly.

"What is it, girl? What were you barking at?" Villem squatted down to pet her.

People were dancing about the nearest bonfire, shouting and laughing. Someone had a drum and was pounding out a merry beat.

"Let's get back to the others," Villem said, standing and heading for Zora.

Duchess started barking again, and when Villem looked at her, he heard scuffing sounds behind him. He whirled about just in time to feel a fist smash into his face, sending him sprawling backward, the sword skittering away into the dirt.

"Got you this time." It was Othar's voice.

Though slightly stunned, Villem rolled to his left and tried to regain his feet. Othar crashed into him and knocked him to the ground again. Though he wasn't large, the man was heavy. He straddled Villem and began raining punches at his face.

With a growl, Duchess leapt on Othar and dug her teeth into his forearm. Villem got an arm up to block Othar's blows. Othar cried out in pain at the savaging Duchess was giving his arm. As the man turned to strike at Duchess, Villem shoved him hard in the chest, knocking him to one side.

Duchess yelped as one of Othar's blows connected. Rage filled Villem's mind. He threw an arm around Othar's neck from behind and squeezed hard. Othar gurgled and flailed his free arm at Villem, while trying to fend off Duchess with the other.

Villem continued to squeeze, but he took several deep breaths and tried to get his anger under control. He did not want to kill the man. Well, he had to admit, a part of him did. Othar went limp, finally succumbing to the lack of air.

"Down, girl!" Villem cried. He let go of Othar's neck and crawled over to give Duchess a hug. His face ached from the battering it had taken. Villem tentatively felt his nose and cheek bones. Nothing seemed broken.

"Are you all right?"

Villem saw that one of the healers had come out of the tent.

"I think so," Villem said. He pointed at the unconscious Othar. "That's the second time this man has attacked me."

"Why? Is he one of the raiders?"

Villem shook his head. "Just a ruffian. Wants my pony. If you can hold him, I'll send a guard to retrieve him."

The healer nodded. "I'll get James and Maynard and we'll tie him to a cot. I can take a look at his injuries."

"Better than he deserves," Villem muttered, then thanked the man.

He groaned as he knelt down to hug Duchess. He thought of the ironies of life. The dog had likely saved his life more than once, yet he would never have had her as a companion had not the raiders butchered the dog's family. Duchess licked his face, and Villem hugged her harder.

He untied Zora and decided to walk her back to the crossroads. He would speak with the captain or Lord Sewell and get some guards to arrest Othar. He rubbed his swelling jaw and couldn't wait to get back to see Livia and the rest.

61
LIVIA

"Why didn't you tell me what you were planning, you silly old man?" Livia asked, wiping Xax's forehead with a damp cloth.

The wizard was breathing much better now, but Livia insisted he rest, so he was lying on a pallet in the former gaol. "I had no idea what I would do. I had several ideas, but I didn't know what might help the situation or simply make things worse. When I saw all the horsemen bunch up together, I realized I had a chance if I hurried. I feel terrible about the horses, though."

Livia felt awful about them as well. Seventeen horses had had to be put down immediately, and others would likely follow soon. All of their ears had been bleeding badly; if any horses lived, they were likely to be deaf. A few refugees would be deaf as well, not having followed the hurried instructions being yelled out to them before the sound blast. Or they had not heard the instructions, and now they would never hear again.

"You had to do it," Livia said, "else many more people would have died. Darus may even have become king. You saved us."

"Don't speak too soon. The sea lords have already declared their independence, and the south is likely to break away as well. I'll go south first, once I'm able, and try to talk sense into Lord Symonidis.

He's the most sensible of the lot, and he could likely sway the other lords. I'll talk up your role as advisor to young Imric. Your bookishness is legendary."

"Would it be so terrible for the realm to split?"

"The more divisions people place between each other, the more excuses they find to cause strife with those who they view as different. It may be difficult to keep peace within the realm now, but a united land is better than otherwise."

"I wish we still had the spire to keep the peace."

"Other than the fact that many have suffered, I'm glad it's gone."

"Why?"

"A number of reasons. People's behavior was tamed by force rather than by teaching. And the entire populace was made too passive, unused to being able to defend themselves when danger threatened. Darus's army could whip ours because his men were hardened warriors."

"But we shouldn't want our people to be like them," Livia said.

"No, but you need a balance. No system is perfect, but a magically-enforced peacefulness left your people vulnerable. It's a dangerous world. A tragedy was bound to happen."

"Then why build the spire in the first place?"

"Hope. And what felt like necessity." The wizard gave a wry smile. "You must remember that your people didn't arrive in these lands for thousands of years after we built it. It was built to reinforce the peace between the elves and dwarves after their great war. The bulk of both races lived outside the sphere of influence, so the tower represented peace in the divide between their respective lands. When we later led your tribe here, it was out of desperation, because the barbarian tribes were uniting against you. We had to get you to safety, and this was the easy path to take at that time."

"I remember you teaching me some of this history when I was a girl, but you never quite put it all together like this."

"My apologies. Sometimes I concentrate too much on what happened and forget to teach the underlying causes."

The door opened and Lord Sewell entered, a hesitant smile on his face.

"How is he?"

"I'm much better, thank you," Xax said. "I could get up, if only my nursemaid would allow me."

Livia laughed. "You'll stay right where you are. You need a good night's sleep."

"I think we all do," Sewell said.

"I am exhausted," Livia said. "But there's so much to do. The refugees can't stay here. Without Valandiria's support, the logistics become impossible."

"It will be hard to get any nobles to agree to take them in, at least in any great numbers," Sewell said. "But if anyone can pull it off, you can."

"I don't know about that," Livia said. "Many lords don't like listening to a woman."

"We need to get your brother crowned as quickly as possible. That way you can tell them you're doing it in his name for the good of the realm."

"Imric is going to hate it. He was never prepared for this." Livia turned back to Xax. "You better stick around for a while and help me guide him."

"Do you think…?" Sewell hesitated. "Do you think I'll be allowed to continue work on the new city?"

"I don't see why not. You've been doing so well, even with limited resources. And you seem to enjoy it."

Sewell's face lit up. "I do. I never considered the prospect before, but I really do like it very much."

"You need a name for it," Xax said.

"Like what?" Sewell asked.

"I don't know," Xax said. "Did this little village have a name?"

"No."

"What about the name of the leading family?"

"The head man is Ebor Panga."

"Well, there you go!" Livia said. "Call it Pangalia."

"Huh. It rolls off the tongue, I suppose. Ebor will be the proudest man in the realm. Now, if you'll excuse me, I'll let you rest and go give him the good news." Sewell nodded good night and departed.

Livia turned to Xax. "Are you hungry?"

He shook his head.

Livia drew in a deep breath. "I've been meaning to talk to you about…about earlier, when you saw what Dinara did." She felt her face flush with embarrassment.

Xax cradled her cheek in his hand. "My dear, you need not feel any shame about it. It is far more common than you imagine, only your people pretend it doesn't exist."

"I never heard of women loving other women."

"Even in societies far more advanced than this one there are often people who frown on this type of love and call it unnatural. The country where I was born was not very enlightened about it, though many other countries had become far more accepting. It is natural."

"I'm not sure I can grow used to it. I…I know what I feel inside, but I also feel so embarrassed, and I don't know if I can go through with it. These people…my people, won't accept it, I don't believe."

Xax sighed. "No, it's not likely they will. I'm sorry to say, but you may have to keep such a romance a secret as well as you can. Luckily, you have many friends who will be understanding and will support you."

Livia's voice fell to a whisper. "Maybe I'd be better off if I married a man and put these feelings aside."

"To repress your true self is to live in regret." Xax looked at her in earnest. "Do you know how long I have lived among your people? This is not nearly the first time I have encountered this. Even among your own ancestors. King Vlodmir liked other men. He had to marry a woman and reluctantly produce an heir, but he also kept some lovers around him as courtiers. I can't speak for what Dinara wants, but you could always see if she's interested in being your lady-in-waiting."

Livia pursed her lips, then leaned in to peck Xax on the cheek. "I never expected you to be so understanding."

"No? I'm insulted." Xax chuckled. "You go on now. Get yourself something to eat. Villem should return with the others soon and they'll be all over you."

"That's certainly true." Livia kissed Xax again before heading out the door. She wondered if she had time to check on Azer and his companions. A surge of affection swept over her at the tribulations the three had undergone to try to help her. Azer had refused the offer of pallets inside the house, insisting on making camp in their old spot among the refugees. When the time came, she meant to ensure the nomads got the honors they deserved from the new king. Livia's stomach grumbled and informed her she needed food immediately. The nomads would have to wait.

She had only just managed to wrangle a bowl of soup from the captain when Villem arrived, escorting Lady Sonia's carriage. Livia put the bowl down and ran to meet them. Villem rode north on his pony before she could get there, so Livia ducked down to embrace both Imric and Soot together. She smiled and nodded politely to Lady Sonia, then gave a tentative embrace to Dinara.

"Where's Villem riding off to?"

"He's returning the arms he borrowed at the healing tent," Dinara said.

"Let's hope he won't need them anymore." Livia stepped back to look at everyone, a tired but happy smile on her face. "I'm so glad to have everyone together. Are you all hungry?"

Lady Sonia stepped forward. "Please excuse me for a little while. I must thank the drivers and see them off. Where will you be eating?"

"There's some good-smelling soup over there," Livia said to Imric and Soot. "Why don't you two run along, and we'll catch up in a moment."

Imric gave her a funny look before taking Soot's hand and leading her to where a cook was ladling out the soup.

Livia looked around to see if anyone else was watching, then looked at Dinara. She was nervous, thinking that the gorgeous woman still might have reason to reject her. When she saw the look in Dinara's eyes, however, she realized her fears were silly. With a smile, she stepped into Dinara's arms and kissed her deeply. When the kiss ended, face flushed, Livia whispered, "I've never done any of this before."

Dinara smiled beautifully. "We'll take things slowly. You hungry?"

Livia grinned and nodded, and the two went to join Imric and Soot. Lord Sewell intercepted them on the way. Imric and Soot brought over their soup bowls.

"I'm glad to see young Imric safe," Sewell said. "I'm sending out couriers to announce his coronation to all corners of the land. We'll see how the lords react. It will be interesting to see who comes to pay fealty."

"Where did you decide it should take place?" Livia asked.

"The most central location of any size is Vimar Keep. Lord Arthanis is my liege. I don't doubt he will remain loyal and would be thrilled to host the coronation. Even better, it isn't a long distance for you to travel from Iskimir."

"Having men like you in the realm gives me hope, Lord Sewell," Livia said, placing a hand on his arm.

"You are too kind, my lady. By the way, before you depart tomorrow, I'd love to show you the new plans for Pangalia."

"That would be lovely."

"I want to see them, too!" Imric said, excitement clear in his voice.

Livia laughed. "I had no idea you would be so interested."

"There will be a castle, won't there?" Imric asked.

"Of course," Sewell said.

Imric beckoned to Livia and she leaned down. He whispered in her ear, "I need to be able to add the secret passages."

Livia grinned and kissed Imric on the cheek. He had seemed so miserable when he first arrived, but seeing him now, hand in hand with Soot, she knew he was going to be fine.

62

VILLEM

The small group of riders—and one dog—rode slowly through the streets of the small city of Iskimir, headed for the castle. The day was overcast, a welcome change from the scorching heat of the past week.

Villem smiled to hear Soot and Imric trading complaints about how badly their bodies ached from never having ridden before. It was funny how he had acquired the horses. He had ridden forth to find his father's body and one of the first people he encountered had been Weevil, sitting beneath a tree, minding a string of horses. The boy had been so deeply asleep as Villem rode up that he did not open his eyes until Villem stood directly over him, still mounted upon Zora.

"Weevil," Villem said, and watched with satisfaction as his eyes popped wide open.

The boy leapt to his feet. "You! Where's Darus? Orderic?"

Villem leaned down in the saddle. "Dead, the lot of them. All dead." He hadn't thought the boy's eyes could get any larger, but he was wrong.

A hand rose unbidden to the boy's mouth. "Can-can't be. No, that can't be."

Villem untied the string of horses from the branch. He looked down at Weevil again. "Which one's yours?"

"You…you can't take my horses."

"I'm not going to take your horse, unless you refuse to tell me which one it is."

"Th-that one," the boy said, pointing at the lead horse of the string. He stared at the ground for a moment, then looked back at Villem. "What happens now? Now that Darus is…gone."

Villem unwound the tethers and tossed them to Weevil. "It's a long ride back to East Gate. Good travels."

"Tha-that's it? You're just cutting me loose?"

"Better than you'd have done for me, I'm certain. Now, I have no desire to ride with you. We'll be heading the same direction for a bit, so I'll ride slowly so you can go on ahead."

Weevil had taken some coaxing to finally mount up and depart. Villem had finished what he needed to do for his father, and returned to his friends with a nice string of horses.

Now they approached the castle gates in Iskimir, and Villem grew more nervous. There was only one apparent guard on duty on the wall above the gate, and Villem did not recognize him.

"What's your business here, traveler?" the guard called down to him.

"I'm Villem Tathis, lord of this castle. Open the gates."

The man looked panicked for a moment. "Umm, please wait a moment, milord. I-I must bring someone who might recognize you." The guard ran off, leaving his pike still leaning against the crenellations.

Villem looked back at Dinara, Sonia, and the two youngsters. Duchess barked twice and wagged her tail. "Guess I should have told him I had the king here as well. Though I suppose he'd want to verify who Imric is. Not sure there's anyone in the whole castle who would know."

"Can I please get off this horse?" Imric pleaded. "My arse is killing me."

"Me, too," Soot said.

"Here, let me help you," Dinara said, and slid from her mount.

Dinara had been quiet for most of the journey from the refugee camps. Villem knew she had not liked leaving Livia behind. Lady Sonia had impressed him. He knew she was as unused to horses as the others, yet she had not complained once about the pain she must be enduring. And she was also feeling nauseous each morning from her pregnancy. He wished he could have secured a carriage for her. The only one available had been Tristopher's, and however bad the man might be, Villem hadn't had the heart to take it from him.

Dinara first helped the children down, and then aided Sonia, who gave a small groan as she dismounted. Sonia and the two youngsters walked around a little, hands pressed to the smalls of their backs, Villem limping with his lame foot. Duchess chased them around as if it were a game, while Dinara, being well used to riding horses, gave Villem an amused smile.

It was some time before anyone reappeared on the wall. Villem was surprised that his step-mother came all this way from the castle. She stood silently above the gate and glared at him, looking a little pale.

"Will you please open the gates, Mother?"

Her mouth compressed in a scowl. "You have no right to call me that, as you well know. Why are you here?"

Villem stared at her open-mouthed for a few moments. "Like it or not, I am now lord of this province. You have no right to keep me from my own castle."

She pointed down at him, visibly trembling. "You are a...a...a bad person. The magic knew it, which is why it made you leave. Just because the magic is gone is no reason to let a bad man return."

Villem felt someone come up beside him.

"Villem is not a bad man." It was Sonia. "He may have felt

resentment toward his situation here, but that was understandable, and it did not make him a bad man."

"Who is this woman, Villem?"

"Don't be rude, *step*-mother! You can address Lady Sonia directly."

"*Lady* Sonia?" His step-mother examined her doubtfully.

"Of Rokentree," Sonia said.

"Never heard of it."

"And I suppose you've never heard of Imric Kaldarion either," Villem said, pointing down at Imric.

"You think you're funny, but you're not, Villem. There is no Kaldarion named Imric, as you're very well aware. Now if you want these gates open, you'll need to bring an army." With that, his step-mother vanished from view.

"Now what do we do?" Villem asked. He looked at each of his companions in turn. He had prepared them for the rude welcome he had thought likely from his step-mother, but he had not expected this. Villem dismounted to join the others. Duchess jumped up, her two forepaws on his chest, and he scratched behind her ears.

The gates began to swing open with a groaning sound.

Surprised, Villem turned to watch, wondering what had made his step-mother change her mind. When the portals had parted enough to see through them, he saw the soldier he had met at the refugee camp. The man grinned at him.

Villem grinned back and walked his pony across the small drawbridge. "It's good to see you again, soldier."

"You as well, milord." The man dipped his head.

Villem held out his arm, and the soldier grasped it. "My apologies, but I never asked your name."

"Timothy, milord."

"Did any more of our men make it home, Timothy?"

"Just three more, milord. They got here before me."

Villem nodded toward the castle, where he could see the stiff-backed form of his step-mother marching up the entrance steps. "What made her change her mind and let us in?"

Timothy grinned again. "Oh, she didn't. She wanted to take my head off when I ordered the gates opened. I told her you're the lord now, it's your castle. Also told her there is an Imric Kaldarion. I was camped at Valandiria long enough to hear about him." Timothy hesitantly approached Imric and knelt in front of him. "You are very welcome in Iskimir, sire."

Imric blushed. "I haven't been crowned king yet."

"It makes no matter to me," Timothy said as he stood up. He grinned and ruffled Imric's hair. "I got to be the first to welcome our new king!"

EPILOGUE

Kathkalan eased his black mare up the mountain road, hoping it would not be much farther. He had never been to the great dwarven city of Kaldorn, having previously visited only the even vaster Suldorn far to the south. If Kaldorn was anything like her sister city, it would be magnificent. If the dragon had not done too much damage.

The horse stumbled slightly on some gravel, and Kathkalan felt a twinge of pain in his mostly-healed ribs. He had run into a small group of dwarves a fortnight past. They were heading north to Faldorn, the most northern of the dwarven realms. The dwarves had been tight-lipped until he told them he was searching for the dragon. Then they told him the dragon had destroyed their city and appeared to be using it as its new lair.

Kathkalan had spent days at the base of the mountain that held the entrance to Kaldorn, enough time to note that the dragon flew forth from the mountain most mornings, spent much of the day away, and returned in the early evening. The dragon usually appeared to be carrying something, though the beast was too distant for even the elf's sharp eyes to tell what it was.

This morning Kathkalan had prepared early, then waited patiently, hoping today would not be one of the days the beast decided to remain in its lair. Around the same time as usual, the dragon flew overhead, heading due west, and Kathkalan whistled to his horse and began climbing the long road to the city entrance. The roads to the dwarven realms were always the best paved that one could find anywhere, and this road was no exception. Only once did Kathkalan have to dismount and lead his steed over a spot mostly buried by an avalanche.

Coming around another shoulder of the mountain, he finally saw the enormous double-doors leading into the underground city. The intricately-designed metal doors stood open, and several small figures were emerging, shielding their eyes from the glare of the sun.

He rode closer and saw the figures were dwarves—twenty-four of them, each carrying a large pack. The lead dwarf glared up at him as they neared one another.

"Ho, friend," Kathkalan said. "It's good to see the living walk forth from Kaldorn."

The line of dwarves halted, and the leader stared at Kathkalan with undisguised suspicion. "Friend remains to be seen. What brings you here, elf?"

By the sound of the dwarf's voice and the lack of beard, he realized the leader was female. "I'm going to slay the dragon."

Some of the dwarves behind the leader laughed, but the leader merely looked grim. "Your fame precedes you, Kathkalan, greatest of the elven heroes. Yet do I doubt that even you can succeed where so many of my brethren have failed."

"You know my name. May I know yours?"

"I am Anlag, one of the few remaining warriors of my people."

"You were in hiding all this time?"

Anlag nodded. "Deep inside the smallest of our tunnels. The beast rooted most of us out, crawling like a rat through tunnels you'd swear she could not fit inside, and when she found a tunnel she could not enter, she blasted clouds of acid to slay as many of us as possible. I fear few of us survived."

"The dragon is a female?"

"Oh, aye. Clear as day."

"I saw more of your folk heading north, a fortnight ago."

"That is welcome news. We plan to head south. But tell me, how do you intend to kill this monster?"

"I must find a means of coming upon it quickly and from behind or the flank."

Anlag shook her head. "You are begging for death, elf."

"That may be," Kathkalan said, "but I've lived overlong already. This is the last great challenge remaining for me in this world."

The dwarf nodded slowly. "I would help you."

"I don't ask it of you. As you said, it is likely suicidal."

Anlag grinned. "I will gladly die if it means helping to kill that beast. You want to get in close to it? Well, I can distract it and give you the time you need."

Kathkalan dismounted and came forward to offer his arm to Anlag. She gripped it with a strength no elf woman could have, causing another twinge of pain in his ribs.

"Your aid is welcome, Anlag."

"I'll see my friends off."

Kathkalan nodded, then turned to his horse. He gathered a few items he figured he might need should he survive. "Go on home, girl. Perhaps I'll see you again one day." He touched her flank and she nuzzled him, then turned and clopped off down the road.

Anlag approached with two others. "This is Bogi and Senvan. They will join us."

Kathkalan noted that all three wore beautifully crafted armor. While Anlag favored a war hammer, Bogi and Senvan carried axes. "Let us hope we are successful this day, comrades."

"Come," Anlag said, "let me show you the main hall where the beast is lairing. There is a simple plan that may work."

The massive double-doors were overlaid in bronze, with gorgeous, intricate designs carved into the metal. Kathkalan halted at the line of sunlight before entering the darkness. His was a people of the air. Purposely going beneath the ground felt unnatural. Even a small cave could make an elf feel uneasy, and before him lay an entire city buried beneath several mountains. When he had visited Suldorn, thousands of years ago, he had refused to go beyond the entrance hall, and even that had given him the shivers.

He stepped over the line into darkness and gave his eyes a few moments to adjust to the gloom. There was no entrance hall to Kaldorn—the great gates opened directly into an enormous chamber, so huge Kathkalan could not see the far end.

Anlag paused to look back at the elf. "We get used to seeing it all the time. I suppose it's something to see it for the first time."

"We build for lightness and nature," Kathkalan said. "For the sense of flying free from the bonds of the earth. Your folk build on a massive scale, for strength and durability. It numbs my mind to look upon this."

"Well, we had best be going. The dragon may return in the next couple of hours, and we will want to be ready."

Kathkalan nodded and strode forward. Bogi and Senvan had lit torches, but the flickering flames offered little to see in such an enormous chamber. Kathkalan saw torch brackets lining the near wall. Then he caught a glimmer from ahead. "What's that?"

Anlag looked at him and grinned. "I'll show you. Come." The dwarf strode confidently ahead, straight down the center of the chamber.

Kathkalan would have preferred to stay close to one of the walls, but he could not show nervousness in front of these dwarves, so he drew in a deep breath and followed. The other two dwarves fell in on either side, providing two small pools of light in the void. The darkness seemed alive to Kathkalan. It had patches of air that were warmer or cooler, slight breezes, and at times faint echoes of far off sounds. Though he was famous for his ability to walk silently, he could hear the slight scuff of his boots on the stone floor, alongside the heavier tromp of the dwarves. The gleams he had seen earlier became more frequent, and now an awesome sight became visible in the flickering torchlight.

A small mound of treasure was splayed out across the floor around a throne encrusted in gold and jewels. Empty sacks and broken chests showed how the hoard had been delivered. Never had Kathkalan seen so much gold and silver coin, along with intricate jewelry, fancy goblets, rubies, diamonds, and so much more.

"I had heard dragons accumulated a hoard," Kathkalan said, "but it is something else to see it."

Anlag sat down on the glittering throne and clapped a hand to one of the armrests. "This belonged to our king. It actually sat over there at the end of the hall, but the dragon hauled it over here for some reason."

"The dragon is just getting started," Senvan said. "It collected much of this from our own troves, but now it's flying out to the cities of man to bring back what it can from them."

"With its large claws, it's hard to imagine the beast can carry all this," Kathkalan said.

"They're cunning monsters, dragons," Bogi said. "They find tools to help them with their tasks."

"Why didn't you take any of this when you were leaving?" Kathkalan asked.

"It's no longer ours," Anlag said. "We lost our city. We have no right to any of this until we can avenge ourselves upon the beast. Win back the city and we win back our gold."

Kathkalan grunted, thinking about the odd sense of honor the dwarves follow, always so alien to the elven people. "So, what is your plan, Anlag?"

The dwarf hopped off the throne. "Let me show you. This way first." She headed toward one of the side walls of the massive chamber.

When they drew close to the wall, Kathkalan saw a large exit passage. Anlag pointed at it. "This was once the only passage leading from the great hall, other than the exit gates. Now this way." She began walking back the way they had just come, toward the treasure trove. Once she reached it, she continued on across toward the far wall. Reaching that wall, she followed it to the left for a few seconds. Here there was a break in the wall, a jagged hole that looked freshly carved out, with rubble strewn all about.

Anlag pointed into the dark maw of the small tunnel. "A few months ago, some of our engineers broke through into a natural cave complex. When we find such things, we explore them in detail before we determine how to work them into whatever form we decide they should take. We knew this end of the caves drew very close to the wall of our great hall, so when we came up from the deeps, we purposely entered the caves and camped just the other side of the wall here. We could hear the dragon's comings and goings, and eventually we learned its patterns. When it departed this morning, we took up our picks and started breaking through the wall here. Took a long time, which is why you found us departing so late in the day."

"I see," Kathkalan said, "so this way we can hit it from two sides."

"Aye," Anlag said, "and the dragon doesn't know about this here crack. You'll hide yourself here; we'll create the diversion from the main hallway; you'll come in quick and silent from behind when it turns to go after us."

"You're awfully brave, dwarves."

Anlag shrugged. "You just make your blow count. Our names will be remembered by our descendants for all time."

Kathkalan looked down at the rubble littering the floor, thinking it might make it harder for him to be silent when making his run at the dragon. The dwarves seemed to read his mind—they pulled shovels out of the passageway and began clearing the mess.

Without seeing the sun, Kathkalan had trouble guessing how much time was passing. "We must be in place before she returns."

Bogi grunted and looked up from shoveling. "Still another hour or more if she follows her habits. We'll clean this up right quick and be off to our hiding spot."

Kathkalan turned and studied the route he would have to take to get close to the dragon. There would be no light, other than the faint dimness coming in from the distant gates. While the darkness would help conceal his movement, he would struggle to see properly to strike the death blow. He sighed. If only he could see the spot where the scale was missing. That would allow for an easier, deeper strike. The dragon would give him no second chance.

"We're done here, elf," Anlag said.

Kathkalan turned to see the dwarves propping their shovels against the wall. They looked grimly determined as they each in turn grasped him by the arm.

"May your arm be strong and your aim true, elf," Anlag said. "You may become the first of your kind to be revered by our people."

"If I succeed, it will be because of you three. I'll tell your kin what you did here today."

Anlag grunted, then strode off across the hall with Bogi following. Senvan held his torch out toward Kathkalan, who took it gratefully.

After watching the dwarves vanish into the darkness, Kathkalan turned to the crack in the wall. He already felt uncomfortable out in the great hall, feeling the countless tons of rock above his head, and now he had to enter this tiny hole. He shuddered, drew in a breath, and ducked inside, holding the torch out before him.

Rough walls pressed in on both sides. The passage was narrow for several paces before coming out into a cavern. Water dripped from the dark ceiling, in some places making pools where the bones of tiny creatures crunched underfoot. Kathkalan had no desire to go exploring, so he sat down on a bare stretch of rock and found a hole to prop up his torch. As soon as he heard any sign of the dragon, he intended to quench the flame in a nearby pool of water. He pulled forth his blade and laid it across his lap, then began to meditate.

How long he sat that way, he had no idea, but eventually he heard a sound reverberate through the small crack in the wall behind him. Quickly he took up the torch and thrust it into the water, where the flame died with a hiss. In the pitch darkness, Kathkalan began to breathe deeply to control his nerves. The magic from the shard of crystal tingled through his blood and muscles, making him feel strong. A sense of power welled up inside of him. He would succeed. He would ensure the sacrifice of the three dwarves was merited.

Now there were slithering and scraping sounds echoing out of the crack. Kathkalan silently surged to his feet and slowly edged through the tiny passage, crouching low and feeling one wall with his free hand, the sword held loosely in the other. He crawled forward until he began to see the faint light provided by the entrance gates. A massive bulk heaved into view. Clinking and tinkling sounds broke the stillness as the dragon slithered onto its small hoard. It appeared to Kathkalan as if the dragon were somehow limping, but as his eyes adjusted, he saw that the beast was holding the bed of a wagon in one of its huge clawed feet. The dragon twisted about and settled its rear onto the floor, then dumped the contents of the wagon so that several dozen chests and bags spilled out. Casually the dragon tossed the wagon to one side. It used its claws to tear and poke at the bags and chests, bursting them open and spilling their glittering contents out to join the rest of the hoard.

Be ready, Kathkalan told himself. He had no idea when the dwarves would make their run, so he tensed himself, ready to go at any moment. Would fear spike their hearts and make them unable to cause the diversion? Kathkalan doubted it. He may have little love for dwarves, but he did not doubt their bravery.

And then he heard it. A rushing of leather-clad feet. A grunt. Then a shout. The dragon's head whipped about, staring toward the other end of the hall. It was time.

Kathkalan eased himself out of the crack in the wall, then began silently loping toward the dragon's flank. He kept an eye on the beast's tail, not wanting to get swatted by its lashings. The dragon's roar shattered the stillness. Kathkalan broke into a full run.

The dragon twisted violently, and whipped its tail in a wide arc. As if from down a long tunnel, Kathkalan heard the cries of the dwarves as the tail smashed into them, but he was too intent on his goal to worry about what was happening to them.

A burning pain filled his head, along with a voice he knew from long ago.

It's my dragon. I'll not let you have her.

"Out of my head, Bilach!" Kathkalan cried, and the unbearable pain vanished as quickly as it had come. But it was too late.

The dragon's head swung around and its eyes settled directly on Kathkalan. He was still a good fifteen paces away, and now he knew he could not possibly make it in time. He skidded to a halt and reversed course, hoping he could make it back to cover before the dragon blasted him with its acid breath. *Too far*, he thought. *I'll never make it.* He ran as he had never run before. He heard the dragon sucking in a huge breath of air, and Kathkalan found the will to run even faster. Suddenly the crack was there. Without pausing, he plunged into the darkness, one shoulder bouncing painfully from one of the walls. His blade clanked against the other. He slowed enough to duck down and quickly slide his blade home in its scabbard. He did not want to lose it, but he wanted to be free to run with every fiber of his being once he broke through into the cavern.

He heard the whooshing of the dragon's breath. Just as Kathkalan burst into the cavern, a warm cloud of burning death blew over and around him. Desperately, he closed his eyes and ran on blindly. He knew it was all over. He had no idea how far the caves went. There was the uneven floor, the pools of water…

That's it! If he could just find a deep enough pool, he might be able to clean himself of the acid, if only for a moment, until he was forced to come up for air. Air that would be filled with acid. Already his face burned and bubbled and hissed as the acid ate at his skin. He wanted to scream, but he wanted to hold in the last of his air for as long as he could. He flailed his arms out in front of him, hoping somehow to guide himself as his feet pounded across the floor. How he had not already crashed into a wall or tripped on a boulder, he had no idea. The acid was like fire, eating at him—his forehead, his nose, his eyelids, his lips. The agony was too much, and yet he had no other option than to continue on blindly. He ran on, much farther than his luck should have allowed, his hands smacking against stone now and again, telling him through the haze of pain that he was somehow following a passageway.

And then the ground wasn't there.

He tumbled into nothingness. He felt both legs break as they smacked hard against the far ledge of whatever crevice he had fallen into. That pain was almost a relief compared to the bubbling agony of the acid. And then he plunged headlong into icy water, a roaring torrent that sucked him under and rushed him along at great speed. The water washed away much of the acid, though Kathkalan imagined it was too late to save him. He had been inside the acid cloud for too long. The iciness of the water began to numb him, which was a relief from the horrendous pain that was assaulting him all over his body. He felt himself bump against the bottom of the underground river, and his lungs were near to bursting. He had to somehow get up for air, yet the weight of his armor and sword was dragging him down. Somehow he got his legs underneath him and tried to launch himself upward. Pain stabbed through him from the broken bones, and his legs could not bear his weight. He flailed his arms and managed to get his head above water enough to heave a quick breath before he went under again.

The torrent slowed a little, and Kathkalan swam as best he could with only his arms, popping above the water and catching quick breaths. He began to see a little of the stone walls all around, a faint greenish glow probably provided by lichens or moss. When he bobbed up for air again, he thought he saw a bend in the river ahead, so he splashed as best he could to the right, hoping he might be able to stop himself against the far bank of the river.

His body whirled through the bend, and he painfully scraped against the rocky edge. He scrabbled at it with his arms and managed to catch an outthrust rock and pull himself to a stop. He hugged the rock and sucked in air, his whole world seeming to be nothing but the roar of the water and the pain scorching his body.

Was there a ledge here? He had no idea, but remaining in the water felt like giving up entirely. Already his body was growing numb, which helped with the pain, but ultimately it meant his death from drowning.

He had no idea if he could pull himself out of the torrent using nothing but his arms, but he intended to try. Holding to the rock with his left hand, he reached out with his right and got hold of another rock on the bank. Three times he sucked in his breath to prepare himself, letting the magic of the shard grant him additional energy, then he lunged upward with all his strength, knowing he likely had but one shot at it. Somehow, almost miraculously, he managed to heave himself up enough to roll his body out of the water and onto a bed of cold stone.

He lay there for a long time, drawing in deep breaths, staring up into nothingness, just a barely visible glow emanating from the growth on the cave walls. His body somewhat numb from the cold, he willed his mind to push aside the pain and think. The magic from the crystal helped lend him strength his body on its own likely could not have managed. With his right hand he felt his face, and groaned at what his fingers told him. His skin was terribly burned. He was fortunate his eyes still worked. If there happened to be some way out of here, he felt there was almost no chance he would have the strength to actually escape, especially with two broken legs.

So this is it, he thought. Countless thousands of years, and this is how it ends for the great hero Kathkalan. He tried to chuckle and choked instead, coughing up more water from his lungs.

And the dragon lives. He felt terrible about the brave sacrifice of the three dwarves. He had failed them. He had failed himself. He shied away for the moment from thinking of those he had failed the most.

How would he die here? Would it be the damage to his body from the acid? Starvation, slow and long in the damp cold of this underground river ledge deep below the mountain?

And then there was no more hiding from it. Those he had truly failed. Alvanaria and their son Linvaris. She had begged him not to go on this quest. Begged him to consider his son, if not her. Did he not love them?

Of course, he did. Alvanaria would never understand. His life had gone on far too long. He had done everything he could imagine doing. Whatever love he held for her, and of course for their son, the ennui of endless repetition through his life was too much. He *had* to have a reason to live on. The challenge of this dragon had been the best reason to come along in centuries. There was no passing on the chance.

And now it came to this. Dying alone on a ledge where no one would ever know what had happened to him. Failing to slay the dragon was a pity, but far worse was knowing that Alvanaria and Linvaris would be left forever wondering about his fate.

The adventure continues in…

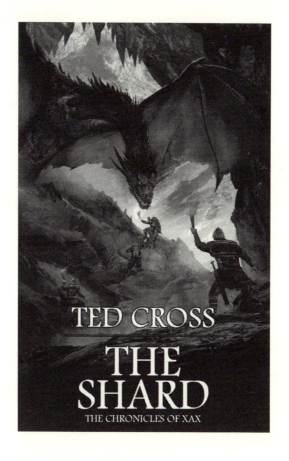

About the Author

Ted Cross has spent more than two decades traveling the world as a diplomat, all the time dreaming about writing fantasy and science fiction. He's visited nearly forty countries and lived in ten, including the U.S., Russia, China, Croatia, Iceland, Hungary, Azerbaijan, The Bahamas, Italy, and Luxembourg. He's witnessed coup attempts, mafia and terrorist attacks, played chess with several world champions, and had bit parts in a couple of movies. He currently lives in Luxembourg with his lovely wife.

Acknowledgement

I would like to thank the wonderful folks who read early versions of this book and helped me make corrections and adjustments to improve it. Rob Andrews, Matthew McNish, Michael Detwiler, and my son Alex—you all did so much to make this book better. Additionally, I would like to thank Scott Toney of Breakwater Harbor Books for his constant support. Thank you all!

Author's Note

I'd like to thank you for reading this book. The publishing industry is changing dramatically since the advent of ebooks. It is now very difficult to get any book noticed, regardless of quality. If you enjoyed this book, you could do some very simple things to help me attract attention. Word of mouth is the number one source of success for novels, so simply telling family and friends about the book is a great start. Here are a few other ways of helping out, if you are so inclined:

- Post a review on Amazon.com
- Post a review on Goodreads
- Talk about the book or write a review on Facebook
- Tell folks about the book in a blog post or on Youtube.
- Perhaps ask your local library or bookstore if they are willing to stock it!

One or more of those options would be a tremendous help! Again thank you, and I hope you will try out my future publications.

Ted Cross, March 2022

BREAKWATER HARBOR BOOKS

Fusion: A collection of short stories from
Breakwater Harbor Books' authors
Gateways

<u>Fantasy</u>
The Ark of Humanity, by Scott J. Toney
Eden Legacy, by Scott J. Toney
Horker's Law, by Mike Lee
As I Awake (and See the World) (The Beholder Book 0), by Ivan Amberlake
The Beholder, by Ivan Amberlake
Path of the Heretic, by Ivan Amberlake
The Firelord's Crown, by Dee Harrison
Firelord's Heir, by Dee Harrison
Firelord's Curse, by Dee Harrison
Firelord's Wyrd, by Dee Harrison
Godhead, by Ken Mooney
The Hades Contract, by Ken Mooney
The Fall Of Bacchus, by Ken Mooney
The Libations, by Ken Mooney
The Willow Branch, by Lela Markham
Mirklin Wood, Lela Markham
The Shard, by Ted Cross
Lord Fish: Chronicles of Xax, by Ted Cross
The Purple Morrow, by Dyane Forde
Wolf's Bayne, by Dyane Forde

Sci-Fi

Fey, by Mike Lee
StarFire, by Mike Lee
Dr. Zimm's Elixir, by Mike Lee
NOVA, by Scott J. Toney
NovaForge, by Scott J. Toney
NovaSiege, by Scott J. Toney
NovaDark, by Scott J. Toney
The Immortality Game, by Ted Cross
Life As We Knew It, by Lela Markham

Historical Sci-Fi / Fantasy

Chasing Pharaohs, by C.M.T. Stibbe

Horror

Doubles, by Melissa Simonson
Snuff, by Melissa Simonson

Dark Paranormal

Limerence, by Claire C Riley
Limerence II, by Claire C Riley
Odium, by Claire C Riley
Odium II, by Claire C Riley
Odium III, by Claire C Riley
Odium Origins. A Dead Saga Novella. Part One., by Claire C Riley
Odium Origins A Dead Saga Novella Part Two, by Claire C Riley
Diary of the Gone, by Ivan Amberlake

Crime Thriller

Hazard Pay, by Melissa Simonson Woman's

Fiction

The Wishing Place, by Mindy Haig
The White Room, by Mindy Haig
Hidden in the Pages, by Mindy Haig
Kiss Her in the Moonlight, by Mindy Haig
Under A Million Stars, by Mindy Haig
The Postcard, by Mindy Haig
Hearts of Avon, by Scott J. Toney
The Young and the Reckless, by Melissa Simonson

Christian

Lazarus, Man, by Scott J. Toney
The Last Supper: John, by Scott J. Toney
Among us, by Scott J. Toney
Zacchaeus, by Scott J. Toney
The Messenger, by Mindy Haig
Glory, by Mindy Haig
Forsaken, by Mindy Haig

Poetry

Dusk Crescence, by Scott J. Toney

Made in the USA
Columbia, SC
10 September 2024